HARD KNOCK HERO

HANNAH SHIELD

Copyright © 2023 by Hannah Shield

HARD KNOCK HERO (Last Refuge Protectors Book 1)

All rights reserved.

No part of this book may be reproduced in any form or by any electronic or mechanical means, including information storage and retrieval systems, without written permission from the author, except for the use of brief quotations in a book review.

Cover photography: Wander Aguiar

Cover design: Angela Haddon

HARD KNOCK HERO

CHAPTER ONE
Aiden

SNOW BLASTED my windshield faster than the wipers could brush it away. The forecast had said a storm was headed for Western Colorado, but it was supposed to hit tomorrow, when I would be warming my hands at the fireplace of my rental cabin. Not when it was already dark, and I still had a long way to go.

I could barely see the car in front of me. Then two brake lights lit up, and I slammed on mine. More red materialized out of the whiteout conditions. Next came flashing yellow.

Damn it.

Snow settled on the hood of my truck. I was going nowhere. Not the ideal start to the vacation I'd been envisioning. Five blissful days in the woods, cooking just for myself. A luxury I didn't often get in my line of work. No roommates. No family, as much as I did begrudgingly love them. I was a loner, and I refused to apologize for that. When I'd been a soldier, my Army brothers had given me the call sign Solo. It wasn't a Star Wars reference. It just fit. If you'd asked any of my ex-girlfriends, they would've agreed.

At an agonizing pace, my truck inched forward. Then I spotted a sign.

Hartley, Next Exit. Gas, Food.

The car ahead of me veered right to take the exit ramp. I wasn't much of a follower, but I figured this was one time to embrace what my neighbor was doing. I took the exit. Hopefully I'd be able to find a warm place to sit and some halfway decent food to wait out whatever snafu had jammed up the highway.

The gas station was just off the ramp, and several highway refugees had stopped here. The town was further afield. Fading signs directed me to Hartley's Charming Historic Business District. *Pop in and stay awhile.*

"No thanks," I muttered. "Just passing through."

My truck rolled slowly down Main Street, wipers droning rhythmically. If there was historic charm on offer, I couldn't see it. But then again, not much of Hartley was visible for all the snow. The sidewalks were deserted, most of the other Main Street businesses dark. A couple had plywood over their entrances.

There was a lonely-looking diner down at the far end of the commercial strip, and the warm glow of its lights called to me. The place looked completely empty, which didn't bode well for the quality of its provisions.

Later, I would understand how deceptive that first impression had been. The diner might've been lonely, but the reason wasn't the food.

The car in front of me made a u-turn, probably heading back to that gas station. But I preferred to risk the diner than to burn gas and go nowhere on the highway. Or far worse, eat warmed-over convenience store burritos. I would rather have starved.

So I pulled my truck into the lot to one side of the building. I did my best to park between two of the dividing lines, though I could barely see them under the rapidly collecting snow. I pushed out into the swirling wind, not bothering with the hood on my canvas coat. My boots left tracks in the white on my way to the diner's door.

A little bell jingled as I entered. "Be right with you," a breathless female voice called from the back.

As far as I could see, she was the only person in the entire place. No patrons. Nobody manning the griddle in the open kitchen, though I could smell something hearty cooking and heard the distinctive gurgle of coffee as it brewed.

I inhaled deeply. Notes of red wine and thyme. Promising.

The place was warm and tidy. Lots of feminine touches, like little lace things hanging over the windows and a collection of tea pots and cups decoratively arranged on shelves like a display at an antique store. The chrome and formica were straight out of the middle of the last century. Everything a bit worn, but fresh paint brightened the walls.

I left wet footprints across the tile floor, choosing the last booth by the long window. There was a hook on the wall, so I hung my snow-damp coat to dry. The leather bench creaked as I eased myself onto it. I'd chosen the seat facing the wall, where a landscape print of summer mountains hung.

The table already had a menu, old-school laminated, and I snagged it with my finger and dragged it toward me.

Jessi's Diner. Please ask about our daily specials.

My skin prickled. I glanced up to find two large eyes fringed with dark lashes and eyeliner peeking out at me from around the side of the opening to the kitchen.

A small gasp, and she vanished.

Something crashed.

"Everything okay back there?" I asked.

"Yes! Sorry. Be right out."

"You are open, right?"

"I am. We are."

"Is something wrong?" I was getting slightly concerned.

"Just *hold on*."

I listened for voices, but heard none. It seemed to just be her back there. After another moment, the woman raced out of the kitchen, leaving the door swinging behind her. "Can I help you?"

She wore a plain white apron over jeans. A sweater with the sleeves pushed up to her elbows. A stray strand of dark hair tickled her cheek, and she pushed it away with a blow of her lips. The rest of her hair was gathered into a ponytail that trailed down her back.

Maybe mid-twenties. Pretty.

"Are you Jessi?" I asked.

One foot stepped back, her jaw going hard. *"Why?"*

I sat back, lifting my hands. Wow. She was wary as hell of me. I'm a big guy, but I didn't think I'd done anything threatening. Except exist and wear my typical non-smiling expression, which some people may have called *grumpy* in the past. I thought *neutral* was more fair.

She was a woman alone, though, so I tried to be sympathetic.

"Just curious, since you seem to be both the back and the front of the house." I gestured at the quiet diner, most of which was behind me. Then my gaze met hers again. "I was instructed to ask about the specials."

Her long lashes blinked. "Excuse me?"

I tapped my finger on the menu. *Please ask about our daily specials*.

"Oh. A joke?" Her mouth twitched. "You might want to work on your delivery."

"Just trying to lighten the mood in here. If you want me to get dinner somewhere else, I can." Maybe. If there was anyplace else in Hartley except the gas station, and I was beginning to wonder.

She exhaled, shoulders sagging. Unwinding a notch or two. "Sorry. I'm a little tense."

"Because of the storm? Or your lack of patrons?"

A smirk. "So many reasons to choose from."

"Now *that* was a joke. I see how it's done."

"Glad you're catching on." Her smirk broadened into an almost-smile.

I changed my mind. She was *very* pretty.

"I am, in fact, Jessi. The special today is lamb stew."

"Is that what I'm smelling right now? Red wine, thyme, garlic. And…fennel?"

Her focus on me sharpened. "You got it."

"Then I'll have that. Plus a cup of coffee."

"Room for cream?"

"Nope. Black. And keep the refills coming."

She walked over behind the counter and poured a mug. "Long night ahead," she remarked. It wasn't a question.

"Looking that way. I'm waiting for whatever's blocking up the highway to clear out."

Jessi hummed as she set the mug in front of me, and I heard skepticism in the sound. But she didn't elaborate on whatever she was thinking. "Where are you heading?"

"Not here."

"Lucky, then," she murmured. She spun on her heel and went to the kitchen.

Well, *that* was mysterious. But I'd never been a big fan of mysteries. They were demanding of attention and time, and I had other uses for both.

I tried to check the weather and traffic, but my phone had no service. So I sipped the hot brew and focused on the view through the large, plate-glass window. Swirling snow. A few cars went by, carving two long furrows in the growing blanket of white. But nobody else stopped at Jessi's Diner.

A few minutes later, Jessi came out with a large steaming bowl. "Here you are. Let me know if you need anything else."

The stew looked and smelled delicious. "This should do it. Thank you."

She pulled a rolled-up napkin with utensils from her pocket, but her eyes were on the window, where I'd just been looking. A frown sank into her expression. I recognized the signs of deep thought. Jessi seemed like a woman with a lot on her mind.

None of my business.

So I surprised even myself when I asked, "Waiting for someone?"

She startled and looked over. "What?" She set the bundle of utensils on my table with a thunk.

"You keep staring out the window." I took the spoon and dipped it into my stew, stirring it around. "And you seemed nervous when I first got here. You were spying on me."

"I wasn't *spying*."

"But you *were* nervous. And you still are. Which suggests the person you're waiting for isn't welcome. You're expecting bad news. Or worse." I took in her mannerisms. Her pupils had dilated. Her hands shook, and she tried to hide it by stuffing them in her apron pockets. "Whoever you're waiting for might be…dangerous."

We stared at each other.

Her chin lifted, and she crossed her arms. "You got all that from a few minutes of sitting here?"

Plus four years as a soldier, I thought. *And two opinionated siblings in law enforcement who refused to shut up.* "Pretty much."

"I don't need help from some random guy."

"I wasn't offering," I said matter-of-factly. I was nobody's hero, least of all hers. "Just being observant. If somebody's about to barge in here and start trouble while I'm eating my dinner, those are facts I might want to know."

"I'm sure you can take care of yourself."

"I'm sure I can, too."

"Then you have nothing to be concerned about," she snapped. "Let me know if you want dessert before you head out on the road. Our desserts happen to be *excellent*."

The door to the kitchen slammed the wall as she wrenched it open and vanished inside.

CHAPTER TWO

I COULDN'T MAKE my hands stop shaking. Couldn't get my breathing to slow down.

My shoe crunched in the shattered drinking glass I'd dropped earlier when I'd been... Okay, *fine*, I'd been spying on him. Because I'd been trying to figure out if my ex had sent him. Just thinking about that bastard made my insides burn with fury. Made old aches rise to the surface, like bruises appearing after the initial trauma has passed.

I grabbed my phone from my stainless-steel prep table. Wi-Fi from my upstairs apartment was still working, but no new messages from Trace. The last one had said, *Flight delayed for weather*.

If my half-brother didn't get to Hartley before Jeremy did, then I would have to sort things out on my own. Meanwhile, rent was due, and the burly, observant guy sitting in my diner right now was the only customer I'd had in days.

Nervous? Oh, I was nervous. As he'd so helpfully pointed out.

I peeked around the opening that connected the kitchen to the front of the restaurant. Not spying this time. Just observing, which he had been so eager to do before. I was returning the favor.

He wore dark jeans and a long-sleeved gray Henley. Ample muscles filled out the soft fabric. He had a trimmed beard and tousled light brown hair. Hard to say how old he was. Maybe about thirty. He had a military vibe, which I knew how to recognize from Trace, though I hadn't seen my brother much in the last several years.

But the odd thing was, my customer had chosen to sit with his back to the door instead of facing it. Most people didn't do that, much less military folks.

He dug into his lamb stew, glancing at the window to the street as he chewed. He licked his full lips. Took another bite.

He hadn't smiled a single time since coming in. But I had learned that men with nefarious intentions often approached with a grin. This guy, whatever his name was, didn't seem to care much what I thought of him, and I appreciated that. If he could just eat his dinner, pay up, and move along, I'd like him even more.

His eyes flicked in my direction, and I darted out of sight again.

"Saw that," he muttered, and despite my terrible mood, I fought back a smile.

"Saw what?" I replied.

I needed something to do. I swept up the remains of the glass, then grabbed a rag and went back to the front of the diner. I wiped off a few of the tables, making sure that everything was spotless, as if I might have a rush of customers at any minute. Hey, maybe I would. Why else had I opened today?

At least I still had hope, ridiculous though it was. They hadn't smothered that out of me yet.

I grabbed the carafe of coffee and walked over to my only

patron. His dinner was nearly gone. "How is everything?" I asked, refilling his mug.

"Not bad."

"*Not bad,*" I repeated. "I'll have to put that endorsement on our website."

"You asked about *everything*. A lot about my current situation is less than optimal." He pointed his spoon at the stew. "You cooked this?"

"Not sure I want to own it now."

"The stew is delicious. I just wanted to compliment the right person."

"Then, yes. I'm the cook. I'm also the waitress and the cleaner too. As you noted before. I'm front of house, back, and everything between."

"Is that your way of asking me not to make a mess?" He still hadn't smiled, but I could've sworn his eyes were laughing.

"It would be appreciated."

"What kind of wine did you braise the lamb in?"

That question tripped me up because he hadn't signaled a switch in topic. But cooking was a subject I could get behind. "A pinot noir."

We went back and forth a few times on my recipe.

"You cook?" I asked.

"I do."

I almost rolled my eyes. Was he angling for me to ask more questions? Or did the guy hate sharing personal info? I was about to call him out on it, or offer to bring him the check. I hadn't decided yet.

Then the bell on the door jingled. I looked up to find Chester Rigsby and his two younger brothers ambling into my diner.

Shit.

My heart launched all the way into my throat. My eye twitched, and the coffee carafe felt too heavy in my hand.

"Evening, boys," I said, impressed by the nonchalance in my tone. "Grab a seat, and I'll be right with you."

"We're not here to eat, Jessi," Chester said. "You know that."

I crossed my arms and shrugged, the coffee pot held like a shield in front of me.

Chester and his brothers were my ex-boyfriend's cousins. They had their reasons to hate me. Mainly, because my ex had been in prison the last two years. I'd put him there.

No, that wasn't true. Jeremy had put himself there. But my testimony had been a key part.

"If you're not going to buy anything," I said, "you can keep moving."

"The only one who's supposed to be moving is you. Out of Hartley."

Keep working on that dialogue, Chester, I thought. "And yet, I'm still here."

Inside, I was quaking all the way to my bones. Jeremy had just been released from prison, and he was on his way back to Hartley. Today was the deadline his cousins had given me to be gone, and I'd ignored it. I'd known somebody would show up here. I just hadn't known who. Though Chester and his brothers had been the most likely suspects.

Unlike Jeremy, they'd never laid a hand on me. Yet.

But there was always a first time.

Chester's eyes shifted to focus on the man behind me, my sole customer, who had his back to us. My mysterious military man sat in his booth, sipping his coffee. His shoulders were bunched up in a way they hadn't been before.

"Who the hell are *you*?" Chester barked.

Slowly, my customer turned, his arm stretching over the back of the seat until his profile was visible. "Who, me?"

"Yeah. You."

For a moment, there was no reply. Nobody moved. But I could feel the air *waver*. Flexing. Like glass just before it shatters.

Then my customer took a loud slurp of coffee. "Just a guy who's passing through."

Chester's shoes squeaked on the tile as he crossed the space, his brothers flanking him. "You must not realize what kind of a place you're eating in. Jessi Novo is a liar and a backstabber. Wouldn't be surprised if she poisoned your food."

The corner of my customer's mouth lifted, the first indication I'd seen that the guy knew how to smile. But it wasn't friendly or pleasant. That smile made ice flow through my veins.

"I don't want any trouble," he said, low and rumbly.

Coiled energy suddenly radiated from him. I didn't know his name, and I didn't want to. I had my own problems, and this man had *problem* written all over him, spelled out in big, muscular letters. If he tried to stand up for me, some military-guy code of honor thing, then I'd be the one to suffer for it. I had to get control of this situation before the rickety house of cards that was my life came crashing down around me.

I walked forward, projecting confidence. I was tall for a woman. The same height as Chester.

"Leave," I said. "Stop harassing my customers."

Beady eyes turned toward me. "You haven't got any, aside from this dumb asshole. Nobody else will come here. You'll be needing a different kind of customer real soon to make rent, but that would fit for you, wouldn't it? Because you're a wh—"

"*Enough.*" I thunked the coffee pot onto a table. "Just stop. I won't let you come in here and talk to me that way."

"No? What're you going to do about it?" Chester advanced, backing me up against the counter and wedging me between two of the barstools. His younger brothers stood like two gargoyles at his shoulders. "Report me to the sheriff and spew a bunch of lies like you did about Jeremy?"

"I didn't lie. You know it. Jeremy knows it. Everyone does."

His fingers gripped my shoulder. Rancid breath met my nose as he leaned in. I angled my face but couldn't escape it.

The bell on the door tinkled, and all four of us turned to look.

Through the window, I watched my customer walk calmly along the sidewalk through the snow. He'd left a stack of cash on the table.

For a moment, I just stared, disbelieving.

I hadn't wanted his help or expected it. I'd even been afraid of it. But I still couldn't stop the crashing wave of disappointment and sadness that my single potential ally was gone.

He'd left me here.

I was alone.

"Guess unlike some people, he knew what was good for him." Chester's head swiveled to face me.

"Guess so." My voice sounded raw. Scraped, like I felt inside.

He was smart to get out of here. Plenty of people had already told me I was a fool for sticking around Hartley. For refusing to let these lowlifes push me out of my home. The diner was all I had.

But I was used to being alone. *Fighting* alone.

I stuck my chin out and glared. "Your turn. Get out of my restaurant."

"I'm sick of that smug, stuck-up attitude." Chester's hand

cinched around my arm. He dragged me through the door to the kitchen. The hinge thumped as it swung. Back and forth.

He pushed me against the ovens. On the stove, the pot of lamb stew simmered. His brothers had stayed out front. Probably keeping watch. But Chester had me in the part of the kitchen that was out of sight of the street.

"Seems like you need to be taught a lesson about knowing your place." Reaching out, Chester swept a baking sheet of tarts off the opposite counter. They smacked onto the floor, and I cringed, thinking of that lemon curd I'd spent hours on.

"You're threatening to put me in the hospital again?" I hissed. "Like Jeremy did?"

"Just keep talking. Keep running your mouth."

"Remember what I did to him? They had to stitch him up before he went to jail. And I'll do the same to you by the time this is finished."

Chester raised his hand. His palm was open, which was good. It would hurt less. I braced myself.

Then a huge shape loomed out of nowhere, moving so fast he was a blur on my periphery.

Chester flew away from me. He slammed into the refrigerator so hard that it left a divot in the stainless steel. He slumped onto the ground, nose gushing blood. He was out cold.

And my nameless customer towered over him, broad chest moving as he breathed. His face was completely blank except for his eyes. Those gleamed like polished obsidian.

Chester's brothers shouted and cursed. The next oldest after Chester—Mitch—ran through the swinging door.

"Back away," my customer growled. "Don't be stupid."

"Listen to him, Mitch," I said.

Mitch charged.

My customer grabbed the handle of a chef's knife and pulled it from the block, already swinging. The knife blade slashed. Whined as it rent the air. A long, thin cut appeared in Mitch's sweatshirt and the tee beneath. A stripe of red welled from his now-exposed skin. Shallow, but a good six inches across.

Mitch stared at his stomach in shock. He made a keening sound.

My customer shifted his weight, balancing the knife in his hand. "Second warning. Need a third?"

I was holding my last inhale, leaning against the ovens. Chester's nose made a wet noise as he breathed, passed out on the floor.

"I don't need this shit," Mitch muttered. He fled and nearly bowled over his younger brother on his way. "Let's go. We'll deal with her later."

"But what about Ches—"

"*Later*."

Both men careened for the exit. The bell rang shrilly.

"They forgot their fearless leader." My customer bent over and grasped Chester by the back of the collar. He dragged Chester like a rag doll through the swinging door. Then outside into the snow, where he dumped the unconscious man unceremoniously onto the icy curb.

Finally, my limbs unfroze, and I sucked in a breath.

Oh, hell. This was bad.

I grabbed another knife from the block and ran after my customer into the biting wind and snow.

Mitch and his younger brother had scampered over to pick up their sibling. One at the arms, the other at the legs. "You're gonna be sorry for this, Jessi," Mitch shouted.

He didn't even look at the man who'd actually done it. My nameless customer stood casually to one side with his hip cocked, coat unzipped, weapon dangling from his fist. Expression still blank.

I shook to my core from adrenaline. Even some idiotic

glee. At least I could enjoy seeing Chester knocked out and his brothers running scared. As briefly as that would last.

I pointed my chef's knife at Mitch, feeling puffed up with bravado and ridiculous because what the heck did I know to do with it? Except dice onions and julienne lemon zest. "Just go. Leave me alone. Never come back."

"You're so gonna pay," Mitch spit out.

The boys stuffed Chester into the back of their truck, snowflakes swirling around inside the cabin, and their tires skidded as they roared away.

My eyes slid over to the man beside me. His dark gaze was there to meet mine.

Quiet fell over Main Street.

"I thought I asked you not to make a mess," I said.

He shrugged one shoulder, the same arm that held the knife. "Oops."

CHAPTER THREE
Aiden

JESSI'S EYES shone with wild energy. Wind ruffled her ponytail. The ice and frigid air brought a pink glow to her cheeks. She wasn't wearing a coat, just her pristine apron, sweater, jeans. Her knife glinted.

I changed my mind again. She wasn't very pretty. She was stunning. I was stunned, looking at her. Which rarely happened to me.

I'd been surprised that she picked up a knife and followed me out here. But she was no doormat. She'd made that clear inside, both to me and to Chester. Not her fault she didn't have the same physical intimidation factor a man like me did, despite her bravery and her height.

Then she deflated. Eyelids drooping, shoulders curving. "Oh, God. This is bad. Bad, bad, bad." With quick steps, Jessi returned to the diner.

I came in after her. The door made a final jingle, and I flipped the lock and the open sign to closed. I figured she was done for the evening.

She went to the bar counter and dropped her knife to the formica surface. I set the one I'd borrowed next to it. A few snowflakes had settled on her neck and shoulders outside, and the shapes dissolved on her skin.

"It's not *that* much of a mess." I glanced around. "I've done worse."

"You have *no idea* what you just did."

"I think I saved you from a beating," I said evenly.

"I was handling things in there."

I raised an eyebrow.

"I *was*. He wasn't actually going to hit me." She didn't look remotely like she believed that. "What happened to not helping me? Minding your own business? *Just passing through?*"

Good questions, all. "I don't like to see someone come into a perfectly nice establishment, ruin my dinner, and threaten the cook. Where I come from, that's considered rude." Plus, he'd called me a dumb asshole, and I hadn't cared for that either.

She gritted her teeth and roared. Her palm slapped into the middle of my chest over the buttons of my Henley. She pushed me up against the bar counter, nearly where Chester had pinned her a few minutes ago. Jessi couldn't hold me here, of course, though I felt the strength in her arm. But I stayed. I let her do it.

"You *left*."

"I came back."

"Why? Real answer this time."

When I'd left the diner, I hadn't intended for one second to leave her there alone. Some people might assume I'd do it. But even I wasn't that callous.

"Because I wanted to." Truest answer I could give.

Her eyes raked over my face. "Who *are you?*"

"Aiden Shelborne."

"That's…" Jessi shook her head, backing away. I still felt the warmth of her like a brand on the center of my chest.

"Fine. I didn't want your help. You should've stayed out of it."

"Then I apologize for interrupting your friendly chat with Chester. I'll get out of your hair. Maybe the highway is clear by now."

"So you just roll into town, screw everything up for me, and then take off?"

I turned my head. "I'm confused. Do you want me to stick around? Or not?"

Her throat moved as she swallowed.

"Go," she whispered. The word was defeated. "Just go."

So I did. I went through the back door, just like I'd done earlier when I'd wanted to take Chester by surprise.

I heard the lock flip the moment the door closed behind me.

The highway was not clear.

I drove to the gas station, where a bored teenager behind the register informed me a truck had jackknifed on a bridge over the canyon, causing some sort of damage. The bridge was closed and would be until it was repaired.

At least I had a stomach full of good food. My altercation with Chester and his boys hadn't given me a moment of indigestion. But Jessi's worry afterward had made me pause. I didn't like to think I'd made things more difficult for her.

But when I'd sneaked around the back of the diner, I hadn't been thinking much at all. I'd just known that three men were threatening a woman who'd made me a damn good meal. I'd taken offense. And I'd known that, with three against one, it was better to come at them in a roundabout way.

When I had seen Chester raise his hand to her? I'd taken a *lot* of offense at that.

What had the woman expected me to do, just walk away whistling without a care in the world? I did prefer to mind my own business, but there were limits. There were rules in a civilized society.

It was like those lines in the parking lot marking one space from the next. Had I put them there? No. Did it annoy me that I had to comply with somebody else's arbitrary setup? Yes. That was why I hadn't enjoyed being a soldier. But I had still parked inside those lines, because I was a grown human and not some kind of animal. And it bugged me to no end when dumbasses like *Chester* and *Mitch* weren't playing along.

Did Jessi expect me to apologize for defending her? I refused.

Now my stomach was churning with annoyance, and that pissed me off.

Matters only got worse when I reached the roadside motel, to which the gas station jockey had helpfully directed me. No vacancy. The other highway refugees had gotten there first while I was busy defending the local diner princess.

I left my number, asking the motel receptionist to call if they miraculously had a room open up. Then I stood in the cramped lobby and used their free Wi-Fi to check my phone, since I still had no cell service in Hartley. There was some info about the jackknifed truck, but not an estimate on when the bridge would be repaired.

As I drove down Main Street again, pondering what I should do, the entire town seemed to have shut its doors. I could see better now that the wind had calmed. There was indeed some historic charm about the buildings. Brick with western-style accents, big storefront windows. Old-timey streetlights that some people might call *cute*. Plus the striking outlines of mountain peaks, just visible in the storm.

Yet there was something off about Hartley. Something desiccated, dried out and slowly blowing away. It made me wonder why Jessi was so determined to stay here. I would've loved to see it disappearing in my rearview.

I passed Jessi's Diner. The lights were off, but I slowed down and studied the windows, trying to see if she was in there. My dirty dishes were still on the corner table where I'd left them. Given the cleanliness of the rest of the diner, I figured that was unusual. But there was no other sign of Jessi. Nor of Chester and the other idiots, for that matter.

There was a second floor above the diner, and the lights were off there too. I wondered if it was an apartment. Maybe Jessi's apartment.

I really needed to stop wondering so much.

Finally, I spotted glowing neon in a narrow window. There was a faint light shining on a sign that said *Hartley Tap & Saloon*. That sounded like the right place to get warm and drown some of my sorrows, at least until they kicked me out at last call. It was either that or get back on the highway going the wrong direction and look for another hotel, which would be at least an hour back. There was no other decent route to my vacation rental except through Hartley because of all the mountains in the way. Freaking Colorado.

So I pulled around to the lot behind the bar, parked, and stomped the snow off my boots on my way inside.

A few faces glanced up from the bar. One of them was Jessi's. She sighed as I made my way to the barstool two down from hers. I took off my jacket, laid it over my stool, and sat.

"You're still here," she said, looking into a glass of amber liquid.

It was warm in here. Both the air and all the wood. Wood

bar top, wood paneling on the walls, wood floors. "Because the highway's still blocked. I haven't been following you, if that's what you're implying."

"I wasn't."

The bartender gave me the hairy eyeball as he wiped a glass with a towel. "Jessi, that guy bothering you?" he called out.

"No, Marco. I'm good. I know him. Kinda."

I huffed a small laugh.

When I glanced over at her again, Jessi was staring. "You're smiling. A real one. Oh, never mind. There it goes."

"I smile enough. Maybe the rest of the world smiles too much."

The humor abruptly left her eyes. "You're right about that." She knocked back the rest of her drink and grimaced.

Now I felt like the jerk my siblings often accused me of being. "Can I buy you a round?"

"No, I'll buy you one." Jessi lifted her hand. "Marco, two more doubles please. On my tab."

She scooted over by one seat, taking the stool next to me.

I pushed my sleeves onto my forearms, getting comfortable. "What're we drinking?"

"Well whisky. Neat."

"Fitting for a saloon.

"It's that Hartley *Historic Charm*. Registered trademark. All rights reserved."

I chuckled.

"Wow, another one," she said. "You must *really* feel sorry for me."

"I never said I was sorry. Definitely not sorry *for* you."

Marco brought over the whiskey bottle and a low-ball glass. It clattered on the bar top. Liquor sloshed into my glass, then Jessi's. I reached for mine.

"Wait." Her hand rested on my wrist, but the touch

vanished almost immediately. "Aiden." She cleared her throat. It was the first time she'd said my name.

"Yeah?"

"Thank you for helping me earlier. I freaked out because…" Her voice dipped even lower. She shifted infinitesimally closer to me, enough that the hairs of my arms brushed the hairs of hers, causing an electric charge to zip through my entire body. "Because I'm in a bad situation, and I don't know what to do."

"Can't you ask your friends for help? Like Marco?" I nodded toward the bartender, who had retreated to the other side of the bar and was watching an old football game on cable.

"No. That's not… I'm not asking for help or your pity or anything at all. I just wanted to say you were right. Chester would've hit me. And I'm glad you hit him instead. That's all." She took a deep breath. In. Out. Like it hadn't been easy to say all those words.

I raised my glass. "To cleaning up messes?" I suggested, hoping she got my meaning, even though *I* wasn't totally sure what I meant.

Her gaze held mine. Dark blue, like a lake that's too deep to see the bottom. "To standing your ground. Even when it might be a mistake."

"I'll drink to that."

We clinked. I tossed back half the whiskey in my glass, enjoying the burn as it slid down my throat. Sometimes, cheap whiskey was just right. Harsh could be better than smooth, depending on the circumstances.

Jessi had only sipped hers. "You know, I don't even like whiskey." She passed her glass over to me.

"Then why are you drinking it?"

Her only answer was another tired sigh. We sat there

quietly for a while, which was the way I usually liked to sit. Yet I was the one who broke the silence first.

"Who's Jeremy?"

Before she could answer, the door to the bar opened. I glanced back to see a man in a cowboy hat parting the curtains that blocked the cold air from the doorway. He had khaki pants that only a cop would wear. A sheriff's department star on his fleece-lined coat.

His eyes landed on me and Jessi and narrowed.

Uh oh.

"I think Mitch went and tattled," I murmured to her.

Jessi sucked in a breath.

The cop stormed over to us. The star said he was Sheriff Douglas. Surprising, considering the guy was around my age. Thirty-ish. Seemed young to be in charge of the whole county, but some people were overachievers.

"Jessi, Mitch just came down to the station saying you tried to have Chester killed. Insisted I arrest you and some friend of yours for attempted murder." The sheriff squinted at me. "Let me guess. The friend was this guy."

"Attempted murder is nowhere close to what happened," I said.

Jessi muttered a curse and grabbed the glass of whiskey, downing the rest of it. Every eye in the bar was on us.

The sheriff rested a hand on his gun, adopting a defensive posture. "I want you to step outside, sir. Right now. With your hands up."

I complied, and Jessi trailed along at my heels. She'd grabbed both of our coats.

Outside, the snowfall had reduced to a trickle. But the temps had plummeted. Jessi shrugged on her jacket, but didn't offer me mine.

"Owen, it's not the way Mitch made it sound."

"Oh really? This guy didn't slam Chester into a refrigerator and break his nose and probably give him a concussion?"

I nodded. "All that happened."

"Not helping," Jessi hissed at me.

"Give me one reason I shouldn't take you into custody right damn now," Sheriff Douglas barked at me.

"Happy to." I kept my hands up as I explained. "I was having dinner at Jessi's Diner. At approximately seven p.m., I observed three male individuals enter the establishment. Jessi asked them to leave. They refused. I observed one of the individuals, whom Jessi identified as Chester, threaten her verbally. Then he put his hands on her and pushed her up against the counter. After that, he put his hands on her again and pushed her into the kitchen. He threatened her a second time. Then Chester raised his hand, and I assessed that he imminently intended to cause her grievous bodily harm. So I acted in defense of her to stop him."

I stopped to take a breath. I didn't usually have so much to say, but I could put sentences together. When I felt like it.

The sheriff and Jessi both gaped at me.

"Well, that's at least one reason," the sheriff said. "Are you a cop?"

"I'm not. But I have friends who are." A lot of them, in addition to my brother and sister.

"What about Mitch's claim that you stabbed him?"

"He was running into the kitchen and making threats. I warned him to stay away from us. He didn't. I scratched him with the knife so he would think better of his choices. Turned out, he did."

"It's all true," Jessi confirmed. "That's exactly what happened."

"Oh, I believe you." Sheriff Douglas wiped a hand over his stubbled face. "But jeez, Jessi. Where'd you dig up this guy?"

Clearly, that was a rhetorical question, because he didn't

let her answer. He pointed an accusatory finger at me. "Here's what's going to happen. You're going to get out of Hartley. I don't care where you go, as long as it's not here. I'm going to say you disappeared, and we're going to forget about this."

I was about to agree because he was right. If I left town, it would save him a ton of paperwork. And it would save me the trouble of making formal statements or turning over my ID. I didn't need this to escalate into a bigger headache later.

But Jessi said, "No way. You can't do that, Owen."

"And why is that?"

"Because..." Her panicked eyes danced over me. "He's my brother."

CHAPTER FOUR
Jessi

I'D DONE some impulsive things in my life, but this was a doozy.

"This is your brother?" Owen asked skeptically.

"Yep." Now that I'd said it, I had no choice but to follow through. "This is Trace. I told you he was coming to town because of Jeremy."

No one in town had ever met Trace or even seen his picture. I didn't have any family snapshots with my half-brother in the diner or my apartment. We weren't close that way. Like many aspects of my life, my relationship with Trace was complicated.

Now, even more so.

I hated to admit it, but I was *scared*. And somehow, for a few minutes tonight, Aiden had made me feel protected. After what he'd done for me, was it right for me to let Owen drive him out of town? On a night like this?

Owen was still frowning, but he finally removed his hand from near his gun holster. Aiden watched me with a tiny smirk curling one side of his mouth.

"You don't look alike."

"*Half*-brother," I said.

"Whatever. But if he's staying in Hartley, Chester and his crew are going to have it out for him."

"Then aren't you supposed to do your job?" Aiden asked. "Protect and serve?"

Owen glared, and Aiden returned it. But when Owen spoke, it was only to me. "I'm trying my best to keep the peace around here. You know how things are, Jessi, and you'd better inform your *brother*." Owen spit the word out like a curse. "He can stay long enough for things to settle with Jeremy and the Rigsbys. But I don't want any more trouble. He'd better keep his head down. And you know I don't enjoy saying it, but the same goes for you."

I nodded. Owen's frown turned apologetic, and then he walked back toward the bar. He'd parked his sheriff's department truck out front.

Snow still gently drifted down onto our bare heads and shoulders. I tossed Aiden his jacket, and he tugged it on. "I don't need you to explain how things are," he said. "I can already guess. Your sheriff is either in somebody's pocket, or he's a coward." Aiden raised his zipper to his chin. "I'm guessing Chester is related to somebody important. The mayor? Or the local judge?"

"You're partly right, minus a few key details. Owen Douglas isn't that bad. He's in a tough situation. I'm sure you don't want the entire history of Hartley, so I'll keep it simple. Chester's last name is Rigsby. The Rigsbys are an important family around here. Owen Douglas is part of the family, too. But Owen tries to be objective."

"Even when it comes to a woman being harassed and threatened on his watch? I don't think that's an issue a person can stay neutral on." Aiden's words were pointed, yet he spoke calmly. I hadn't heard him raise his voice once. Not even in the diner with Chester and Mitch.

"And I doubt Owen would have stayed neutral if I'd

shown up at the station tonight bleeding and with my jaw broken. But understand, Chester's friends would've given him and his brothers an alibi. They all would've sworn that nobody with the last name Rigsby attacked me. And it would've been my word against theirs. Trust me, I've been through that bull before, and I know how it goes."

"With Jeremy?"

I sniffed, my eyes and nose stinging. I insisted to myself that it was just from the cold. The guy seemed determined to get my life story. Maybe it was a way for him to pass the time while he was stuck in Hartley. Rubbernecking on his way through town. But I knew that thought was unfair. Aiden hadn't wanted to get involved, but he genuinely seemed to care about right and wrong.

Don't trust it, part of me said. Instincts honed by harsh experience.

Yet I was the one who'd proclaimed him to be my brother, even though I'd known him for the sum of…two hours? I had *vouched* for him. Claimed this stranger as mine.

I was all over the place tonight. I felt *lost*.

"I'm going back to the diner."

Aiden hooked his thumb toward the bar. "I'm parked in the lot out back. I can drive you."

"It's a few doors down. I'll walk." I paused. "You can walk with me if you want."

I started down the sidewalk, and instead of getting his car, Aiden fell into step beside me. Snowflakes tumbled across the few puddles of light from the street lamps. "I'm not from Hartley. I grew up near Colorado Springs, and that's where I met Jeremy. I thought I was in love."

Aiden nodded, as if this revelation didn't surprise him in the least. I hated the thought of being a cliche. But every story, no matter how classic, had its shades and nuances.

When I'd lived it, I hadn't seen how my love story would go so wrong.

My mother was an unrepentant romantic. Married four times and currently working on a fifth. My dad—Trace's father—had been her second, and that marriage hadn't lasted long. Mom loved the anticipation and the chase, but living as a married couple usually proved unsatisfying.

I'd wanted a life for myself outside my mother's shadow. Big dreams of traveling the world, creating beautiful and delicious food like the celebrity chefs on TV. But not much money to make all that happen. I hadn't minded paying my dues, though. The most inspiring successes had a lot of hard work behind them. I'd thought, why not me? I hadn't wanted to be rich or famous. I'd just wanted a place of my own.

I'd been working three jobs and barely paying my bills when I'd met Jeremy. He'd walked into the restaurant where I was a waitress, all confidence and flashing his killer smile. A fancy sales associate at some white-collar company. I'd ignored him at first, but after he asked me out at least six times, I'd finally agreed.

"He was on his best behavior in the beginning," I said.

"But?" Aiden asked.

"Jeremy had a thing for getting into bar fights." He'd had a temper and couldn't bear the slightest insult. He'd gotten jealous easily, which I'd convinced myself was sexy. A hint of jealousy could be a turn-on if it was tempered with trust and respect, plus a hefty dose of common sense. But Jeremy was too quick to anger, as if it was always simmering inside him and could leap to full boil at any minute.

"The local cops in the Springs warned him again and again. He had some friends in the police department because his dad had been in the Air Force, stationed at the base there. But after too many close calls and near arrests, Jeremy realized it wasn't going to end well. Not unless he learned how to manage his temper, and *that* wasn't going to happen. So he decided to move to Hartley and asked me to come with him."

"And let me guess. Jeremy's last name is Rigsby?"

"You catch on fast." I smiled without any humor. "His family was from Hartley, including his cousins like Chester and Mitch. And his uncles. After we moved here, Jeremy only got worse. One night, he came home drunk, and we argued. Same old story. He was jealous over some imagined thing. That time, he hit me. I was pretty shocked, because he had never done that before. But the warning signs had been there. I decided to leave him. Packed my stuff and left that night."

Probably because I had known, deep down, that if I let it go that one time, I might let it happen a hundred more. That wasn't me, and I couldn't ever let that become me.

I would never presume to judge another woman's story. But this was mine.

"And then?" Aiden asked, his tone softer than before.

Then I'd taken my beat-up car and driven to the motel. The owner was a touch paranoid, security cameras all over the parking lot. So a camera spotted Jeremy when he showed up later that night.

"When Jeremy caught up to me, he put me in the hospital." I said it with as little emotion as possible. I'd talked about it a lot in the past, and though it hadn't gotten easier exactly, I'd gotten further away from it. As if I could step back from the incident now instead of feeling like I was still inside of it. Living in it.

"I'd had a pocket knife with me that night," I added, "and he needed stitches to his face. So at least there's that."

Aiden and I started walking again. We were going slow, but we'd almost reached the diner. No cars out front, no sign of anyone nearby.

"Was he arrested?"

"Yep. By Owen. There was camera footage proving my side of the story, so there was no way for Jeremy or anyone else to deny it. Plus a woman staying at the motel happened to be a witness, and she made sure to tell anybody and everybody what happened. All of that was enough to get Jeremy to plead guilty to the charges. He got four years in prison, which everyone told me would be two years in reality. And that's exactly what happened. He just got his parole."

"Only two years for putting you in the hospital? After his history of violence?"

"It was his first official offense, and he had a parade of character witnesses at the sentencing."

Aiden exhaled a white cloud of vapor. "What about your family? Your brother? Didn't they come to Hartley to help you through that?"

"I never told them. Trace and I weren't close. Our father divorced my mom when we were kids, and Trace and our dad moved to the east coast." I chewed my lower lip. "I chose to make Hartley my home. I loved it here. In spite of everything, there are a lot of good people in this town. People who never doubted my side of the story."

That, and I'd refused to run. When I'd left Colorado Springs, I'd been running *to* something. A man I'd thought I loved, a new home. There was no way I was going to slink back, my dreams dashed, literally beaten down. No, even then I'd had too much defiance in me. All you had to do was ask my mother for confirmation of that fact. The battles we'd had when I was a teenager were epic.

"Then why is Chester Rigsby trying to run you out of town now?"

"Because Jeremy is heading here. And he's made it clear that we can't exist in the same town together. It's him or me."

We'd reached the front of the diner. Aiden turned to face

me and shifted his weight from one boot to the other. His large hands were tucked into his coat pockets. I returned his gaze as he studied me. "I expect that you feel the same?" he asked.

"Sure. But I'm in no place to make demands. I have friends in Hartley, but it's complicated. There are a lot of dynamics at play in this town, more than I've explained." This entire conversation had been draining enough already. "That's why I asked my brother to help me. I didn't know where else to turn. But he's coming all the way from Virginia, and this storm is causing delays. I got a text at the bar saying his flight to Grand Junction had been canceled. Even when he gets there, he'll still have to rent a car and drive to Hartley. I have no idea when he'll get here."

"That answers another of my questions."

I cringed. "Yeah, the brother thing. I spoke without thinking. Nobody in Hartley knows much about Trace. It just didn't seem right for Owen to make you leave because of me, and that was the solution my brain came up with. To say you were my brother."

"I don't mind. I won't be here long, anyway. I guess I'll have to answer to the name 'Trace' while I'm in Hartley."

"Either that, or I'll have to admit to Owen that I lied. I'll delay that as long as possible, thanks."

"It'll be obvious when the real Trace gets here, and he's not me."

"That's a problem for tomorrow. I'm still working on today." My usual motto these days. I took out my keys and unlocked the front door. Then I glanced back at him, my throat going dry. "Uh, I guess you'll need a place to stay tonight."

Aiden shrugged. "I'd been planning to bundle up in my car. I've slept in worse places."

"Military?" I guessed.

He nodded. No elaboration.

I huffed, a cloud of white appearing in front of my face. "You can't sleep in your car. That's ridiculous. It's freezing out here, and if you die of hypothermia, I don't want that on my conscience. But I need to know something about you. I can't invite some stranger to spend the night with me."

I realized my poor word choice. Aiden's expression remained in its usual impassive state, but his eyes were smirking.

"I mean, spend the night in the building where I live," I corrected. "Nothing more than that."

"Nothing more than that had even crossed my mind. So you do live here? Upstairs?"

"Yes."

"I agree that it's not a good idea to ask strange men to spend the night with you." That smirk continued to ricochet in his eyes. Aiden took his wallet from his pocket. "So how about this? I'll give you my driver's license to keep while I'm here. You can take a picture of it and email it to whoever. I could give you my family's contact info, too. If you want, you can call them to vouch for me. Assuming you have reception, because I don't."

"My phone has decent reception. Only certain carriers work around here. But I've also got Wi-Fi in my apartment upstairs. It works in the diner, so I'll get you the password." I held out my hand for his driver's license, and he plucked it from his wallet and placed it on my palm.

West Oaks, California, I read. I'd never heard of it.

I crossed my arms over my chest. "But I want to know something more about you. Something *real*. After the saga I just gave you, it's the least you can do. It had better be interesting, too, or I just might decide to let you freeze in your car after all."

He pursed his lips sardonically. "All right. Don't know if

it's interesting, but here goes. I was in the Army a few years back. Now I'm a chef. I rented a cabin way out in the woods for a few days. That's why I passed through Hartley, and that's where I'm headed as soon as the road's clear. Eventually, I'll end up in Steamboat Springs."

"Steamboat is a long way from Hartley."

"The cabin is between here and there. I had a hotel booked for tonight an hour east of Hartley. Was supposed to finish the scenic drive to my cabin in the morning."

He'd told me just barely enough to answer some of my questions from earlier. And he'd told me in the *least* interesting way possible. Like he was determined to be mysterious and make me ask more questions. Questions he'd no doubt ignore.

But I couldn't resist.

"Are you on vacation or is your trip to Colorado work-related?"

That made him pause for a moment. "Both. I have a work engagement in Steamboat Springs. But the cabin is just for fun. I like snowy woods. And quiet."

"See? That wasn't so hard. Are you meeting up with anyone for your vacation? Friends or family who'll be worried when you don't show up?"

"No. I'm going by myself."

I frowned. "Alone. In a remote cabin. Is this like a meditation retreat or something?"

"I *am* from California," he deadpanned. "I've planned a week of solitary contemplation and vegan food. Nothing but raw kale."

"I think that was a joke."

"You catch on fast."

I snickered.

"Did I pass?" he asked.

"Barely." I unlocked the door. "Come on. Before either of

us freezes or more Rigsby cousins decide to come by." *Or I think better of this.*

Aiden cast a final glance at the snowy street before following me inside.

I grimaced as I noticed the dirty dishes I'd left, but that was another problem for tomorrow-me to deal with. When I reached the kitchen, I flipped on the light. All I'd done in here was put away my lamb stew and other perishable ingredients. But my poor lemon tarts were still splattered over the floor. That made my heart hurt.

"This isn't how I usually leave things," I said. "Sorry about the mess. I know I blamed you earlier, but it wasn't your fault."

"It was a rough evening." Aiden bent down and swiped a fingertip through one of the less mangled tarts. He sucked the filling off his finger. "Wow. That lemon curd is..." He grunted instead of finishing the sentence, and a sudden thrill of pleasure flooded my body, leaving my pulse pumping. He'd complimented my lamb stew at dinner, but my desserts were my real passion.

His eyes flicked up to me as my face heated. I was clearly praise deprived. That explained it.

"Thanks," I forced out. "Uh." Why did I keep saying that? "I hope you don't mind bedding down in the dining room. My place upstairs is a studio. So."

He nodded quickly. "No problem at all. I'm just glad I'm not out in the cold."

"I thought you were a big, tough military man who could sleep anywhere."

"Doesn't mean I was going to enjoy it."

I smiled. "I'll go up and grab some blankets and pillows for you. There's a bathroom down here." I realized he didn't have anything with him. "Shoot, your travel bag is in your car, isn't it? With your toothbrush and all that."

"It is. But I'll survive."

"You could've grabbed your stuff before we walked over here."

One of his thick eyebrows lifted. "I wasn't going to assume you'd ask me to stay."

There went my pulse again. "What kind of sister would I be otherwise?"

"I have two, and they can be pretty ornery. Probably because I piss them off, but still. I'm used to it."

I smiled even wider at the fact that he'd just shared another small detail with me. Which was dumb. He wasn't going to stay more than a day or two in Hartley, anyway. What did it matter if he shared his story with me?

I had his driver's license. He'd offered to let me talk to his family, though I hadn't taken him up on it. I knew enough to let him stay here. But I was still going to lock my apartment door upstairs.

"You ate dinner?" he asked, catching me off guard again. "Not just whiskey?"

"I did." Two mini lemon tarts before he'd walked into my diner and radically changed my evening. "I'll be right back."

Aiden waited at the bottom of the stairs for me to grab some makeshift bedding for him, along with a new toothbrush from a bulk pack and some travel toothpaste. I handed it all over, taller than him now because I was on a higher step. Our hands brushed when he took the stack of blankets. I shivered. "Is it cold down here?" I asked. "I could turn up the heater."

"But then it'll be too hot for you upstairs."

He was totally right.

"Thank you." Aiden's voice dipped with sincerity. "I'm sorry for putting you out like this."

So he did know how to apologize. "It's no trouble. Sorry for getting so upset earlier about what happened with

Chester. I'm the one who caused this whole situation, not you. You were just trying to help."

He stared at me for a long moment with that hard, inscrutable expression.

Then Aiden turned and walked away from me, disappearing through the door to the dining room.

"Goodnight," I said, but I didn't hear an answer.

In the morning, I came downstairs to find the blankets folded neatly on the bottom step, the pillow placed on top.

The kitchen was spotless. The lemon tarts were cleaned up and the dishes were done. The dining room was clean too.

"Aiden?" I wandered around looking for him.

I'd been awake half the night thinking about the guy I barely knew who was asleep downstairs. Wondering what his deal really was. Army made sense. He was a chef, which explained a lot of the comments he'd made about my cooking. Plus the comfortable way he'd swung around that chef's knife.

He was a man who would go on vacation in a cabin all alone, yet also risk himself for a woman he'd just met and then *clean her kitchen*.

It was weird. But also endearing.

"Aiden?" I said again. But the bathroom was empty. So was the pantry. The storage closet. Cold disappointment seeped in as the minutes passed. There was no *I'll be right back* message. Nothing.

He was gone.

But in the short time I'd known him, Aiden had proved to be unpredictable. He'd cleaned up my mess from last night. I just hoped he wasn't going to cause any new ones.

CHAPTER FIVE
Aiden

I TRUDGED through the snow on Main Street. A truck with a snowplow pushed its way down the road, and shopkeepers shoveled their sidewalks clear.

First off, coffee.

While I'd tidied up Jessi's kitchen for her this morning, I wasn't about to go digging around for beans and filters in there. I wouldn't have been okay with some stranger getting handsy in *my* kitchen. That just seemed disrespectful.

White-coated peaks towered to one side of Main Street, while red sandstone cliffs provided color on the opposite. Spruces and pines added a rich hue of dark green, muted by the evidence of yesterday's storm.

I could see a little better why Jessi liked this place. The town didn't seem nearly as run-down and desolate as it had last night. The historic charm was on display, with far more *open* signs and inviting interiors in the windows, though at least half of the storefronts were closed down and marked for lease. Yet the fresh air and hum of activity on the street made the town pulse with energy. It was awake. *Alive*.

I wandered until I found a coffee shop, which turned out to be next door to the Hartley Saloon. Bean grinders whirred.

Sugary muffins and fresh Columbian brew scented the air. The line was five deep, and the baristas looked harried, making espresso drinks as quickly as they could. From the chatter I overheard, I gathered that most of the people in here were fellow refugees from the bridge closure and the storm.

While I waited for my turn, I used the free Wi-Fi. The vacation rental host had confirmed my stay at the cabin. *Nonrefundable*. I wrote back that I probably wouldn't arrive today, but I'd hopefully be there tomorrow.

I *really* hoped I'd be there tomorrow.

The rental host had promised true isolation. Nobody around for miles in a place that didn't even qualify as a blip on the map. That was what I'd wanted. A scenic drive to an even more scenic, isolated locale. I pictured the cozy fireplace of my vacation rental again. Quiet woods surrounding me, no sounds but the thump of falling snow. And a kitchen for me to try out some new experiments. Nothing too fancy, but I wasn't fancy at home either. And after that, my catering gig for the wedding in Steamboat. Then back to California and my usual life.

Jessi's real brother would be in Hartley by then, and her problems would once again be her own. As they should be. She had made it clear that she wanted to maintain some distance from me, and I had no problem with that. This was just an interlude. A brief crossing of paths.

But…that didn't mean I couldn't make myself useful during my brief stay.

I reached the front of the line and ordered a black brewed coffee. The girl at the counter smiled with relief at my simple order, though she did a brief double-take when she looked up at me. I wasn't sure what that meant. Was it just general interest, or had she heard about the incident last night?

The town I was from, West Oaks, wasn't that big. But it

was far from the tiny footprint of Hartley. My hometown was on the Southern California coast to the west of Los Angeles, and it had new people constantly churning through. I'd never spent much time in a true small town like Hartley, hours and hours away from the nearest real city and cut off by geography from everything else.

Maybe news around here just traveled that fast. It didn't seem like something I would enjoy. Having my neighbors so aware of my business? Nope. I liked my privacy, thank you very much.

After I paid, I tucked a dollar in the tip jar, thanked the girl, and went on my way.

The cold air braced me when I got back outside. It was a pleasant contrast, thin warmth from the sun peeking through the layer of clouds combined with the dry, pine-scented air. I took a sip of hot coffee, enjoying the flood of heat down my throat and the bitter tang on my tongue, before my cup was suddenly knocked out of my hand and my coffee splattered over the snow. Steam rose.

Mitch Rigsby stood next to me, teeth bared in a snarl.

I blinked at him. "Now that wasn't nice. I was having a moment."

He had a baseball cap pulled low over his eyes, his overgrown hair sticking out from beneath. "What the hell are you still doing in Hartley? After the shit you pulled at the diner, anybody with sense would've been in Utah by now."

Had he heard the news that I was Jessi's brother? Probably not, unless Sheriff Douglas was the talkative type. I was sure Owen intended to downplay my presence here more than that.

I'd been up most of the night, but not because I'd been uncomfortable bedding down on the dining room floor. I'd kept my ears trained in case any other Rigsbys came near the diner, but mostly I'd been contemplating the woman asleep upstairs. And wondering if she was up too, thinking of me.

I'm the one who caused this situation, she'd said. I doubted she'd realized at the time how it sounded. Like she was the one to blame for her ex's actions. It probably wasn't something she believed on a conscious level. Maybe it had only been a slip of the tongue, a result of exhaustion after a long night.

But all the same, I hadn't liked it. If Jessi believed her situation was her fault, then I blamed Mitch and Chester Rigsby and their band of lowlifes.

I glanced pointedly down at Mitch's stomach, which was hidden within his parka. "How's your tummy? Bothering you? It just seemed like a scrape to me, but I don't know your pain tolerance."

"Shut your mouth." Mitch took a menacing step toward me. I didn't move.

"You're going to attack me in broad daylight with a hundred witnesses around?" I asked. "Keep in mind, most of them aren't related to you. They're tourists or travelers from other towns. I'm sure they'd be excited to post videos online of you attacking an unarmed guy who was just trying to drink his coffee."

Mitch's eyes darted to the coffee shop behind us. Like most of the storefronts on Main Street, it had a huge window, and I didn't have to look to know at least some of the people were watching this confrontation with their phones at the ready.

Mitch seemed to be thinking along the same lines. He backed off by a centimeter. "I don't know who the hell you are, or why you'd step in to defend a slut like Jessi Novo, but—"

I advanced on him fast, edging him backward toward the curb until he was teetering off of it. I grabbed a fistful of his parka. From a few feet away, it would look like I'd saved him from dropping into the street.

"See, that's where you've gone too far," I spoke in a near whisper, gathering myself to my full height and glaring down at him, though I probably only had an inch on the guy. I was tall and bulky, and so was Mitch Rigsby. But it was all about presence, and Little Mitch didn't have it.

"You don't talk about Jessi like that. Or any woman, for that matter. You don't come near Jessi. You don't look at Jessi. You don't think about Jessi. And then I won't have an issue with you. I'll be generous and forget about your other bullshit. If you don't? I'll have to teach you a more vivid lesson than the one you and your brother already got."

I let go of his coat, and his arms pinwheeled as he lost his balance, stepping hard into the street off the curb. I spun on my heel, continuing down the sidewalk. I'd have to get more coffee later because I wasn't going to wait in that line again.

"Next one to be getting a lesson is you!" Mitch shouted after me. Not exactly eloquent. But what I'd expected. Jessi's brother was going to have a cluster on his hands when he got to Hartley. But that would've been the case whether I'd passed through this town or not.

For now, *I* was in Hartley, and her brother wasn't. So I was going to do my damnedest to stand in for him. I was going to do what a brother should for his sister, the same actions I would take if Madison or Regan had been in Jessi's shoes. My sisters drove me nuts, but I would always have their back if they asked.

Chester Rigsby and his brothers were bullies. They liked to talk big. Show off. Smack around somebody who was weaker. But every bully had a pivot point. That moment when they thought better of it and backed off. Last night, Mitch had found it when I had the knife in my hand and his brother was bleeding on the kitchen floor. This morning, it had been all the witnesses.

The question was, what would it take for the Rigsby boys to decide Jessi wasn't worth the effort?

With any luck, my next encounter with them would nip this problem in the bud. The sooner I could get that out of the way, the better. Because I had that nice, cozy cabin waiting for me and days of solitude to look forward to. I would clean up this little mess for Jessi, and then I'd be on my way.

———

After going a few blocks, I saw the sign for the county sheriff's department on the next street over. I came through the front entrance, stomping my boots on the mat on my way in.

The officer on desk duty, a young woman with hundreds of tiny braids pulled into a ponytail, looked up. "Help you, sir?" She had big brown eyes, and her uniform identified her as Deputy Marsh.

"I hope so. I'd like to speak to Sheriff Douglas, please."

"What about?"

The station wasn't very big. There was an open door beyond the desk that I suspected belonged to the sheriff. Blinds were drawn over a window in the wall, but I spotted movement coming from behind it.

"Could you tell him Jessi Novo's brother is here?"

Then Owen Douglas stepped into the open doorway, already frowning at me. "Is Jessi all right?"

"For now. That's what I'm here to talk to you about."

His mouth worked like he was chewing up something especially disgusting. "Fine. I've got five minutes, but after that I have to see to the motorists who are stranded because of the bridge being closed. We're organizing a coat drive."

Motorists. I liked that. Here, the speech had a different clip to it than in Southern California. A different drawl.

I followed him into his office. "People drive through Colorado in January without a coat?"

"You'd be surprised," he muttered. Owen shut the door to his office and plopped into the chair behind his desk. His cowboy hat rested crown-down on the console table behind him. Owen's hair was buzzed in a high and tight. Made me wonder if he was ex-military. "Thought I asked you to keep your head down," Owen said. "Yet first thing the next morning, you're parading over here like you want everyone in Hartley to see you. Like you're asking for trouble."

"Not asking for it. But not turning down any invites, either. Should they come my way." Though I decided it was best not to share my encounter with Mitch outside the coffee shop.

Owen's scowl darkened. "You know what? I don't appreciate that attitude. You might be Jessi's brother, *supposedly*, but that doesn't mean I won't throw you in jail if you step out of line." He pounded the desk with his index finger. "I want to see some ID. For all I know, you've got outstanding warrants in other places."

My respect for him grew slightly. "Don't have ID. Sorry."

He stood up from his chair, palms landing with a smack on his desktop. "Turn out your pockets. Now."

I did. I tossed my wallet, phone, my car keys, and the keys I'd borrowed from Jessi onto the surface. Owen grabbed the wallet and flipped it open. "Where's your driver's license?"

"I must've misplaced it somewhere last night." Specifically, when I gave it to Jessi. She still had it. And my credit cards were back at the diner, too, tucked safely in a drawer in the kitchen. I hadn't thought it wise to walk through town with a credit card for "Aiden Shelborne" if I was supposed to be somebody else.

"You're playing games with me, Novo, and I won't stand for it. If you're hiding things, I'm going to find out." He plopped into his desk chair and rolled it up to his computer. "I want your state of residence and date of birth. I'm going to run a background search on you right now. So park yourself in that seat."

"I'm from…Virginia." Jessi had said her brother was from there, and I decided to be honest in case she'd already mentioned it to Owen. I plucked a date of birth from thin air, recited it, and sat. But the weaknesses in this story were quickly becoming apparent. I knew nothing about Jessi's brother. Hell, maybe there were arrest warrants out for the guy. Or pictures all over social media of a man who clearly wasn't me.

We were about to find out.

Owen started tapping on his keyboard. I waited to see if I would land myself in jail for false statements to a peace officer. Maybe this entire charade was about to go up in smoke. If that happened, I would explain and hope that Owen's sympathy for Jessi extended to the guy who was helping defend her. I was in this office for *her* wellbeing, not mine.

But after several long minutes, Owen sat back in his chair and glared at me. "I can't seem to find anything about you. You're a ghost, which is pretty rare in this day and age. Especially with such an unusual name."

Rare indeed. Trace Novo must've hated social media as much as I did. "Maybe the problem is with your internet connection," I supplied.

"Or you're a *liar*. I didn't even find a driver's license record in Virginia."

"Are you calling Jessi a liar too?" I asked calmly.

Owen's jaw clenched. Released.

"I'm not here because I want to cause problems for you," I said. "I'm here for my sister. She's got nobody else to stand up for her the way she needs. You going to deny that?"

He stared me down a bit longer before reluctantly shaking his head. "But you weren't around for Jessi before. Were you?"

That was something that had bothered me last night about Jessi's story. She hadn't called her brother after Jeremy Rigsby put her in the hospital. Seemed like a glaring omission. If she had trusted him, why wouldn't she have called him back then?

But my questions about Trace could wait until later.

"I regret that," I said. "But I'm here *now*. Let me do what I can for her. We'll say that you called me in this morning to question me. Nobody has to know if you answer a few of mine as well."

"All right," he grumbled after some more glaring. "This is only because it's for Jessi."

"My thoughts exactly." I wondered just how much interest he felt toward her, but I pushed that aside. "Jessi told me that Jeremy Rigsby is on his way back to Hartley. What do you know about that?"

"Jeremy just got his release papers. He was at a correctional facility near Denver and he's heading home. The bridge closure has delayed him, and the last I heard, he was going to wait it out instead of taking the long detour around. But for weeks now, his cousins have been trying to clear the way for him in a more figurative sense. When I've asked them about their intentions toward Jessi, they've denied and denied some more."

"So you *have* tried to stop them from harassing her?"

He leaned his forearm on his desk. "Of *course* I have. When Jessi tells me something specific, I look into it. But the problem is that she doesn't tell me much. And then, when I talk to Chester and Mitch and their guys, nobody knows a damn thing. So don't sit there and accuse me of not doing enough when you *haven't been here*."

I considered my next words carefully. I was already pissing him off, which I didn't necessarily mind. But if Owen threw me out of his office, or decided to arrest me after all, that wouldn't help anyone. "You booked Jeremy after he attacked Jessi. You gathered the video footage, made all the reports. You must've been a witness against him."

"Yes. The case didn't go to trial because he pled out, but I led the investigation and turned over the case to the county prosecutor."

"Even though you're related to the Rigsby family?"

Owen's eyes narrowed to slits. "I will explain this one time to you. Not because I owe you anything, but for Jessi's sake, because I consider her a friend. And this is off the record. You got that?"

I twirled my fingers. *Go ahead.*

"This story starts a few decades ago. Before you or I were born. In the 1970s, when the whole country was in recession after recession, Hartley was on its last legs. Tourism had dried up around here, and the businesses were shuttering. A man named Sawyer Rigsby came to town. Invested, started up new enterprises, brought in new jobs. He saved Hartley. And ever since, anybody with the last name Rigsby has had a special shine on them around here. Especially Sawyer Rigsby's sons."

"Is one of them your father?"

"No," he snapped. "Sawyer Senior was my grandfather. His daughter was my mother. I'm talking about my uncles: Sawyer Junior, Dale, and Gary." He hunched forward. "Are you following this so far? Should I draw you a diagram?"

"I'm no genius, but I'm keeping up."

"Good. Uncle Sawyer is the eldest. He took over his

father's empire after my grandpa died. Expanded investments all over Hartley and in the surrounding towns too. Real estate, mining, even a candy-making company. He's the president of the town's Board of Trustees, founder of half the charities. He's well-loved."

"Does he deserve it?"

"I'm biased."

I inclined my head, appreciating Owen's honesty. But he hadn't said if he was biased for Sawyer, or against.

"The next son after Sawyer Junior was my uncle Gary. He set out to fight for his country and make Hartley proud. He became an Air Force captain. He was shot down during Operation Iraqi Freedom. KIA."

"Jessi mentioned him. Stationed in Colorado Springs. Jeremy's father?"

"That's right. My favorite uncle, and I hope he rests in peace."

"And Dale?"

"He's Uncle Sawyer's right hand. The problem solver. Contract negotiations that turn ugly, evictions. Trying to boss around law enforcement. That kind of thing."

Ah. Now I was getting a clearer picture. It didn't sound like Owen was fond of his Uncle Dale. "And let me guess. Chester and Mitch are Dale's kids."

"Plus two daughters and Theo, who's the youngest." Theo must've been the third guy at the diner last night. "Uncle Sawyer has no children. After Gary died, Sawyer wanted Jeremy and his mom to move to Hartley. Join the Rigsby clan. She declined because she had family and a life in Colorado Springs. But three years ago, Jeremy finally moved here, and he brought Jessi Novo with him. I assume you know what happened then."

"More or less." Jeremy had beaten up his girlfriend and gotten himself sent to prison. And Owen Douglas, disfavored relation, had helped prosecute him. But Owen hadn't been driven out of town for it. Interesting.

These were some of the town dynamics that Jessi had mentioned last night. She was right—it was complicated. And yet, it was a common enough story. Fathers, sons, brothers. Men who ruled over a place, and the women who sometimes got caught in between. In other variations of such stories, women were the ones in charge, but that didn't seem to be the case with the Rigsby family.

Owen hadn't mentioned much about his own mom, and I figured there was another story there. Maybe something that explained why he was on the outskirts of the group. But nothing I needed to know about.

"I'm worried about what's going to happen when Jeremy gets back," Owen said. "A protective order bars Jeremy from going near Jessi. He's also on parole, which puts further limits on him. If Jeremy was smart, he'd just leave her be. But Chester and Mitch have made it clear they don't approve of Jessi sticking around anymore. I've told them to stay away from her. They don't listen to me. They see me as a nuisance and only tolerate me because I'm technically family. But if I can get hard proof that Chester or anyone else has crossed the line, I'll take it to the district attorney."

"And your uncles? What about them?"

Owen turned contemplative. "Sawyer keeps himself above the fray. That's what he did when Jeremy was arrested. He stayed out of the mess entirely. Dale is trickier, but he cares about their finances, not petty grievances. My hunch is that my cousins are plotting against Jessi on their own."

"But do you think your uncles will welcome Jeremy back?"

"Jeremy's out of prison, and he's paid his debt. That's how they'll see it."

"Is that how *you* see it?"

"That's how our justice system works, so yes. But we were talking about my uncles, not me. Dale is kind of a jerk. Uncle Sawyer is tougher to predict. If he has to choose between his prized nephew and a woman who isn't a Hartley native?" He heaved a sigh. "I like to think he'll make the right choice."

I stood up. "It's more important that you know what *you'll* choose."

I left Owen Douglas's office without waiting for a reply.

CHAPTER SIX
Jessi

CARRYING A FOIL-COVERED TRAY, I used my back to push open the door to the Hart-Made Sweet Shop. As usual, twangy country music played, this time the heartfelt melody of "Cowboy Take Me Away."

I'd always been a rock and roll girl myself, but my friend Scarlett Weston loved her 90s and 2000s country hits. The more sappy and romantic, the better. It reminded me of the music my mom listened to. And I had listened to it, too, back in the day. When I used to believe some cowboy-prince would sweep me off into the sunset. I did still harbor silly fantasies like that, but I kept them to the realm of daydreams and late-night musings. Where they belonged.

Reality wasn't so pretty.

Case in point: I'd invited my mysterious savior to stay last night. I had trusted him. And he'd vanished, taking the primary set of keys to my diner with him. Including the key to *my safe*.

When I'd realized that, I had checked the safe and found my dwindling stack of cash intact. But I couldn't sit around all day waiting for Aiden to return. Today was Monday, and I didn't open the diner on Mondays. I had other work to do. I was going to focus on my tasks, not on Aiden Shelborne and what he might be up to.

But if he robs me, I swear I'll be using my chef's knife in new ways later.

"Hey," I called out. "Where do you want me to set these?"

Scarlett poked her head out from behind a massive stand-mixer. Her dark auburn hair was swept in a high ponytail, with wavy tendrils falling into her face. "Anywhere, sweetheart. Thanks."

I put the tray of tartlets on the marble-topped counter. The sweet shop had the vibe of an old-fashioned soda fountain, with a stamped tin ceiling and a checkered tile floor. The glass cases were packed with Hart-Made's red and white packages, each filled with chocolate-covered treats and their signature brown sugar brittle.

The Hart-Made Candy Co. was one of the few Hartley businesses that was still thriving. Expanding, even. Probably because Sawyer Rigsby owned it. Well, he owned a lot of things around here, including the building that housed my diner and apartment.

So I was all the more grateful for the risk Scarlett was taking—selling my tartlets in the sweet shop and passing me the proceeds. They sold some other third-party products here too, so it wasn't entirely unheard of. But Sawyer didn't know about our side deal.

It wasn't as if the Hart-Made Candy Co. lacked for demand. In the last year, Sawyer had converted a nearby commercial kitchen to increase production. They had a warehouse to pack and ship orders to stores throughout the region. Sometimes, Scarlett had trouble keeping the sweet shop stocked. So really, I was helping them out, too.

Scarlett came over and peeked beneath the foil. "Lemon? These look incredible."

"I hope so." There were only half as many as I'd originally

made, but the other half had ended up on the floor thanks to Chester Rigsby.

Okay, *fine*, I'd eaten some too, before I'd realized how scarce they would be. Before Aiden had shown up and then suddenly disappeared, leaving his driver's license behind and taking my keys.

Admittedly, leaving his license was an odd strategy if he intended to rob me. I assumed that meant he'd turn up again, but I had no idea when. Or even if he was all right. What if Chester's brothers had grabbed Aiden off the street and done something to him as payback? What if *Chester* now had my keys?

I was about ready to stuff another lemon tartlet into my mouth, just to shove down all my worries.

Everybody in town knew about Chester Rigsby's warning: *Jessi's Diner is off limits*. The threat was more implied than explicit, whispered rather than yelled. That gave them deniability when Owen Douglas came sniffing around. And it kept the ugly truth out of the ears of Sawyer Rigsby, the town benefactor who hated to sully his hands.

It was like I'd told Aiden last night. I did have friends who were helping me as much as they could. I was supplying bar snacks a couple times per week for Marco, and Scarlett was selling my tarts. But they were at the mercy of the Rigsby brothers, too. Everyone was afraid to step out of line, as they should be. I didn't want them to take risks for me, even if it meant I was standing out front all alone when Chester made me a target.

It hadn't always been like this. Right after Jeremy's prison sentence, the town had been squarely on my side. The evidence against my ex had been too damning. Jeremy's Uncle Sawyer had been kind to me, at least on the surface, keeping my rent low as I was just getting started with the diner. Dale and his sons had ignored me, which had been fine by me. I'd thought the town had begrudgingly accepted me as one of their own.

But after two years, Hartley was ready to welcome back its prodigal son and to sweep me away with yesterday's trash. The Rigsbys wanted to give Jeremy his fresh beginning, and there I was, the rotten reminder of his past.

The problem was, I didn't intend to go so easily.

I had no idea how much Sawyer really knew about his nephews' scheming. But if I could keep making my rent payments, then Sawyer couldn't kick me out until my lease was officially up next year. My brother Trace, the real one, would help me weather the storm. And soon, I hoped that public sentiment would sway back in my favor. Somehow.

There were a lot of *ifs* and *maybes* in my plan. A whole lot of hope. Sometimes, that was all I had.

Scarlett went to the register and pulled out a small envelope. "Here's what you earned for last week's chocolate and pecan. If you can make more, we'll take them. Any flavor. Whatever inspires you."

"I'll try to whip up more, but I'm still hoping to make the diner work. I'm not giving up on it yet." I accepted the envelope, unable to resist the urge to check the cash inside. It would help, but I would be short on rent unless something changed.

Scarlett's mouth turned down sympathetically. "Of course not. You shouldn't give up."

"If Hart-Made has my baked goods dominating the shelves, wouldn't that make it more likely that somebody will ask about your new supplier?"

"I can sweet-talk Sawyer. I talked him into hiring me, didn't I? And I don't care what Dale Rigsby or his caveman sons think. They can kiss my sugary butt."

I held back a smile. Scarlett was around my age, twenty-seven, but she talked like a quirky grandma in a small-town movie. Yet she was also an avid outdoorswoman, fishing in summer, off-roading in her Jeep Wrangler during mud season and scouting the best spots for back-country skiing in winter.

"You don't want that attention," I said. "Trust me."

"Speaking of the Rigsbys." Scarlett drummed her fingers on the counter. "I heard there was a dust-up at your diner last night. Involving Chester and Mitch?"

Of course she'd heard about it. "Who told you?"

"People who were at the bar. Sheriff Owen marched you and some mystery guy outside to question you. Are you okay?"

"I'm fine." My pulse kicked up. I had to lie to her, and it was my own fault. "My, um, brother was there. He's the mystery guy."

"Oh? I remembered you said he was on his way, but I was worried the storm put a wrench in his travel."

It definitely had. I'd gotten a text from the real Trace that morning, saying he was still trying to get a new flight after his was canceled.

"He managed to sneak through," I said sheepishly.

"Good timing, then." Scarlett lowered her voice, as if we were in a crowd and not alone in the sweet shop. "Jeremy will be back any day. I'm sure the storm and the bridge are making it harder for him to get back, but I'm glad your brother beat him here."

"Me too. I'm just hoping that with Trace around, I can ride this out and somehow Jeremy and his family will forget how much they hate me. But my brother beating up Chester isn't likely to help defuse things."

Scarlett probably thought the same. But then she surprised me. Her kind smile turned devious. "Maybe not. But if you have to go out, better to go out swinging. You've always seemed like the fighting type to me."

"You're right, I am." Even if I sometimes took a leap without checking how far I was from the ground.

"So," Scarlett said. "When do I get to meet this brother?"

I glanced at the window to the street at that exact moment, and guess who was sauntering down the sidewalk? "Sooner than you might think," I muttered.

I crossed to the door and pushed it open. "Trace!" I yelled. Aiden continued to walk away from me on the opposite side of the street. Had he already forgotten his fake name? "Hey!"

Finally, he glanced over and paused when he saw me.

It was still frigid out, but the sun had a broken through the clouds, making all the snow on the nearby rooftops glitter. Aiden had a beanie over his hair, a bag slung over his shoulder, which I assumed he'd gotten out of his car. His mouth quirked slightly as he crossed the street toward me. I went out to meet him.

"You took off with my keys," I said. "I had places to go, and I was nearly locked in."

"Yet you obviously used the spare key that I assumed you would have. I couldn't leave your doors unlocked with you asleep." He tossed me my keys, which I barely managed to catch.

I should've thanked him for cleaning up my kitchen. And thanked him *again* for the way he had helped me last night. But that wasn't what came out of my mouth.

"Where have you been?" I demanded.

"Busy," he said in his rumbly, stoic voice. "Have you had breakfast yet?"

"That's hardly an answer to my question."

"Do you have a snow shovel? If you haven't cleared your sidewalks yet, I can take care of it. I finished the other things on my to-do list."

To-do list? I moved in closer, glancing up and down the street. "*Aiden*," I whispered. "You're supposed to be my brother, but you disappeared this morning without leaving me a note or your phone number or anything. I had no way to reach you. What if somebody had grabbed you and dumped you off a cliff into a ravine?"

He shifted toward me, and I could feel his warmth even through our layers of clothing. Aiden's dark brown irises had tiny flecks of gold in them. "You were worried about me?"

I opened my mouth, my response stuck somewhere in my chest.

Scarlett cleared her throat behind us. She had the door to the sweet shop open. "Is this the brother I've heard so much about?"

I spun around, pasting a smile over my face. "Scarlett." My voice cracked. "This is Trace."

Aiden shook her hand politely, but made zero effort at conversation. The awkwardness was palpable. I was lying to my friend, and that knowledge crawled over my skin.

When the real Trace Novo got to Hartley and very much *did not* match up with Aiden Shelborne, Scarlett would find out I'd lied. Everyone would find out. And that sucked, because it would confirm what Jeremy had been saying about me all along. That I couldn't be trusted with the truth. Plus, every moment that Aiden played my brother, he could be in danger. Which should've been obvious to me last night. And having a man like him around me, so *close* like this...

No. It wouldn't work. How had I *ever* thought this would work?

I couldn't do it.

"Actually, the thing is—"

Then another voice rang out across Main Street, interrupting me. "Miss Scarlett Weston. Just the woman I wanted to see!"

I turned and groaned when I saw who was jogging toward us. Sawyer Rigsby was in his sixties, but was one of those men whose looks had both softened and improved with age. I'd seen pictures on Jeremy's computer of his family when he was younger, and his uncle Sawyer had been dazzlingly handsome. Now, between his white hair and the smile lines around his eyes and mouth, he was less intimidating. Attractive in a warm and easygoing way.

But I no longer trusted men who smiled that much.

Sawyer reached us, his grin flickering when he noticed me and especially when his eyes landed on Aiden. "Morning."

"What can I do for you, Mr. Rigsby?" Scarlett asked.

Sawyer was outwardly friendly to everyone around town, and when he stepped in to defuse a controversy or argument, he acted more like a disappointed grandpa than a stern authority figure. He'd never been outright rude or dismissive of me, even after Jeremy's arrest. But he was still my landlord. And Jeremy's uncle.

He might as well have had a big yellow *caution* sign right above his head.

Sawyer got down to business. "With the bridge out and the snowstorm, no one will be getting any deliveries today. The coffee shop is running low on supplies already. I wanted to see what we had ready to go at the sweet shop."

"Plenty," Scarlett said with a glance at me. Would Sawyer see the lemon tarts and ask where they'd come from?

But Aiden interrupted before I could finish that thought. "I heard there was a drive for winter coats, too," Aiden said to Sawyer.

Mr. Rigsby gave him another assessing glance that set my nerves on edge. "That's right. We've got extra people to feed and keep warm, and we want to make them feel welcome. Even if it's not the best timing." He stuck out his hand. "Sawyer Rigsby. You are?"

"Trace Novo," Aiden said. "Just got in yesterday."

"My brother." The words left bile on my tongue. But the

thought of admitting my lie now, in front of Sawyer, made my insides seize up.

I was really having a day, wasn't I?

"And what do you think of our fair town so far?" Sawyer asked.

Oh, no.

"Mr. Rigsby owns the Hart-Made Candy Company," I said to Aiden. "And he's my landlord."

Translation: please don't say anything stupid.

But in the twelve hours or so I had known Aiden Shelborne, had he seemed like the type to shy away from controversy?

"Hartley has its charms. I'm not so sure about the Hartley welcoming wagon, though. Your nephews didn't seem too friendly last night."

Sawyer's smile deflated. "I did hear about an incident. That was unfortunate. A misunderstanding, I'm sure."

Aiden nodded. "Even more unfortunate is how Chester and his brothers have been keeping people away from Jessi's Diner. Another misunderstanding?"

I wasn't even breathing. My eyes stared daggers at my fake brother.

"I can look into it," Sawyer said stiffly. "Later. When the current crisis has been averted."

Aiden suddenly broke into a wide smile. Lots of teeth. It came nowhere near his eyes. "Actually, this is a perfect opportunity. The diner hasn't been busy lately, so Jessi has all kinds of supplies. Don't you, sis?"

Sawyer and Scarlett both looked to me. I shrugged. "Absolutely. What do you need?"

Sawyer opened his mouth, but again Aiden spoke over him. "The Hartley Board of Trustees should host a free dinner at Jessi's Diner tonight," Aiden said. "To show everyone just how welcoming this town can be. Of course,

I'm sure you'll compensate her for the cost of the food. Your company could make it a charity tax deduction."

"Sounds like a perfect solution," Scarlett chimed in. "You wouldn't mind, Jessi?"

Sawyer glanced between me and Aiden, while I was racking my brain for some way to get out of this. Owen had told us to keep a low profile. This was calling attention. A lot of it.

Aiden slung his arm around my shoulders. "She wouldn't mind at all."

———

After Sawyer and Scarlett had gone inside the sweet shop, I grabbed Aiden's arm and started marching him down the street toward the diner. A few people watched us curiously. When we were far enough away from anyone else that we wouldn't be overheard, I pushed my fake brother into a narrow passage between two buildings. Deep snow nearly swallowed my boots.

"*Host a dinner tonight*? I thought you were going to help if Chester's brothers came around again. Not run my business for me!"

He leaned against the brick wall of the building behind him. "Sawyer Rigsby cares about public opinion. We're using that against him."

"How do you know anything about Sawyer Rigsby?"

"Owen told me."

"You and Owen are besties now?"

Aiden's eyebrow twitched sardonically. The man had some expressive eyebrows, considering the rest of him was so matter-of-fact. "This charity dinner will get Hartley back on your side. And even if the stranded tourists are getting a free meal, they'll leave tips. They'll be grateful for what you're doing."

"It...might not be a bad thought." In fact, I wished I'd come up with it. It was kind of brilliant, actually. "But how the hell am I supposed to host a dinner for a hundred or more people on a few hours' notice?" Sawyer had set the charity dinner for six o'clock. Guests wouldn't come at a slow trickle like regular customers. It would have to be a buffet, food made to scale, and I had no experience with that.

"It's not ideal, but I do this for a living. I'm the executive chef for a catering company." Aiden said this like I already should've known it. As if I possessed more than a handful of details about this man. "I saw what was in your pantry and fridge this morning," he went on. "We can do chicken parmesan. Pasta and vegetables on the side. I'll keep it simple. Something hearty for a cold night."

Okay, that did sound really good. And possibly even doable. "But Trace Novo isn't a chef," I said. "As far as I know, my brother doesn't know how to cook an egg."

"What does he do for a living? I was wondering about that."

I rubbed the skin between my eyes. "Some kind of government work overseas. I barely know. My point was that I don't like lying."

"You're the one who said I was your brother. What did you think would happen?"

I threw up my hands. "I wasn't thinking!"

"I'm not a fan of lying, either. I'd much rather say nothing at all. But these people are fighting dirty against you, Jessi. You might have to get dirty, too. And you can't feel bad about it. Last night, you said you were glad I stepped in. Right?"

I glanced out of the alley at the street. We were still alone. "Yes."

"And it was my choice to get involved. So long as I *am*

involved, I'll do whatever I can. I don't half-ass things. But it's your choice if we keep this going. If you want to call it off, then do it. Just be ready to deal with the consequences. Because there will be consequences, either way."

I crossed my arms. "You're arrogant, you know that? Maybe you do have something in common with my brother."

"Maybe we should stop talking and get started on cooking. You've got over a hundred people coming to dinner tonight. In case you forgot."

"You're obnoxious too."

"Drown me in compliments, why don't you? Clock is ticking."

"Fine," I said begrudgingly. "Thank you for doing this."

"No problem at all." He hitched his bag onto his shoulder and marched out of the alley. My eyes followed him for a few seconds before my feet moved.

I did need his help. But I was a fool if I'd imagined I could control this man. Or even predict what he might do next. Aiden Shelborne was more than I had ever bargained for.

What had I gotten myself into?

CHAPTER SEVEN
Aiden

THE CHARITY DINNER WENT SMOOTHLY, all things considered. Until what happened after.

Jessi and I spent most of the afternoon in the kitchen. If she was chopping, I was sautéing. If she was minding the pasta as it boiled, I was stirring extra seasonings into the tomato sauce. We were a relay team, working instead of talking. Just how I liked things when I ran a kitchen. I'd brought my knife roll with me on the trip, and it gave me some comfort and satisfaction to have my own knives in my hands. No offense to Jessi's, of course. But a chef liked to use his own tools.

When I reached a break in my preparations, I mentioned that I could use a shower. It had been way too long since my last one, all the way back when I'd left the house I shared with my roommates in West Oaks. But Jessi hesitated. Then there was more awkwardness when she realized I would need to use *her* shower.

Her cheeks went rosy as she minced onion into minuscule bits. "Go ahead. Fresh towels are in the closet."

"All right. Thanks."

I tried to be quick about it. Stripping down and starting

the water, barely pausing to notice the details of her upstairs studio apartment. The vase of fresh flowers, which must've come from a greenhouse, a touch of beauty that she'd probably bought just for herself. The abstract paintings on the walls that I suspected she had made. All the feminine touches that transformed the simple space into a home. It wasn't a cabin in the woods with a fireplace. But it was damn cozy in its own way. Infused with a floral, powdery scent.

I came downstairs in my jeans with my T-shirt over my shoulder, water droplets trailing over my bare shoulders. "Have you checked on the chicken in the oven?"

Jessi glanced over. Then she started coughing.

"You okay?"

"It's nothing."

I poured her a glass from the tap, but she waved it away and disappeared into the diner bathroom. She didn't emerge until I'd put my shirt back on, which I doubted was a coincidence. I hadn't been trying to upset her or get any particular reaction out of her. My body temperature ran hot even in winter, that was all. Especially when I was cooking. But from then on, I tried to give her some extra space. Clearly she wasn't comfortable having me around if I wasn't fully dressed.

I spent the rest of my cooking time contemplating asshole ex-boyfriends and the way they made us decent guys look bad.

Part of me hoped that Jeremy Rigsby would fall off the edge of the earth before he made it back to Hartley. But the other part? That part of me couldn't wait for Jeremy to show his face in Jessi's vicinity. Just so I could even the score.

What? It was the kind of thing a brother should do.

Before we knew it, dinner guests were arriving, drawn by the promise of a warm Hartley welcome. Then it was a whirlwind of serving, eating, and more cooking, as every event tends to be. A bunch of Jessi's friends, like Scarlett and Marco, showed up to help and socialize. Stranded tourists shared stories about where they were going and where they were from. The little diner was hopping, the way it probably used to be when the town of Hartley had been on Jessi's side.

And she was *basking* in it. Smiling and joking and making her guests feel comfortable. Making them laugh. Jessi looked good out there. Happy. She was the kind of woman who got joy out of feeding people and making them feel at home. Feeding people was important to me too, given my chosen profession. But I liked keeping my mouth shut and letting my food say everything for me.

Jessi, though. She wore her heart right there on the outside of her apron. In her gestures, words, and her smiles. And in the despair I'd seen in her expression last night, too.

A few people asked about her brother, but I just saluted a greeting from my spot in the open kitchen. I grabbed a plate of food to eat when I got a chance, making sure that Jessi did the same. As for Jeremy's trouble-making cousins, none showed to the dinner. Sawyer was the only Rigsby there, shaking hands and giving out boxes of Hart-Made candy like he was running for mayor or something.

Around nine o'clock, Jessi dropped into a booth, marveling at the stuffed tip jar in front of her. "I have no idea how we pulled that off."

I was in the kitchen, looking at her through the cut-out archway, as I had all evening. "We did it together." I toweled off a plate and set it in the clean stack on the counter.

She dumped the tip jar upside down. Bills scattered everywhere. "Pretty sure it was all you. I believe your story about being a chef for a catering company now."

"You thought I was lying?"

"I don't know what I've been thinking about *anything* for the past twenty-four hours." Tendrils of dark hair fell over her face as she sighed. If I'd been sitting across from her, I might've tucked them behind her ear. That woman deserved a hell of a lot more than she'd gotten out of life.

Hopefully, she'd find the right person to give it to her.

I finished the last of the dishes, and Jessi stacked her tips into neat little piles. She stared at the money for a moment, eyes damp.

"How much?" I asked.

"Enough to cover the rest of my rent this month and help out with my other bills, too. If Sawyer pays me back for the cost of the food like he promised."

"Oh, he will. I heard Scarlett thanking him over and over again and making sure everybody at the dinner knew he was footing the bill. She's a smart one."

"I know it. Scarlett's one of my favorite people in Hartley. If it wasn't for people like her, I might've given up a while ago."

I pushed through the swinging door and came around to the front of the counter, leaning against a barstool. "Not sure I believe that. I think you would've stuck it out. You're tough."

She shrugged dismissively.

"No," I argued. "It's true." Jessi had a soft femininity that some might mistake for weakness. That was probably what Jeremy Rigsby had seen. A beautiful girl he could mold into whatever he wanted. But her backbone was steel underneath. "I'm not saying it to flatter you or cheer you up. I don't say things I don't mean."

She studied me like she was searching my words for some agenda. There wasn't one.

"I would've stuck it out," she said. "And I'll keep doing it. Easier when things actually go *well* for once." She pointed at the money. "I'm going to put this in the safe before it wanders off." She gathered up the cash, went into the back, and then reemerged in the kitchen, where I'd gone back to the dishes.

The diner didn't have a liquor license, so I grabbed a bottle of orange juice from the fridge. "Another toast to standing your ground?"

She laughed. "Maybe later. After the mess is cleaned up. That was *your* toast yesterday, don't forget."

"I haven't. Those are words I live by." I didn't like leaving things unfinished.

Despite some vague promises of road-repair crews from Sawyer Rigsby, the bridge was still closed. *Maybe tomorrow*, I thought. I still hoped to make it to my vacation cabin rental. That meant I had, at most, another day to see Jessi settled. But things were looking up for her. We were on the right track.

I smiled a little to myself, enjoying the feeling of progress. Of order re-established in the world.

Jessi took over the dishes, and I went to take out the trash, which was full to bursting. I didn't bother to put on my coat as I hefted the trash bag and pushed through the back door.

The diner had a small dumpster out here. I lifted the lid and tossed the bag inside, relatching it carefully to keep any curious bears out.

My breath puffed in front of me, barely visible in the shadows. Faint light came from the windows of the houses on the surrounding streets. Hartley had returned to quiet again. I wasn't sure if it was because of the snow, which still blanketed the streets despite all the efforts to clear it away. Or if Hartley usually closed up after nightfall.

The town had a sleepy vibe, but having two siblings in law enforcement had taught me that sometimes, there's a lot more beneath the surface of a place than you might think.

I'd grown up in West Oaks, which seemed like an idyllic seaside enclave. But some messed-up things had gone on there too. Organized crime, kidnappings, murders. According to my sister Madison, who was a West Oaks cop and hostage negotiator, less than half of the worst crimes got any publicity. From what I'd seen in the Army, I believed it. The world could be a lawless, cruel place.

Every town had its secrets. *Especially* a charming, historic, and isolated place like Hartley. But the quiet was nice. The sweet, clean mountain smell in the air... The girl running the local diner. She was awfully nice as well.

Staying here another day wouldn't be so bad.

Noise and movement caught my attention from further down the street. I was on the rear side of the diner, the wide sort of alleyway behind the commercial strip. I'd just spotted someone coming out the back door of another building. The brief rise and fall of music suggested he'd just exited the Hartley Saloon. Same parking lot where I'd left my car last night, and where it still sat now, obscured by a covering of snow.

My eyes followed the figure as he stumbled along toward a vehicle. A security light shone like a spot over him, illuminating the massive dark bruise and white bandage over the man's nose.

It was Chester Rigsby.

Chester sat against the hood of a car and lit up a cigarette. I backed slowly toward the rear wall of the diner, just in case he might look over and see me. But he seemed preoccupied with his thoughts. The end of his cigarette burned orange as he inhaled.

Then another car pulled into the saloon lot. Chester glanced up. The newcomer parked beside him and got out.

This was an older man who looked a lot like Sawyer Rigsby, but had darker hair and was leaner around the middle.

I guessed he was Dale, Chester's father.

Then Dale pushed Chester roughly up against the car. The angry tones of his words carried toward me, but not their meaning. As I'd claimed countless times in my life, I preferred to mind my own business. But for my remaining time in Hartley, brief though it was, Jessi's business *was* officially mine. And it was possible this father-and-son argument pertained to her.

I wanted to find out what they were saying.

Stepping carefully, I stole toward the saloon parking lot along the edges of the buildings. I was regretting my decision not to wear a coat. It was way below freezing, and I only had my jeans and long-sleeved tee to keep me warm. But I wasn't going to retreat now just because of a little chill.

Their voices were getting louder.

My boots slipped on the slick ice. Finally, I got close enough to make out the words they were saying.

"—not the right time for this fucking nonsense," Dale said.

"But Jeremy's on his way. He's just waiting for the bridge to open up again. You told me to make sure she was gone by the time he—"

"I gave you permission. But I didn't tell you to be a damn idiot about it, drawing Owen's attention and half the town's. We can't afford prying eyes. This conflict with Jessi Novo is over now, you hear me?"

"But what about that brother of hers? What he did to me?" Chester pointed at his face, which filled me with enough satisfaction to stave off the cold. "What about *Jeremy*?"

"You both have more important—"

I missed the rest of it. Dale was heading back to the

driver's side of his car, and Chester got in along with him after a few more seconds of arguing. Dale started his engine. They drove away, leaving me wondering what that had been about.

"There you are." Jessi poked her head out of the diner's back door. "Where'd you go?"

I strolled toward her. I had waited until Dale and Chester were out of sight before I walked back. "Worried about me again, like you were this morning?"

She rolled her eyes and went back inside.

After locking the door behind us, I followed her to the dining room. She'd finished the dishes. "I just overheard an interesting conversation."

Jessi's eyes brightened as I told her about Dale and Chester's argument. She opened up a variety box of Hart-Made candy that Sawyer had left behind. There were filled chocolates inside, plus some shards of caramelized sugar that the box called brown sugar brittle. Jessi selected something that looked like a chocolate-covered cherry.

"I wonder if Sawyer said something to Dale," Jessi mused. "Maybe Sawyer told him to make Chester stop bothering me."

"Could be. If Sawyer said Dale's boys were making the family look bad, it would explain why Dale called them off. Dale clearly knew that Chester had been trying to intimidate you. Maybe Sawyer knew it too, or maybe not. Either way, the elder Rigsbys have put the kibosh on Chester and Jeremy's plan to push you out."

"*Kibosh*? What is this, an old black-and-white movie? A film noir?"

"Isn't that how you talk here in Hartley?"

"Maybe. But it's extra cute when you do it."

"*Cute?* That word doesn't describe me."

"Too bad. I say it does." She was in a more buoyant mood than I'd seen before. Grinning, cheeks flushed. Jessi popped another chocolate into her mouth, then pushed the candy box over to me. I picked up a shard of brown sugar brittle. It had some spice and salt to it. Not bad.

"I'm not flirting with you, by the way," she added. "Just so we're clear."

"Didn't think you were." I felt a smile tease my lips. She seemed to have that effect on me. She was happy, and I liked seeing that. It was a simple pleasure. Maybe as good as relaxing in front of a fireplace in a remote cabin.

Jessi turned thoughtful as she chewed. "But what is it that Chester and Jeremy are supposed to be focused on instead of me? What did Dale mean by 'not the right time'?"

"Are you afraid they'll decide a later time is better to harass you again?"

"Or maybe I just don't trust anything they're up to."

I shrugged. "I wouldn't either."

Her phone pinged, and she checked the notification. "That's Trace. He's finally on his way." She glanced up, cringing. "But he's driving instead of flying. The airlines are having some kind of major computer meltdown because of the storm, and he wasn't going to get another flight until later in the week."

"How long will it take him to get here?"

"Couple days, I guess? Assuming the weather doesn't get bad again. And then there's the bridge. But at least he's moving instead of sitting in Virginia."

Jessi stuck the lid on the box of candy and shoved it away. I didn't like to see that frown. I wanted to keep our easy, meandering conversation going. "Do you have any more of your lemon tarts?" I asked. "Those are much better than this candy."

Her smile turned shy, but I saw the pride beneath. "I took the rest to the sweet shop. Scarlett is selling them for me so I can make a little extra money. Though that's probably not necessary any more if the diner gets going again."

"But you'll keep making the tarts, right? To serve here?"

"Sure." She twisted the closed candy box back and forth on the table. "I have a bunch of flavors I've been testing out. Chocolate and pecan, coconut-mango. I've been perfecting the crust, too."

I nodded. I understood that process. How people might say they loved a dish, yet I still might not be happy with it. "You have a vision for it, and you want to capture it."

Her dark blue eyes flashed. "Exactly. When I really got started baking, I wasn't sure what I wanted to do with it. I did pies and cookies and brownies. Different things for the diner. I still make those, because they're always hits. But then I tried a tart recipe, and it just clicked for me. And then —" She rolled her eyes at herself. "Never mind. It's not that exciting."

"Tell me." I wasn't a baker, but cooking was something I could talk about endlessly.

She pursed her lips. "No. I don't think I will. Because I've already told you a ton about me, and I know next to nothing about you."

"You know plenty."

She lifted her fingers, counting off. "California. Army. Chef. Friends who are cops. And...see? That's next to nothing. A person is a lot more than just four things. I need *details*."

"I guarantee that's not interesting. I'm boring."

"Too bad." She spun the candy box. "You answer a question for every one of mine. Or we're done. I'll grab your blankets for you and say goodnight."

I grunted. *Done?* I didn't want to end the night yet. I wanted to talk cooking with her. Trials in the kitchen, failed experiments. Unexpected flavor combinations. I wanted to see that passion light up in her eyes.

"Okay, you win. You can ask—"

The high-pitched cacophony of shattering glass filled the air.

Shards rained onto us. Something heavy slammed onto the tile floor. Jessi screamed. I reached across the table. Grabbed hold of her and shoved her down, taking us both to the floor and under the tabletop. Time had slowed, as it always did when a battle started. It was a feeling that had branded my soul during my time as a soldier. Those were things I could never unlearn, even though I'd been out for years.

"Are you hurt?" I asked.

"No."

I lifted my head. Through the window, I spotted a figure running. The brake lights of a pickup. "Get upstairs. Lock the door."

"What about you?"

I didn't answer her. Just pushed her toward the back of the diner, while I went the opposite direction. I flipped the latch on the front door, wrenched it open, and ran through onto the street.

The dark figure was way ahead of me. He jumped onto the tailgate of the truck. The truck's engine gunned. It slalomed forward on the ice-slick road.

I was slipping too, my boots barely keeping traction.

But then the truck's tires spun out. The back fishtailed. It gave me enough time to close the distance. The guy who'd just broken Jessi's window was only halfway into the truck bed. I grabbed hold of his coat and yanked him out. He sprawled hard on the ice. He was wearing a ski mask, and I pulled it off.

It was one of the Rigsby brothers from last night. The third one, Theo. The youngest. He stared up at me in fear and shock.

At the same time, the truck's tires had stopped spinning. The vehicle lurched forward before it managed to stop, swung into a wide u-turn, and started to come back to Theo's rescue.

I had seconds.

I fisted Theo's jacket and pulled him up until our noses were an inch apart. "She's an innocent woman. What is wrong with you?" Theo looked too terrified to speak. So I kept going. "If you don't stop this, then I won't either. I'll hunt you down. You'll spend the rest of your days breathing through a *tube* and regretting you ever heard my name." In that moment, I couldn't remember what the hell my name was supposed to be. I only knew that I wouldn't let this go. Because Jessi deserved *better*.

The truck was heading straight toward us. I let go of Theo, giving him a shove. His arms pinwheeled as he raced toward the vehicle. The truck slowed enough for Theo to leap over the tailgate and into the bed. Then it sped up again. Heading straight toward me.

I took out my phone and hit record. Held up the device as I stood in the middle of the road.

Headlights bathed me in a yellow glow. In my head, I counted down. *Three. Two. One...* I was about to leap out of the way, but at the last moment, the truck veered around me.

I had a brief glimpse of two men in the driver's seat. Both wore ski masks. The eyes of the driver, I knew. Mitch Rigsby. Chester's brother. The asshole I'd had the displeasure of seeing this morning outside the coffee shop. The man riding shotgun, I didn't recognize. But he had an actual shotgun nestled against his chest.

Mitch's eyes were furious. His lips mouthed the words, *You're dead*.

And then, tail lights glowed as the truck roared past me down Main Street. The vein in my head throbbed, like I was still counting down.

Jessi. I had to make sure she was okay.

I spun to face the diner and looked up at the second level. I found her framed in one of the apartment windows. Her eyes were wide and frightened. She waved for me to come back inside, and I gave her a signal meaning *stay there*.

Silence had returned. I breathed, coaxing my pulse to slow. Using my phone, I recorded the broken window of Jessi's Diner, narrating aloud exactly what had happened a few minutes before. For evidence. Next, I went inside and found the brick Theo had thrown. It had skittered to one wall, but I grabbed the projectile and removed the rubber band and the paper that the Rigsby brothers had attached to it.

It said, *You and your brother better leave town while you still can, bitch*.

I thumbed the button on my phone to end the recording. "Now you've done it, assholes," I murmured. "It's on."

CHAPTER EIGHT
Jessi

THE LAST FEW minutes played in a loop in my mind. "*Get upstairs,*" Aiden had said. "*Lock the door.*"

But I hadn't wanted to run. I had wanted to *fight*.

Those jerks had just broken the window of my diner. The place I had worked my butt off to establish in the last two years, and they were trying to destroy it. I shook with fury as I watched Aiden run outside, chasing after the fleeing figure. And I was half a step from running out there after him.

But I forced myself to think better of it. *Be smart, Jessi.* Aiden needed backup, and I was hardly the one to do it. What if the Rigsby brothers had been trying to lure us outside? Aiden was unarmed.

I had to call Owen.

I hurried to the kitchen as I pulled out my phone. I grabbed a chef's knife from the block and raced up the stairs to my apartment. By the time I had the door closed and locked behind me, Owen picked up my call. "Jessi?"

I nearly tripped over Aiden's duffel bag. He must've left it here earlier when he showered. Maybe his sudden presence in my life had complicated matters, but I was still glad that Aiden was here. He'd stepped up for me in a way nobody else had. Probably *ever*. If he got hurt while defending me, how could I forgive myself?

The words rushed out of me. "Somebody just threw a brick through the window of the diner. Aid—" I closed my mouth on the rest of Aiden's name. "Um, Trace is running after them. You have to help. *Please*."

Owen cursed. I heard a sound like clothing rustling. "I'll radio a couple deputies to get there. I'll be right behind them. Stay out of sight, Jessi. Don't do anything stupid."

I ended the call, annoyed that the second man in just as many minutes had told me to stay out of the way.

I went to the window and yanked up the blinds. My throat seized as I saw what was going on outside. Aiden was snarling at Theo Rigsby, who lay sprawled on the icy road. And Mitch Rigsby's truck had just swung around. Aiden let go of Theo, who scampered toward the truck and leaped into the bed.

But now the truck was barreling straight toward Aiden, who just stood there in the road. I banged on the glass, as if he'd be able to hear me. I'd never met a man so absurdly reckless. If he got himself killed out there—

I almost passed out from relief when the truck swerved around him, and Aiden looked up at me in the window. Then his hand flattened, as if saying, *Stay there*. But I'd had enough of that particular instruction.

Still holding the chef's knife, I threw open my apartment door and hurried down the steps. I found Aiden in the dining room, kneeling to yank the rubber band off the brick that had trashed my window. He unfolded the piece of paper attached, muttering something to himself.

"What does it say?" I asked.

Aiden did one of his eyebrow things. He glanced at the knife still dangling from my hand. "Careful with that. Could hurt someone."

I wasn't in the mood for his deadpan sarcasm. I thunked the knife down on a table. "Aiden, *the note*."

He showed it to me. He had his finger partly over the word *bitch*, like he was trying to hide it from me. Lovely message. As if the broken window hadn't been enough.

I slowly surveyed the room. Broken glass was everywhere, and frigid air pumped through the jagged hole. An hour ago, we'd been cleaning up after hosting dinner, and I'd been awash with optimism and good feelings. Like things were really going to work out for me for once. But that was how they got you, wasn't it? Waiting until you'd lowered your guard again, and then, *boom*.

I was so sick of getting knocked down.

The sheriff's deputies arrived, followed soon by Owen himself. I sleepwalked through explaining what had happened. Aiden filled in his part. Somehow, he made running into the street after potentially armed men sound reasonable. But I knew if I asked him about it, he'd say the same thing he did the first night we met. He had done it because he *wanted to*.

That was the thing about Aiden. Who could say what was going through that mind of his. Why he was sticking around. Why he cared enough to protect me. I just knew that *he did*. Maybe that was the craziest thing of all. I had no idea what he would do next, but I still trusted him.

I'd known him for one day. But I trusted him.

The deputies found some pieces of plywood to cover up the hole in the window. A few neighbors had also wandered over to investigate the noise, and they joined in, nailing the plywood into place. Owen told them he was investigating and shooed them away when they tried to ask more questions. But Owen was simmering with a quiet but palpable fury. I knew that Aiden had sent him the video he'd taken of the Rigsbys' truck.

After the plywood was in place and we'd nearly finished sweeping up broken glass, Owen turned to me. "It was the Rigsby brothers who did this. Maybe not Chester, but definitely Theo and possibly Mitch. I'm going to make sure someone is held accountable for it."

Aiden stood behind Owen, resting an arm on top of the broom handle as he eavesdropped.

"Because you have video evidence this time? We both know my word alone is never good enough," I said.

Owen frowned. "I hate that as much as you. I've always believed you, Jessi. That's never been the issue, and you know it."

But things aren't always fair. And justice doesn't always work the way it's supposed to. He didn't need to say it because I knew it already. That was the reason I often hadn't bothered to report the Rigsby brothers' harassment at all. With Jeremy, the video evidence and the impartial witness had been enough, but I didn't usually have so much to back me up.

The sheriff fitted his cowboy hat back on his head and said goodnight. Finally, the diner was quiet again. I was beyond exhausted. I didn't even know if I'd be able to open tomorrow, much less have the energy to run this place.

I sank into one of the booths. "This is my mess. Not yours. I'm grateful for everything you've done to help me. Pretending to be my brother and putting on the dinner tonight. It's okay if you're ready to bow out."

Aiden still leaned against the broom handle. "Do you want me to leave?" As usual, his voice didn't betray much. He'd asked matter-of-factly, as if he didn't even care about the answer. But for some reason, he *did* care what happened to me.

"I don't want you to get hurt," I said firmly.

"I haven't yet."

"But you *could*. That would be on me." It was one thing to

ask my real brother to take the risk, but this man didn't truly know me. It wasn't right for me to put this responsibility on him.

Aiden set the broom aside. He lowered himself onto the seat across from me. Rested his elbows on the table between us. "Why do you want to stay in Hartley? You said you would stand your ground, and I admire the hell out of that. In my mind, that's reason enough for you to stay. But I suspect there's more to it for you." His mouth quirked. "Simply because you're not as contrarian as me. Though you come close at times."

I returned his subtle smile. I was tired, and he'd just asked a big question. But Aiden genuinely seemed to want to know.

How could I explain what I felt about Hartley? Describe the way this place had sunk into my soul, even though I'd started out a stranger just over two years ago?

"From the first day that Jeremy and I pulled into this town, I loved it. The mountains and the canyon. The aspens and the evergreens. The architecture of the buildings and the history and the local stories. The kindness of a lot of the people here, if not all. I fell head over heels." I glanced at the building around me. "And this diner, too. When I moved into town, the previous owner was ready to retire, and it seemed like the stars aligned perfectly to make this place mine. What happened with Jeremy was a roadblock, but I didn't let it stop me. If I give this place up and leave, then I'm giving up on every dream I've ever fought for." My voice broke. I swiped at my eyes. "And I just can't."

Aiden held my gaze a moment longer. "Makes perfect sense to me."

His hand was on the table, close to mine but not touching. I moved my hand so our pinkies brushed. We sat like that for a while. Neither of us spoke. The tightness in my chest loosened, bit by bit.

Finally, he pushed up to standing, stepping out of the booth. "You should get ready for bed. It's been a long day. I can stay up a bit longer to keep an eye on things."

Aiden stretched his arms over his head. And suddenly, I had my eye on some things as well.

I was trying and failing not to notice the sliver of skin between the waistband of his jeans and the edge of his long-sleeved tee. Just like I'd tried not to notice the beads of water on his bare shoulders and chest earlier after his shower.

I'd had no romantic inclinations of any kind since what had happened with Jeremy. Aiden was the first guy I had noticed *that way* in the last few years, and I was supposed to be related to him. Keeping a respectful distance seemed like the wisest course.

"I'll grab your blankets, then. And your duffel." I looked around at the floor. We'd gotten most of the glass, but there were probably stray bits around. Plus the dirt that had blown in through the window. "Wait, you can't sleep on this floor. It's a mess."

"Don't worry about it. I'm not picky."

"Are you sure?"

"I've slept in worse places. I promise."

But as I passed down the hallway toward the stairs, it didn't feel right. After all Aiden had done for me, he'd earned something better than a cold, glass-strewn floor.

The day before, he'd been a stranger. I didn't know what we were now. But strangers wasn't it.

I turned around. "You can sleep on the couch in my apartment," I said in a rush. Without waiting for his response, I climbed the stairs. Aiden's footsteps followed a moment later.

CHAPTER NINE

WHAT AM I DOING?

I rinsed shampoo out of my hair as thoughts ping-ponged around my brain. Aiden was in my bedroom right now. Just beyond the thin bathroom door. Well, it was my studio apartment, but it was essentially one big bedroom.

What if he thought my invitation to sleep up here had meant more than it did?

Did I *want* it to mean more?

I'd practically run into the bathroom as soon as I'd made it up here. My heart was racing, but it was nothing like the terror that I'd felt after that brick sailed through my window. The sprint that my heart was currently on wasn't necessarily unpleasant.

The bathroom lock was broken. It had been like that when I moved in, and I hadn't seen any reason to fix it. I hadn't planned to have anybody up here, except Scarlett a time or two. I'd never had a man in this apartment before. Ever. I had moved in here after everything happened with Jeremy.

But I was the one who'd invited Aiden up here, which meant I was in control, right? Except my impulsive streak was as wide as the county. And as for Aiden, I never could predict what he might do next.

I didn't think he was going to grab me, shove me to my bed, and ravish me... Not unless I asked him to.

Oh, boy. Now I had those images in my head.

I dried off and put on the pajamas I'd brought in with me, wrapping the towel around my head. When I stepped out of the bathroom, Aiden was kneeling on the floor over his duffel, digging around inside.

"It's all yours," I said.

His eyes lifted to mine, his mouth curving. "Thanks." He carried some clothes in the bathroom and shut the door. The sink turned on. Aiden probably wasn't showering because he had done that just a few hours ago. Already, the scent of him had permeated the entire room. I'd noticed it before after he'd been in here, but now I couldn't smell anything else. It was salty and fresh, a bit herbal, like an ocean breeze. Or at least, what I expected an ocean breeze would smell like, since I'd never been anywhere near a coast.

He had a tattoo of ocean waves cascading over his shoulder and along one side of his upper back. I had seen it earlier in the kitchen when he'd come downstairs with his shirt off.

And now I was imagining him in the bathroom, probably with his shirt off right now.

I pulled the towel from my hair and started combing it out, tugging roughly at the strands. I was being ridiculous. But my heart refused to slow down. Now that Aiden was in my space, I realized how much I wanted to have him here. Wanted...things I hadn't desired for years. But I was scared of those things too.

In short, I was a mess.

I just *wanted*. Even though I knew how foolish it was and how I'd probably end up disappointed.

When Aiden emerged from the bathroom, I was laying out the spare blankets and pillows on the floor at the foot of my bed, which was the only open space where a man over six feet could fully lie down in here. Except for *my bed*, of course.

"I know I offered the couch," I said without looking at him, "but I forgot it's too small for even me to sleep on, so there's no way you would fit."

"Whatever is fine."

I turned around. He was wearing a soft-looking T-shirt and a pair of boxers. My eyes snagged on the view of muscular, long legs.

"I didn't pack any more pajamas than this." Aiden sounded only a fraction as awkward as I did, which was still a contrast to his usual cool demeanor.

"No problem. It's…great." *Great?* Was I saying his boxers were great? I turned toward the window, grimacing at myself. Aiden sat on the couch. He took up more than half of it. I was facing the window, but I could see him in the reflection. I'd already switched off the main overhead light, leaving just the lamp by my bedside.

"Mind if I stay up and read my phone for a bit?" he asked.

"Not at all. I'm pretty wired. It'll take me a few minutes to settle down." That was an understatement. My vital signs were surging like I'd just run all the way up Refuge Mountain, my favorite local trail.

"You're okay?" he asked.

"I will be. Never had a brick thrown into my window before. But if they think they can intimidate me, they're wrong."

I could see him in the window's reflection, watching me. I hadn't moved.

And then Aiden started talking.

"My parents own the catering company I work for. Mom is the business brains of the family, and Dad does the book-keeping. We specialize in big events, weddings. We're always overbooked. This is a quieter time of year, after the rush of the holidays, so I like it. January is a perfect time to get away. Technically I have the event in Steamboat to cook for next weekend, but I was sick of all that California sunshine anyway, so a vacation in the Colorado mountains sounded ideal."

I turned to face him, leaning my weight against the windowsill. He had his hands clasped between his knees, his gaze down at them.

"I know what you're doing," I said.

"And what is that?"

"Sharing things to try to make me feel better."

"I thought you wanted to know about me. I did warn you. I'm not that interesting." He sat back against the couch, eyes gentle. "Should I keep going?"

I shrugged. Yep, I was determined to be difficult. I felt too confused and mixed up inside to do anything else. And I'd already opened up to him multiple times. If he chose to do the same, it would be because he wanted to. No more and no less.

He looked at me with his eyes glinting. Like he was issuing a challenge. I looked back at him.

And dammit, I gave in.

"Did you always know you wanted to be a chef?" I asked.

"To understand that, you need to know more about my family."

So he told me about growing up one of five kids. Aiden was the second oldest, and he'd felt like the polar opposite from his siblings. The only introvert. And unlike his golden-boy older brother, Aiden was a loner and a contrarian at heart. If somebody told him he had to do something, automatically he felt the urge to do the opposite.

"My brother Jake always knew he wanted to join the

Army. He went to an ROTC program for college. But nobody ever asked if *I* had a big plan like that. And that pissed me off. So I thought, what the hell. After high school, I enlisted. I actually beat Jake to the Army, since he was still getting his degree. I was such a shit." Aiden laughed softly, and I went over to the couch. I sank onto the cushion beside him, keeping a narrow line of space separating us. "I didn't mind the structure. But I didn't like not being able to determine things for myself, especially when I thought my orders were bullshit. I chose not to reenlist after my four years of active duty were up."

"Do you regret enlisting?"

He looked confused. "Not at all. I met a lot of great people. I was proud to serve with them. Learned a lot. I don't do regrets."

"What did you do after that? Culinary school?"

"Isn't it your turn to answer a question?"

"Hardly. I've answered way too many. You have a backlog."

He smiled, broad and brilliant, and I felt a physical tug behind my belly button. His smile was a weapon. It was probably a good thing he didn't unleash it too often. "I started culinary school after I left the Army, when I was twenty-three. Seven years ago."

He told me what culinary school had been like. Long days of watching his chef-instructors prepare dishes, then having to replicate them. Memorizing recipes and techniques. Having to pay his dues and work his way up in the first restaurants where he worked.

"Then my mother offered me the job as head chef of her catering company. I thought hard about it. My mother is opinionated as hell, and we clash constantly. But I got to be the boss of my own kitchen far earlier than I could have in a restaurant."

"And maybe you wanted to be closer to your family too."

"Why would I want that?"

"Admit it. You like them."

"What would give you that impression?"

"Your voice when you talk about them. Like they're people who matter."

He grunted. "I guess. They've always loved me and supported me. And forgiven me for all my nonsense."

"No, you're right. That sounds awful."

He snickered. We'd turned toward one another, propping our heads on our hands and our elbows against the back of the couch. I had no idea what time it was, but I wasn't the least bit tired. "What about you?" he asked. "How did you start cooking?"

I told him about my makeshift culinary training based on YouTube videos and TikTok tutorials. So many failed experiments. Saving every penny so I could spend them on ingredients. Thrift-shop cooking tools and hand-me-down cast iron pans.

"My favorite videos were the ones taught by chefs in France. I even watched the ones in French and tried to figure out what they were saying. I wanted to learn different cuisines from all over the world." I rolled my eyes at myself. "I've never left Colorado, though."

Aiden didn't miss a beat. "Out of anywhere in the world, where would you want to go most?"

"Paris," I said, no hesitation on my part either. "Have you been there?"

"Yeah, and it seemed nice. Great food. But otherwise, I didn't really get it. The mystique it has."

"Are you kidding? You did it wrong if that's what you think. Paris is magical." I shrugged. "Or so it seems in the YouTube videos I watch. I'm sure it's disappointing in real life. It's a cliche to want to go there, anyway."

"Don't say that," he said softly. "It's okay to want what you want. Maybe if I went to Paris with you, I'd see it differently."

Aiden's eyes were on me. And I didn't know how to respond. What he'd just said had probably been a throwaway comment. Yet it had touched the soft, eager hopes of my heart. The part that wanted someone to care about how I saw the world. To see *me*.

We'd been talking for so long that I didn't feel like I was in my studio apartment anymore. I wasn't in Hartley. I was in some dreamlike place where I could let my mind wander, and somehow, this handsome man was wandering with me.

His hand was resting on his knee. Inches away. I knew this was a risk, but I didn't let myself question. I crossed that gap between us and placed my hand on his.

His eyebrows lifted, this time curious.

Aiden rotated his wrist so our palms touched, and my breath hitched. His fingers stroked against mine, and I held my breath. We were hardly even touching, but suddenly lightning was shooting off everywhere inside me.

"This all right?" He must've noticed my reaction because his hand went still. "Should I stop?"

"I just…" I cleared my throat. "Sorry. I haven't touched anyone like this in a long time." I squeezed my eyes shut, wishing I hadn't admitted that.

We were *holding hands*. It was nothing.

But for me, it was major. I'd hugged Scarlett plenty of times, because Scarlett was affectionate. But that wasn't the same as *this*. Aiden's large hand beneath mine, our palms together, his heat, his calloused fingers making tingles race over every inch of my skin. As if my hand was an erogenous zone connected to every other part of me.

"No one since Jeremy?" Aiden asked.

"I haven't let anyone get close enough."

"That's a shame." Slowly, he flipped my hand so his was now on top of mine. Aiden's fingertips dragged along each of my digits until they reached my palm. Then his thumb brushed a circle there, and I actually *moaned*.

"Feels good?"

"Yes," I whispered. *So good.*

"I might be emotionally stunted," he said wryly, "but I like to be touched, too." He was watching our hands. "You feel *very* good, Jessi."

Those words coming out of his mouth set off fireworks at my nerve endings. I imagined him pressing that mouth to my hand. My arm. My lips. *More*.

Too much. Too, too much. My vision feathered. I was lightheaded.

I pulled my hand away. "I don't want to give you the wrong idea. Inviting you up here wasn't for…that."

"I didn't think it was. And I don't expect anything else." With aching slowness, he reached over and carefully took my hand again, this time in both of his. Cradled it like a fragile, precious thing. "This is perfect. If it's good with you. Just this."

I felt exposed right now, and if he'd wanted to, he could've singed me down to my center with a careless word. "How long are you staying in Hartley?" I didn't want to ask this question, but I had to know the answer. I *deserved* to know. "If the bridge opens up tomorrow, will you go?"

"This morning, I would've said yes. Probably would've said yes a couple hours ago."

As I had expected. Aiden had never promised more.

"But now?"

He traced the tops of my fingertips again. "That cabin in the woods will still be there another time." He shook his head. "I wouldn't feel right leaving you until your brother gets here."

I forced myself to take a breath. My heart kept racing. "I'd appreciate that. Thank you."

"I have a hard deadline, though. I'm catering a wedding in Steamboat. The bride is the daughter of my parents' friends, and my family will be there. I can't let them down. The wedding is on Saturday, and I have to be there by Friday."

I nodded. Of course he wouldn't let them down. I'd known that Aiden wasn't going to stay in Hartley. Obviously. He lived in California. *Just passing through*. Yet his answer settled something within me. He was the kind of man who kept his word, who loved his family, even if he also claimed to be a loner who didn't fit in with them.

He would remain until Trace got here, or until Friday. Today was Monday, so he'd leave at most in four days.

I liked Aiden. I wanted to know more about him. And *God*, I wanted to be touched. To be close to a man who was kind in the ways that counted, who cared enough to keep me safe. Even if it only lasted four days.

Just this. This is perfect.

You feel good, Jessi.

Aiden was the kind of man who said exactly what he meant. Wasn't he? I'd been wrong about so many things in my past, but I wasn't wrong about this. Was I?

His fingers moved over my own. Caressing my knuckles. Drawing stars on my palms.

"Do you like that?"

Yes. Yes, please don't stop.

I nodded. I didn't trust myself to speak. My heart was running too crazy. Like a wild horse. I was scared of making *myself* run away, and I didn't want this to stop. I wanted, *needed* him to keep touching me.

But that sliver of fear still lay embedded in my heart, and it wouldn't disappear so easily. I was holding my breath again. Waiting for him to cross the line we'd set. *Just this*.

He didn't.

He talked and talked as he ran his fingers over my hand. He told me more than he'd said in the entire last day, and the rhythm of his caresses lulled me, the gentle cadence of his deep voice.

I was hypnotized. And it really was perfect.

CHAPTER TEN
Aiden

SOMETIME DURING THE NIGHT, I woke with Jessi's head resting on my shoulder, both of us slumped into one another on the couch. Her slender hand was still nestled in mine.

I looked at her for a moment. How her lips were slightly open as she slept, and her lashes spread like a fan below her eyelids. Her damp hair had dried into soft waves.

Damn, she was beautiful.

Earlier, as we'd been talking, I'd wanted to do more than just touch her hand. I'd wanted to smooth my fingertips over her face. Run them through her hair. And then kiss every place that my fingers had touched. Of course, I didn't. Because she didn't want me to.

The last man she had been with had put her in the hospital. I couldn't get my head around it. The way an experience like that would mess someone up.

And yet, she was trusting me.

Her chest rose and fell. I didn't want to wake her, but I couldn't leave her here either. So I scooped her up and laid her on her bed, lifting the covers over her to tuck her in. I took my own place on the floor at the foot of her bed. I got back to sleep pretty quick, but my dreams—those had my pulse racing for the rest of the night.

The next time I opened my eyes, sunlight had infused the room with a soft glow. I blinked, inhaling as I came fully awake.

Then I noticed Jessi.

She was peering down at me over the edge of her mattress. Her eyes widened, as if she hadn't meant to get caught watching me.

I tucked an arm behind my head. "Enjoying the view?"

"Just seeing if you were awake yet."

"I'm awake."

Her hair fell around her face, and she pushed it back. "I see that."

"Hmmm." My eyes wanted to move to her lips. It took a lot of effort to keep them steady as I returned her gaze.

"You must've carried me to my bed." Her cheeks were turning pink in that way I liked so much. "Thanks."

"No problem." I lifted my hand, offering it to her. She was lying on her stomach, and she stretched out her own arm to twine our fingers together.

"You feel good," she said softly. Like I'd said to her last night.

Something strange was happening in my chest. Like I couldn't get enough air. Maybe it was the altitude.

This was nothing like my typical morning after. Usually, if I went home with a woman, I'd wake up naked beside her and we might indulge in some more fun before I took off. Jessi and I hadn't removed one stitch of clothing, nothing more than we'd intended to sleep in, yet this felt more intimate than every other encounter I'd ever had.

And I didn't want to leave. I wanted to keep lying here on the cold floor, just like this, holding her hand and staring up at her.

I didn't know what was wrong with me.

"Can I make you some coffee?" I asked. I'd gotten to know her kitchen yesterday while making food for the charity dinner. But I still wanted her permission.

"Okay," she said, voice husky. Her dark blue eyes strayed over me. Lingered on my lips.

Oh, wow. My body was getting ideas that it had no business having.

Coffee. Breakfast. Focus on that.

I slid my hand away from hers, ignoring the shower of sparks that ignited across my skin at that friction, and rolled away. I kept my back to her as I tugged on my jeans. First stop was the bathroom. When I emerged, she was still lying stomach-down on the bed, feet near her pillow and her head at the end.

"I'll be right down," she said.

"I'll see you then."

Jessi smiled. "You will."

And there it was again. The too-tight sensation in my ribcage. The uneven thrumming of my heart.

I felt fucking *giddy*.

Something had shifted overnight, between last evening and the early hours of the morning. I didn't know what was happening between us. But I liked it.

Downstairs, the lower ambient temperature of the air hit me like a splash of cool water. I'd been right. The heater kept the upstairs a bit too toasty, the down a little chilly. The building needed better insulation. Maybe Jessi could complain to Sawyer Rigsby about it. Or I could…

No, I probably wouldn't be here long enough to fix anything big like that. But if I had time before leaving, I'd see what else I could do. Wouldn't hurt.

In the dining room, the large front window was covered over with brown plywood, but the remaining glass showed that a fresh layer of snow had fallen overnight. The world looked blank. New. Full of possibility.

A few minutes later, I had the coffee brewing and some eggs scrambling in a pan. I'd envisioned creme fraiche and brioche toast, but I had to settle for sour cream and sourdough. But I had found some chives, and I was chopping them on a cutting board.

I heard the door open upstairs, and the wooden steps squeaked as Jessi made her way down.

"Smells great." She leaned her hip against the counter. She was wearing a different sweater and jeans. "Is this for me?"

I'd left a coffee mug there, ready for her. I grabbed the carafe and filled it. "Your eggs will be right up."

"My goodness." She warmed her hands around the mug. "I don't think anyone's made me such a fancy breakfast before. I didn't realize you could be so charming."

"I can. If the moment inspires me."

She tilted her head thoughtfully. "I like that about you."

"I like a lot of things about you." I'd said it without thinking and was glad when a cautious yet gratified smile hovered over her lips.

She took a sip of coffee. When the eggs reached the perfect combination of opaque and silky-soft, I plated them, adding a dollop of sour cream, finishing salt, and a sprinkling of chives. But when I handed her the plate, Jessi set it on the counter instead of digging in.

She stood in front of me, still holding her mug, but she took my hand with her free one. My fingers slid into the spaces between hers. I liked how tall she was. Just a few inches shorter than me, which put her at near six feet. I barely had to look down at all.

"Aiden," she whispered.

Ask me to kiss you. Please, just ask me. Because I didn't know if I could hold myself back when she looked at me that way.

I leaned in.

Loud knocking broke the spell, and Jessi and I leaped away from each other. Owen Douglas was banging on the diner's front door. And *shit*, we'd just been standing an inch apart, holding hands. We were in the kitchen, so only part of us had been visible from the front of the restaurant. He probably hadn't seen the way our fingers were entwined.

But if I had kissed her? Kissed her in the exact way I'd wanted to?

It would've been hard to explain a kiss like that between a brother and sister.

And Owen wasn't alone. There was someone standing behind him. It was the same man I'd seen last night outside the bar with Chester.

Dale Rigsby.

Jessi rushed through the swinging door to unlock the front. I followed, moving more slowly with my hands tucked into my back jeans pockets. Through the glass, both Owen and Dale wore serious and unreadable expressions. Jessi opened the door, and they stepped inside. Owen was first, and he took off his cowboy hat and tucked it beneath one arm.

"Dale is here to have a word with you, Jessi. If you're willing to hear it." Owen's eyes narrowed as they slid over to the other man.

I glowered and crossed my arms, staying at Jessi's shoulder.

"Are you going to tell me that someone was arrested for breaking my window last night?" she asked.

"Theo was. He spent the night in jail. Dale is here to apologize." Owen's tone held a warning.

The lines around Dale's mouth deepened. He had a goatee and sun-weathered skin. Probably in his fifties, though his hair was still so dark it was nearly black. He didn't seem like the type to bother dying it. "Ms. Novo, I apologize for the actions of my son last night. Theo regrets what he did. Let me know the cost to have your glass repaired, and I'll take care of it."

"What about Mitch?" I asked. "He was there too."

Dale's eyes slid over to me. "You're the brother?"

I felt both Owen's and Jessi's eyes on me.

"That's me. The big brother."

"You took the video Owen showed me this morning. I couldn't recognize any person in the truck other than Theo."

"Because they were wearing masks," I pointed out. "Did you recognize the truck?"

"It might have been my son's, but anyone could've been driving it. You can rest assured, though, if anyone else of my acquaintance was there last night, he won't be bothering Jessi again."

I opened my mouth, but Jessi beat me to it. "What about Jeremy when he gets back to town? Are you going to tell him to leave me alone, too? Because that's all I want. Just to live my life."

Her voice wavered, and I touched my fingertips to the small of her back.

"No one will bother you," Dale said through clenched teeth. "It was a misunderstanding."

I scoffed. That word again. The same thing Sawyer had said. "You have a lot of misunderstandings here in Hartley. Too many. I want your word that Jessi will be left alone."

Dale gave me a single nod, holding out his hand. We tried to strangle each other's grip, and it was a draw. Then he turned and wrenched open the door without another word.

We all watched Dale disappear down the sidewalk, boot prints marring the snow. Then Owen turned around to face us. "I agreed to let Theo out of jail without any charges on the condition that they pay for all repairs and stop any further harassment of you. If they go back on their word, I'll send the video from last night to the district attorney." Owen pinned me with his gaze. "But I need your word, Trace. This ends here. No retribution, even when Jeremy Rigsby gets back to town."

"I don't get a say in this?" Jessi grumbled.

Owen hadn't taken his eyes off me. I understood Jessi's annoyance, but everybody in this room knew I was the most likely one to demand blood for the treatment of my "sister."

Hell, Jessi wasn't my sister. But payback on her behalf still seemed to be in order.

"It's done," I said. Then added silently, *For now. So long as the Rigsbys keep up their end*. "You realize why they're doing this though, right? Dale was telling Chester last night that the timing was bad. They're up to something else. This is supposedly your town, so you might want to look into it."

"That's none of your concern." Owen jammed his hat back on his head with a scowl. "Jessi, if you decide to open up the diner today, I'll be sure to send all the customers I can your way. Otherwise, enjoy your day."

"What about the bridge?" Jessi asked. "Is it repaired?"

"Not yet. But they're working on it. Should be soon." Owen didn't say goodbye to me before he left.

Jessi and I went back to the kitchen.

"I don't think he or Dale saw us holding hands," I said. "Almost blew my cover. That could've been awkward."

Jessi pursed her lips and didn't comment on that. She didn't take my hand again, either. Or even look at me. She took a bite of the eggs with a neutral, bored expression. It didn't seem right on her.

"Did I do something to upset you?" I asked.

"No. I'm just wondering why Dale is so eager to make

nice with me all of a sudden. But I guess I should be grateful and stay quiet about it. Let the men worry about such things."

"I didn't say that. Owen didn't either." But she was unhappy about the way Owen had spoken to me like I was her keeper. That was clear.

She stabbed at the eggs. "I'm going to open for lunch. You can help. If you want."

"I do want."

"All right." She shrugged, as if she didn't care either way. But I *did* care. I wanted her smiling again. Laughing and content.

I only had a handful of days until I had to be in Steamboat. And once I left Hartley, I couldn't imagine that I'd ever be back.

But dammit, when it came to Jessi, I really did care a lot. Which wasn't convenient.

The diner saw brisk business over lunch. I cooked, and Jessi's mood seemed to improve the more she got to order me around. I didn't mind at all.

After the dining room quieted down, I made us a couple of burgers. I whipped up a bacon-onion jam and some sauteed mushrooms to go on top. As the last customers shuffled out, satisfied and grinning, Jessi flipped the sign to closed and locked the door.

I held out her plate as soon as she walked into the kitchen, and she washed her hands quickly before taking a huge, hungry bite. "Oh my goodness," she said with her mouth full. "This is insane. You're a way better cook than me. First the eggs, now this? No wonder everybody was cleaning their plates."

"So you did like the eggs."

She rolled her eyes and chewed.

I took a bite of my own burger. It was pretty damn good. Maybe some cheese next time. "I'm glad you like my cooking. But you make better desserts."

"Don't flatter me to win points. All you've tried is my lemon curd. You can hardly judge based on that."

"Sure I can. I don't even like sweets, and your lemon curd was amazing."

She dropped her burger onto the plate. "You don't like sweets? What kind of monster are you?"

The frustration she'd shown after Owen and Dale's visit was fading, but I didn't think I deserved credit. It had been the customers flooding the diner. Some had been tourists still stuck in Hartley, and they'd seemed happy enough to be spending time with Jessi. Others were locals who'd hugged her on their way in. And Jessi had soaked it all up, radiating joy as she bustled around the dining room, filling waters and delivering food and getting everyone laughing. And I'd been perfectly content in the open kitchen, keeping an eye on her and on my cooking at the same time.

If business continued like this, Jessi was going to need more employees. Another cook, because obviously I wouldn't be around for long.

While I took another bite of my burger, she went to her freezer and dug around until she pulled out a plastic bag. "I keep some brownies in here in case of emergency. Time to break the glass." She made a face, glancing at the dining room. "Ouch. Too soon for that joke."

I realized I was straight-up grinning. Jessi had a way of getting me to do that.

She warmed up a brownie in the microwave, which I thought was sacrilege, but by the time we'd scarfed down our lunches, there were two brownies oozing with chocolate.

Jessi held up the plate between us. We each lifted our forks and took a bite. I groaned. Rich dark chocolate spread over my tongue. The brownie had the perfect chewiness despite the microwaving, and the ideal balance of sugar to intensity.

"Still don't like sweets?" she asked.

I dipped my chin and looked at her. "I like yours."

Her fork broke off another piece of brownie. "Stop flirting with me," she muttered.

I don't flirt, I thought. *Except with you.*

"What should we do the rest of the day?" Jessi asked.

"Since we won't be occupied with seeking revenge, you mean?"

She nibbled more of the brownie. "Exactly. My schedule just opened up." Was I mistaken, or could Jessi be flirting with *me*? Whatever this was, I wanted it to continue. Preferably without any Rigsbys showing up to ruin Jessi's mood again.

"Any ideas?" I asked.

"You asked me yesterday why I was so determined to stay in Hartley. I could show you part of the reason." Her eyes lifted with hope and vulnerability.

It already felt like she was showing me something that she usually kept hidden. *Show me more*, I thought. *Show me everything.*

I tamped down those wild thoughts. "Let's do it."

CHAPTER ELEVEN
Aiden

"THESE ARE SNOWSHOES?" I asked. "Are you sure? They don't look anything like tennis rackets."

She studied me a moment before she cracked up. "Shut up. I thought you were serious."

I was decked out in all the winter gear I'd brought to Colorado. Heavy jacket, black snow pants. Gloves. Jessi's gear was a mixture of pink and purple. She'd brought me over to the shed behind Marco's saloon, where he kept various sporting equipment and loaned it out first-come, first-served.

Jessi had dug out two pairs of snowshoes to fit our sizes, along with two sets of poles. Now we were carrying everything to her beat-up hatchback, which had balding snow tires and a thick layer of ice encasing it. I'd offered up my truck, but Jessi had wisely reminded me of my California plates. Best not to drive around Hartley displaying those if I was supposed to be Trace. So my truck remained safely covered with snow behind the saloon, my state of origin obscured.

She'd also insisted on driving, arguing that she was the one who knew where we were going.

"We do have snow in California," I said. "Not in West

Oaks, but within driving distance. The Sierras are gorgeous and covered in snow in the winter."

"Does that mean you know how to ski?"

"Nope. I snowboarded once. Do you ski?"

"My mom didn't have the money for lift tickets or ski school when I was a kid. I haven't as an adult, either. Hartley doesn't have anything fancy, but people go back-country skiing around here. And cross country. Scarlett loves all that stuff. I've been wanting to try it. Just haven't had the chance."

"Same here."

"I know this isn't the winter vacation you had in mind. You wanted to be alone meditating in a cabin."

"That's okay. I'm starting to think this might be better." I loaded up the trunk with our snowshoes. She was smiling as she got behind the wheel, her cheeks a pretty pink.

We drove away from Main Street, taking a small side road lined with homes. The road got narrower and the houses sparser until we were climbing in elevation. The mountain was all glittering snow and evergreens and blue sky above. Jessi pulled her car off the road, parking just at the border of where the snowplow had stopped.

"This is Refuge Mountain," she said. "There's a trail here that leads up to the summit. Hard to see right now since it's buried, but that's what the snowshoes are for."

"An adventure. I like it."

"I figured you would. You seem like a guy who enjoys an adrenaline rush."

"Maybe. On occasion."

We were *definitely* flirting.

We strapped on our snowshoes. Jessi had to help me. Then I nearly tripped over myself, which she thought was hilarious. She cackled when a tree branch dumped a load of snow right onto my beanie. But soon enough, we had our poles in our gloved hands and we were trekking along, following the trail that Jessi claimed she had memorized.

If we got lost and never made it back, at least I'd go out in good company.

The landscape was epically stunning. Somehow it grew more beautiful at every turn. Spindly pieces of ice formed sculptures on the branches, and sun transformed the snow crystals into cut diamonds. Our snowshoes sunk through the powder, resting on the layer of thicker, compacted snow beneath. Nobody else had been through here except for some animals whose dainty tracks were left behind as evidence.

This was exactly what I'd been hoping for when I'd rented that cabin in the woods. I did enjoy the occasional adrenaline rush, but I wasn't the thrill junky my brother seemed to be, with his heroics as a federal agent. I liked my peace and quiet. I liked balance—between silence and motion, salt and acid, spice and caramelized notes. Too often, other people rocked my boat, and not in a good way.

Yet being here with Jessi wasn't just fun. It was *easy*. There was an effortlessness to being around her. Jessi did rock my boat some, but this was a motion I liked. If we really got going, I had a feeling I'd enjoy that rhythm a hell of a lot.

If she wanted that, I was game.

"Where exactly are we going?" I asked.

She glanced back at me. "There's a reason this is called Refuge Mountain. During World War I, Hartley was just a tiny enclave. A handful of families. Some of the men left to fight in the war, and then after a rough winter, more of them went to other towns hoping to find work. The people left were isolated."

"Cue the bad guys?"

"You guessed it. They saw a bunch of women and children, grandparents. Easy pickings. They planned an attack, and the people of Hartley realized what was about to happen.

They ran to a cabin here on the mountain. Gathered to protect one another. Make their stand."

"Did they succeed?"

"Be patient," she teased. "Wait until we get there."

Jessi led me through the steep curves of the invisible trail along the mountainside. Finally, we reached a clearing. Pine trees made a semi-circle, standing straight and tall like sentinels. In the center of the clearing was a lopsided old wooden cabin, one end half buried by snow. Behind us, a clear view of the valley expanded downhill into the distance toward faraway mountain peaks. Wood smoke curled from chimneys in the town below. I saw the neat lines of Main Street, Jessi's Diner at the far end.

I needed a moment to take it all in. *Wow*. I took out my phone to snap a picture, noticing as I did that I had no service. Typical.

But Jessi wasn't ready to stop. "Come on," she said, wading into the deeper snow.

We went closer to the old cabin. I spotted a rusty corrugated roof beneath the thick layer of winter white, and I was amazed the place was still here.

"Is this it?" I asked. "Hartley's last stand?"

"If you look close, you can see bullet marks in the wood. The townspeople fought back against the bandits, but they were penned in here. It was a standoff. One night, a couple of brave townspeople sneaked into the enemy camp and attacked. Drove the bad guys away. Just two of them against a dozen men."

I whistled. "Do you think it's true?"

"It's a legend. I like it either way. But the best part is the romance." Her cheeks were rosy from our hike, but they were getting even pinker as she spoke. "In some versions of the story, a stranger came to Hartley to warn them. He was a soldier who'd been wounded in France and was on his way home to some other remote Colorado town. He'd seen the bad guys on the road and heard what they were planning. He helped defend the townspeople here, and he fell for one of the young women. They were the ones who made the final attack on the enemy camp. The two of them, together."

"It's a good story," I said. "Far-fetched, though."

"I don't know. I think it could've happened. But this place, right here, is where I fell in love with Hartley." Jessi's eyes were on the cabin, a soft smile on her lips. I was watching *her*. She unstrapped her snowshoes and laid her poles aside. I did the same, and we brushed snow off a flat rock to sit down.

"It had nothing to do with Jeremy," she explained. "Scarlett brought me up here and told me the legend. After I got out of the hospital and was trying to decide whether to stay or go, I came up here a lot. It became my refuge, too. I realized what I had to do. I wasn't from Hartley, but this town was my home, and I didn't want to leave."

"You decided to stand your ground."

"Yep."

"I'm glad you did."

"So you could walk into my diner?"

"No, I'm glad you did it for *you*."

Her smile drooped. I wasn't sure why. I hoped I hadn't offended her by what I'd said.

Jessi got quiet, so we stared at the view. We could see for miles and miles. The canyon was a ribbon through the valley. I could barely make out the repair trucks near the bridge. Most of the highway was invisible from here, creating the illusion that this valley was cut off from the rest of the world. Carved out of the surrounding rock. Despite the high altitude, my lungs filled with the clean, dry air. A calm feeling settled over me. This place was a little wild. A lot rugged. I felt *free*.

And damn, I wanted to hold Jessi's hand.

Because this was her spot, and she'd shown it to me. Shared this with me. There were probably a thousand corners of Colorado that looked like this, but this one was hers.

Right now, it felt like mine, too.

I tugged off my glove. Held out my hand. She side-eyed me, took off her glove. Slid her cold hand into my warmer one. It felt just right.

"What do you think about when you're up here?" I was enjoying the comfortable quiet between us. But I liked her voice, too. I wanted more of her stories.

"Well." She closed her eyes and smiled. "If I tell you, you have to tell me something too."

"Deal."

"I have this idea." She blew out a breath. "There's a ranch downhill, closer to the road. The owners closed it up a few years ago. You probably noticed businesses shut down around Hartley? It was part of the same thing. The town has had ups and downs. But recently, people have trickled away from here again as opportunities dried up and other Colorado towns seemed more promising."

"Not you," I pointed out.

"True. But anyway, that ranch is in the perfect spot for a bed and breakfast. There could be a real restaurant, too, with French food and pastries." Her eyes twinkled, her smile infectious. "Hiking trails lead up the mountainside, and in the summer, there's a creek and a waterfall. It's incredible. The view from the ranch is almost as good as up here. The other side of the mountain is national forest, and there are no other neighbors."

"Sounds like an exclusive resort. Throw in a spa, and you're talking five stars."

She wrinkled her nose. "That wouldn't feel like Hartley. I would want it to be rustic, but *real* rustic. Not the fake kind that costs an arm and a leg. Except it probably would cost that much to buy this land and build it."

"I like how you described it. I love good food, but five-star resorts aren't my thing, either. Seems like you've put a lot of thought into it."

"Just daydreaming."

I rubbed her palm with my thumb. "My mother built her catering company out of nothing. Why not you? It would take a lot of work, but it sounds worth it." Our knees brushed, and Jessi didn't pull away.

"You don't have to give me a pep talk. Right now, I'm just trying to get by with the diner day by day. This place is a pipe dream, and that's okay. I have to be practical. Dreaming isn't enough to make something real."

"But the fact that you're showing me means that you want to make it real."

"Maybe." She closed her eyes. "No, I do. I really do." When she opened her eyes again, the dark blue reflected the periwinkle sky. Her gaze fixed on me. "Since that first time Scarlett brought me, I've never come here with anyone else. Until now."

"I'm glad you brought me." My thumb traced the ridges of her knuckles.

"Me too," she whispered.

"My turn to share something, huh?"

She nodded.

"I've been thinking all day about kissing you. Can't get it out of my head."

Jessi's breath hitched, and her pupils nearly swallowed the blue of her irises.

Holding her gaze, I slowly brought her hand to my mouth. Paused. Then pressed my lips to one knuckle. I raised my eyebrows in a question, and she gave an almost imperceptible nod.

I pulled my other hand out of its glove and did the same to hers. Now I was holding both her hands, skin to skin, but I kept pressing kisses to just the first one. To the back of it. To each fingertip. Her skin was starting to warm, although it was still cool against my lips. Smooth and soft. Jessi opened her hand and let me kiss her palm, and she made a tiny sound of pleasure.

Oh, I wanted more of that.

I had never kissed a woman's hand like this before. Never felt the urge to. But with Jessi, even the smallest thing was heightened.

I sucked the tip of her index finger into my mouth, and she gasped, her eyes bright with dark blue fire.

"Aiden."

"It drives me crazy when you say my name like that," I rumbled. My tongue licked between two of her knuckles, and she groaned. She pulled her other hand from my grasp and brought it to my face. Her fingers stroked along my cheek.

My self control was loosening at the edges. My veins roared with heat. Before I knew it, my arm had circled around her, gathering her against me. We were still sitting on the icy rock, snow all around us. Her breaths came fast and shallow. Warm on my cheek. Her fingers moved along my beard to my jaw. This moment was cold and warm, ice and fire.

My hungry lips found hers.

For a second, it was a perfect combination. Jessi and me, the two of us coming together in a blend of want and need and fiery chemistry. Her hands moved to my chest over my coat.

Perfect.

Then she pushed.

I broke away from her. The fire in Jessi's eyes had been doused by uncertainty. Maybe even fear. She stood, arms crossing over her middle, and walked a few feet away. Turning her back to me.

Shit. I'd messed up.

When I'd started this trip, I had craved nothing more than solitude. Time to myself, alone. But now, even this small distance between me and Jessi was like a vast, empty canyon.

I was here by myself, and suddenly, I didn't like the cold.

CHAPTER TWELVE
Jessi

"I'M SORRY," Aiden said. "That was out of line."

But it wasn't, I thought. *I wanted you to kiss me.*

Yet I kept wading out into the deeper snow of the clearing. I touched my cheeks, my mouth, scarcely able to believe what had just happened.

Aiden's lips had felt so warm. So soft and gentle. First, on my hand. The way he'd kissed my fingertips and my palm had sent liquid fuel into my veins. His *tongue* between my *knuckles*? How had that felt so good? I'd wanted that to keep going. More of his mouth on my skin. More of his warmth and attention. *More.*

And then, his lips on mine. A spark that had ignited every part of me. His mouth had stayed sweetly closed. Not demanding too much too soon. The scratch of his whiskers on my cheek had been the perfect amount of friction. But he'd felt so *big* up against me. His muscular chest. The power in his arms as they'd held me.

I'd pushed him away.

"It won't happen again," Aiden said. I turned around. He was standing by the rock. He'd pulled off his knit cap and had it in his hand, hair unruly. "I know you've been through a lot. I promise, you have nothing to fear from me."

"I'm not afraid. Not in the way you're thinking."

"It's okay if you are. It's none of my business, and you don't owe me anything."

I tipped my head back and huffed in frustration. Not at him, but at everything else. My conflicted emotions and this complicated *stuff* in my head.

The contradictions that were *me*.

It had meant a lot for me to bring Aiden here. Show him this cabin and tell him my dreams for what Refuge Mountain could be. And he had *gotten* it. He'd said such wonderful things, and I knew he'd meant them. Aiden could be gruff and standoffish and blunt, but when he opened up? He was genuine. He was the sexiest man I had ever met. Bar none. That feeling had snuck up on me, and now it was all-consuming.

I wanted him so badly.

And he clearly wanted me. Maybe that was the part that had freaked me out.

Aiden was staring at me. Waiting for me to say something. Do something. If I'd told him to get lost, then he would. Of course, I didn't want that. I wanted to tell him what was in my head and my heart. To see if he might understand this part of me, too.

"I've healed from what Jeremy did. Inside and out. I did that work because I didn't want him to have any hold on me. I also knew things wouldn't always be easy in Hartley, but I chose to stay and make my home here. I stayed even when Chester and Mitch threatened me. And I'll *keep* staying. I'll stand my ground. Because I've always been a dreamer, too. I have big ideas and hopes, and I won't apologize for it. Even if sometimes, those hopes have steered me wrong."

"Like falling for Jeremy?"

"Yes. I was so wrong about him. But Jeremy brought me to Hartley, and I love it here." I loved my diner. I loved Refuge Mountain. These places were part of me now, under my skin. "Some people might say that everything happens for a reason. Who knows? But the work it's taken to get on my feet and have a life here? That was all me."

Aiden nodded, listening with a single line carved between his eyebrows.

"After I got out of the hospital, I swore two things to myself. The first was that I would go after what I wanted and not give in to fear."

"What was the other thing?"

A bird soared through the sky, far above us. Smoke continued to curl from chimneys below.

"That I would be careful. Not jump into something just because it seems like a great idea in the moment." Even if it was *exactly* what I wanted.

His chest moved as he inhaled, as if understanding had just hit. "Like jumping into bed with a man you just met two days ago?"

Desire bloomed in my stomach as I imagined what jumping into bed with Aiden might be like. "In the last couple years, that hasn't been a problem. I haven't wanted any man like that. Until *you*."

Aiden's eyes darkened, and I craved what I saw there. The hunger that mirrored my own.

He stood still. Waited.

"I have to be careful. I know all you did was kiss me, but I have to make sure you know where I stand. If I'm going to get physical with someone, I need to take things slow. Slower than a lot of men would prefer."

"I understand."

I took a step toward him. Then another. Erasing the distance I'd put between us. I kept walking until I stood right in front of him. Close enough I could feel his heat again. Smell the sunshine and salt on his skin, so different from the evergreen scent of Hartley.

"But I also promised myself I'd go after what I wanted." I lifted my hand and touched his cheek, the way I had a few minutes ago. It felt every bit as good. "I want you."

Aiden's eyes dragged down my body. Then back up to my face, lingering on my lips. "I'll stay until Friday. But that'll be it for me."

"I know. You were never supposed to be in Hartley at all."

He tilted his head. "Some say things happen for a reason." I could tell he was joking. But the corners of his mouth turned down again with seriousness. "I'm fine with taking things slow," he said. "I could touch you. Kiss you. Give you other things you want."

Tremors of anticipation spread through me. *Yes, please.* My thumb traced along his cheekbone, running the edge of his beard.

"Or we don't have to do anything at all," he said. "But I can't offer you more than that. Jessi, I like you. A lot. You deserve more than just a few days of attention. But even if I had more time, I'm not the right man for…" His gaze darted away toward the expansive view of the valley. "For everything you deserve to have."

"You're not going to fall in love with me?" I asked wryly.

He had to know I was kidding, but he looked sad when he replied. "I don't think I have that in me."

The funny thing was, it didn't disappoint me to hear it. He was being honest with me. He had been honest since the moment we'd met, and that was what made me want him. Not just his muscles or his rugged features or the fierce way he'd defended me, though those aspects of him were incredibly sexy too.

I had been alone for over two years. And alone in reality

for longer than that, even when Jeremy had been buttering me up and pretending to be my Prince Charming. I wanted to be touched and kissed the way that I *knew* Aiden would touch and kiss me. The way he already had. Like he cherished me. I wanted to feel passion, even if it was only for a few days.

Dreams were like that, weren't they? You always woke up. But you could still enjoy it for as long as the dream lasted.

"I just want what you have to give," I said. "If you can be satisfied with what I'm able to give *you*."

Aiden's tongue traced his lower lip as he made a low, growly sound in his chest. He dropped his forehead to mine. "You have no idea what you do to me. Just touching your hand would be enough for me, and I can't even explain it. I know I tried to take more when I kissed you, but—"

"I did want you to kiss me. You were right about that. I still do."

His eyes flashed. "Are you asking me to?"

There was a low, percussive boom. The ground beneath our feet trembled slightly, and snow cascaded from tree branches. I gasped and grabbed Aiden's arm.

"What *was* that?" I breathed.

"I didn't think you had earthquakes in Colorado."

"We *don't*. That came from somewhere uphill."

He cursed. "An avalanche?"

That had been my first thought, too. I scanned the parts of the mountain I could see. No telltale puffs of white that would signal an impending tsunami of snow. Refuge Mountain didn't have the kinds of sheer slopes that were prone to avalanches. It was a baby mountain compared to the huge fourteeners in the distance.

Then voices carried to us. People were shouting.

"Someone could be hurt," I said.

"Can you call emergency services? My phone has no bars."

"Nobody gets reception on Refuge Mountain. It's a dead spot."

"Then we should go see if we can help."

I nodded. "We have to." I rushed to my snowshoes and strapped them on. Aiden did the same. They weren't easy to move fast in, but it would be quicker than wading through deep snow.

I found the trail and started uphill toward the ridge. The sound had come from somewhere up here. Or maybe the other side, the national forest land.

"I've heard there are caves around here, but I don't know where any entrances are. Scarlett said the townspeople hid the children in one when those bandits attacked during the First World War."

"Could a cave have collapsed?"

"I guess it's possible. If someone was inside at the time…" I worried about those tourists who'd been stuck in Hartley for two days now, probably getting desperate for something to do. Had they gone wandering in the wrong place?

"Maybe I should go ahead myself," Aiden said. "You should return to town and tell Owen. Notify mountain rescue."

"But you don't know the trail." I'd walked this path hundreds of times in all seasons. I knew every tree and landmark along the way, and the snow could be deeper than it looked. There were ravines. Slopes where you could slip and twist an ankle or worse.

"Then lead the way," he said.

We followed the trail around the side of the mountain. There was a split in the path here, one fork leading uphill to the summit, and the other down along the far side of the mountain, opposite from the way we'd come up.

Someone had been through here. The snow was tamped

down. And there were fresh ATV tracks on the lower trail. "They must be on the national forest side," I said. "This is all federal land over here. But parts of that trail have been closed for at least a year. There was a flood. It washed out some of the path."

"I don't see any barriers."

"There's a sign somewhere, but it's probably covered in snow. Maybe tourists were out here exploring and didn't know about the damage."

Voices carried toward us again.

"That's where they must be," Aiden said. "Downhill. I can go check. You stay here."

"Would you stop trying to leave me behind? I'm going."

We ventured onto the lower trail, entering the national forest. This was definitely the right way. The voices were getting louder. And then, the sound of an engine, which fit with the ATV tracks.

But just as we came around a curve, Aiden pulled me back, his grip a steel vise around my arm. He pointed at one of the trees. "Do you see that?" he whispered.

It took me a moment to figure out what he meant. I kept blinking at it, because it didn't make sense. It looked like a high-tech camera was perched on a tree branch. It was black, which made it stand out against the snow. "It could be there to track wildlife," I said. "But I haven't heard about anything like that. And there haven't been any forest rangers around here in ages." If they didn't have the budget to repair the trail, why would they be setting up expensive looking cameras?

"Maybe it wasn't the rangers. Whoever put that camera there, they could've spotted us if they've been watching. Where else does this trail lead?"

"Just into the national forest. It's huge. The trail leads into the forest access roads, and those go for miles and miles.

But they aren't easy to reach from Hartley, and they're all unpaved."

Then an ATV roared into sight. Aiden pulled me behind a tree. Peeking out, I saw a familiar face riding it, bundled up in a heavy coat and hat. It was Mitch Rigsby, following a perpendicular path to the trail we were on. But unlike last night, his face was exposed. And he looked *furious*. He shouted something into the radio perched at his shoulder.

Aiden pulled me closer and murmured into my ear. "He's got a rifle strapped to his back. I can see the muzzle."

What on earth was Mitch Rigsby doing out here on national forest land? With a *rifle*? I'd almost taken him for a hunter at first, except I didn't think Mitch was that sporty. Like Chester, he was more into drinking and causing trouble than the outdoors.

And what had caused the ground to shake beneath us?

Maybe it wasn't such a good idea to find out.

Aiden tugged on my arm. "We need to go back before he sees us."

"Just what I was thinking."

Whatever Mitch was doing out here, I didn't want to run into him on a mountainside while he had a weapon and we were unarmed. Didn't seem too wise after that confrontation last night. Dale had promised this morning that the Rigsbys would leave me and my brother alone, but I had a hunch that Mitch being out here meant something far bigger than his family's vendetta against me.

I thought of the conversation between Dale and Chester last night that Aiden had overheard. Dale saying it wasn't the right time. Warning Chester not to draw attention. Whatever the Rigsbys were up to, they wanted to keep it hidden.

What would Mitch do if he found Aiden and me here?

We waited until Mitch had gone past, and then I led the

way going back uphill. "We should get off the trail," Aiden said. "Mitch could easily see us if he comes back."

"But it's dangerous to go off of it! And if he spots our tracks, couldn't he just follow them? He'll catch up to us." My pulse had already been racing when I thought that someone was injured, but now my heartbeat was a constant roar in my ears.

Suddenly, a gunshot rang out, the high-pitched snap echoing over the mountainside. At the same moment, a nearby tree trunk splintered.

Shit.

Mitch had definitely seen us.

Aiden leaped onto me, and we went sprawling in the snow. He pushed me uphill. "Go. Get out of here. I'll hold him off."

"With *what*? A trekking pole?"

"Get out of here, Jessi," he snarled. He rolled over into a crouch, unstrapping his snowshoes. He left them behind, along with his poles.

Then he bounded up and took off in the direction the gunshot had come from. Once again heading straight into danger.

CHAPTER THIRTEEN

I CAREENED DOWNHILL between the trees, moving parallel to the trail. My legs sank knee-deep into the snow. It was awkward and slow-going. But I had to stay off the path.

I didn't hear the ATV engine, which had to mean Mitch was on foot. Probably trying to sneak up on us. And sure enough, a figure raced uphill along the trail that Jessi was on. I dove between two trees before he could spot me. He was carrying his rifle, breathing heavily.

The bastard had shot at us. And right now, Jessi was up the slope from him. I'd basically left her as bait, knowing he would follow her as she ran in her snowshoes along the trail. It had worked. He'd seen prey, and he'd reacted, not stopping to look around for other predators.

For *me*.

But that meant I had better hurry the hell up and stop Mitch before he caught up to her.

I waded out of the tree cover and emerged on the trail behind him. Mitch was ahead of me by a few yards. Jessi was up the mountain from us and moving fast, following the zig-zag shape of the trail. But she wasn't fast enough.

Mitch raised his rifle to his shoulder. Aimed.

I slammed into his back. We both went down, Mitch sprawling face-first onto the trail. He lost hold of his rifle, and I grabbed for it, but Mitch rolled surprisingly fast and got his hands around the barrel. We grappled, the rifle held between us. I barred the weapon against Mitch's chest. He forced me onto my back. Then I spun him again, driving the rifle hard into his solar plexus. He wheezed.

Distantly, I heard other noise. Shouts and engines. I assumed that Mitch had friends. It had looked like he was out on a patrol of some kind. He must've seen us on the cameras. That was the only way to explain how quickly he'd gotten here.

His friends could be on their way.

Mitch's knee raised and smacked me in the side, knocking me off balance. My gloved hands slipped from the rifle. We rolled again. Mitch straddled my middle and tried to ram me with the side of the gun. I deflected it. He got a better grip on the weapon and forced it forward, the muzzle catching me on the nose. Not enough to do damage, but enough to sting. Pushing back against the rifle with one hand, I drove my fist into his body with the other. But snow was in my eyes. Blinding me. The thick padding of his winter clothes meant my punches weren't landing nearly as hard as they should've. I'd never fought on a snowy mountainside before.

I shook my head, blinking the icy wetness away. Mitch had maneuvered the rifle so it pointed at me.

His fingers searched for the trigger.

Then a long, thin stick flew at Mitch's head out of nowhere. It was *Jessi*. "Get off of him!" She let out a rage-filled scream. Hit him again. She was using her trekking pole. Swinging it like she was going for a home run. "You *asshole*! Leave us alone!"

Mitch raised a hand, grabbing for Jessi's pole, and I took

advantage of the distraction. I grabbed the rifle and chucked it away from us.

"Grab it!" I yelled to Jessi. She dove.

Mitch tried to scramble after her. I got to him first. Grasped him around his lower body and heaved, trying to throw him down the slope.

Mitch's hands closed on my jacket at the last moment.

I was dragged along with him. We somersaulted down the slope, end over end like a couple of snowballs. Mitch was shouting curses. We both landed hard where the slope evened out, and I saw shadows just past us where the snow and the trail fell away. Open air. Holy *hell*.

We were inches away from a ravine.

We were both absolutely covered in snow. Mitch got to his knees. Blood oozed from the cuts on his forehead, a frenzied, bloodshot tinge to his eyes visible through the coating of white on his face. He wasn't looking at the drop-off. Only at me.

"You're *dead*," he yelled. Just like last night when he'd driven past me on Main Street. Mitch launched himself forward, hands going for my throat.

It barely took a shove. A rotation of my body.

Mitch sailed over the side of the trail into the open air. Thudded once. Twice.

Then silence, marred only by distant ATV engines.

"Oh my *God. Aiden!*" Jessi ran down the slope, slipping and sliding. She had the rifle, and she'd slung the strap across her body.

"Be careful." I held out my hands to keep her from getting too close.

"He went over the edge!"

"Yep. I know. Better him than us." Once I was sure Jessi was on stable footing, I scooted on my belly and peered sideways down into the ravine. Mitch lay on some rocks far below, legs buried in snow, his neck bent at an unnatural angle.

I inched backward away from the drop-off. Jessi was on her knees beside me, panting to catch her breath. I didn't want her looking down there. "Mitch is gone. He's not coming back."

Her face turned to stone. She nodded.

"We need to go."

I grabbed her hands and pulled her up. We raced up the trail, grabbing our snowshoes and the remaining poles along the way. Snow was churned up in the woods, on the trail. It was going to be obvious to anyone who came through here that a fight had taken place.

And there was at least the one camera.

We had to get the hell out of here before anyone else stumbled on us. I just had to hope that, whatever had shaken the mountain before, it was proving a distraction to the rest of Mitch's friends.

We were both covered head to toe in snow, which probably provided some decent camouflage as we trekked our way over the trail and back down Refuge Mountain. Jessi kept the rifle and tightened the strap so the weapon was nestled against her back. At one point, she paused to check the chamber. Closed it up again. Flicked on the safety. She knew what she was doing.

After we'd made our way down the other side to the road, I scouted ahead, but nobody was waiting near Jessi's car.

We stowed our gear and snow-laden coats in the trunk, then buckled in and locked the doors. I'd taken the driver's seat this time. Jessi had kept the rifle with her. Her hands shook slightly on the barrel.

"You all right?" I asked.

"Yeah. You?"

"Just fine." But if Jessi had thought it was bad when I

confronted Chester on the first night I'd arrived, there was no comparison to what we'd just done.

I thought about Mitch riding that ATV. The explosion. The possibility that we might still run into company. "Do you think Mitch's friends are parked near here somewhere?" I asked. "It didn't seem like they were following us on the trail. Could they be flanking us?"

"You can't reach the forest access roads from this side of Refuge Mountain. They're miles out of the way. They would have to circle half the mountain to get over here, and we can definitely beat them back to Main Street."

That was good. I didn't want to give them a chance to catch up to us. I started the engine, and we rolled slowly across the icy road back toward town.

Jessi squeezed the stock of the rifle. She had the muzzle pointed down into the wheel well. "I can't believe Mitch is dead."

"He tried to kill both of us."

"I know. But did you…did you know he would go over the edge?"

"Yes," I said evenly. "That's where I intended for him to end up. You can't feel bad about it." I certainly didn't.

"I don't feel bad." When she turned her eyes to me, they were like two blue gemstones. Hard and shining. "What do we do now?"

I sped up. Trees flew past. "We'll go back to your place. Wait to see what they'll do. If the other Rigsbys come for us, we'll call Owen." I was glad we had that rifle. It would help in case things got really bad. Our chefs' knives had limited utility.

Though what I wanted most was to get Jessi to safety. Away from the diner. Where, though? There was nowhere else.

"You don't think we should go to Owen now?" she asked. "Try to explain? It was self defense."

"Whatever they're up to on the national forest land, Mitch was patrolling to keep anyone from stumbling upon it. They're keeping it a secret. And that's our leverage. For tonight, we stay quiet and wait. If we're lucky, they'll do the same. They'd be idiots not to."

"We're talking about Chester and Theo."

"True. But I think Daddy Dale is involved in what they're doing, too. He'll be calling the shots."

"Because of what Dale and Chester were talking about last night? How they can't afford to draw attention?"

"Exactly. That camera was there for a reason."

We reached the diner, and I parked Jessi's car behind it in her usual space. We went inside. I made sure all the doors were locked and shut as many curtains as possible. Jessi and I stripped off our outer layers. Left them piled by the back door. Puddles formed as the snow melted.

We sat huddled together in her kitchen. We were both high on adrenaline. Primed for the next fight. But I'd lived this before. Jessi hadn't. This wasn't like the other night, when Chester had threatened her. Not like the brick either. This had been far more intense.

But maybe it was like what Jeremy had put her through.

I was worried about her. I wrapped my arm around her and held her tight to my side.

Neither of us had any appetite, but we stayed there on the floor of the kitchen. We were far from any windows here. Out of sight. Hours passed, the shadows lengthening as it started getting dark, and I thought of the conversation we'd had outside the cabin, right before the earth shook. Everything Jessi had shared with me. Her dreams for building a hotel and restaurant on Refuge Mountain. The longing in her eyes when she'd looked at me.

I promised myself I'd go after what I want, she had said.

I wanted to give that to her. And protect her, too. After what we'd been through today, it was a feral instinct, clawing at my insides. Jessi had made me care for her in ways I usually didn't care for anyone. Like if she got hurt, it would threaten *my* survival, not just hers.

It was a dismaying feeling. I didn't know what to do with it, except follow it for as long as I was here.

"Where did you learn how to handle a weapon?" I asked.

"My mom taught me. She had a rifle and a shotgun for the times that she didn't have a man around."

"Was that often?"

"Not really." Jessi chuckled, and that sound did a lot to calm the tension that still had me wound as tight as a bowstring.

"Tell me more about your family. How you grew up."

Jessi recounted stories from her childhood. The brief time that Trace had been around before he and her father moved away. Her mom's series of husbands and boyfriends that followed, which Jessi agreed could've been awful and traumatic, but most of the guys had been harmless and comically nerdy. We both laughed as she told story after story. It was dark in the kitchen, but we didn't bother with a light.

"And your dad?" I asked. "Is he in Virginia like Trace?"

She stilled. "He passed away. I don't have any family that I'm close to. Not my mom. Not even Trace."

I rested my head against hers. Put my hand on her bent knee and rubbed circles into it with my thumb.

I wanted to kiss her right now, but not just because she'd asked me earlier. And not simply to make her feel good, though of course that was important to me. It was more that I wanted to prove to Jessi that she was safe. Safe with *me*. Prove that I hadn't made things worse for her just by my presence.

Jessi probably wouldn't have been on Refuge Mountain today if not for me. But some people said things happened for a reason.

Hell, I didn't know. My brain was going in circles. I didn't usually deal with this kind of shit as a chef. Life and death decisions. I had thought my Army days were far behind me, and I had said good riddance. I was no hero.

But if I had to be a warrior for her, I would be.

For the next few days that I was in Hartley, I would be whatever Jessi needed me to be.

CHAPTER FOURTEEN
Jessi

MAIN STREET WAS QUIET. Nobody had come for us.

At about two in the morning, we trudged upstairs. We brought the rifle. Aiden locked the door to my apartment and shoved a chair beneath the knob. Then he went to the window and looked out. "Still nothing," he reported.

"Maybe they know Mitch is dead and there was a fight, but not that it was us." I tried to reason through it. "We had our beanies on. The camera was above. The angle was more to detect intruders, not capture faces."

"It's possible. Even if they suspect us, Dale knows if they come near you again, Owen will be pissed enough to take action. And I'm guessing Owen doesn't have the slightest clue what they're up to on that mountainside. Whatever it is."

"I'd bet not. Like you said, we have leverage. What do we do with it?"

"How about you get some sleep, and we'll worry about that tomorrow."

I rubbed my face and stifled a yawn. I had dozed off in the kitchen, my head against Aiden's shoulder as we sat and he ran his fingers through my hair. Now I was dead on my feet, but also wired, much like last night. How could I sleep?

Aiden's presence dominated my thoughts. Our conversation earlier, the terrifying moments on the mountain trail when he'd nearly followed Mitch into that ravine... I had seen it *all*. Aiden had almost gone over the edge, and my heart and lungs had been choking me as I watched.

I could still smell the fear on me. In fact, I stank.

"I'm going to shower," I said.

Aiden lifted one of those thick eyebrows, but he didn't invite himself to join me. Of course he didn't. He was being good. And I wasn't quite ready to make that move myself.

Yet as I closed the door and stripped off my clothes, I stared at the broken lock. Nerves had me on edge, but having Aiden right outside that door both made me feel safe and so eager that my heart was skipping beats. I was too restless to spend long under the hot water. And I didn't want to take it all. I figured Aiden would take a shower next.

And there went my heart again. Even under the warm spray of the water, goosebumps pebbled all over my skin.

I dried off and ran my fingers through my hair to break up the tangles. I didn't usually wear much makeup, and now my face was scrubbed clean. Still pink from the cold air and the harsh, dry wind on the mountain.

I wrapped the towel around my body and gathered up my discarded clothes. When I opened the door and stepped into the room, Aiden was by the window, the rifle propped near his feet. He'd been watching the street through the gaps in the blinds. But then his head turned, and he looked at me, his eyes flashing with heat when he saw that I was just in a towel.

"Still quiet out there," he said. "I think we're good. Until daylight, at least. If they were going to do something rash, they would've done it already. Either they don't know we were involved, like you thought, or they're waiting for us to make a move."

"Are we going to make a move?" A drop of water slid from my hair down my shoulder. His gaze followed it.

"Remains to be seen."

"Okay," I said, lungs tight. "Your turn for the shower."

Aiden nodded once. His Adam's apple bobbed as he swallowed. He grabbed a folded piece of clothing from his duffel. He headed for the bathroom, and I said, "There's no lock on that door, by the way."

He paused. Turned his head slightly, not facing me. "I noticed. I don't mind." His voice had dropped a whole octave from the last time he had said anything.

Then he went into the bathroom and closed the door, but not all the way. He let it touch the frame without the latch catching.

Oh… Boy.

My pulse was going crazy now. I stood in the middle of my apartment, still in nothing but the towel. And Aiden was probably getting undressed at this very moment.

The water turned on.

Without letting myself think, I went to the door and knocked. "It's me." I closed my eyes. Of course it was me. Who else?

I heard amusement in Aiden's voice when he responded. "I know it's you. And you know the door's open."

My hand was poised on the door, hesitating. Taking a deep breath, I pushed the door wider.

Water pattered against the tile. Aiden hadn't stepped into the shower yet. He was wrapping a towel around his waist, his large hands tucking it into place. It hung low enough on his hips to make very clear that he was naked underneath. He lifted his head and looked at me.

I held my towel closed at my chest and took another step

toward him. The warm water in the shower was fogging up the mirrors. The humid air prickled my skin.

"Need something?" he asked with an almost-smile.

Fire spread across my abdomen. A flush that I'd never experienced before. Maybe this was impulsive. But I *wanted*. And after our conversation by the cabin, he knew it. He knew I needed to go slow.

"Turn around?"

I could tell he had questions, but he didn't ask them. He rotated slowly until he was facing away from me. His back muscles were broad and sculpted. Carved beneath his skin. His ocean wave tattoo moved over them, cascading over his shoulder and down half of his upper back. His spine was a deep furrow down the center, ending in the swell of his glutes just beneath the towel.

"Can I touch you?" I asked on a sigh.

"Please." He sounded just as short of breath as I had.

I started at his neck. Brushing my fingers over the short hairs there. His skin was golden and warm. Cords of muscle lay beneath. My fingertips trailed along one shoulder. Over the curves and divots. Then down the furrow where the knobs of his spine lay, to his lower back, which was beading with sweat from the humid air.

My eyes were eating him up. Every freckle and mole and small scar. "I like touching you."

He made a low, needy sound that made me shiver. "That's really nice. But I thought you wanted me to touch *you*."

"Not yet."

His back expanded as he breathed. Touching him with one hand wasn't enough anymore. I tucked my towel again at my chest to secure it, then rested both of my palms on his shoulder blades. They dragged down. Lower and lower, until both my hands rested at his hips, where the muscle flared out again in generous, firm curves. My thumbs dipped slightly beneath his towel at his lower back, finding hard, compact muscle.

I felt delirious. "Can I?" I didn't even know what I was asking exactly. My thoughts weren't coming through clearly. I just wanted more of him.

"Jessi, you can do whatever you want to me."

A small, desperate noise made its way past my lips. My fingers tugged at his towel, and it fell to the floor with a soft whoosh.

Aiden turned his head to look over his shoulder at me, and the unguarded lust in his expression set me on fire. I wrapped my arms around him at chest level. My hands found the swell of his pectorals, and we both inhaled sharply. I rested my cheek at the base of his neck. Inhaled him, salty from sweat and that scent that made me think of the ocean. My tongue darted out to lap at his skin, and Aiden groaned. He tasted salty, too.

Only my towel separated us. His ass tightened against me. My nipples beaded, the rough Terry cloth rubbing my skin and Aiden's skin at the same time. Aiden's entire body seemed to be clenched so hard he was vibrating.

I loved it.

"Are you testing me, Jessi? Trying to see if I'll lose control?"

"I know you won't. But if you don't like what I'm doing, you can tell me." My hands moved down again as I closed my eyes. I touched the ridges of his abs. Found the soft trail of hair that started near his belly button.

Another groan. "I like it way too much."

I swirled a finger around his belly button. I felt the heat and desire radiating from him. His musky scent. He didn't move, just let me stand there, pressed to him, my arms around him. He was very turned on, and I knew it. So was I.

If I moved my hand even slightly, I'd be able to feel *everything* he had for me.

My hands didn't go any lower, but I pressed kisses to the base of his neck. The moment grew. Gathered weight and substance. A pulse throbbed between my legs.

He looked over his shoulder at me again, pupils dilated. Dark and intense. "I need to be alone now, Jessi. You should go."

Unless you plan to stay, his tone warned. But if I did, my towel was coming off. We both knew that. Aiden would press our bodies together, lift me up, and I would feel every achingly hard inch of him. And that wouldn't have been going slow. That would've been full-speed ahead. I did want that. I *so* wanted it. But I also wasn't ready.

Reluctantly, I separated from him and backed away. "Sorry. I'm wasting your hot water."

"A cold shower isn't a bad idea after all that."

My hand pressed to my mouth, covering a laugh. I got a brain-searing eyeful of his naked, sculpted butt before I spun and left the room. Then I pulled the door all the way closed and leaned against it, panting to catch my breath.

Going slow with Aiden was going to be more difficult than I'd thought.

He took a long shower, even though the water had to be cold.

I hung my towel on a hook, dressed in my pajamas, and spent way too much time arranging the blankets and pillows on my bed. When he came out, his hair was tousled and he was wearing gray boxer briefs. No shirt. He set his folded dirty clothes on the floor. Then looked up, probably having noticed I hadn't set out his bedding like last night. "Where would you like me to sleep?"

I scooted over on the bed. "You can sleep here. With me."

The mattress compressed as he lay down, getting under the covers. I switched off the light, blood thumping at my throat. But my nerves settled as the minutes passed. I wanted him here, and he wasn't going to take things any further than I wished. I had the reins. We'd proven that in the bathroom.

I had *really* enjoyed proving that in the bathroom.

Aiden was a comforting, solid presence. And my bed had been lonely for such a long time.

I curled on my side, facing him. I could see his eyes in the low light. "Hi," I said.

"Hi," he rumbled.

My hand reached over to him and touched his arm. I trailed down his thick bicep and corded forearm until our fingers laced together. He lifted our hands. Kissed my knuckle. I scooted closer to him until my head found his shoulder. We both readjusted, his arm going around me and tucking me against his side.

"Just this," he whispered.

I smiled against him. We didn't say anything else. My breaths found a rhythm with his, and it was exactly what I needed.

I dreamed about cozy wooden cabins surrounded by snow. Breathless kisses. Fear and danger blotted out by broad shoulders and strong arms. Safety.

A refuge.

CHAPTER FIFTEEN
Jessi

WHEN WE WOKE, the sun was bright yellow, forcing its way through the blinds. I didn't usually sleep this late, and if I was going to open the diner, I had a ton of work to do.

Yet I didn't want to move.

I was cuddled against Aiden's rib cage. The size of him had unnerved me before. But now, he felt like a perfect fit. I was lounging on him like he was my own personal body pillow. My leg was draped over him, foot tucked beneath his calf. I could tell by the way he was breathing that he was awake. But he hadn't moved either. As if he was just here for me and wanted me to enjoy cuddling up to him to my heart's content.

"I would love to stay here as long as possible," he finally said. "But I have to go to the bathroom."

I laughed, propping my chin on his chest. "So do I. You can go first."

I kept my eyes averted when he got up. I knew he had an erection. I'd felt it brush my hip. He'd had one in the bathroom last night, too. I'd felt the heat of him when my hand got near. The pheromones in the air had nearly made me drunk.

I'm being careful, I reminded myself. *I'm going slow*.

Even though I wanted to maul him right now. Or better yet, for him to maul me.

While Aiden used the restroom, I tugged on some jeans. Then we traded places, and when I left the bathroom, I found Aiden was dressed as well.

"You opening the diner today?" he asked.

I nodded. "For lunch, at least. Like yesterday." Although I would have to get creative with the special because I was running low on supplies, and I still hadn't had any deliveries come through. Technically our town was accessible right now if you approached from the west, since that part of the highway wasn't damaged. But a lot of delivery trucks weren't eager to make the trip just to Hartley before turning around. We were an awkward, isolated spot for a dead end.

But the bridge repairs had to be getting close. Trace had been on the road for almost a day now. "I'm going to check on the bridge repairs," I said, reaching for my phone on my nightstand. "And I'll see if my brother has any updates."

"Sure. I can get things started downstairs." Aiden went to the door and removed the chair that he'd used last night to barricade it. He flipped the lock.

But before he could twist the doorknob, I said, "Aiden. Wait."

He turned around. I set my phone down without even checking it and crossed the room toward him. Stopped less than a foot away. His nostrils flared as he inhaled.

"Would you kiss me?" I asked.

His gaze softened and he took a step, his hands lifting. His palms cradled my face. We still hadn't kissed, really kissed, since outside the cabin on Refuge Mountain yesterday. And that one had been pretty tame. But now, we had an understanding between us. And I knew what I wanted. What I *needed*.

I needed his mouth on mine.

This time, the touch of his lips was pure electricity. A spark that jolted my body entirely awake. He pressed his mouth to my upper lip, my lower. My tongue darted out, and he responded by opening up. His tongue stroked into my mouth. Petted mine sweetly.

I put my hands flat on his chest. His heart thrummed into my palm. We kept going like that. Gentle yet deepening kisses. Tasting each other. Aiden was fresh like mint on the surface, but with something richer beneath. Hungry. And he hummed the same way he had when he'd tasted my lemon tart a few days ago. Like I was delicious and he wanted more. Yet at the same time, he let me take the lead, responding to my every cue.

I was the one who escalated things.

I slid my hands down and under his T-shirt. I pulled it upward, and Aiden helped me take it off of him, tossing it aside. My hands went back to his chest and rubbed his bare skin and the dusting of dark hair. Blood was rushing in my ears. Distantly, I thought I heard a noise downstairs. Maybe a knock? But I didn't pay it the slightest bit of mind. The diner's doors were locked, and I was too wrapped up in the gorgeous man before me.

Aiden's lips found mine again, but now he wasn't nearly as controlled. He took my mouth with dominant strokes, his hands sinking into my hair as he walked us backward into the center of the room. Closer to my bed.

Then the door to my apartment flew open, and somebody *screamed*.

Aiden and I both turned to look, his hands still in my hair and mine on his chest. Scarlett stood in the doorway with a look of pure, scandalized shock on her face. "What are you—but you, I—"

"Shit," Aiden muttered. He let go of me.

"How did you get in here?" I asked.

Scarlett's pale skin was turning crimson. "I texted you a million times, and you didn't respond. And then I was knocking downstairs, and you didn't answer. I used that key you gave me for emergencies." She was talking fast, gesturing wildly. "And your apartment door was unlocked, so I just…" Her eyes scanned over Aiden's naked chest, and she spun around in the doorway. "Jessi, we need to talk."

I glanced sheepishly at Aiden. "I'll take Scarlett downstairs." I needed to talk her off the ledge she was teetering on.

He went to pick up his T-shirt from the ground. "I'll be there in a bit."

I nudged her out of the doorway and closed it behind me. "Let's go to the kitchen. I'll explain." But the minute Aiden was out of sight, she grabbed my arm, holding me there on the landing.

"He's your *brother*," Scarlett hissed. "How can you possibly explain…" She waved her hand at me. "What you two were just *doing*?"

Oh, Lord.

I clapped my hand over her mouth. "Please, for the love of dessert, stop talking. He's not my brother. He's not Trace."

Her eyes bugged. Then narrowed. "You lied to me?" Her voice was muffled behind my palm, but I could make out the words.

"I'm sorry. Let me explain?"

A few minutes later, I was arraying every dessert from my freezer on a plate in front of Scarlett in the hopes that she would forgive me. "So not only is he *not* your brother, you'd never even met him before a couple days ago?"

"He was stuck here because of the bridge being out. He was heading to a rental cabin."

"Yet now he's living with you and clearly enjoying the

benefits? Not that I'm judging. Since he's not related to you, I guess you can have at it."

Scarlett broke off a piece of chocolate-chip cookie.

"Please don't be mad?"

She huffed. "I'm not." A bigger chunk of cookie popped into her mouth. "In fact, I'm jealous. Where's my sexy out-of-towner for a meaningless fling? All the stranded tourists who've stumbled through the sweet shop have been either children or a hundred years old."

"It's not a fling, exactly. He's been protecting me. Helping me hold off Chester and Mitch Rigsby."

How could I explain the connection that Aiden and I had after just a couple of days of knowing one another? How I could suddenly trust this man more than anyone else in Hartley? Maybe even more than my actual brother?

Scarlett didn't know the real Aiden, so there was no way she could understand. I barely did either. But there was something special about him. I was drawn to him, and I didn't want to deny this connection that we had. Or deny the attraction that I was feeling.

"Aiden got into a fight with Chester because he was defending me. Then Owen tried to make Aiden leave town. That's why I said he was my brother. And the lie just grew from there. But the chemistry between us grew as well. I didn't expect that. I wanted to tell you, I really did. I'm so sorry."

She rolled her eyes. "I guess I sort of get it. You've been in a really tough spot with the Rigsbys, and Owen hasn't always jumped instantly into the fray. I heard all about the brick they threw at your window. That was so awful. I would've come by yesterday if I'd been able to. I *should* have. You needed a protector."

I smiled and squeezed her hand. "You're offering?"

"I would've tried."

"That's kind of you. I'd been doing pretty well on my own. But Aiden makes for excellent backup."

"With those muscles? No wonder." She smirked and nudged my shoulder. "So he's not your brother, and he ended up in Hartley by chance. But who is he aside from that? I just saw the man half naked with his tongue down your throat. I should know a few non-scandalous details about him so I don't blush when I face him next."

We shared bites of brownie and half-unfrozen cheesecake while I told her about Aiden Shelborne. Nothing too personal, not that he'd shared a ton of personal stuff with me. But I felt myself smiling even broader as I talked about him.

"You really like this handsome stranger. Are you catching feelings?"

"I can't. He has to leave in a couple more days for work, and he's not planning to come back to Hartley." That thought sobered me.

"So this is a little free dessert to thank him for his help?"

I snickered. "I know it seems that way, but that part is separate. Being close to him… Scar, it's amazing. He won't be here long, but I still need to be cautious, and Aiden has been great about that. He's…" I sighed and snagged another bite of brownie. "If I'm really lucky, maybe the bridge won't get repaired and he'll have to stay longer. Because I swear, my body feels like it's been mothballed the past couple years. I need him to sweep out all my corners and pump some sunshine into me."

We leaned our heads together and giggled.

"It's good to see you like this," she said.

"Like what?"

"Like stress isn't about to drive you into the ground."

"It's good to *feel* like this." Desired. Seen. Like my world was opening up with possibilities instead of closing in around me. "After Aiden leaves, I might be ready to try dating again. He's breaking the seal on my forgotten love life."

Though the thought of any man but him made my stomach sour.

Suddenly Scarlett gasped, covering her mouth. "Shoot, the bridge. That's why I was trying to get ahold of you in the first place. The bridge was repaired as of this morning. Which means Jeremy could be back any minute."

My stomach fell all the way to the tile floor. But at least I didn't have to worry about Aiden leaving yet. He'd said he would stay until Friday, and he had all the more reason now, judging by that fiery kiss we'd shared before Scarlett had barged in.

But my real brother would get here soon, and so would my ex. And things were so much worse between me and the Rigsbys than ever before. Scarlett didn't know the half of it.

Then someone else started banging on the diner's front door. Scarlett and I both jumped.

Sheriff Owen Douglas was outside, and he looked *pissed*.

CHAPTER SIXTEEN
Aiden

I HADN'T MEANT to eavesdrop. But I had been starting down the stairs and heard Scarlett and Jessi talking. Their voices had drifted up from the kitchen.

"You really like this handsome stranger. Are you catching feelings?"

A question like that should've filled me with the urge to run. I'd had girlfriends, but never anything serious. That was how I preferred things. But as I listened to Jessi's answer, I wasn't running for the exits. I was just thinking about *her*. Pondering what else I could do for her in the time we had left together. And wishing we had at least a few days more. Jessi was saying the same thing downstairs.

But as I kept listening, it sounded like Jessi was just talking about sex. I was more than willing in that department. And able. Yet I was almost…disappointed.

Then she said, "After Aiden leaves, I might be ready to try dating again." Those words hit me like a punch to the solar plexus. Jessi had every right to date other men, to be happy, but the thought still made me nauseous. I wanted to know who these other guys were and see proof that they were good enough. Jessi deserved the best.

Loud knocking interrupted their conversation. Somebody was at the door, and that knock wasn't a friendly one. I raced down the stairs and joined Jessi and Scarlett in the kitchen, where they were looking through the cut-out toward the front of the diner.

"Owen," Jessi whispered at me, eyes wide.

"I'll handle it."

I guessed we were about to find out if he knew about Mitch. It was still possible I'd see the inside of a Hartley jail cell, and that would've put a damper on any romantic plans I had for Jessi.

Really hoped that wasn't about to happen.

I went toward the door and unlocked it. Scarlett must've flipped the latch after she'd come inside, and I appreciated her carefulness. She was a good friend to Jessi, despite her lack of caution about entering apartments without knocking.

I opened the door and looked out at Owen. "Can I help you, Sheriff?"

Owen's scowl deepened. "Is Jessi all right?"

I nodded my head toward the kitchen. "She's here. Why wouldn't she be all right?" *What have you heard?* I wanted to ask. Was the rest of Mitch's family out for our blood, or not? The suspense was killing me.

Never mind. Insensitive choice of words, considering Mitch's broken neck.

Owen pushed his way past me into the diner. I re-locked the front door and stepped in behind him. Jessi and Scarlett were already coming through the swinging door and into the dining area.

Owen yanked his hat off, then rubbed a hand over his buzzed hair. "I just got a call from one of my deputies. Jeremy is back in Hartley. Drove in this morning almost the moment the bridge opened. I'd made it known to the Rigsbys that I wanted Jeremy to check in with me first thing, and he didn't. I had intended to remind him of that protective order barring him from seeing you, Jessi, and I was worried he'd decided to be stupid instead."

"I haven't seen him." Jessi pressed her lips together. Her gaze darted to mine. I walked over to her and touched her arm. She leaned subtly into me.

Owen exhaled. "That's good. Apparently, Chester's been out and about as well, riled up about something. I'm sure I'll hear the details sooner or later, but if it's nothing to do with *you*, I can breathe a little easier for the moment."

I had no doubt Chester was riled up about his brother falling to his death in a ravine yesterday. But it seemed nobody had reported the death to Owen. Just as I'd suspected they wouldn't. The Rigsbys couldn't afford to let the sheriff know what they were up to.

Of course, Jessi and I had secrets too. Scarlett had just found out I wasn't really Jessi's brother. That secret wasn't going to stay under wraps for long. Not because Scarlett would tell everyone, but because I doubted Jessi and I could keep our hands off each other.

I'd never been a model soldier, but my time in the military had taught me—secrets were commodities. It was all about whose secrets were more dangerous. And that was exactly where our leverage would come in.

"Owen," I said, "there's something I need to show you. It could explain why Chester's upset."

"Can't you share now? Instead of being all mysterious about it?"

"It's more of a show and tell."

Jessi frowned at me. Clearly she wanted to discuss this, so I tugged her into the kitchen. "Hold that thought, Sheriff. We'll be right back."

We stood out of sight of the dining area, where Owen and Scarlett waited. "You're going to tell him?" she whispered.

"Yep. Everything. It's the wisest choice."

"Are you sure?"

"Do you trust him?"

She considered a moment. "Yes. I do. Owen's a good man, and he's been proving that again lately."

That strange feeling shifted around in my chest. "Do you think he's got more than a friendly interest in you? He seemed pretty worried."

She smirked. "It's not like that between me and Owen. Never has been, never will."

"It's not really my business." But hell, I did want it to be my business. I leaned closer, my nose brushing her temple.

Her lips moved against my cheek. "Then why did you ask?"

I brought my hands to her waist. "You can probably guess."

"Trace, are we going somewhere or what?" Owen called out.

"Five minutes," I replied, though my eyes stayed on Jessi. "Can you drive us, Sheriff?"

"I'll meet you out front. Four minutes, or I'm leaving. I have plenty of other things to do, you know." The bell jingled as the diner door opened and closed.

Scarlett pushed through the door to the kitchen and peered at us. "Hello, Aiden," she said, a smug smile on her face. "Nice to meet you. Officially."

"You, too." I nodded politely, then turned and leaned to kiss Jessi's lips, nice and slow.

When I pulled away, Scarlett's grin was even wider, and she was fanning herself with her hand. "All right, enough of that. I'm too young for hot flashes."

Jessi laughed and pulled me by the shirt for another kiss, this one quick and soft. "You're going now?"

"Yeah. Sounds like it. But I don't like leaving you with Jeremy back in town."

"I'm opening the diner for lunch service," Jessi said. "If I can get things organized around here. It's broad daylight. I'll be just fine."

"I can stick around to help," Scarlett added. "I have a girl working the register at the sweet shop today."

So long as Jessi wasn't alone. "Good. I'll hurry back." I sneaked in for one last kiss before dashing to the door.

"Not fair," I heard Scarlett say as I left. "Is there a rescue shelter for sexy, stranded men, and where can I sign up to foster one of my own?"

―――

"Where to?" Owen asked, arm slung casually over the steering wheel like he was a cabbie. But if he thought his sarcastic tone bothered me, he was wrong.

I settled into the passenger seat of his Hartley Sheriff's Department truck and buckled my seatbelt. I glanced around at Main Street. Already, it looked like the numbers were thinning out. I had no doubt a lot of those stranded tourists were back on the road, eager to get where they were going. But Hartley residents were bound to be watching us right now. It wouldn't be good to linger.

"I hear there are access roads into the national forest on the north side of Refuge Mountain."

"There are. Why?"

"Because that's where we need to go for this show and tell."

Owen put the truck in gear. "Fine. You can show me when

we get there, but the telling needs to start right now. I want to know what's going on."

"There's a lot. I'm not sure where to start."

"How about with the part that I'll hate the most. I'm a bad-news-first kind of guy."

He was going to hate all of this. "That doesn't help."

"Jeez, the universe is determined to ruin my day, huh?" he muttered. "Start anywhere. We'll go from there."

"I'll start with my real name. It's Aiden Shelborne."

He punched the brakes, bringing the truck to a shuddering halt in the middle of the road. Glared at me. "No wonder I couldn't find anything in the databases. 'Trace Novo' has fake name written all over it. Would have been smarter to go with something generic."

"Nah, he's a real guy. Jessi's brother is on his way, like she said. But he's not me."

"Then who the hell are you? 'Aiden Shelborne' doesn't tell me much."

I dove right in. Started with my arrival in Hartley the night of the storm. Just a guy from California, passing through on his way to other parts of Colorado. How I stopped at Jessi's Diner and got mixed up with Chester, Mitch, and Theo. Then Jessi's impulsive claim that I was her brother.

"You can't blame her," I said. "She was freaked out."

He waved a hand dismissively, pressing the gas. "I'm not mad at her. Keep going to the rest of the stuff I'm going to hate."

Get ready, I thought.

I told him about what we'd seen on Refuge Mountain yesterday. How it had started as an innocent hike. I left out the kissing, though my pulse kicked as I remembered Jessi's cold hand and how I warmed her skin with my mouth. And back in her apartment afterward, her hands on my naked body in the bathroom...

Nope. Couldn't let my mind stray to that.

I moved on to the loud noise and the rumbling of the mountain. Then the camera monitoring the trail into the national forest and Mitch patrolling by ATV with a rifle slung over his back. Owen kept his eyes on the snow-packed road ahead of us, but I could tell he was hanging on every word.

"Mitch spotted us. Took a few shots. We fought, and he and I ended up rolling downhill. I stopped before I reached the edge of a ravine. He didn't." That was close enough to what had happened. He didn't need the blow-by-blow.

"Did you leave him down there? It wouldn't have been easy to climb up with all the ice. Or..."

"He broke his neck. It was obvious. There wouldn't have been any point in sending a rescue mission."

"Fuck," Owen whispered. "I see why Chester's upset this morning. Either his brother is missing, or they found Mitch's body."

"I assume so. After that, I got Jessi out of there. There were more ATVs on patrol. I didn't want to run into them. And we didn't come to you because I had no idea if Chester or somebody else was going to come after us. I figured our silence was the only leverage we had. Whatever the Rigsbys are doing on Refuge Mountain, they're trying very hard to keep it quiet."

Owen pulled the truck over, stopping again. He kept the engine idling, but rubbed a hand over his jaw like he was thinking. "You're right. I do hate all of this."

"I realize Mitch was your cousin," I said. I hoped he didn't expect an apology or remorse because he wouldn't get that from me. Not about Mitch Rigsby.

"It's not that. He and his brothers are all assholes. Always have been. I half-expected one of them to get killed in a bar fight one of these days. On a mountainside is at least more creative. But this is a whole new layer of complications I didn't want to deal with. Fuck," he muttered again.

Then he resumed the drive.

"Doesn't seem like you get along well with the rest of your family," I said.

"I told you that the other day when you came to my office."

"More or less. But you didn't explain why."

He tapped his fingers on the steering wheel. "I told you Sawyer Junior and Dale are my uncles, along with Gary, who died. And that my mom was their sister."

"I remember."

"The extended Rigsby family didn't approve of my dad. He was the second son of a rancher. No money whatsoever. My mom got pregnant with me, and they married. Her brothers helped some, Sawyer and Gary especially. But they didn't go out of their way. Didn't disown her or anything like that, but everybody knew that my dad was second class around here. So I've always been on the outside compared to the favored Rigsby boys. Which is fine with me, by the way. I wouldn't change anything."

We'd been driving on smaller roads for a while now. Stretches of Hartley I'd never seen. We'd long since left the town proper behind.

"Are your parents still around Hartley?" I'd noted his use of the past tense, but I didn't want to presume.

"My mom died of cervical cancer. Probably would've been okay if they'd caught it earlier, but they didn't. Then my dad passed a year later. He had a stroke. People around Hartley say he died of a broken heart."

"Sorry to hear that."

Owen nodded. "I was in college at the time, and I took it really hard. I know how it sounds, but my mom and dad had been my best friends. They'd been so in love. The kind that embarrassed me as a teenager because of how they were always kissing and touching each other. The kind of love that's unattainable for regular folks." He blinked at the windshield. "After they died, I decided to join the Marines."

A new life far away. I could understand.

"Army," I said, gesturing at myself.

"I'm sorry to hear that."

I cracked a smile, and then he did too.

We talked for a few minutes about our military service. Sounded like Owen's had been more illustrious than mine. Even if he'd been a jarhead.

"Finally, I was ready to come home," he said. "The previous sheriff of Hartley was a friend of my parents, and he hired me as a deputy. Chose me as his successor, even though I was young. And here I am. Doing my best to manage a county that's got far more acres than it does people, and with only four deputies out on patrol."

"A fact I'm sure Dale is counting on."

"Dale? Do you think he's involved with this?"

I recounted the full conversation I'd overheard between Dale and Chester a couple of nights ago.

"I don't like this," Owen said. "Not at all. But it doesn't surprise me that Chester and Mitch would go around making noise and getting into trouble at the worst possible time. My uncle Dale is smart. Like a rat who waits until you're asleep to sneak out and forage. But his sons have never had that much sense. Back in high school, they were the ones drag racing down Main Street or egging the teachers' houses."

"But what about Jeremy? He didn't grow up here, did he?"

"He didn't, no. He was out in the Springs. But even so, he was still Hartley royalty whenever he came to visit. Because of his dad in the Air Force. Gary was my favorite uncle. He made my parents and me feel welcome. But Jeremy was young when his father died. Even though he stayed out in the Springs with his mom, the rest of the Rigsbys influenced him too much. And now he's back in town. I have to believe that he's got a role in this mess, too. Whatever it really is."

I propped my elbow against the passenger door. "Honestly, I don't care what they're up to. I care if it's going to hurt Jessi."

"Why? You barely know her."

I bristled at that comment more than I should've. He had a point. "Because Jessi has nothing to do with it. It's Jeremy and Chester and his brothers who've brought her into it."

Owen gave me a side-eye glare. "Well, I care what they're doing, regardless of how it impacts Jessi Novo. This is my town. *My* county. It's all well and good that you want to stick up for Jessi while you're here. But my job is bigger than that."

"You were plenty concerned about Jessi this morning."

"She's a constituent. And a friend. Are you trying to give me a hint that you've staked a claim where she's concerned? There's no need."

"Then I'll stop hinting."

"Keep in mind. I've never claimed to be her brother or any other relation to her. But if you don't do right by her, I'll be more than happy to kick your ass. And I'll follow you back to California to do it."

"Noted. Though it seems like Jessi would do the same to me on her own."

Owen smiled. "You're right. She would."

Finally, we'd skirted around Refuge Mountain and had entered the national forest. "This road just follows the edge of the forest. The turnoff for the unpaved access roads is up ahead. What exactly am I supposed to be watching for?"

"I'm not sure. Unusual activity, I guess. Anything that

strikes you as out of place. Like you said, this is your county, not mine."

Owen drove slowly past the turnoff and kept going. "There are a lot of tire tracks. Way more than I would expect considering the storm we just had, and how quiet this area is even in the summer. This is off the beaten path. We haven't had any federal forest rangers come through in ages."

"Which would make it a great place to use if you needed room to spread out and a lot of privacy."

"But for what?"

Owen parked in a secluded spot, his truck sheltered from view by a stand of trees. We got out and walked to the turnoff for the unpaved national forest roads. We weren't going to get very far without snowshoes or better equipment if we left the path, but it seemed like Owen just wanted a better look at things and to do it more discreetly than his large truck would allow.

As we got further into the national forest land, the powder from the last storm had been tamped down by vehicles coming through. Owen's first impression had been right. There were numerous tire tracks. Not just ATVs, but larger vehicles as well. Jeeps. But unlike what Jessi and I had witnessed up at the top yesterday, it was deathly quiet over here. We were at least a mile from the base of the mountain. Maybe we were too far from the action.

We went ahead and hiked along the forest access road for a while, watching the tire tracks. Then we came to a metal gate that crossed the path. It had a padlock on it. "This is new," Owen said. "There were no barriers here before. The forest service didn't put this in."

He tugged a pair of binoculars out of his uniform coat and held them up to his eyes, clamoring onto the gate to get a better view. "I see a camera further along the trail, in a tree like the other you described. Good thing we aren't going any further or they might spot us. The tire tracks keep going all the way toward the mountain. The tracks are definitely fresh."

"The Rigsbys might have been moving vehicles in and out at night. Less likely to be seen that way."

"That would be the way to do it. Assuming they're transporting something to or from Refuge Mountain."

We went back instead of pressing our luck. Once we were in the front seat of Owen's truck, he turned on the heat and drummed his fingers anxiously on the dashboard. "My first thought is illegal mining," Owen said. "Wouldn't be unusual on federal land, especially in an area like this that isn't being patrolled by law enforcement. My uncles have invested in some mining operations around Hartley over the years. But I'd have to get closer to find out for sure, and I would need backup for that since they have people tooling around on ATVs with rifles." He pointed a finger at me. "And do not say you. We might have some decent military training between us, but two guys don't make an army. If they caught us, Chester would probably shoot you on sight. Maybe even me."

I had no doubt about that. "I have another idea. My older brother is a federal agent."

His face twisted like he'd tasted something moldy. "No thanks. I don't need any feds barging in here, telling me what to do, and wrapping everything up in so much red tape that we don't get a thing done anyway. Dale and my cousins would probably sweep away all the evidence and move on to some other scheme. Meanwhile, it seems like they're treating Hartley like their own personal playground to exploit with no consequences. That's not okay with me."

"And that's not what I had in mind. I'm not a fan of bureaucracy either. Neither is my brother Jake. I mean unofficial help." I was thinking of methods Jake had used to investigate sophisticated illegal operations. Technology we might be able to apply here. *Without* bureaucracy getting in the way.

Jake's nonstop heroism annoyed me at times. It was a cry for attention. *Look at me, look how awesome I am. Look at my two cute kids and wife and golden retriever.* But when a situation warranted discretion, Jake knew what he was doing.

"All right," Owen said. "I'm listening."

CHAPTER SEVENTEEN
Jessi

I ESCORTED a family of three to a booth and grabbed some glasses and the water pitcher. "Today our special is a burger with sauteed mushrooms and bacon-onion jam." I'd been inspired by Aiden's creation yesterday. I took their drink orders and went to the kitchen, where Scarlett was finishing a last bit of prep. But we'd done what we needed to open up for lunch.

With the bridge now open, word had gotten around that bulk deliveries would be coming through later this afternoon. I sorely needed more supplies. I needed to hire some new servers, too. Chester and Mitch had scared away my previous ones, and I'd been doing more business at the diner in the last couple days than in the last month, thanks to Aiden. It was locals too, not just the stranded tourists who were heading out of town.

I hoped that whatever Aiden was doing with Owen, it was going well. And that Owen wouldn't react too badly to hearing that I'd lied to him. I owed him an apology for that. But he was practical. Owen might not like it, but I had to believe he would understand my reasoning.

Luckily, Aiden had a way of convincing people. Some of

his methods involved brute force, and I assumed he wasn't going *that* route with Owen. I did not want to see Aiden in a jail cell. But he could be convincing with his words, too. When he chose to use them. That intense look he got in his eye, the growly quality to his voice. His very presence, so commanding and soothing at the same time…

Or maybe he just had a unique effect on me. Some kind of pheromone-related magic.

A thrill ran through me as I remembered touching him last night when he was naked, the shower filling the bathroom with warm, humid air. *Yikes*. His skin had been like touching a hot stove, and I did not want to learn my lesson.

Hopefully he wasn't using any of *those* methods to convince Owen, either.

"What are you laughing at?" Scarlett asked me.

"You really don't want to know."

"Something about Aiden, I'm sure?" She grinned knowingly.

"Am I that predictable?"

She hummed. "I don't blame you for a second, hon."

Scarlett and I had been friends since I'd moved to Hartley. Like me, she hadn't grown up here. She was a native of another part of the county, a far more remote and desolate spot than Hartley. The kind of place you had to cross a steep mountain pass to get to.

She had hinted about troubles in her past. A dark backstory that belied her sweetness and smiles. Yet I hadn't gotten close enough to her for Scarlett to share the details. Really, I hadn't gotten close to *anyone* in Hartley. Not the way they deserved. I'd just been so focused on surviving. Reaching for my dream little by little and trying to make things work day by day.

But suddenly, I was imagining *more*. A more secure standing as a member of this town. Friends I could open up to and truly count on. I was so tired of holding people at arm's length.

Once things got busy enough with the lunch crowd, I had to stay in the kitchen and devote myself entirely to pushing out orders. "Hey, two more burger specials," Scarlett called out, pinning up an order slip. "Plus chicken tenders and a large basket of fries."

"Coming right up."

As we'd done our prep work, I'd told Scarlett everything about our investigation of the Rigsbys, even what had happened with Mitch on Refuge Mountain, and it had been a relief to share it. She'd been shocked, of course. But also swept up in the excitement of a mystery. And she'd never liked Mitch.

The strange thing was, the news that Jeremy was back in Hartley had actually given me hope. After two years of dread and sleepless nights, Jeremy was back, but he couldn't hurt me anymore.

I wouldn't let him.

But at the very end of the lunch rush, when the last customer had just left, the bell on the front door jangled. My guts plummeted to somewhere around my feet.

Jeremy Rigsby had just walked inside.

Scarlett had been dropping off some dirty dishes, and she nearly dropped them as she muttered a curse. "Oh, hell no," she whispered. "This is not happening. I'll get rid of him, Jessi. Don't you worry."

"No," I said under my breath. "Get him a menu. I'll have to see him sooner or later. Might as well get it over with."

She leaned over the counter and lowered her voice further. "But like this? Him coming in here as if he has a right? There's a protective order. We should call Owen and have Jeremy arrested."

But I knew Owen was busy. And having Jeremy thrown in

jail would just make things worse with the Rigsbys, not better. "Jeremy's uncle is my landlord. And your boss. We'll be civil, and we'll get through it."

This was my chance to prove how far I'd come. Jeremy didn't control me. He had no hold on my life.

I could do this.

Distantly, I heard Scarlett taking his order. She used a clipped tone, not nearly as polite as she'd been with the previous customers. I tried to ignore him, though I couldn't help glancing at him from the corner of my eye. He looked different than I remembered. Thinner and more haggard. When I'd met him, he'd had thick blond locks and a strong jaw. Now, his hair had lost its golden color, turning a sallow beige, and he had a threadbare scruff on his chin, with the scar I'd given him visible beneath. He wasn't as filled out as he'd used to be, leaner, but he sat with his shoulders back. There was something harder and compacted about him. Like granite.

I was stronger since I'd last seen him. I hadn't thought about prison doing the same to Jeremy.

My vision started to tunnel, but I fought it. I sipped a glass of water. Took deep breaths. And in a few minutes, that brief panic had passed.

I couldn't hide back here in the kitchen. I refused to cower. So after I finished his order, a BLT, I carried the plate out to the otherwise-empty dining room myself. I went straight to Jeremy's booth and set the plate on the table.

"Here you go." *Asshole*, I added in my head.

"Thank you, Jessi." He nodded at me, and I saw a touch of humility in his expression. I didn't believe it for one second. "I'd like to have a word with you. There are some things I need to say."

Scarlett took a few steps toward us, but stopped when I held up a hand. "I'd rather you didn't," I said.

"I'll say whatever I like," he insisted. "And you'll listen." His mouth puckered in a frown I knew well. I had known his civility wouldn't last. And suddenly, I was done with this little reunion. I'd been willing to serve him lunch, but I had no interest whatsoever in anything this man had to say.

I grabbed his glass of ice water and dumped it over his head. Jeremy's hands flew out, and he sputtered.

"Scarlett, get Mr. Rigsby a to-go container," I said. "His lunch is on the house. He's going to be leaving now." I started for the kitchen, but Jeremy leaped out of his seat. I heard his footsteps as he followed me.

I'd been full of bravado and indignation, but now uncertainty was sneaking through again. *Fear*.

Jeremy grabbed my wrist. Forced me to turn around. "I was going to apologize, you little—"

The door to the diner flew open, bell ringing like an alarm. Aiden stalked inside. He crossed the dining room in two strides and grabbed Jeremy by the neck. Scarlett yelped. Instantly, Jeremy fought back, trying to yank Aiden's hands away. But Aiden forced him down against the bar counter. Leaned in. Jeremy kept struggling.

"This is him?" Aiden asked me. "Jeremy?"

I rubbed my wrist where Jeremy had grabbed me. "Yes," I said breathlessly. "It's him."

Aiden's voice came out low. Steady. Dangerous. "You made a mistake coming here today, Jeremy. Not a good start to your return home."

Jeremy grabbed at the hand squeezing his neck. "You're the brother?" he choked out. "Is that who you are?"

"I'm the man who's telling you that you should've stayed out of Hartley. I don't care *what* your last name is."

I should probably put a stop to this, I thought.

Probably.

The bell jangled again. Owen ran into the diner, as if he'd

been on Aiden's heels but hadn't been able to keep up. "Let him go, Aiden. Right now. This isn't helping!"

Jeremy squinted, confused. He knew that Aiden wasn't my brother's name.

Aiden acted like he hadn't heard Owen's warnings. "I can throw you out, or you can walk out of here yourself. The second option will be a lot easier on you. Less fun for me." Jeremy kept pulling at the thick fingers squeezing his neck.

Owen tapped Aiden hard on the shoulder. "I'm *serious*. Last warning."

Aiden let go of Jeremy, shoving him toward the door. Jeremy stumbled. Scowled and opened his mouth. I still had no interest in what he might say, so I stepped forward. "Get out. You're not welcome in my diner."

Fuming, Jeremy banged the door open and went onto the street. I couldn't see him anymore because of the plywood, and I was momentarily glad for that broken window.

My heart was shaking my ribcage.

Owen and Aiden were still facing off near the bar counter. "I like you, Shelborne, but I won't hesitate to arrest you if you flaunt the law."

Aiden walked forward until his chest bumped Owen's, though his voice remained calm. "Arrest that asshole for violating his protective order."

"I might have. Before you wrapped your hands around his neck. Now it's better for us all if we let this go."

"Let it go, like everything else going wrong in Hartley?" Aiden asked.

"That's uncalled for," Owen spit out.

"Next time I'm protecting Jessi from harm, don't get in the way."

"Next time you do something stupid, don't expect me to stop you."

I pushed my way in between them, a hand on each broad

chest. "Enough. Stop arguing when Jeremy's the one to blame, not either of you."

Owen shoved his cowboy hat low over his eyes. He spun on his boot heel and left. Aiden turned and pressed his hands flat to the bar counter, looking down at it.

Scarlett blinked, watching me and Aiden.

Then she came over to me, stepping carefully. Like she didn't want to rile the large man in the room. "I'm guessing you're ready to close for the afternoon?"

"Yeah," I said with a sigh. "Thanks Scar. You've been a huge help."

"What about cleaning up?"

"Aiden and I can handle it."

"You sure you're…" She gestured vaguely at Aiden.

"I'm fine. I promise."

She grabbed her jacket and gloves, gave me a hug, and left through the back. I locked up. Set a few dishes in the sink.

Then I came back to the dining room, where Aiden hadn't moved. He was still leaning against the bar counter. But the calm he'd displayed earlier was gone. His nostrils were flaring, and his chest heaved as he breathed. His hair looked like he'd been digging his hands into it. He hadn't even taken off his outdoor coat.

Yet I felt strangely relaxed. Like some inner tension I'd been holding for a long time had finally released. I stopped right next to him, and he stepped back, putting more distance between us.

"I don't get like this," Aiden said, so quietly I felt his words more than heard them. "I'm not an angry person. I'm not someone who gets caught up in emotion and just…reacts."

"You didn't seem that angry when Jeremy was here. If that's what you mean."

"Well, I was. I was so furious I couldn't see straight.

Owen was right that I wasn't helping you. I'm still pissed, and I don't think I should be around you when I'm like this."

"Are you saying you would hurt me?" I asked, already knowing the answer. This was nothing like when Jeremy had gotten high on jealousy-fueled rage. I knew those warning signs. Aiden wasn't remotely like that. I knew it all the way down to my bones. He was respectful. Careful with me. I wouldn't have been standing here with him otherwise. I'd come too far for that.

"I would never hurt you," he said firmly. "But I'm not always polite. I have a tendency to say whatever I damn-well please without caring how it's received, and that's on a good day. Right now, polite is the furthest thing from what I feel."

"What *do* you feel?" I asked.

Every time I'd seen Aiden fight, he had been eerily calm. Cold even. But that wasn't the way he looked at me now. His gaze was an inferno of heat and desire and even uncertainty. A chaotic mix of emotions. As if he didn't know how to deal with what was happening inside him.

"Same thing I did when I saw Jeremy's hand on you. Like I needed to defend what's *mine*."

Warmth bloomed in my belly. I edged closer to him. Reached for the zipper to his coat and tugged it down. I rested my hands on his chest, which still moved up and down with his labored breathing.

"But you don't need to defend me right now. I'm safe. In fact, I was about to slap Jeremy across the face before you tried to choke him. I'd already dumped a glass of water on his head and told him to leave." I got even closer. Until my breasts were pushing into him through his long-sleeved tee. My mouth was an inch from his.

Aiden swallowed. His eyelids were heavy. "I know that. But the issue is that you're *not* mine. I have no right to you. I'm leaving in two days, Jessi. You *can't* be mine."

There was frustration still in his voice, but it had ebbed into resignation. Like maybe, just maybe, he wished that things could be different, like I did. Oh, I wished. Even though what he'd said was true.

"Then make me yours while you're here," I whispered. "Take me upstairs."

CHAPTER EIGHTEEN
Jessi

AIDEN GRABBED me by the hips and lifted me. My legs went around him, my arms at his neck. Someone could've seen us through the remaining windows or the glass door, but I didn't care. I didn't care about anything except the fire in Aiden's eyes. This soul-deep ache inside of me.

I wanted him, and it was long past time that I got to have what I wanted.

My lips found Aiden's jaw as he carried me through the kitchen and upstairs to my apartment. The door slammed open, and Aiden brought me straight to my bed, standing at the foot of it.

He crushed our mouths together. I was still in his arms, clinging to him as his lips and tongue claimed mine. Firm strokes. Nips of his teeth. His strong hands squeezed my hips, and I could feel each one of his fingers as they gripped me through my jeans.

Then he forced himself to break the kiss. It seemed to take a lot of effort. "You're gonna need to tell me *exactly* what your limits are, Jessi. Because my mind isn't sharp enough right now to puzzle it out."

I carded my fingers through his hair. Sucked his earlobe. "What about you? What do *you* want?"

"Everything you'll give me."

I wanted everything too. But I'd made that promise to myself. *Be careful. Take things slow.* Two more days wasn't much, but it was something. More than I'd ever had before with a man like him. I couldn't rush this. Someday, when Aiden was back in California and just a memory, I wanted to look back on our time together without a single regret. I didn't ever want to feel like this moment between us was a mistake.

"I want to undress you," I said.

Aiden set me on my feet. His hands moved to my face, kissing me deeply again. But instead of the bed, I nudged him toward the couch. He stripped off his coat. I tugged at Aiden's shirt, and he immediately yanked it off as he walked backward. My fingers popped open the button on his fly and fiddled for the zipper. "Jeans off too?" he asked.

"Yes. Um, leave your boxers?"

"Perfect," he said, kissing me again. "Whatever you want, Jessi. Whatever you want is perfect."

I was flying on a cloud of eager desire, but contentment too. The knowledge that whatever I gave him was enough. But if anything, that made me want *more*. Then Aiden stepped out of his jeans, and my throat went dry.

I wanted a *lot* more.

All the muscle and masculinity, I'd seen before. His ocean tattoo, the golden skin. But now, I saw the hard, thick cock tenting his boxer briefs. Liquid fire cascaded across my body. My tongue felt too large in my mouth.

Aiden's mouth curved. "Okay?"

"Shhh." I nudged his chest, and he sat heavily on the couch, bouncing on the cushion. I couldn't take my eyes off him. There was a nearly naked man in my apartment. An *aroused,* nearly naked man. Who was also honest and honorable and kind.

All for me.

Slow, I told myself. *No need to tackle the entire buffet all at once. You can go back for seconds.*

I pulled off my sweater. Undid my jeans and pushed them over my hips, wiggling my legs until they fell to the floor. His eyes traced over me, up and down. I'd left my bra and panties. My nipples pressed insistently at the cotton, showing how turned on I was. My panties were damp.

"Okay?" I asked.

He pressed his lips together and made a rumbly sound. The tent in his boxers had grown. I loved that I could see his desire for me. It made me feel powerful. But what I truly wanted was Aiden's body up against me, showing me how good he could make this for the both of us.

I wanted Aiden taking charge. His hands directing this show.

I kneeled on the couch to either side of his thighs. Sat down so that I was astride him. Aiden's lips were parted, tongue at the corner, but his eyes were smiling. "Want to come closer?"

I scooted forward until I was all the way seated in his lap, and *finally*, I made contact. His dick pressed against my core through two thin layers of fabric, but I felt his heat. The steely hardness of him. Tremors of pleasure zinged from my center to my extremities.

"Oh. *Wow*. That is...*wow*."

His lips ghosted over my cheek. "You like feeling me?"

"I...*love* it."

"You want more?"

"Yes. I want to feel you." Oh, please.

He rolled his hips. I grabbed for his shoulders. "Aiden," I whispered. Every other word had fled. He unleashed his full smile, the one that lit up his face and made him beautiful. Irresistible. He nodded. His hands found my hips, holding me against him. And he arched up, rocking our bodies into one another. His cock rubbed between my legs. Liquid arousal flooded my veins.

I fell forward, kissing him and touching his chest. His face. Anything I could get my hands on. I'd done stuff like this back when I was a teenager, but there was no comparison. Aiden's movements were the exact opposite of fumbling. He was confident and virile, moving his hips to rub my clit exactly where I needed it. His hands placed me just right. His fingers gripped with possessive pressure. His tongue just added to the symphony as he teased my mouth lightly one minute, then owned me the next. Kissed me into oblivion.

Nothing could be better than this. Even if we'd been naked, I couldn't imagine how I could feel more pleasure. It wasn't what we were doing so much as *him*, Aiden. Every detail of him and the way he brought us together.

Delicious tension built inside of me, every moment better and brighter than the last, until stars exploded behind my eyes.

"*Aiden*." I bucked into him. Rode him hard.

"Oh, fuck." Aiden held me tight to him, face buried in my neck as he shook, soaking his boxers with heat. Kept thrusting against me, on and on, as tingling aftershocks lit up my nerve endings.

I went limp. Lightheaded. Completely overwhelmed by the passion of what we'd just done without even getting fully undressed.

Aiden held me there with his arms around my waist. We both were apparently comatose.

But after a little while, he picked me up and brought me over to my bed, gently laying me down. He kissed my cheek and said, "I'll be right back." He went to the bathroom. I snuggled up to my pillow, and a couple of minutes later, he returned. He'd changed into a fresh pair of boxers.

He stretched out on the bed beside me, lying on his side so we were facing one another. His fingers traced along my forehead and down my cheek. "How are you?" he asked.

I snuggled in closer to him, fitting my head into the crook of his shoulder. "Still regaining the power of speech."

I heard the smile in the sound he made. Not quite a laugh, but pleased. Satisfied. "You're happy with what we did? It wasn't too much?"

"Just enough. For now."

"Good." Another soft kiss to my forehead. "Did the rest of lunch service go all right?"

"Uneventful, except for what you saw. I got a new update from Trace. He's made it to Missouri. He'd been trading off driving with somebody who was supposed to be on his flight, but the guy's car broke down. Another big delay." But he still expected to reach Hartley before Friday, so I wasn't too concerned about it.

"I hope I get to meet him before I leave."

I burrowed against Aiden's chest. I didn't want a reminder that tomorrow was his last full day in Hartley. And I was surprised that he actually *wanted* to meet Trace. It was…thoughtful.

"How did things go with Owen earlier?" I asked. "What did he say about Refuge Mountain? And Mitch?"

Aiden told me everything that had happened while he'd been away from the diner. How he'd confessed the truth to Owen, and how they'd seen evidence of unusual activity over in the national forest.

"I called my brother Jake. I had to use Owen's phone because mine refuses to work in Hartley except on Wi-Fi, but luckily Jake answered. He's a drug enforcement agent, and he works a lot with drones. The feds use them for surveillance. I thought we could do the same on Refuge Mountain. Find out what the Rigsbys are really up to without risking them seeing us."

I lifted my head. "That would be amazing. What did Jake say?"

"He knows a retired DEA agent who's now a drone operator here on the Western Slope. He's making it happen."

"When?"

"Tonight. The drone operator is driving down, and Owen will meet us. We have to do it when it's dark." He rested his head on his hand. "The operator just wants a late dinner in exchange. I'm sure a dessert or two would also be welcome. I can pack everything up and take it with me tonight. Maybe some for Owen too, since he's not too happy with me."

I shrugged. "Or *I* can bring the desserts. Because I'm coming with you."

He frowned. "I don't think that's a good idea. It could still be dangerous."

"I want to see this drone in action. But more than that? I want to help nail the Rigsbys to the wall. You are *not* leaving me behind."

Aiden's thumb caressed my cheekbone. "All right. Not my place to tell you no. Even though I want to."

I smirked. "I wasn't going to *accept* no. But it's your place to try. I'm yours while you're in Hartley." I shivered as I said it. Aiden rolled us both so I was flat on my back, and he was gazing down at me.

"That's true. I did just claim you as mine. I'd like to do it again." He leaned in for a slow, tender kiss that had me lost in him for a while. Then he pulled back. "But I haven't eaten all day, and I'm starving. I'm going to make us some food. You can lie here and look pretty, or you can come with me. I'm good either way."

"I'll come. I like watching you cook."

"I like that, too." Aiden sat up and held out his hand. "I'll teach you my best tricks if you teach me yours."

"You're on."

For one more day, I thought with a pang of longing. I was already in deep with this man. Deeper than I should've been.

And when he left on Friday, I knew it was going to hurt. Probably worse than I even imagined.

CHAPTER NINETEEN
Aiden

JESSI ZIPPED UP HER COAT, tugging a knit cap over her hair. I handed her a to-go mug of coffee. "You ready for this?" I asked.

She sipped her coffee, and her eyes flashed with anticipation. "I can't wait. I'm so tired of people named Rigsby bringing trouble to me. This time, I plan to bring some trouble to them."

"Couldn't have put it better myself." I nodded as I grabbed my own infusion of caffeine. That fire in her eyes made her even sexier. And Jessi was a *very* sexy woman.

It was after midnight. I went through the back door first, glancing around to make sure that all was quiet. The only sign of life was Owen's truck idling in the alley. Jessi and I piled into it, shutting the doors carefully so the noise didn't echo over Main Street. I had taken the backseat, leaving Jessi shotgun.

"Bring any of that coffee for me?" Owen asked. He was using an unmarked vehicle tonight, rather than one emblazoned with the sheriff's department logo. He'd also dressed in plainclothes rather than his uniform, though he'd worn his usual cowboy hat.

"You bet." I dug into our picnic cooler, where I'd carefully stowed an insulated travel cup. I handed it over. "Does this buy me forgiveness for trying to choke out your cousin earlier?"

Owen snorted. "Already forgotten."

Jessi and I had spent the afternoon cooking. I'd made roasted chicken with a bearnaise sauce, and Jessi whipped up three different flavors of tarts, feeding me tastes of each filling. That had led to an animated make-out session, during which my sauce nearly separated on the stovetop.

I'd enjoyed having Jessi by my side. Fighting over burners, teasing me, arguing about the proper techniques and seasoning levels. We'd been able to ignore the rest of the world for a while. As if we could suspend time, create something magical together that would last and last beyond any expiration date.

But cooking wasn't like that. Life wasn't either.

Now, we were scheduled to rendezvous with my brother's friend in about twenty minutes for the surveillance op. We'd packed a roasted-chicken sandwich, chips, and as many tarts as Jessi could fit into the cooler for the retired DEA agent we were about to meet.

"I heard from the drone operator," Owen said. "She sent me the coordinates of where she wants to set up. Apparently, she was all over Google Earth. I made a few suggestions for where we would be safely out of sight, but she's very particular."

"She?" Jessi asked.

"Yep," I said. "Just wait till you meet her. Jake said she's a character."

Owen took the road into the national forest. We'd long since left the streetlights behind, and the moon was just a sliver in the sky. The truck's headlights lit up a pair of glowing yellow eyes. Maybe a bobcat. The animal darted away, back into the darkness of the trees.

Though Jessi was in the front seat, she'd stuck her hand around the side so she could grasp mine. We'd been touching almost constantly since our sexy session on her couch and through our joint cooking efforts in the afternoon. I wasn't a possessive guy by nature. That feeling had snuck up on me with Jessi.

The thought of having only one more full day with her was making something go haywire in my brain.

Maybe it was the sexual tension. Usually when I hooked up with someone, my mind dove straight for home base. I wasn't the type to play up the romance and the anticipation. But Jessi had set the rules, and I had given her everything she'd wanted right up to the edge. I'd forgotten how hot it could be to have some limitations in place.

Not that I viewed her as a challenge, like we were playing some kind of game. It wasn't that. It was more like Jessi had created a multi-course menu, and I'd been enjoying each dish, even if some people might've called them appetizers or starter courses. I was hungry for more, but I could make a meal out of what she'd given me so far. And if that was all I'd get, I wasn't complaining.

A single kiss from Jessi, a single touch, sent my world spinning. It was going to be hard to leave.

We pulled off onto a side-spur of the road. An Expedition was already here, the massive SUV mostly hidden by a grove of aspens.

"That's her," Owen said. "License plate matches what she gave us. Right on time."

As Owen put the truck into park, a woman jumped out of the SUV, waving. Jessi and I got out and went to meet her. Owen was just a few seconds behind us. Ice crunched beneath our boots.

"I'm Shonda," the woman said. She grasped my hand and pumped it. "Which one of you is Aiden?"

"That would be me."

"Your brother said that the next time you leave the state and go off the grid, you might want to inform your family."

Shonda was in her sixties, barely tall enough to reach Jessi's shoulder, much less mine or Owen's. She had ebony skin, and her gray hair was cropped close to her head. A pair of wire-rimmed glasses perched on the edge of her nose. Her eyes were as sharp as the santoku knife I'd left back in Jessi's kitchen.

"You can tell Jake he's not the boss of me."

Jessi snorted a laugh, while Owen shook his head.

Shonda winked and tapped her nose. "But our boy Jake thinks he's the boss of everybody, doesn't he?"

I cracked a smile.

Shonda slapped her leg. "Jake bet me I couldn't get a grin out of you. Now he owes me twenty bucks and a case of Coors. I beat the over-under."

"That was impressive," Jessi said. "It took me a couple of hours to get Aiden to smile the first time. Please, teach me your ways. I can pay. I brought you some spiced chocolate tarts, but there's more where that came from."

"I'm always open to negotiation."

Shonda ate half of the sandwich we'd brought her, followed by a sample of Jessi's chocolate tart. Between bites, she showed us what she'd packed into the back of her Expedition. "Ever since I retired from the DEA, I've run my drones as a contractor for government agencies as well as private companies." She took the lids off of two packing crates. "These are my babies. The little one, I use for law enforcement. It's a precision instrument of aerial surveillance. I can follow all those legal limitations the police are required to observe. But when you *really* want to have some fun…"

She pointed at the second crate. The drone inside was sleek black plastic, with arms protruding from its body like a spider. "This handsome fella is Big Jim. Named after my late husband. Big Jim is a lot to handle, but he sure can get the job done and leave you satisfied." She added a wink. "If you know what I mean."

"I think I do." Jessi glanced at me.

I lifted a brow while Owen pretended to study his fingernails.

"Now, I've loaded up Big Jim with all the fancy stuff. Infrared camera, the longest-range zoom, the latest in weapons recognition. With this guy, we'll be able to read the logos on their underwear. If that's the kind of thing you're into. But your drone choice depends on how strictly you need to follow search-and-seizure rules."

Jessi jumped in before Owen or me. "We're definitely going with Big Jim. I want their underwear tags and anything else they might be hiding. I want *all* their dirty secrets." Her eyes were narrowed like a villain in an old TV show. If I'd been a Rigsby, I would've been worried.

Owen and I looked at each other.

"I'm not usually the one urging caution, but can we get away with that?" I asked.

He shrugged. "This is public land. The Rigsbys have no right to privacy here. We don't need to worry about warrants or anything like that. Let's give Jessi what she wants."

Shonda rubbed her hands together with glee. "Then let's get this rodeo riding, cowboys."

She set up the drone and got it ready to fly. We stood behind her and watched, Jessi's hand tucked into mine. Shonda put on an elaborate headset, which held the controls.

She'd also set up a tablet for us to watch the camera feeds from the drone.

"I've got the coordinates that you sent me, Sheriff Douglas, along with the topography. We can take a look around. If they're operating underground, like you think, I've got a few tricks to see what we might be dealing with. But first I need to get up there and see what's what."

The drone took off, propellers whirring.

Jessi let go of my hand and edged in right beside Shonda, watching the tablet. The two women chatted quietly as Shonda explained all the readouts. Owen and I stood behind, watching over their shoulders. "They don't even need us here," I said to him. "Jessi is more than happy to run this investigation herself."

"If she wasn't busy with the diner, maybe I would hire her. She's got more backbone than most of my deputies. Except maybe Marsh."

On the tablet screen, we watched the drone's night vision camera feed. There were ATVs parked halfway up the mountainside. One drove along the snowbound trail, out on nighttime patrol. The driver had a rifle slung over his back. Just like Mitch.

Shonda moved the camera over the mountain in a grid. Searching for more clues. We spotted power generators with wires snaking around through the trees, and a large collection of metal canisters. When the camera zoomed in, it revealed the words *Caution: Flammable* along with warning symbols. Then another stack of canisters labeled *Liquid Nitrogen*. But the most interesting thing? The large, round patches of snow-free ground all over that side of the mountain. As if someone had carefully cleared the snow away. Or it had melted.

"Let's try the infrared," Shonda said.

She switched the camera feed, and multiple blobs of red

appeared. Heat. A lot of it. Which explained the melted snow. There was heat bleeding off into the air as well. Like it was being vented from an unseen source.

"Is that coming from underground?" Jessi asked.

Shonda nodded. "Must be. Fits with what you observed before."

Owen shuffled forward for a better view. "Illegal mining?"

"But that wouldn't generate this kind of heat." Shonda pointed at the screen. "This looks more like industrial processing. They're making something."

"Meth?" I suggested. That could've explained the quake that shook the mountain. Meth labs exploded all the time.

"This would be an odd setup for a meth lab." Shonda tapped at the screen. "And nobody uses liquid nitrogen for making meth, either."

"Another kind of drug?" Jessi asked. "It has to be something that makes money. The Rigsbys wouldn't bother with it otherwise."

"I have some suspicions, but I can't answer with any certainty from what we've got here. You'll need more on-site surveillance. Probably on the ground."

Shonda continued surveying the mountainside and the forest access roads.

Then, movement.

Three jeeps had just pulled onto the unpaved road. Passengers jumped out to open the padlocked gate, and they continued onward. Through the drone's camera, we watched as the jeeps climbed partway up the mountain, and more people suddenly appeared, loading up the jeeps with boxes. The drone's weapons detector pinged again and again.

Lots of firepower was present on that mountainside. Heat and energy and a sense of singular purpose. This was a serious operation. It had seemed that way from the moment

I'd spotted that camera on Refuge Mountain. The drone's surveillance only confirmed it.

Finally, the jeeps started heading back down the access paths and toward the main road.

"Can Big Jim follow them?" Jessi asked. "See where they go?"

"His battery is getting low. I need to bring him in. Afraid you'll have to switch to old-fashioned methods."

Jessi moved first, already heading to Owen's truck. "Then let's go!" she shouted at us. "Before they can get too far ahead and we lose them."

"Thoughts?" I asked Owen.

The sheriff shrugged. "I feel like I'm just a chauffeur at this point. But we're staying back. Observing only. Once we see where they're heading, we're turning around. Got that?"

"*I've* got it."

But I suspected Jessi might have other ideas.

CHAPTER TWENTY
Aiden

WE SAID a quick goodbye to Shonda while she set up Big Jim's landing. Owen pulled out onto the road.

We kept the headlights off. It was dim, but our eyes had adjusted, and all the snow helped amplify the little light coming from the sky.

The brake lights of the jeeps winked in the distance. They were headed back toward Hartley's commercial district. Owen was careful to hang back, but Jessi had her hands on the dashboard, as if she could urge the truck forward. The jeeps turned before they reached Main Street, taking a road that branched northwest.

"They're not going to the freeway," I said. "What's out this way?"

"Not much," Owen replied.

"Except for..." Jessi trailed off as we saw the jeeps pull off the road in front of some kind of warehouse. The sign was too far away for me to read in the dark. "The Hart-Made Candy Co.'s shipping center," she finished. "Where they package up candy for big orders and ship it out."

"Sawyer sells that much candy?" I asked. "I didn't think the brown sugar brittle was *that* good."

Owen frowned at me. The man insulted his own family members constantly, but apparently, shit-talking Hartley's local delicacy was a step too far.

Jessi turned in her seat. "The sweet shop in town is just the local flagship. Scarlett said they fulfill orders for stores all over the western United States."

I smoothed a hand over my beard. "But what would those jeeps be doing at a candy shipping warehouse? I doubt they're cooking up caramels on Refuge Mountain."

"Clearly not," Owen said. "But if they need to ship out what they're processing, this place could be their cover."

Jessi bit her lip, her expression devious. It was a good look on her. "Then we have to get closer. Whatever it was they were offloading from Refuge Mountain, they're probably using Hart-Made's shipping trucks to take it out of Hartley. Now is our chance to find out what it is before it leaves the warehouse."

The sheriff held up his hand like he was saying, *Hold on*. "I can't just go barging in there. I've got no probable cause. Certainly nothing to excuse the lack of a warrant. And I guarantee the judge would kick me in the ass if I got her out of bed on so little evidence. No way would she sign a warrant based on this."

Jessi and Owen continued to argue. Meanwhile, I debated within myself. Finally, I spoke up from the back. "But I'm not a cop."

"I'm not either," Jessi said with a sweet smile.

Owen pushed his frown so hard that furrows appeared around his mouth. "No. Absolutely not. They had guns on the mountain, Aiden. They have guns in those jeeps."

"I'm aware of that. You want to loan me a weapon?" I'd left the rifle I took from Mitch back at the diner.

"Hell *no*, I will not. Are you crazy?"

"We'll be careful," Jessi said. "If this is our shot to nail them, I refuse to miss it."

Owen looked at me like he expected me to transform into the voice of reason. But that had never been my forte. I had no intention of putting Jessi in danger, but as she had said, we didn't want to waste this opportunity. Tomorrow was my last day in Hartley. I had no idea what she might try to do once I was gone. If she wanted to investigate this, shouldn't I help her with it now, while I was still around to protect her?

"Even if you do find something, I can't use it as evidence," Owen said.

I shrugged. "We'll worry about that later. Perhaps you'll receive an anonymous tip, complete with photos. After we get out of this car, you won't know for sure where we go or what we do. I'm sure it would be better if you *didn't* know."

Jessi and I jumped out of Owen's truck, just barely latching the doors to avoid making noise. He backed his truck up carefully, then turned around and drove away.

"Wait," I said to Jessi before she could start toward the warehouse. "I'm doing this with you, but I won't put you at unnecessary risk. This is recon only. We see what we can see, and when it's time to get out of there, you need to follow my lead. If I tell you to run and leave me behind, then you'd better go."

She pulled me into a quick kiss. Warmth zipped through me despite the cold temps. "Whatever you say."

I suspected she was placating me. I'd just have to stay close to make sure this didn't go sideways.

Jessi and I crept along the tree line so we'd be in shadow. By the time we reached the warehouse, the drivers of the jeeps had finished unloading. They were standing around casually, smoking cigarettes and chatting with men who I assumed had emerged from inside the warehouse.

Owen had loaned me his binoculars. I lifted them to my

eyes. "There's Jeremy," I said, recognizing him from the diner that afternoon.

Jessi took the binoculars, then touched my arm and pointed. "And Chester's with him."

The Rigsby cousins stood just outside the open loading bay. Light spilled out from within, illuminating their faces. The bandage on the bridge of Chester's nose shone like a beacon, and I could still make out the bruises spreading beneath his eyes. That made me smile. Jeremy's sandy hair was neatly combed, and he wore a scarf around his neck, as if he was hiding some bruises of his own.

That made me smile even wider.

"So Jeremy's in on it," I said. "The Rigsbys wasted no time bringing him in. Maybe he already knew about it before he arrived today. Could this have been going on two years ago before he went to prison?"

"I don't think so."

We watched them for a few minutes, trading the binos. Boxes were stacked inside the loading bay, but there was no clue to their contents.

After a while, the drivers got back into the jeeps and left, but the Rigsby cousins stayed, trading sips from a metal flask.

"The real question is whether Sawyer knows about this," Jessi said. "Are they using his warehouse under his nose? Or is he part of their operation?"

"No way to know from here."

"Exactly why we should get closer."

"*Jessi*. That's not what we—"

Before I could finish my sentence, Jessi had dashed away in a crouch, heading for the warehouse.

Shit. I had known this would probably happen, yet I'd ignored those warnings in my head. Jessi had me wrapped around her manicured fingers, didn't she?

I raced after her. When I reached her, I pulled her back against me, wrapping my arms around her so she couldn't step out into the open. "That's close enough."

We were only a few yards away from a side entrance into the warehouse's office. Jeremy and Chester continued to chat. We no longer needed the binoculars to see them, and their voices traveled clearly.

I caught the name *Mitch*.

"You still haven't gotten his body out?" Jeremy asked.

"Can't exactly call mountain rescue, and we've been too busy trying to get things back on track." Chester took a swig from the flask. Anger and grief were clear on his face. "Everything was chaotic yesterday after the cave-in. We saw some things on the camera, some intruders, and that's who Mitch must have gone to investigate. We found a whole mess of snow, and when I looked down, there he was. His neck..." Chester took a bigger gulp of liquor. "So *no*. I haven't figured out how the hell to get my brother out of that ravine yet."

Chester shuffled his feet, and Jeremy looked away.

"Who were the intruders?" Jeremy asked.

"It wasn't clear on the camera. Two people, big one and a smaller one in pink. They were bundled up. Everybody has gear like that. I have plenty of suspicions though."

Jeremy scowled. "Yeah, so do I. A big guy, like that douchebag Jessi's been hanging around with? That son of a bitch attacked me at the diner today."

Chester pointed at his bandaged nose. "I already told you what he did to me. He's her brother."

"He's not. Guy's name is Aiden, but her brother's name is Trace. Figures. Jessi's a liar. We all know that."

Chester nodded, but I thought I spotted an eye roll. Like he was more skeptical of his cousin's claims than he ever admitted aloud. "Why did you go to the diner at all?"

"Because I was trying to apologize like Uncle Dale told

me to do," Jeremy spit out. "Make nice after you and Mitch screwed up. But I thought at worst, her real brother would be there, not some asshole that slut is banging in our town. If you had gotten rid of her before now, none of this would be happening."

Jessi tensed in my arms. Her body radiated with fury, as if she felt the urge to run straight at them. To throw every caution aside and give them a piece of her mind. I had to get her out of here.

But when I took a slow step backward, a twig snapped.

Both Chester and Jeremy turned in our direction. "Who's out there?" Chester yelled.

"Keep absolutely still," I whispered. Jessi trembled against me.

We were concealed by the inky shadows between the trees. The light shining onto Chester and Jeremy from the loading bay effectively blinded them to what else was out here. But if we moved by an inch, that might be enough to make our shapes stand out against the rest of the darkness.

Chester started walking across the gravel, but Jeremy put an arm out to stop him. "Where's your weapon? With the shit that's been going on, we need to be armed. At all times." Chester picked up a rifle from the loading bay and handed it to Jeremy. Then Chester took a handgun from beneath his winter coat. While they were distracted for those few seconds, I backed Jessi slowly away.

"We're going to have to run," I whispered.

"What if they catch us?"

Then that would be bad, I thought. I figured Jessi's question had been rhetorical.

Chester and Jeremy started toward us. Jeremy nodded at his cousin, a signal for them to separate. They were going to try to come at us from two directions. A decent strategy. I planned to do the same thing.

"When I tell you," I murmured, "get out of here as fast as you can. Run and get to safety. Then call Owen."

"I can't leave you."

"You had damn well better."

She was breathing hard. She didn't acknowledge what I'd said.

Jeremy had taken the lead. He was aiming the rifle with it braced against his shoulder. Staring hard into the darkness right at us. His eyes narrowed. Any sudden movements on our part, and he or Chester would see us.

Every second brought them closer.

I breathed out. "Get ready," I whispered.

"*Aiden*," she hissed.

I prepared to shove her in the opposite direction, then run into the open and create a diversion. Basically what I'd done on Refuge Mountain. Except I intended to run faster this time instead of lying in wait. I wasn't a sprinter. I was more bulk than speed. But I also doubted that Chester or Jeremy were expert marksmen. I'd seen Mitch's skills on the mountain, and he'd lacked accuracy. His brother and cousin were probably no better.

I counted down in my head. My muscles tensed.

Suddenly, a gunshot rang out on the other side of the warehouse. Jessi gasped, while Chester and Jeremy both dropped to the gravel, though I didn't think either of them had been hit. A moment later, the Rigsbys were scrambling up and running for the cover of the loading bay, shouting curses.

I didn't wait to see who was shooting or what else they would do. I grabbed Jessi and got us both out of there.

CHAPTER TWENTY-ONE
Jessi

AIDEN and I ran through the woods, dodging between the trees. Everything was in varying shades of gray. Our breaths puffed in white clouds. My boots kept tripping over brush and fallen logs covered by snow.

Aiden didn't let go of my hand.

We'd been running parallel to the road, heading roughly back toward town. We stopped running at one point and glanced around to get our bearings. It didn't seem like Chester or Jeremy were following us. I hadn't heard any more gunshots, either. I had no idea what *that* had been about. But it had drawn the Rigsbys' attention away from us, so it was fine by me.

The possibility of catching the Rigsbys in their schemes had been so tantalizing. And we *had* gotten more info. Everything Chester and Jeremy had said was bouncing around in my brain, but I couldn't slow down and examine it yet. We had to get back to safety first.

"That way," I said, pointing. "We need to stick closer to the road or we'll get lost. These woods go for miles."

"That's what I figured."

We approached the road, hanging back to listen and

watch for vehicles. We weren't that far yet from the warehouse. But I didn't hear a single thing. Nothing man-made, anyway. And it was winter, so there weren't many animals or insects filling in the silence.

"We'll have to walk along the road," Aiden said. "We're too slow in the woods. Our tracks will be less clear on the road, too."

We left the cover of the trees and started jogging along the road in the direction of town. I kept glancing behind, and so did Aiden, in case Chester or Jeremy set out in search of us and we somehow didn't hear the engine.

But then Aiden stopped. He shuffled to the side, pulling me so that I was behind him. "There's a truck up ahead. Lights off."

I peered past his shoulder. There was a pickup parked in the road, its tailgate facing us. Just waiting there. I couldn't make out the license plate. Aiden started drawing me to the trees. But then I saw the outline of a cowboy hat on the driver's head through the back window.

"That's Owen!"

I took the lead this time, pulling Aiden by his hand. The truck's engine roared to life as we got close. I heard the locks thump, and Aiden and I both jumped in. Owen didn't waste a second, driving off the moment our doors were closed, though he kept his lights off.

"What are you doing out here?" I asked. "I thought you were going back to the station. You didn't want to be involved in what we were up to."

Owen steered the truck down the middle of the icy road, gunning the accelerator. "I didn't want to be involved. But I couldn't abandon you. You could've moved faster, though. I certainly did."

Aiden was in the backseat, his arm stretched forward to touch my shoulder. "We were trying to stay out of sight."

"Maybe you should've tried *that* earlier, too. Chester and Jeremy nearly caught you."

I made the connection. "It was you who fired the gun. Drew their attention away from us. Thank you."

"And if anyone asks, I will deny it. Please tell me you got something useful from that boondoggle."

We shared what we had overheard and seen.

"I would guess they've used the warehouse before," Aiden said. "They were comfortable there and in no hurry to leave."

"I was hoping to get close enough to find out what's inside those boxes," I added. "But that…didn't work out." I didn't have to look back at Aiden to know he was lifting an eyebrow at me. Of course he was. "Any possibility that what we've got is enough for a search warrant on the warehouse?"

Owen shook his head. "Not even close."

I tipped my head against the seat in frustration. We'd learned so much. It was obvious the Rigsbys were doing something illegal. What evidence would be enough?

Owen took the turn onto the far end of Main Street, switching on his headlights. The road was still clear. Nobody was out, and the only business with any activity was the Hartley Saloon. We were nearing last call.

We overshot the diner. Owen turned at the next corner.

"What now?" I asked.

He stopped the truck halfway down the next block. "We all get some sleep. We can regroup tomorrow. As far as I'm concerned, this investigation is still off the books. I need to sit down and puzzle this out."

"Today's my last day in Hartley," Aiden reminded him.

My heart seized. *Today*. It was way past midnight. Time was slipping past too quickly.

Owen turned to glare at Aiden in the backseat. "Which has no bearing on my plans whatsoever. Something like this can't be rushed. If you don't want to be involved further, that's fine. But don't go thinking you've got a crucial role to play in this, Shelborne. Hartley is my job. As far as I'm concerned, you're a passing ship in the night. And judging by the interactions you've had with the Rigsbys so far, it's a hell of a lot better for you if we keep it that way. It would be best if you left town sooner rather than later."

We got out of the truck and Owen took off. Aiden and I walked back toward the diner. He reached for me again, but his hand felt stiff on my shoulder.

His last day.

Maybe he was going to take Owen's advice and decide to leave now. Get it over with before any new trouble started.

Please don't, I thought. It didn't matter to me that he would leave in a little over twenty-four hours. I wanted every moment with this man, even if that would make it hurt more when he finally left.

Then his touch softened, his gloved hand sliding down along my arm, and I exhaled. I hadn't even realized I'd been holding my breath. Aiden's hand glided to the small of my back, massaging lightly at my waist. He kissed the top of my head. "Glad you're safe."

"Me too." I raised my chin to kiss him. Our lips met softly, right there on the street in the dark. As if neither of us could wait long enough to get inside. We had to kiss right here, right now.

"Let's go to bed," Aiden said, and my heart beat faster at all the meanings of that phrase. We started toward the diner again.

We saw the silhouette at the same time and stopped in our tracks. A man was leaning against the back wall of the diner.

"Stay relaxed," Aiden said under his breath. "We were

just out for a walk. Be cautious, but don't act like we have something to hide."

All of which I could've figured out for myself. But I appreciated Aiden's calm. His presence made me a lot braver than I would've been alone. He'd had that effect on me since the first night we met.

"Okay," I whispered. Aiden's hand remained at my waist.

The two of us started forward again. The figure by the door shifted his weight. He had a large backpack with him, resting by his feet. But I couldn't see his face.

"Can I help you?" I called out.

"I thought *I* was here to help." He stepped forward. Broad shoulders, though his clothes hung loosely on him. His hair had grown past his chin, hanging into his face over a scraggly beard.

But I knew my brother's voice.

"*Trace?*" I let go of Aiden's hand and dashed over to him. "I didn't even recognize you." I pulled him down into a hug. He was just as tall as always, an inch or two taller than Aiden. But he was nowhere near as bulky as the last time I'd seen him. He'd lost weight.

"What are you doing out here in the dark?" I asked.

Trace pushed the hair out of his face. "The guy I carpooled with dropped me off. It took us long enough to get out here. I didn't want to bother with finding a hotel." His eyes moved past me to Aiden. "Is this your…?"

"He's a friend."

Aiden came forward, holding out his hand. "Aiden Shelborne. I've heard a lot about you. Glad to finally meet Jessi's brother."

"Heard a lot about me, huh?" Trace squinted at me.

I shrugged. In truth, *I* didn't know that much about my brother. He looked like hell right now, and I had no idea why. "It's freezing. Let's go inside."

Trace picked up his pack, which was overstuffed and looked like it was set up for a backpacking expedition into the wilderness. He, Aiden, and I went into the diner. Trace was walking slowly, though I couldn't tell if he was limping or just exhausted.

I turned on the light in the kitchen, and Trace dropped his pack on the ground just inside the back door. But his eyes were moving everywhere. Taking in the kitchen and the dining room.

Aiden leaned against the prep table, crossing his arms.

Trace pointed at the plywood-covered window. "I'm guessing that's courtesy of your ex's family?"

"Yes. That's why we were out tonight. Gathering evidence to use against them. We think the Rigsbys have some illegal enterprise going, but we're not sure yet what it is."

"We were out on a recon mission," Aiden added.

"How'd it go?"

I glanced at Aiden. "We made it back," he said.

"Okay, then." Trace exhaled and shook his head. "Sorry it took me a while to get here. And I'm sorry about…everything you've been through."

There was an awkward pause. I didn't know what to say, and I was so worn out by everything that had happened today. Jeremy appearing, the drone surveillance, the warehouse.

And today was Aiden's *last day*. It was awful of me, but I found myself wishing that Trace had taken a day longer.

"It hasn't been that bad," I said. "Aiden's been helping me. I can tell you the rest when the sun's up. We should all get some sleep."

My brother looked at each of us in turn. I had no idea what was going on in his head. But finally, he nodded. "I'm not tired, so I might as well stay up and keep watch. Just in case your nighttime excursion prompts a response. The two of you can go ahead." Then he started opening the kitchen cabinets and glancing through them. Making himself at home.

Aiden had a curious look. I just shook my head. When it came to my brother, I had very few answers.

"You didn't tell me your brother is ex-military," Aiden said.

We were taking turns brushing our teeth and getting ready for bed. Aiden had stripped down to his boxers. I was wearing an oversized Rolling Stones T-shirt.

I pulled the toothbrush from my mouth. "I didn't?" I rinsed my mouth and the toothbrush, stepping out of the way so Aiden could do the same. "He was in the Army, like you, but it was a while back. He's been doing some kind of work overseas for the government. Dispersing foreign aid money?" I waved my hand. "Something like that."

Trace had always been an enigma to me. Not just because we hadn't spent that much time together growing up. But when I'd called him a couple of weeks ago, desperate for any kind of assistance, he'd said he was in Virginia and agreed to come out. In some ways, I didn't know much more about Trace than I did about Aiden.

"Yeah, you mentioned that part. But now, the impression I'm getting is totally different." The look in Aiden's eyes was sardonic. "Jessi, your brother is a spy."

"A *spy*? What are you talking about?"

"*Aid work overseas?* It's no wonder there were no official records on him when Owen looked. Trace does something clandestine. Probably CIA. Or he did."

I was shocked, but it did seem plausible. Trace was secretive enough for that. "And I just thought he didn't like social media."

"How long is he staying here in Hartley with you?"

"I don't know. He wasn't that specific. Before, I didn't know who else to turn to. So I tried him. I was surprised when he actually said yes. I didn't know *you* were going to turn up."

Aiden wrapped his arms around me. "Well, if I'm right about him, then he's the kind of operative you want on your side. Even if you two aren't close, I'm sure you'll be in good hands."

The rest went unsaid. *When I'm gone.*

I wasn't ready for that. Everything was happening too fast. We'd just barely made headway in the investigation against the Rigsbys. We'd just barely started exploring each other, too. And Aiden was about to leave.

We finished up in the bathroom. Then he took my hands and walked me slowly into the bedroom. "Are you tired?"

"Yes. But I don't want to sleep yet. I want to kiss you."

"Easy enough to arrange."

Aiden kept pulling on my hands until I'd walked into his arms. We shared slow, tender kisses, standing together at the foot of my bed. After all the stress of today, he relaxed me. Jeremy's cruel words in the diner and the fraught moments by the warehouse when he and Chester had almost caught us —it all melted away in Aiden's arms. My safe place.

I slid my hands along his bare chest to his stomach. The room was dark, and I regretted that. I wanted to see him. I had to memorize this man so I could call him up in my imagination later. Hopefully in my most vivid dreams.

He leaned forward to kiss me again, but I was busy yawning. I clapped a hand over my mouth. "Sorry."

He chuckled. "You need rest."

"I want to do more than that." But my body wasn't cooperating. Plus, Trace was downstairs, and that would be awkward. The walls were thin.

"We have one more night after this," Aiden murmured in my ear. "We can make it count."

"You promise?"

"I'm not a big fan of making promises. But for you? I'll make it happen." He gently gripped my chin between his thumb and forefinger. "I promise."

We crawled beneath the covers. Aiden held out his arm, and I snuggled into him, finding that perfect spot between his chest and shoulder to lay my head. He stroked my hair the way I liked. Just a couple of days since he'd first touched me, and he'd unlocked me like a key. We'd clicked together as if we'd always been meant to fit.

But on Friday, he's walking away.

"I'm glad you were there with me tonight," I said into the quiet. "Or last night? It's turning into a blur."

"No kidding."

"Not gonna lie, I was nervous outside the warehouse. But I wasn't scared. I kind of loved it. I was out doing something, bringing the fight to Jeremy and the Rigsbys. You have no idea what that meant to me."

"Now who's the adrenaline junkie?"

"I don't know about that." I rested my hand on his firm stomach. "I like a safety net."

"I'm glad I could be that for you. Even though I hated you being in danger."

I was braver with Aiden beside me. And yet, I also felt more *myself*. Vibrant and alive. Like I could do all the things I'd imagined. Things I'd always wanted. Maybe even going to Paris and taking real French pastry classes. Building the restaurant and hotel on Refuge Mountain…

I could make those dreams into something real.

Aiden would be gone soon, and that was going to hurt. Hurt so damn much. But I was determined to hold on to this bold, fearless feeling all the same. To be enough on my own, after Aiden and even Trace had gone. I wanted the life that I'd dreamed of. And I finally had a fire within me that said, *Yes, Jessi, you can go out and get it.* I could do more than just survive day to day. I could have *everything*.

Everything except Aiden.

I burrowed into him, getting as close as I could. Aiden held me. His leg nudged in between mine, and I felt his erection, hot and thick against my thigh beneath the cover of his boxers. I *wanted*. More than I ever had in my life.

But I was also falling asleep.

Aiden kept humming contented sighs, as if this closeness was exactly what he needed right now. Just cuddling, listening to each other's heartbeats and breaths. Soft kisses and touches as we both drifted toward sleep.

One more night wasn't enough. I doubted another month of Aiden would be enough.

I was in way over my head with this man, but I didn't want to come up for air.

CHAPTER TWENTY-TWO
Jessi

THURSDAY. Aiden's last full day.

We slept later than I'd intended. When I went downstairs close to noon, I found Trace asleep, sitting in the booth in the far corner with his back to the wall.

I grabbed the coffeepot and filled it under the tap. I'd decided not to open the diner. With my brother's arrival and all the developments since yesterday, there was too much going on. Or maybe that was an excuse. I wanted every minute with Aiden that I could get. I wanted him to be *mine*, as long as that lasted. He was still asleep, and I planned to get the coffee going. He'd made breakfast for me yesterday, so now it was my turn.

While he was in Hartley, Aiden was my man. Was it wrong to want to spoil him the way he'd spoiled me?

"Morning." Trace wandered into the kitchen. He looked just as tired as he had last night. Dark circles under his eyes, a weariness to his face that had been carved into the lines around his eyes and on his forehead. He looked far older than thirty-two.

"You all right?" I asked.

"Coffee?" he grunted instead of answering my question. So I let it go.

"Coming right up. I'm making breakfast too." I started getting out the ingredients for chocolate chip raspberry muffins, one of my personal favorites.

"So what's the deal with your friend who spent the night?"

I shrugged. My brother hadn't answered *my* question. It wasn't his business what I was doing with Aiden. But on the other hand, I didn't mind talking about him. "He got stuck in town when the bridge was damaged in the storm. He stepped in to help me when he didn't have to. I like him."

"That's obvious. How did he help?"

I recounted what had happened the last few days. How Aiden had stopped Chester from hurting me, set up the charity dinner that helped me earn my rent money. How he'd defended me when the brick sailed through my window, and again on Refuge Mountain. "He was pretending to be you," I said. "I told people he was my brother."

Trace looked amused. "And why would you do that?"

"Somehow it seemed like a good idea at the time." I measured out flour and sugar into a mixing bowl. Trace leaned his hip against the counter.

"Then you haven't changed that much. I remember when you posted signs around our neighborhood looking for a best friend. Then Dad went around, taking them all down before some creep responded."

"Aiden's not a *creep*."

"Didn't say he was."

But I knew the point Trace was making. That I was a dreamer full of ridiculous, impulsive hopes. I was well aware of my tendencies.

I was stirring the milk and eggs into the batter way too hard. I forced myself to stop before too much gluten could form. "Aiden chose to spend his vacation time here," I said. "Changed his plans for me. But tomorrow's the end. He has to go. I've always known Aiden would be leaving, and he never misled me about that."

"Leaving isn't a bad idea. It sounds like you're in the middle of a mess here in Hartley, one that doesn't even have much to do with you. Why don't we pack up your stuff, and we can get out of here for a while. Or forever. Either way, if trouble's coming, the best thing for you to do is get out of its way."

I set the bowl of batter aside with a thunk. "That's not why I asked you here. Hartley is my home. If I wanted to leave, I could've done that myself."

"Honestly? I wasn't even sure why you called. I was surprised."

"As surprised as I was that you said yes." I glared at him. He looked impassively back. What was it with these stoic ex-military men? At least Aiden had started showing more to me.

I stirred in the chocolate chips and the raspberries. Then dished out batter into muffin cups. "Trace, you've never told me much about your life. I know about the Army, and things that Dad said about your work for the government overseas. Then suddenly you're back in Virginia. You've lost weight. You look like you haven't slept in months."

"That's true. I haven't."

I laughed without any humor. This was the one decent family relationship I had after our father had died, and my brother wouldn't even share the basics about his life with me. "I know I'm not the only one with problems. The world doesn't revolve around me. Whatever is going on with you, you can tell me. I'm your sister, and I want to be here for you. We could help each other."

He didn't respond. Instead he looked down at the tile floor, his long hair falling across his face.

"Even now, you don't want to tell me. Do you not trust me? Or you think I'm too weak to hear it? Aiden thinks you're a spy. I'm just a girl working in a diner in a small town. A girl who fell for the oldest story in the book—a no-good boyfriend—and wound up in a bad situation. But I'm not weak, Trace. I'm so much stronger for all I've been through, and Aiden sees that. After knowing me for three days, he *sees me*. What does it say that my own brother can't?"

"It says I'm a coward," he said softly. "If anybody can't handle their own shit, it's me."

I waited for him to explain. Finally, he raised his head.

"When you called me asking me to come here, it was like a damn sign. The possibility of something new that would wipe my slate clean. When I packed up my stuff a few days ago, I did it knowing I wasn't going back to Virginia or DC. The work I was doing before, my old life, is *over*. Whether I stay in Hartley or some other place, it doesn't change the fact that I'm *here*. And you're all I've got."

That soliloquy had barely scratched the surface of what was inside my brother's mind. But what else could I do?

I pulled him into a hug.

Trace and I had never been very affectionate. Even now, he held himself stiffly in my arms. But I realized how much I needed this. No matter what else happened from now on, Trace planned to stay with me.

He had his own issues. So did I. But together, maybe we could start figuring it out.

The muffins were just starting to brown when Aiden ventured downstairs. His hair was messy from sleep, but he was dressed. A fresh T-shirt clung to his muscles, and his legs filled out a different pair of jeans.

"Smells good down here. What're we having?"

"My special muffins. Trying to develop your latent sweet tooth." I poured him a cup of coffee. Aiden took it from my hands and gave me a kiss. It started out as a peck, but our lips kept coming back together. Then our tongues got in on the act. I brought my hand to Aiden's left butt cheek and squeezed it through the denim.

Over in the dining room, Trace cleared his throat.

I stepped back from Aiden, biting my lip. *One more day*. I really needed to get him back upstairs.

Aiden turned toward the prep table and subtly adjusted himself. "That was a nice way to start the day."

"Could be even nicer. You made some big promises about later."

He turned around and winked. "I did. I'm game whenever you are."

I almost pushed him up the stairs right then. But the muffins weren't done yet, and I had no doubt Trace would let them burn.

Somebody knocked at the diner's front door.

I flinched. *Now what?*

But it was only Scarlett. I went over to let her into the diner. "Jessi, just heard that—" She dashed in, already mid-sentence, but clammed up as soon as she saw Trace. My brother slowly looked over at her, his hair falling across his face. He didn't smile.

"Scarlett, this is the real Trace Novo," I said. "Trace, Scarlett."

Their eyes locked. And held.

I pulled Scarlett by the wrist into the kitchen with me so I could watch the muffins. "You said you heard something. What was it?"

"Um." Scarlett blinked, as if getting her brain back on track. "Let's see. Right. I heard Chester and Jeremy are going around saying Mitch is missing."

My stomach twisted. "Did they say Mitch is dead?"

"Nope. Which I thought was interesting, after you told me everything that happened on Refuge Mountain the other day. I came straight here."

Aiden leaned a hand against the prep table. He'd been listening. "They're trying to get distance, so to speak, between the mountain and Mitch's death. Just like we expected. They can claim Mitch was last seen somewhere else."

"That's good, right?" I asked. "They're not accusing you or me because they haven't got anything on us. And they can't admit where it all happened without drawing attention to their secret operation."

But after the warehouse last night? I wasn't sure what it all meant. Aiden nodded, though his pensive expression said he was still thinking.

After breakfast, we were all sitting in the dining room when Aiden's phone chimed with a text message. He pulled it out. "That's Jake. My brother. I've been texting him and Owen about setting up a video call so we can share what we found last night."

Trace was sitting over at the bar. He leaned his elbows on the counter. "This was the drone recon you did last night in the national forest?"

Aiden raised an eyebrow at me, and I explained. "I filled in Trace already about what's been going on. The Rigsbys' underground operation and the jeep deliveries to the warehouse." I hadn't updated Scarlett yet, but I knew she would catch on fast.

"Good," Aiden said. "Welcome to the team." He nodded at Scarlett as well. "Both of you."

Trace grunted, while Scarlett curtsied.

Aiden's thumbs moved over his screen. He got the video call set up, with the two of us sitting together on one side of a booth, Scarlett on the other. Trace hadn't budged from his stool, so I guessed he was going to be a passive participant. Given our conversation a few minutes ago, I had no idea what Trace might have in mind. I'd gone from being almost entirely on my own to having two unpredictable ex-military men defending me. Plus a close girlfriend who could whip up a mean batch of brown sugar brittle. It was a lot to keep track of, really. I'd never had so many allies. It felt amazing and overwhelming and so incredibly good.

Beneath the table, I laced my fingers with Aiden's. His gaze met mine, somehow a mixture of both heat and gentleness. Like a promise of how he'd kiss me and touch me later.

I was *so* ready for it.

Owen joined the call first. It looked like he was in his office at the sheriff's department. He had his uniform back on after going plainclothes last night. "Morning, Jessi," he said. "Was the rest of your night uneventful?"

I glanced at my brother. "Mostly." I introduced Owen to the real Trace Novo. Trace barely said two words, and Owen just looked wary. "And Scarlett's here, too," I added. She waved a hello. I wanted all of them in on this. I trusted every single one of these people, and I had nothing to hide from any of them.

Then Jake jumped onto the video call. "So you're Jessi," Jake said with a bright, lopsided smile. "I wish I could say Aiden had told me all about you, but then he wouldn't be my brother, would he?"

"Is it true that Aiden didn't tell you he was in Colorado

until he called you asking about the surveillance drone?" I said.

Jake laughed. "I'm supposed to see him over the weekend in Steamboat, but I'd had no idea he was already in the mountains. Or that he was having such an adventure. Good thing we didn't need anyone to man a barbecue. That's usually Aiden's domain."

"My roommates know better than to go near my grill," Aiden grumbled.

"Trust me, nobody would dare." Jake crossed his arms over his broad chest, where the word ARMY was emblazoned on his T-shirt. "Tell me what you found last night with Shonda. She offered to send me a copy of what her drone recorded, but I didn't want to create more of an electronic trail. This is my private number, not my DEA phone, since you asked to keep this unofficial. Trying to hold up my end of that."

Aiden, Owen and I recounted what we'd learned and seen. The picture on Aiden's phone switched back and forth between whoever was talking. Trace got up from his stool and wandered closer, seeming to be absorbed in the conversation though he still hadn't said more than a brief hello.

I kept studying Aiden. The strong line of his jaw and his calloused fingers stroking my wrist beneath the table. The warmth and solidity of his body as we sat there together.

At first glance, Jake looked nothing like Aiden. The older Shelborne brother had dark-blond hair and vivid green eyes. His demeanor was easygoing and friendly, yet also commanding. He had a Captain America vibe. He didn't have anywhere near the intensity that Aiden did, though they both looked like they could bench press two of me.

But as we spoke, I saw hints of Aiden in his brother. Small twitches of Jake's mouth and the way he narrowed his eyes, his gaze clever and even devious. I had the feeling that both

Shelborne men showed the world only what they wished, and most of their true selves they kept underneath.

Jake tapped his chin. "Given the heat you saw on the infrared camera, it does suggest they're processing drugs of some kind."

"They were using something flammable in metal canisters," Owen said. "And also liquid nitrogen."

Scarlett's eyes widened as she listened.

"I'm curious," Jake said. "Jessi and Aiden, did you smell anything when you were up on Refuge Mountain? If they're processing some kind of marijuana product, the scent would be a giveaway."

I shook my head and looked over at Aiden.

"I didn't smell anything," he said. "But it was cold. And I'm pretty sure the cave-in happened downhill from where we were standing once we reached that side of the mountain. The heat would rise, along with the scent, but the cold air also could've kept it down."

"But marijuana is legal in Colorado," I pointed out. "Why would they go to so much trouble?"

"It's legal when all the proper procedures and regulations are followed," Jake explained. "But there's a very active black market. I'm sure Sheriff Douglas knows all about that."

Owen nodded. "Sure. There's particularly a black market for shipping out of state."

"Illegal marijuana farms are a big problem on federal land," Jake went on. "I've never seen this kind of processing going on in a national forest, but I can't say I'm surprised either. If they're processing marijuana into a concentrate, they'd be using flammable solvents and liquid nitrogen both. The end product could be an oil, or a grainy form that resembles wet sand. There are also thin sheets known as shatter. Those concentrated forms are far easier to transport."

I leaned my elbows on the tabletop. "They're probably

using Hart-Made's shipping warehouse to pack up and distribute whatever they're making."

Scarlett's mouth dropped open. "That is despicable. Somebody's got to tell Sawyer. Unless…do you think he knows?"

I shrugged. I had no idea what to tell her. Sawyer was her boss, and she was a Hart-Made employee. It had to be awful to hear the company was being used for something illegal. I had no clue how much Sawyer knew about Dale's schemes.

"This is exactly the kind of thing the DEA investigates," Jake said, "since it could involve the drug trade over state lines. But you're going to need a lot more evidence to get wire taps or search warrants. Evidence of what it is that they're processing and proof that the warehouse is shipping out something illegally."

Owen chimed in. "But I don't have the manpower to devote to that level of surveillance. I guess I could try to follow one of the shipping trucks as it leaves the warehouse, wait for them to make a traffic violation, but—" Suddenly, Owen looked away, listening to the voice of someone who'd just stepped into his office. His hand partially covered his phone.

"I'll be right there," Owen said.

Then we heard a door close, and Owen's face reappeared in the camera frame. "I need to go. Something else just came up."

Aiden and I exchanged a glance.

Owen signed off. Not long after, Jake said goodbye too. We all promised to talk again soon and share any updates.

"I hate waiting," I muttered. "It makes me nervous."

Aiden's lips quirked, and he planted a kiss on my temple. "I've noticed."

What were the Rigsbys up to? And what the heck was Owen doing? We still hadn't heard from him.

My brother paced across the dining room. Scarlett followed him with her eyes. And every time I looked at the clock, another ten minutes had passed. The sun was already moving downward in the sky. The day was bleeding away. But with Trace and Scarlett hanging around, it was impossible for me and Aiden to sneak away for some privacy.

My patience was so thin it was transparent.

After a while, Aiden went into the kitchen to whip up something for dinner. Trace was in a corner of the diner, repacking his ratty backpack. And Scarlett and I had taken up a booth on the far opposite side, whispering to one another.

"You're jittery," she said. "Because of the Rigsbys? Or because Aiden's leaving in the morning?"

"Both. But mostly the second."

She smiled mischievously. "I could take Trace off your hands."

"What exactly are you planning?" I'd noticed the way she kept staring at him. I didn't want things to get awkward between the two of them. Hartley was tiny, and Scarlett was quickly becoming my closest friend.

"I'll give him the nickel tour of Main Street. We'll grab a few drinks at the bar. And I've got a spare room at my place. Trace can stay with me tonight, which would give you and Aiden some private time. If I do it right, I might just get Trace to crack a smile. You'd think somebody had burned his caramel. He's so serious."

"That's what I thought about Aiden at first."

"Why would Aiden need to smile more? That man's always got a twinkle in his eye around you."

"Not true."

She nudged my arm. "It is. You make him light up.

Anyway, let me introduce Trace to Hartley. I'll bring him back tomorrow."

"Can I trust you with him?"

"I promise his innocence will remain intact. Though if things get really wild, we might break out some boxes of Hart-Made brittle."

"Hey, now. Don't go *too* crazy."

"I should be saying that to you." Scarlett winked. "Enjoy your last night with Aiden."

"Believe me, I intend to."

CHAPTER TWENTY-THREE
Aiden

WHILE JESSI and Scarlett were conspiring about something in the corner booth, Trace came into the kitchen. He didn't say anything at first. Just watched me as I seasoned a pork shoulder. I'd found the chunk of meat in Jessi's freezer and had let it defrost in the fridge over the last day. I was going to make some rolls to go with it too, for pulled-pork sandwiches. One of my go-tos.

"Need something?" I asked Trace.

I wondered if I was going to get a brotherly lecture from him. Something along the lines of, *Careful with my sister*. It seemed odd that he would jump into the overprotective brother role at this point, considering the fact that I was the one who'd been protecting Jessi the past few days.

I'd come into the kitchen to keep my hands busy. Whenever I was near Jessi, I had this irresistible habit of touching her. It had been getting worse by the hour. We had plenty of other issues to concentrate on, such as the Rigsbys and their machinations. Yet Jessi was always at the forefront of my thoughts, both conscious and unconscious.

It was dismaying, actually. I wasn't the kind of guy to get so attached, especially after knowing a woman for less than a week. But Jessi made me feel a lot of things I wasn't used to. We'd already established that fact.

Finally, Trace spoke. "I hear you're leaving tomorrow."

"That's correct."

"Jessi likes you."

I met his penetrating gaze with my own. I had nothing to hide. Jessi was an adult. If she wanted to share her bed with me, that wasn't her brother's concern. "I like her too. A lot."

"Thanks for being here for her. When I couldn't."

I nodded and went back to dry-rubbing the pork. I hadn't expected him to say that, but I appreciated hearing it. In fact, I was relieved.

It shouldn't have mattered what her brother thought of me. I would've sworn up and down that I didn't care. But as soon as he'd said thank you, I felt how much it did matter to me. Because this guy was Jessi's family. Somebody she loved, no matter how complicated their relationship may have been in the past.

Everything about Jessi mattered to me. So much that I didn't know how to deal with it. These possessive, protective feelings she evoked in me.

The past few days that I'd spent in Hartley, it had felt like the rest of my life was on hold. But that would change tomorrow. I had my job with the catering company. My family. A bride and groom counting on me to feed their wedding guests. If I didn't show up in Steamboat Springs by Friday afternoon, a lot of people would be scrambling, and they didn't deserve that.

But if it had been anything less, I wasn't sure what choice I'd make. Whether I might ask Jessi if she wanted me to stay. Just a few days more. Maybe a week. At least until this mess with Jeremy and the Rigsbys was sorted out.

I didn't like leaving things unfinished.

I also didn't consider it my job to run around the world

playing police. That was Jake's style, not mine. Even though I *certainly* didn't like the idea of Dale, Chester and the other Rigsby assholes getting away with illegal shit, because nobody should get away with that.

But for Jessi, I wanted to make everything right. To stop the bad guys and make her smile.

I wanted to be her damn *hero*.

I hardly recognized myself.

"I know there's a lot I missed over the last few years," Trace said. "I haven't been the best brother."

"Jessi kept things to herself."

"But I suspect that's my fault more than hers."

We were speaking quietly, but I glanced into the dining room to make sure that Jessi wasn't in earshot. She was still talking with Scarlett over in the corner.

"Has she told you about the hospital?" I asked. "And what it's been like for her in Hartley since then?"

"She told me a little bit when she called me a couple weeks ago, asking me to come out to Colorado. I looked up the court filings and police reports. I know what they said."

I didn't ask how he managed to get access to all of that. Some of it was public record. Not all. But I figured that in Trace's usual line of work, access to documents wasn't a difficult thing. I also didn't bother to ask because there was no way he'd talk about it. Trace's past wasn't my concern. But his future? That was.

I washed my hands, then turned to face him. "Are you going to be here for her the next time she needs you?"

He brushed long strands of hair out of his face. "Whatever Jessi needs from me, I'm in. I'm not planning to go back. I need a new start myself, and I'm not… I'm not in the best place in my own head. But I'm going to take care of my sister. I guarantee that."

I should've been glad to hear it. I *was* glad. Jessi needed her brother.

But when I pictured Jessi here in Hartley, and me back in California moving on with my life, I didn't like the image. Not one bit. Even though I didn't see any possible alternative.

Once the pork was roasting low and slow in the oven, and the rolls were rising, I went upstairs for a shower. I hadn't cleaned up since the day before. The warm water sluiced over my head and shoulders, down my stomach. I scrubbed shampoo through my hair, my thumbs rubbing circles at my temples.

I'd hoped the tumult of thoughts in my brain would calm under the water. But I'd been wrong.

I was calculating the exact amount of time I needed to get to Steamboat. Just under five hours. If I skipped making any stops, I could stay a little longer in Hartley tomorrow. Get going before lunch…and maybe I could call ahead and give my sous chef more instructions to get things started without me…

This was not like me. At all.

Yet how many times had I told myself that same thing since I'd met Jessi? When would I get it through my skull that she *wasn't* like anyone else? Not to me. The way I felt about her was different. Overwhelming.

I wasn't a hesitant person. I didn't get paralyzed by uncertainty. I decided, and I *acted*. Then I dealt with the consequences without regrets. I didn't do regrets. But the things that were happening in my head? In my chest? I didn't know what the heck this was.

I was still underneath the shower spray, mind spinning in

circles, when the hinge on the bathroom door creaked quietly. I knew it was Jessi. My whole body tensed, but it was the good kind of tension. The kind that pumped my veins with anticipation and energy.

"Hey," I said.

"Hi," Jessi responded. She shut the bathroom door. I could barely make out a silhouette moving on the other side of the fabric shower curtain. "Scarlett left, and she took Trace with her. She's going to show him around Hartley."

"Is she going to show him around her bedroom, too?"

Jessi laughed nervously. "I told her not to. Trace is kind of a mess right now."

"Yeah. So he said." I finished rinsing every last bubble of shampoo from my head. Wisps of steam filled the air. "But he sounded sure about staying here with you. That's good news."

"It is," Jessi said softly. She paused. "But I'm glad he's not here at the moment. Can I join you?"

I made a low sound in my chest. More an animal response than a word. But the answer was very much *yes*.

I grasped the edge of the curtain and pushed it open. The rings slid across the metal bar. I leaned one hand against the tiled wall, all of my body on display. Water continued to fall along my side, a fine mist raining on the rest of the bathroom.

Jessi's eyes moved down to my feet. Back up again. Biting her lip slightly. I let her look. Arousal slid down my spine, and Jessi made a sharp inhale when she saw how my cock was reacting to her. Filling and thickening.

"Get over here," I said.

She crossed the small space, stripping off clothes as she went and leaving them on the bathroom floor. Sweater, jeans. Bra and panties. My eyes devoured the soft curves of her body. Her nipples were blush pink against her smooth, creamy skin.

"I knew you'd be beautiful," I said, admiring her. "But damn."

She stepped into the shower, and I closed the shower curtain. We were in a tiny, steamy, warm space. Just us.

I hooked my arm around her waist and spun us around so she could reach the water. Her head tipped back under the spray, her throat elongating. Drops of water streamed from her neck, down between her breasts, all the way down. They got lost between her legs.

This was too much.

I pulled Jessi against me and kissed her. She didn't hold back. Her arms circled my neck. Her mouth opened to me. Our tongues danced and slid.

Then Jessi's hand reached between us. She circled the base of my shaft and stroked me, root to tip. I had to quickly brace a hand on the tile because my whole body swayed.

I cupped my hand around the back of her head. My tongue surged into her mouth as I switched our positions again and pushed her up against the rear shower wall. I dipped my head to suck gently at her neck. My beard rubbed over her wet skin. Between breaths and kisses, soft murmurs left my lips. "You're stunning, baby," I whispered. "Breathtaking."

"We have hours. Nobody will be looking for us. Everything's locked up downstairs."

"Good." I would need hours for everything I wanted to do to her. "But we can still go slow. I have no expectations."

"I do." Her eyes dragged over me. "I don't want to miss the chance to have you."

"Then take your pleasure from me. Let me give that to you."

Her eyelids were heavy. "Yes, *please*."

I felt a smile ghost my mouth. "I'll need a little more guidance than that. We can do whatever you want, Jessi. How should I touch you?"

Her throat worked as she swallowed. "Put your mouth on me."

"Where?"

"*Everywhere*. All over me."

That, I would happily do.

I quickly finished washing us both. Rinsed. I switched off the water and dried Jessi with a fluffy towel, then myself. But we were still dripping water as I carried her bridal-style into the bedroom. I set her on the edge of the mattress. Then I knelt on the floor at the foot of her bed.

Jessi's eyes were round as she propped onto her elbows and looked down at me. I heard her breaths skipping in her chest. Her heart was beating so hard I could see it, blood jumping in her veins.

I draped her legs over my shoulders and pressed an intimate kiss to her center. She gasped. My tongue flicked over her pussy, and her hands grabbed at the blanket beneath her.

Jessi's sounds were so expressive. Conveying how much she enjoyed this. How much she wanted it.

I reached up to take her hand. Our fingers tangled together, and she held on tight as I licked and sucked at her clit. My tongue slid inside her. Every moan of pleasure zinged through my veins and made me want to give her more. My free hand gripped her thigh and pushed it to open her wider for me. The uninhibited noises she made were giving me life.

"I can't last much longer," she said.

"Then give in. I want to taste how good I'm making you feel."

She cried out my name when she came. Nothing had ever sounded so good. And the taste of her... I was developing a sweet tooth after all.

Jessi sat up. Leaned forward and kissed me, trying to pull me up by my shoulders, though obviously I was way too heavy for her to handle me like that. I got up and crawled onto the mattress. But as soon as I was beside her, she bent over my lap and took my cock into her mouth. Her damp hair fell forward as she sucked. She gripped my thighs, nails digging in.

I groaned involuntarily. The sensation… It was epic.

She seemed to be tasting me and enjoying what she found. I'd been in this very position plenty of times before, but it had never been so beautiful. So perfect. The warm, tight suction of her mouth made pleasure dance up and down my spine. But it wasn't what I wanted most. I liked giving pleasure even more than receiving.

"Jessi." I gently pulled her up and guided her lips to mine in a soft kiss. "Don't worry about me. Let me make you feel good."

I lifted her into my arms and moved her further up the bed so she was lying down. I lavished her body with kisses, trying to press at least one to every inch of her arms and legs. Breasts and nipples and belly. All the way down to her feet, where my thumbs massaged her arches. Jessi smiled and hummed and turned over onto her stomach. I pressed my lips to each knob of her spine. My hands cupped her smooth, round cheeks.

She was absolutely gorgeous.

Jessi lifted her head and looked at me over her shoulder. Her eyes said she wanted more, and I waited. "Tell me what you want, sweetness," I said. "I'll give it to you."

But instead of replying aloud, she wriggled toward the edge of the mattress until she could reach her nightstand. She dug around inside. Pulled out a condom.

"That's what you want?" I asked. "My cock?"

"Yes. I want *you*."

I crawled forward and took the condom from her hand. Set it close by on the mattress. But Jessi rolled onto her back, looking up at me. Her fingers grasped again for the condom, trying to push it into my hand. She was that eager.

I got myself ready. Then I went back to kissing her for a while. Smoothing my hands all over her and searching out the places that made her purr.

"Now. *Please*. Don't make me wait any longer."

"All right. I'll give you what you want."

We both gasped and moaned when I pushed inside her. She was tight, and I didn't want to hurt her, so I kept my thrusts small and shallow as she made room for me. Finally she'd adjusted, and I slid all the way in. Her body gripped me.

Jessi stared up at me in wonder, eyelids heavy. "Aiden," she breathed. "I feel you."

I kissed her forehead. "I know you do, baby. I feel you too. And it's so good." I pulled almost out of her and thrust back in. Jessi moaned and held my face, pulling me down so our foreheads touched.

I lifted my upper body onto one hand so I could look down at all of her. Watching as we moved together. My legs were bent and splayed, knees pushing against the mattress for leverage. My free hand caressed her face, her neck. Jessi gripped my biceps.

This incredible woman. Mine for this moment. For tonight. That was what my mind said. But all my heart heard was, *Mine*.

Something strange happened to time. This moment was endless, *everything*, yet I also knew it would be over too soon. I had to make it last. Jessi tilted her head back, moaning, and I kissed the long curve of her neck. She held my face there against her, legs wrapped around my waist, and she came apart. Shuddered and cried out.

"That's it, sweetness," I groaned. "Love hearing your pretty voice drunk on pleasure."

A few more thrusts inside her snug, slick body, and I was done for.

I already knew I would be thinking of this night, picturing the incredible heat of this moment, for the rest of my days.

CHAPTER TWENTY-FOUR
Jessi

I HAD my head pillowed on Aiden's chest, my hand resting on his stomach. His fingers smoothed through my still-damp hair. The sun was dipping toward the western horizon outside, and I was hungry. A delicious smell wafted upstairs from the kitchen. Yet it was so hard to move. I was pretty sure I could exist right here until the sun swallowed up the earth, and I'd be content.

Except I also wanted to do what I just did with Aiden. Again…and again.

Having him inside me had been everything I'd needed. More, even. Because no man had ever made love to me like that. Attentive to my every reaction, finding out what I liked best and playing my body like it was an instrument, and he was some kind of virtuoso. Or like a chef who'd made himself completely at home in the kitchen, elevating an everyday thing into an art form.

How was I so gone for him after four days? How could it only be that much? It felt like a different lifetime since Aiden had walked into my diner out of the snow.

And changed *everything*. Changed me.

When tomorrow morning came, it would be over. That

thought made my throat tighten up. I was determined to stay in this moment and enjoy it, as if I could stop time altogether by concentrating hard enough. By ignoring everything else but the two of us, right here and now, in this bed.

My finger traced a line down his shoulder over his tattoo. "Why did you pick this design? The ocean waves. Is it because you grew up by the coast?"

He blinked lazily at me, a hint of a smile curving his lips. "Probably. The ocean represents freedom to me. It's dangerous and untamed because that's its nature. It exists according to its own rules."

I lay my cheek above his heart. "Freedom is important to you," I remarked.

"Sure. It's not *everything*, but it's close. Don't you think? Choosing the life you want for yourself. Not letting obstacles stand in your way."

I nodded. I did want that kind of freedom. But I liked the idea of belonging to a place, too. Belonging to the right person. Compromising so we could have a life *together*. I'd been dreaming of that since I was a kid. Listening to my mother's romantic songs. I was a lot more cynical now. Yet I still wanted that kind of connection with someone.

That wasn't what Aiden wanted, though. He wasn't that kind of man, and he'd told me days ago after we'd first kissed. *I don't think I have that in me.*

My brain had listened. But my heart hadn't. Yet I didn't blame myself for it, either. Aiden was the cowboy who showed up in town, made the woman fall for him, and rode off into the sunset. It was inevitable. That was who he was. If anything about him had been different, would I have felt this way?

I ignored the hunger gnawing at my belly until Aiden insisted on getting up. He tugged on his jeans, went downstairs, and returned with a plate holding two pulled-pork sandwiches. I couldn't begin to describe how delicious they were. Tangy sauce and smokiness and buttery, yeasty rolls. We sat on my bed, blankets over us as we shared the one plate. Aiden got sauce in his beard, and I wiped it away, laughing.

The next time I glanced at the window, it was fully dark outside. We still had the whole night ahead of us.

Aiden set the empty plate on my nightstand. He stripped off his jeans so we were both naked again. We kissed and talked and cuddled. He told me about the wedding on Saturday, the prep he needed to start tomorrow. The long list of ingredients his sous chef was supposed to hand-select from local Colorado markets, everything grown in greenhouses or hydroponically since it was winter. The bride and groom were family friends, and that was why they'd hired the Shelbornes' catering company to come all the way out for this destination wedding. It sounded like a fancier party than I'd ever attended in my life. Jake would be there, along with his wife, Harper. And Aiden's parents and other siblings too.

That was the life Aiden had chosen. Glamorous events and expensive ingredients. California sunshine, blue waves, and his big family close enough to drive him crazy on any given day.

But me? I loved Hartley. The mountains and the history and small-town feel. I had fought to make this my home.

I belonged here. Aiden didn't. It wasn't anyone's fault. I was never supposed to get attached to him. To have *feelings* for this man who had insisted from the beginning that he wouldn't stay.

So why did this hurt so damn much?

We hadn't turned a light on. It was dark in my room when Aiden pushed aside our blankets. Laid me on the bed and kissed me as our bodies met, skin to skin. I was glad for the darkness because it meant he couldn't see the tears in my eyes.

He kissed me and touched me until I was breathless. Gasping and clinging to him. Begging again for more. I had more condoms in my nightstand, and I got another one out. They were actually Scarlett's. Before leaving earlier, she'd dashed home quickly and brought them back for me, passing them surreptitiously so Trace wouldn't notice.

Aiden lay on his back and lifted me up. He set me in his lap this time so I was straddling him. His cock slid into me, pushing so deep. His hips bucked up to meet me, concentrating all the pleasure of my existence into the joining of our bodies and the rhythm and heat we built as we moved. He whispered things to me, how beautiful I was and how incredible it felt to be inside me, but I couldn't utter a single word in response. Just bitten-off gasps and shouts.

I never wanted this to end.

Then he flipped us over. I was on my back. Completely in his control. Aiden held my arms above my head, his weight almost too much as he pressed me into the mattress. Drove his thick shaft into me. But it was perfect. His eyes moved over me reverently, as if he wanted to memorize this. Every detail. He captured my mouth with his and swallowed each one of my moans like he was greedy for every part of me.

I wanted him to hold me down. Stay here with me. Be every dream I never thought could come true.

Even though I knew he couldn't.

———

When Scarlett had given me a whole strip of condoms earlier, I'd never thought I could use them all in one night. But we'd already gone through three of them. That last time, he'd been behind me while we both lay on our sides, his cock pumping inside me with such delicious friction I could hardly believe it was real. I'd actually screamed, it had felt so insanely good.

So much for going slow.

I wasn't anywhere near tired. Aiden showed no signs of wearing out either. The world beyond my window was pitch black. I could almost pretend morning would never come.

Almost.

"You'll probably need to rest at some point," I said. We were tangled up together under just a sheet. Aiden was so warm that I didn't need the blankets. "I don't want you to be sleepy on your drive."

He propped up on his elbow. "How about we make a pot of coffee, then? It's…" He checked the clock on my nightstand. "Only one o'clock. We have hours more. I want to spend them all with you." He pressed a gentle kiss to my cheek. "I don't want to waste a minute."

My heart swelled painfully in my chest. "Works for me. I'll go start the coffee. In a bit."

But I ended up stretched out on top of him, getting lost in another make-out session, until I finally pulled away with extreme reluctance. "Okay, coffee. I can do this." I scooted off the bed and went to my dresser, pulling out an oversized sweatshirt.

"And one of your chocolate tarts," Aiden said. "I've been craving it."

I pulled the sweatshirt over my head and grinned at him over my shoulder. "We can share a tart now, and I'll pack up the rest for you to take with you."

"I would like that." His gaze went soft. "I'm going to clean up a little, and I'll be down to help with the coffee."

"Hurry up or I'll miss you," I teased.

"I *already* miss you."

My cheeks flushed. I was shocked he'd said that, and Aiden looked sheepish, like he'd surprised himself. I turned away and headed for the door before tears could burn in my eyes.

Every perfect moment with Aiden was such beautiful agony. But I wouldn't trade a single one.

In the kitchen, I found everything cleaned up and put away. A container of pulled pork and extra yeasted rolls waited in the fridge. Aiden had made way too much, as if he'd wanted me to have plenty of leftovers for the next several days.

I started the coffee, then got out the chocolate tarts, glancing around with a sigh. The diner already felt lonely. The signs of Aiden that I spotted—his knives, the leftovers in the fridge, the sound of water running upstairs—told me the exact shapes his absence would take later on. Later on *today*. I drummed my fingers as the coffeemaker burbled.

But suddenly, a different sort of noise made the hairs on my skin rise.

It was something outside, in the alleyway behind the diner. Heavy boot steps. Cold lanced down my spine. Nobody should've been out there at this time of night.

I gasped, anxiety flooding me, when a fist pounded on the diner's rear door.

"*Open up,*" a harsh voice said. "*Police.*"

CHAPTER TWENTY-FIVE
Jessi

AIDEN'S FOOTSTEPS made the stairs creak as he sprinted down. He wore his jeans and nothing else. The button of his fly was still undone. "What was that?"

"Police. But it wasn't Owen's voice." And he wouldn't show up in the middle of the night this way, banging on my door. "I don't know what's going on."

Another sharp knock. *"Open up. Hartley Sheriff's Department."* It sounded like they might break down the door. *"Last warning."*

Aiden cursed. I unlocked the door and cracked it open. Freezing air rolled into the warmth of the diner. One of Owen's deputies stood there, a guy I'd never liked much. "Ms. Novo? Could you step outside, please?"

"What's this about?" Aiden asked, standing close behind me. His heat warmed my back.

"We got an anonymous tip, and we'd like to ask you about it. Both of you. Please step outside."

"I don't see why I should do anything," I said. "Where's Sheriff Douglas?"

The deputy didn't answer my question. "We got an

anonymous tip," he repeated, "and we want to search your dumpster."

"*Excuse* me?"

"Do you consent?"

Aiden wrapped his arm around me, nudging me aside so he could push in front. "Absolutely not. She's not agreeing to anything."

I followed Aiden out, ignoring the icy cold that immediately seeped into my bare feet and legs. There was a small crowd of people emerging from the bar a few doors down, drawn by the presence of the sheriff's department cruiser. Its lights were flashing. I hadn't seen because my building didn't have windows on the alley side.

Then my blood turned to ice.

Jeremy and Chester Rigsby were out there among the crowd. No way was that a coincidence. Something *very bad* was about to happen. I felt it in my gut.

"If you won't consent," the deputy said, "I'm proceeding anyway. Your trash is abandoned property." Raising his flashlight, he flipped the latch and opened the lid of the dumpster. Then he reared back. "Oh, *shit*."

Aiden grabbed my arm. "Jessi, go back inside the diner."

"*No*." I pushed forward to see, dread flooding me. I spotted a snow boot in the dumpster. It was attached to a leg. I saw a blue-tinged face.

Mitch Rigsby's body was in my dumpster.

I screamed.

Aiden pulled me back. Another deputy had just arrived, Deputy Marsh, and she was trying to hold back the onlookers. Shock spread like a wave through the gathering crowd. Gasps and cries. Murmurs as the news passed from one person to the next. Chester and Jeremy weren't surprised. They looked *smug*.

They'd done this.

"Jessi Novo, you're under arrest," the first deputy barked at me.

"Whoa, hold on." Aiden stepped in front of me. "You have no probable cause. Jessi had nothing to do with any of this."

"This is her property! And we have witnesses who've reported that Mitch was last seen with Jessi, and that she had motive to kill him. She's coming to the station."

Witnesses? Chester's friends, I had no doubt. They were setting me up.

"She's staying here," Aiden said calmly. And then he did the dumbest thing possible. The very thing I'd already realized he was about to do. "I'm the one who killed Mitch. Arrest me. Leave Jessi out of it."

"*Aiden,*" I cried.

A sheriff's department truck roared into the alley. Owen's official vehicle. He jumped out. "What the hell is going on?" He had his coat over pajamas, his hat askew. He glanced at the deputy, then at me.

"It's Mitch Rigsby," his deputy said. "The tip said there was a body in Jessi's dumpster, that she'd killed him, and it was right."

"And who do you think called in that tip! Who are the witnesses!" I cried. Aiden was talking too, but everything was turning to chaos. People jostling to get closer. Staring and pointing. Shouts.

Owen stalked over to the dumpster and swore.

"I confessed," Aiden said. "You can take me into custody, but Jessi has nothing to do with it."

Owen stared hard at him. Then nodded. The deputy slapped cuffs onto Aiden's wrists.

"No!" I yelled.

I started to rush after them, my bare feet going numb, but Owen grabbed both my arms and held me back.

Aiden looked over at me, shaking his head. "Call your brother," he shouted at me. "You shouldn't be alone." The deputy pushed his head down and shoved him into the backseat of the cruiser.

I couldn't let them do this. I *couldn't*. I struggled to escape from Owen's grasp. "Owen, *please*," I begged. "Chester and Jeremy set this up. You *know it*."

"Of course I know," he said. "This is nonsense, and I intend to discipline my deputy over it. Chester and Jeremy seem to think they can pull my department's strings like we're a bunch of podunk puppets. But this is a hell of a lot worse than any of us could've expected. For now, you have to let Aiden go."

"Absolutely not!"

Owen pulled me through the back door of the diner and away from prying eyes. I stumbled into the kitchen, clutching my stomach. I was going to throw up. How was this happening?

A better question—how had I failed to see it coming? *Of course* Jeremy had done this. He was never going to stop. Never leave me alone.

"Listen to me," Owen said. "We will sort this out at the station. He confessed, and that was his choice."

"He was trying to protect me. Like a big stupid *idiot*."

Owen frowned. "Well, technically he did kill Mitch. He all but admitted that to me already. Self defense, but still."

"*Not helping*," I spit out.

"Here's what's going to happen. I have to call in the state authorities to run the forensics, because we don't have the facilities to handle a murder investigation. And when they do, it'll be obvious that Mitch died elsewhere and got dumped here. They'll find evidence it's a frame-up."

"Are you sure? Do you promise?"

He chewed his lip. I took that as a *no*. And that was not going to satisfy me. "I won't let them do this."

Owen boxed me in, a hand on either side of the prep table. "Get yourself dressed and meet us at the station. Find your brother and keep him with you, like Aiden said. Do not go anywhere alone."

"I'll do those things. But first, I'm going to *kill Jeremy Rigsby*," I snarled.

Owen pointed a finger in my face. "Get that nonsense out of your head right damn now. Don't you dare go near any of the Rigsbys. For *your* safety. Now I need to get control of this scene and make sure nobody tampers with anything else."

"How? For all we know, the Rigsbys have people in your department who are helping them."

"That's a serious accusation. I'll leave Deputy Marsh here with you. She's trustworthy. She'll secure the diner and make sure nobody else gets in. Now get what you need to, and get down to the station." He stormed back outside. I stood in the doorway and watched the police cruiser pull away with Aiden inside. Jeremy and Chester stood at the front of the crowd, grinning.

And just like that, everything had gone straight to hell.

I was a lit firecracker, ready to go off.

I raced up the stairs to my apartment. Deputy Marsh was right behind me. She was the one who'd been holding back the crowd, not the deputy who'd arrested Aiden. I had no specific reason to suspect her. She was around my age and a transplant to Hartley like me. But I wasn't in the mood to trust anyone.

"Could I have a moment to get dressed?" I asked.

"I can't leave. Sheriff's orders. You know that."

"Then at least turn around? I'm naked under this shirt."

"I really shouldn't, but I happen to despise Jeremy Rigsby and what he did to you. So consider this your single favor." She turned in the doorway to face the stairs. Her back was to me.

I had to act fast.

I rushed over to the corner, where we'd stowed Mitch's rifle. Owen knew that Aiden had killed Mitch in self defense, but it probably wouldn't help if the state investigators found that rifle here. It could be evidence against Aiden. So I quickly wiped the barrel clean with my sweatshirt sleeves and hit it beneath my bed. Nowhere near good enough, but I'd have to deal with it later. Maybe I could claim I'd found the rifle somewhere. If I was lucky, it wasn't registered to Mitch at all. That would make sense, considering their illegal operation on Refuge Mountain.

"Almost done?" Deputy Marsh asked.

"Working on it!" I tugged on the first pair of jeans I could find. Put on a bra, then gathered my shoes and socks. "I just need to get Aiden's things. He's not even wearing a shirt or shoes."

Deputy Marsh turned around. "Sheriff Douglas told me to leave everything for the state investigators when they get here. Someone at the station will give Aiden clothes to wear for now."

I picked up Aiden's wallet and phone. He hadn't packed yet, as if he'd been avoiding the reality that he would have to leave soon. And now, he was on his way to jail. The state investigation could take days. He'd probably miss the entire wedding in Steamboat, and I knew how much that would agonize him. Letting people down when he'd given his word.

I wanted to believe Owen about the evidence proving Aiden's innocence. But what if it *didn't*? What if the Rigsbys figured out some other way to punish him for helping me?

I had to get him out of this. There was absolutely no other outcome I would accept. But how?

"Can you drive yourself to the station?" Marsh asked.

"I'm going to call my brother."

"He's new in town, right? I thought at first that Aiden was your brother, but Sheriff Douglas said it was some kinda misunderstanding."

"Something like that." We went downstairs to the kitchen, and I called Trace's number. I was worried he wouldn't answer since it was the middle of the night, and I wasn't sure if his phone's reception was as spotty as Aiden's. But he picked up on the first ring.

"Jessi?" His voice sounded sharp and alert. Like he hadn't even gone to bed yet.

I told him as quickly as possible about the disaster that had just unfolded. Trace paused for a moment.

Then he launched into action. "Are you at the diner?"

"Yes. I'm about to leave."

"Stay there. I think Scarlett's asleep. I'll go wake her. We'll meet you in ten minutes in front of the diner. Are you alone?"

I glanced at Deputy Marsh. "No. One of Owen's people is here. She's going to secure the scene and keep everybody else out."

"Good. Both of you stay put until Scarlett and I pick you up."

Nine minutes and thirty seconds later, Scarlett's Jeep Wrangler pulled up out front.

"Good luck," Deputy Marsh said.

"I'm going to need it." I jumped into the front seat. Trace was driving, and Scarlett was in the backseat, looking bleary-eyed. My brother peeled away from the curb, then took a U-turn to head toward the sheriff's department headquarters. Scarlett must've already given him directions.

"Planting a body in a dumpster?" Scarlett said. "That's crazy. Even for Jeremy Rigsby."

"Maybe. But now he's got his other family members helping him. Even a bunch of idiots can put together a strategy when they work together."

"You've got family helping you, too," Trace pointed out.

Scarlett reached forward and grabbed my shoulder. "We're going to fix this."

I nodded. "We have to."

———

A crowd of people met us outside the sheriff's department. Some I'd seen outside the bar earlier. Others had clearly just rolled out of bed, wearing puffy coats over their bathrobes. Apparently half the town had been woken by the news about Mitch's body in my dumpster.

And Dale Rigsby was in the center of them. Shouting for justice and retribution. He pointed an accusatory finger the moment he spotted me. "*You*. You never should've been allowed to stay in this town in the first place. Now my son is dead."

Why would I put him in my own dumpster? I wanted to ask. But I knew better.

Trace wrapped an arm around me, angling us both so I was inside his shadow. Scarlett was on my other side. They rushed me into the station.

But it wasn't any better once we'd made our way inside.

I came face-to-face with Sawyer Rigsby. He stood having a tense conversation with Owen. Both Sawyer and the sheriff looked over at me as I entered.

"Jessi." Sawyer's face was bright red. "Please tell me this isn't true. You couldn't have had something to do with Mitch's death."

"Innocent until proven guilty," Scarlett reminded him. "With all due respect, Mr. Rigsby."

Sawyer nodded vigorously. "Of course. That's all I'm interested in. The truth."

I'd wondered before whether Sawyer knew about Dale's operation on Refuge Mountain. I still wasn't sure. But right now, everything about Sawyer screamed *false*. And somehow, his saccharine concern was even worse than Dale's shouting outside the station.

I had a sweet tooth, and desserts were my passion. But there was something rotten about the founder of the Hart-Made Candy Company.

"Take Ms. Novo and her friends to a conference room," Owen told a deputy. "I'll interview them later."

I was more than happy to get away from Sawyer. The door shut, and I sank into the seat at the head of the conference table. "Scarlett, you shouldn't be here," I said. "Sawyer is your boss. He controls half of Hartley. He's going to blame you for standing by me."

Better yet, I should've left Hartley on my own, I thought. *Weeks ago*. I never should've pulled anyone else into this. Not Aiden, not Scarlett. Not even Trace.

My fault.

Scarlett placed her hand over mine on the tabletop. "It's like Trace said in the car. You've got your family beside you. Maybe you and I weren't always this close, but I'm not going anywhere. You hear me? You're my friend, and nothing matters more than that."

I nodded, squeezing her hand.

My brother paced the length of the conference room, arms crossed, hair obscuring half his face. "Start at the beginning," Trace said. "Everything that happened after I left the diner. I need every detail about how this unfolded. Because it doesn't make sense."

Scarlett raised an eyebrow at me. She was probably thinking of the condoms she'd given me. Trace didn't need *those* details.

I kept things vague, focusing on the events of the last half hour. The sudden knock at the door. The deputy's claim of an anonymous tip, and the discovery of Mitch's body in the dumpster. Trace listened with a tense frown.

"It's not the best setup to frame someone for murder," he said. "Not if they want the charges against you or Aiden to stick."

I combed my hair back with my fingers. "That's what Owen thought. The state police will investigate, and the evidence will show that Mitch's body was planted in the dumpster. This is pure harassment. Either I would get arrested, or Jeremy probably guessed that Aiden would step in to defend me. Did he want to get revenge for Aiden embarrassing him? Or is this because we went near the warehouse? Somehow they figured out it was us."

It wouldn't have been that hard to guess. We'd overheard Chester say that he blamed me and Aiden for Mitch's death. They hadn't seen us distinctly on the camera footage, but they suspected we'd been poking around Refuge Mountain. Afterward, Chester and Jeremy must've recovered Mitch's body from the ravine and figured out how to use it against us. They wanted to make our lives hell. That was reason enough.

But Trace was shaking his head. "It's the timing. That's what bothers me."

"What do you mean?" I asked.

Before Trace could answer, Owen stepped into the room, closing the door quickly behind him.

I got up. "I want to see Aiden."

"That's impossible. Besides, Aiden is fine."

"What was Sawyer saying to you?" I asked.

"Just digging for info." Owen rubbed a hand over his face. "I'm trying to do things mostly by the book, even though I agree with you that it's bullshit. The Rigsbys have been planning this. When I had to leave the video call with Aiden's brother yesterday afternoon, it was because Chester and Jeremy were asking for me. They wanted to file a missing persons report on Mitch."

Scarlett sat forward, dropping her elbows onto the tabletop. "That's what I'd heard. They were going around telling everyone that Mitch was missing. Probably because they were already plotting to stick him in Jessi's dumpster. Sheriff, if you know what's really going on, then you have to do something about it."

"I will. But we have to be careful. Dale is out there shouting for blood. Sawyer…I don't know what he has to do with this."

"That's what I'm trying to figure out, too," I said.

"The way I see it, Aiden's safer in custody than out on the street," Owen continued. "Once the state investigators get here, everyone will calm down. We'll get the forensics, and they'll find that the evidence doesn't line up. And hopefully, the Rigsbys will slip up and we'll learn more about the illegal operation they've been running. But for now, you all need to sit tight and let this play out."

Owen left the room. I wanted to run after him and shout my frustration. We knew so much that the Rigsbys were responsible for, yet we couldn't prove a single thing yet.

We had to wait. That was Owen's answer to everything. "I can't just trust that this will work itself out," I said.

Scarlett sighed. "I can only imagine how you feel. But Owen is right that we can't act rashly. It won't hurt Aiden to sit in county jail for a bit until we come up with something."

"I disagree," Trace said softly.

My brother had been brooding over in the corner during

Owen's brief visit. He had a dark look in his eyes. A *dangerous* look.

I walked over to Trace. "You mentioned timing before. What did you mean?"

"This isn't just a sloppy attempt to harass you. The Rigsbys must know that the murder charge is weak at best. This is a ploy. They wanted to get Aiden into custody at the jail because they're going to make a move, and it'll happen before the state investigators arrive. Before sunrise. While they've got surprise on their side and things are still chaotic."

It felt like a hand had closed around my throat. "You think they'll try to kill him?" I whispered.

Even as I said it, I knew it was true. I'd seen the look in Jeremy's eyes yesterday at the diner when Aiden had pulled him off of me. Jeremy would want Aiden dead for that alone. Add in the fact that Jeremy believed Aiden was my new boyfriend?

Trace nodded. "The jail will have three shifts, probably manned by one correctional officer each, given how small this place is. If it were me, I'd do it at the shift change. Sometime this morning before the state police arrive. That's their window. And ours."

"Then what do we do?" Scarlett asked. "How do we get Aiden out of there?

"What about calling Jake?" I said. "Aiden's brother might be able to help somehow as a federal agent."

"No." Trace's eyes had gone even darker. "No law enforcement. If we're doing this, it's the three of us in this room. Unless you want out, Scarlett. If we get caught, we could be in worse trouble than Aiden is already."

She scoffed. "Are you kidding me? I'm all the way in."

"Then I have a few ideas." My brother's head tilted in my direction. "Now, the real question is how much you're willing to risk. What is Aiden's safety worth to you, Jessi?"

What was I willing to risk for Aiden?

Stand your ground. That had been my motto for the last two years. I'd been fighting for my place in Hartley. But I had more to fight for now. Even if Aiden was leaving Hartley and I'd never see him again, I wanted him safe. I needed to know I'd done everything I could for him, the way he'd done for me over the past few days.

Even if I had to risk my home, my very life, to do it.

"Everything," I said. "I'll risk everything."

Trace nodded. "Then you'll need to do exactly as I say."

CHAPTER TWENTY-SIX
Aiden

I HAD NEVER BEEN ARRESTED before. It wasn't something I wished to make a habit. Especially when I rolled into the station in no shirt and no shoes, with it below freezing outside.

The deputy un-cuffed me once we were indoors. They finger-printed me, took my mugshot. Asked for all my info, and this time, I told them my real name. This wasn't the time to play around. I probably needed a lawyer. Maybe my brother's help, too. I could just imagine Jake's expression when he heard about this.

And the wedding. *Shit*. The bride and groom in Steamboat were in for some disappointing news.

But my biggest concern was Jessi. The Rigsbys had done this for revenge, but perhaps also to get me out of the way. What were they going to do to Jessi? I hoped she'd called Trace. He would protect her. But if the Rigsbys got to her first...

"I want my phone call."

"You'll get it when we say you get it."

The deputy made me turn over my jeans as evidence. That left me naked, since I'd been going commando. He gave me thin cotton sweats and a sweatshirt to wear, plus sneakers that were too small. Then he took me to the jail, which was a drab building behind the sheriff's headquarters. Four cells, all of them empty. Except for the one they locked me inside.

The deputy who'd arrested me and the guy on correctional duty both sneered from the other side of the bars. They looked like carbon copies of Jeremy. Not his exact features, but the same age and type. Maybe not high school buddies of his. Nothing that would make their bias so obvious. But these two clearly had made up their minds about me.

"Hope she was worth it," the deputy said.

"Why would I go after Mitch Rigsby?" I asked. "If Jessi wanted me to kill someone for her, wouldn't it be Jeremy?"

The correctional officer's hand flinched toward his gun. "Watch it."

I backed off. I doubted they would shoot me, but I might accidentally "trip" a few times. I didn't need that headache.

Jeremy's clones left me alone. The deputy returned to his usual duties, while the correctional officer took up his post beyond the cell block. I hoped Jessi was at the sheriff's office being interviewed. Better yet, with her brother by her side. Trace and Owen wouldn't let anything happen to her.

I sat on the metal bench and tried to relax, even though I was keyed up with anxiety over not knowing if Jessi was safe.

A few minutes later, I perked up when I heard voices. A visitor had just arrived. The correctional officer buzzed my guest in.

Sawyer Rigsby strolled toward my cell.

I stood up and went over to the bars, bracing my hands against them. "You walk around here like you own the place."

"That's an exaggeration," Sawyer said stiffly. "I'm just a visitor."

"Does Sheriff Douglas know you're here?"

Sawyer glanced up. He was probably searching out the cameras. "Owen knows what he needs to know," he said quietly. "Nothing more. My nephew means well, but he gets in over his head."

"What do you want?" I asked.

"Look, I know who you are now. They told me your real name. I know you're from California. The night that Chester and his brothers ran into you in the diner, you said you were just passing through. Clearly, you were being honest. I'll bet you were only here in the first place because of the bridge closure. Wrong place, wrong time."

"What's your point?"

"It's admirable of you to try to stand up for Jessi. It really is. But it's misguided."

I squeezed the bars. Said nothing.

"This has all gotten out of hand. The mess between Jessi and Jeremy should've been over with. They never should've escalated things the way they have. And now, look where we are. You're in a jail cell instead of wherever it is you actually belong. People around town are upset. My nephew is dead."

"I didn't want that either," I said. I could tell by the shrewd look in Sawyer's eyes that he knew. This murder accusation was bogus.

"Neither one of us needs this trouble, Mr. Shelborne. I think we can reach a mutually advantageous arrangement. For the greater good of Hartley."

And for the sake of whatever you're trying to hide, I added silently. That had to be what this was really about. He and his brother Dale wanted an end to all this drama. When you were running an illegal operation, drama was extremely bad for business.

But I had to admit, I was curious.

"What's your proposal?" I asked.

He clasped his hands behind his back. "I'll clear up this

misunderstanding. Make the murder charge go away. In exchange, you'll leave Hartley and never come back. As for Jessi, I'll give her a choice. She can join Hart-Made Candy Company as our full-time head of recipe development, with a very competitive compensation package. I know Scarlett has been selling Jessi's tarts in my shop. I chose not to say anything. Jessi's got talent, and I've always preferred making friends rather than enemies. But if Jessi doesn't like that option, I'd be happy to cut her a check so she can make her way elsewhere. Away from Hartley and all the bad reminders of the past."

"Very generous of you."

"You don't believe me?"

I didn't know *what* to think of this guy. But his offer? It wasn't all that bad.

I had to leave Hartley anyway. I'd never planned on returning. This was my get-out-of-jail-free card. And maybe Jessi would like the proposal when she considered it in a practical light. She could take Sawyer's money and go to Paris, like she'd wanted. Go to pastry school. Escape from all her problems.

But the woman I knew? She would never choose the easy way out. I admired a lot of things about her, but that might've been number one.

I remembered that wistful look in her eye when she'd shared her dreams with me. When she'd shown me why she had chosen to stand her ground and make a home in Hartley. If Jessi were standing next to me right now, what would she say? I honestly wasn't sure.

But *I* knew exactly what I had to say.

I beckoned Sawyer closer. Then I announced, nice and loud for the cameras, "Go fuck yourself."

Sawyer's face turned beet red. He wasn't used to people talking to him like that. "You're being stupid."

"Probably. But I'd rather be stupid than sell out Jessi to buy my freedom. I care about her. I—"

"You what? You'd throw your life away for her, just on principle?"

I turned around and went back to the metal bench. Sat my weight heavily on it. "Yep. That is *exactly* what I would do."

I was right on the edge of something. Some big realization. A decision. Things were swirling around in my head. A storm that wouldn't settle.

I'd been the same guy for thirty years. My siblings would've told you. Jake used to call me an ornery little shit. I was being one right now. But I was also different. These past several days with Jessi had done something to me, and I couldn't put my finger on it. All I knew was that I would never choose my own wellbeing over hers.

Jessi. *My Jessi*.

It was worse than Sawyer even knew.

"This is your one chance," Sawyer said. "I can't account for what might happen next. Or what else my nephews might do."

I closed my eyes and leaned my head against the cold cinderblock. "Guess I'll just have to wait and find out."

———

I knew something would happen. I just didn't know when.

After a while, the long night caught up with me. I dozed. The officer guarding me binge-watched some TV show on his phone. Episode after episode played in the background, accentuated by the guy sniffing his nose or coughing.

Then the noise suddenly stopped, and that's when I woke. A second later, the lights shut out, plunging the entire cell block into darkness. That made me sit bolt-upright. Shit was about to go down.

A hinge moved. Someone had just opened the door into the cell block.

I got off the cot and crouched behind the end of it. Footsteps padded toward me. Stopped outside my cell. I saw a faint shape behind the bars, and a flashlight flipped on, the beam fixing on me. Beyond the bright light was Chester Rigsby's face, bandage and all.

He pointed a gun at me.

This was not good.

"Look what we have here. Not so big and brave now, are you?" Chester stood close to the bars. I would have to rush him. *Fast*. Try to get the gun away. He'd probably get off a shot or two, but it was also probable he would miss unless he was an excellent shot against a moving target. And the truth was that most people weren't.

He opened his mouth, probably to spout more triumphant nonsense. I tensed my muscles to spring at him. But before I could make a move, the flashlight beam abruptly lurched upward to the ceiling, then fell to the ground and winked off.

There was a choked-off gasp. A rapid clicking sound. A crash.

Then another flashlight flicked on. Trace stood outside of my cell with a taser in his hand. He tossed the taser onto Chester, who lay in a heap on the ground.

My pulse thudded. "Thanks," I said.

"No problem." He bent to pick up Chester's gun. "I'll be right back."

When Trace turned around, I caught a glimpse of another handgun in a holster at his lower back. He hadn't even drawn it. I approached the bars, and Trace returned a moment later with a set of keys and a pair of handcuffs. He opened my cell with the keys, then used the cuffs to secure Chester's wrists.

"Give me a hand?" he asked.

Together, we dragged Chester into my cell.

I had many questions, but only one was pressing. "Where's the officer who was guarding me?"

"He stepped outside the jail just as Chester came in. I was watching from the roof of the building across the street. I'd expected Chester would wait until the shift change, but having an inside man worked even better. The guy switched off the cameras and everything. Very convenient. For Chester, and for us."

We went into the small lobby. The guard lay on his back on the floor, passed out, hands cuffed behind him. His taser holster was empty.

"You used a submission hold on the guard?" I asked. I could just imagine Trace sneaking up behind the guy and cutting off his airway until he passed out. I bet Trace hadn't even broken a sweat.

"He'll wake up soon. Probably around the time of the shift change, unless someone comes to investigate the loss of power sooner, so we'd better get moving."

We rushed out of the building. The lights were still bright around the jail and the sheriff's department. It seemed like the guard had only switched off the power inside. But the sky was turning pale as well, the sun on its way up.

Trace led me across the street and toward a well-worn Jeep Wrangler. He was limping slightly. But I doubted he'd been injured just now. I figured it was a past injury, maybe before he'd left whatever secret work he'd been doing. Spy stuff. That tended to be dangerous.

"What about Jessi? Is she safe?"

"The sooner we get you out of here, the sooner she will be. We're meeting her and Scarlett outside of town. Hopefully they're on their way."

We got in the Jeep, and I turned to him sharply. "Why wouldn't they be?"

"They had some things to take care of."

Then we heard a siren, and Trace perked up. A firetruck roared across the intersection in front of us. At the same moment, I noticed the dark streak of smoke in the dawn sky. It was coming from Main Street.

From the end of Main Street where the diner was located.

"Something's on fire!" I yelled.

Trace pushed the accelerator, and we raced away from town. "It's fine. That means Scarlett and Jessi finished their part of the plan."

"Are you kidding me? What did you have them doing? You said you were going to look out for your sister."

He glanced at me wryly. "In case you hadn't noticed, you're the one who needed rescue this morning. Not Jessi."

"Thank you for that," I said through gritted teeth. "It wouldn't have gone well for me if you hadn't shown up when you did."

"Glad I could help. I owed you for taking care of Jessi before. But you should know that Jessi was willing to do anything to get you out of that jail. I couldn't have stopped her. You mean a lot to her."

My insides lurched. "She means a lot to me too."

"Maybe. But you can't give her false hope. I may not have been the best brother to her in the past, but this is me doing what I can to protect her. Out of everything in Hartley at this moment, you probably have the greatest power to hurt her. If you're leaving, then make it a clean break. Don't look back."

I sank into my seat, holding my clenched fist against my mouth. Knowing and *hating* the fact that he was right.

I barely breathed until we turned onto a quiet, deserted road, and I saw a familiar truck up ahead. *My* truck. We pulled up behind its bumper. Jessi and Scarlett both jumped out. Scarlett was holding a rifle. She hung back, but Jessi ran toward me.

"You're okay!" she cried.

I opened my arms. She jumped, grabbing me around the neck, her legs holding me at the hips. And I held her back. I held her like the only thing I could possibly need in the world was her. Right now, that was how it felt.

Don't give her false hope, Trace repeated in my mind.

"I brought everything," she said breathlessly. "Your duffel and phone and your wallet. Your truck was still in the bar parking lot, covered in snow, but we got it here."

"So you went back to the diner?" I asked. "Is *that* what's on fire right now?"

I set her down, and she stepped back. Her hands went to my face, eyes searching mine. I held onto her waist, keeping her close.

"Not the diner," she said. "That would've looked like we were destroying evidence. I set a fire in the building next door. It's unoccupied, but it used to be a local newspaper office. Plenty of paper stuff to burn."

I was incredulous as Jessi quickly explained. Trace had known they would need a diversion to break me out of jail. The fire was supposed to keep Hartley's emergency services busy and their communication lines occupied. But Jessi had also needed to get my belongings and Mitch's gun out of the diner. There would be questions when the state investigators arrived, but it had been the best she could do.

"Deputy Marsh had been sitting in her cruiser in the alley," Jessi said. "Keeping watch over the diner. Scarlett boosted me up to reach a window on the side. I was in and out of my apartment fast."

"What you did was insanely dangerous."

"I did it for you." She pulled me down so our foreheads

touched. "I have no regrets when it comes to you. Not a single one."

Dammit. This incredible woman. I couldn't go yet.

I crushed my mouth to hers. Kissed her desperately. We kissed until we couldn't breathe, and then we kept our heads together, gasping the same air.

"Aiden, *go*," Trace said. "The fire will cause some chaos for a while, but somebody is bound to notice the jailbreak any moment. You need to be out of Hartley by then."

"We'll handle Owen," Scarlett chimed in. "You know he's on your side anyway, and when he realizes what Chester was planning, he'll be furious with the Rigsbys. Not you. We'll get it all sorted out. You just get going to Steamboat Springs."

I looked at Jessi. She was nodding. A single tear slid down her cheek. "Aiden, the past few days… It was like a dream, and dreams have to end. But I will never, ever forget a moment of it."

My chest had winched tight around my heart. I didn't want to let go of her.

"Aiden," Trace warned. "You gotta go."

A clean break.

"I'm working on it." I kissed her again, slower this time. Dragging out every gentle press of our lips. *One more. Just one more.*

A million more. That was what I wanted.

How was it possible that I'd never felt freer than when Jessi was in my arms? Why did leaving her feel like the worst kind of burden? But I knew that Trace was right. I had the power to hurt Jessi, and I couldn't allow myself to do it.

Jessi held onto my shirt. "Go," she whispered.

She wasn't pushing me away, though. She needed me to take the first steps. We both knew this was how it had to be.

A clean break. Don't look back.

I forced myself to back away from her. She let go of me, hands outstretched. I went to the truck. The keys were still in the ignition. My duffel was in the backseat. My regular clothes, which I would change into later. I started the engine and put it in drive.

I wasn't supposed to look back, but I did. Couldn't stop myself.

In the rearview mirror, Jessi had her head against Scarlett's shoulder. Hiding her face. And for some reason, that made the moment so much worse. I'd wanted one last look at her. I'd wanted her to be holding her head high as I drove away.

I gripped the steering wheel and took the next turn, aiming the truck toward the freeway. Trace had told me the best route on the drive from the jail. I needed to bypass Hartley's main drags and stay out of sight until just before the freeway entrance. From there, I'd cross the bridge, and I'd be on my way. Leaving Hartley behind.

No regrets. That was how I'd lived until now.

Until her.

CHAPTER TWENTY-SEVEN
Jessi

"LET IT OUT," Scarlett said. "You're going to be okay."

I soaked Scarlett's jacket with my tears. *Two minutes*, I told myself. I would wallow for two minutes, and then I would be done. We had so many other things to deal with. Trace radiated with impatient energy a few feet away. I had to push these feelings down.

I had *known* this was coming. From the first moment Aiden had kissed me, I'd known. But I'd had no idea what it would really feel like.

No matter how much else I'd been through, my heart had still been that same fragile dreamer underneath the thick skin I'd worked so hard to develop. And Aiden had pierced me down to my center. From the *first kiss*, he had exposed me. Stripped me down and made me feel purer pleasure than I'd ever experienced. True safety and contentment. He'd been my refuge.

My foolish heart hadn't stood a chance. It had ripped itself right out of my chest and gone with Aiden when he'd driven away. So damned impulsive. *Still*. But unlike when I'd fallen for Jeremy, Aiden had been exactly who he claimed to be.

And with Aiden, I'd known exactly what I was doing.

"One more minute," I whispered to Scarlett. "I promise that's all I need."

"Honey, it's going to take longer than that."

"We don't have the time."

But the stress of the last several hours had weighed heavily on me. Knowing how close the Rigsbys had come to hurting Aiden because of me.

And if Owen reported Aiden's escape to the state police, then highway patrol would be looking for him. It made me sick to imagine it. I clenched my teeth and grabbed Scarlett's jacket in my fist. Trace came over and laid a hand on the middle of my back. I guessed that was the only comfort he could offer, but I was still grateful for it.

"We need to go," my brother said softly.

"I know."

I heard an engine. Someone was driving this way. *"Jessi,"* Scarlett said sharply.

I wiped roughly at my eyes. *You can do this*, I told myself. *Push it down, just like you did after Jeremy. Push it all down and away. Bury it deep.*

"Let's go." I went toward Scarlett's Jeep. But she held onto my arm.

"Jessi," she said again. Softer this time. There was something different in her voice. Not fear. It was shock. Wonder.

I turned to look. The approaching vehicle was almost here. And I couldn't believe it, either.

It was Aiden's truck.

He stopped and parked directly in front of us. In the windshield, his expression was intense and fierce, yet more untamed than I'd ever seen him. I'd never seen that much emotion written on his face.

His door flew open, and his boots landed hard on the ground. He walked toward me with long, purposeful strides.

I launched myself at him. I didn't even feel my feet hitting the snow-packed road.

We collided. Kissed. Grasped each other like we were trying to fuse ourselves together. My heart was back in my chest and it was going absolutely *wild*. "What are you *doing*?" I asked. "You're supposed to be gone. The Rigsbys and the police are looking for you. It's not safe."

He kissed me again. Hard. Gazed into my eyes. "I couldn't. I just...*fuck*, I couldn't."

"What does that mean?" I ran my hands over his face. This didn't seem real.

"Come with me to Steamboat Springs."

"*What*? Aiden, I…"

"Come meet my family. I'll bring you back to Hartley after. Just *come with me*."

I stared back at him.

I felt Scarlett and Trace standing close by, both of them tense. Aiden's words ran through my brain. Go to Steamboat Springs. Meet his family. I wanted that. Of course I did. I wanted more of Aiden.

But what about after? He would bring me back to Hartley, and then…

Be careful, I told myself.

Because for all my impulsive dreaming, I wasn't the same woman I'd been years ago. I couldn't let myself make those mistakes. Not because I didn't trust Aiden. But I knew what this would mean to me.

I hugged him, dropping my forehead to his neck. "I can't." Saying those words ripped me open anew. "I want to go with you. But it would just be drawing out the goodbye, and it's going to hurt so much worse later on." Because then I'd know Aiden even better. I would meet Jake and the rest of Aiden's family in person, and I'd probably fall for them too. I would find out all the other ways that Aiden was an incredible man, a man I could never have, and my hopeful heart just couldn't take that.

Nothing Jeremy had ever done had broken me. But Aiden could.

"What if we don't say goodbye?" he asked.

Scarlett inhaled sharply, hand flying to her mouth in my peripheral vision.

I lifted my head, telling the runaway muscle in my chest to get ahold of itself. "What are you asking me?" It was possible that I'd just blown up my life in Hartley by breaking him out of jail. To save Aiden's life, I had been willing to risk it all. Yet I was still determined to fight for my place here. "If you want me to leave Colorado…"

But he was shaking his head. "No. You love Hartley, and I would never ask you to give that up." His thumb caressed my cheekbone. "But what if I stayed?"

Everything went still. I could've sworn the world had stopped turning. "You would stay in Hartley?"

His eyes searched mine. "I never expected this to happen. I thought I had the life I wanted, and I didn't think that would change. But then I met you. I saw Hartley through your eyes. And it's different. With you, I'm different. It's confusing as hell."

"I know," I said, laughing as tears filled my eyes.

Sirens blared in the distance.

"We need to move," Trace said. "This has taken *way* too long." He pushed Scarlett to her Jeep.

But Aiden didn't move. His grip on me tightened. "Jessi, I can't promise this is going to work. I could still hurt you, even if that's the last thing I want to do. But I'd be hurting us both right now if I left without you." He pressed a kiss to my temple. Kept his lips there. "We can take things as slow as you need, and you don't have to decide this minute, but I do have to go to Steamboat. Please come with me. I *need* you with me."

The sirens were getting louder. Scarlett was backing away toward her vehicle. Trace shifted his weight from foot to foot. Any moment, a police car could turn onto this road.

But Aiden stood there, all his attention on me. Waiting for my response. Like this was the only thing that mattered. *Us*. My decision.

"Yes," I blurted. "I'll come with you."

A grin split Aiden's face. The biggest I'd ever seen. Not just on him, but maybe on anyone.

"But I don't have anything. Clothes or a toothbrush..."

"We'll get whatever else you need." Aiden laced our fingers together. "Later."

Scarlett dashed for her Jeep and grabbed my purse from the front seat. I'd had it with me when I went to the station, and Scarlett had been keeping track of it for me. At least I had that much. My ID and phone. Scarlett gave it to me, followed by a hug. She was beaming.

I turned to my brother. Trace frowned, but he didn't try to argue with me. "Can you deal with things here in Hartley until I'm home?" I asked.

"I'll do what I can. I'll talk to Owen and make sure nobody's looking for you. Same things we'd already planned." His eyes shifted to Aiden. "You'll bring her back like she asked? You're going to try to make this work in Hartley?"

My brother's stare said a lot more than that. And Aiden nodded like he understood.

"You have my word." Aiden held out his hand, and Trace took it. They shook.

"Then get the hell out of here." Trace pushed us toward Aiden's truck, and we ran, hand in hand.

The engine roared as we took the entrance ramp for the highway.

I couldn't believe I was doing this. Running away with Aiden. It was the most impulsive, crazy-romantic thing I had ever done. And I knew all the way down deep that it was what I wanted.

Aiden kept glancing over at me. He was driving with one hand on the wheel, the other tangled with mine and resting on my thigh. "Did you mean it?" I asked. "You would actually move to Hartley?"

"If you didn't believe me, why did you say yes?" Aiden's calm demeanor had returned. His eyes were smirking.

"I believed you. I believed…that I was willing to take the chance."

He lifted my hand and kissed it, eyes darting between me and the road. "I meant every single word. I knew if I left without you, I would regret it. That's not my style. Only thing I could do was turn around."

He made it sound simple. As if he'd been calm and collected the whole time. But I'd seen that look in his eyes when he'd pulled up in his truck. I'd heard it in his voice.

"You said you need me."

His thumb moved over my knuckles. "I do. I need you, and it snuck up on me. I never claimed to be a genius. But once I finally figured it out, I knew what I had to do."

"You're giving up a lot." No one had ever given up this much for me. Even Trace had confessed that he'd needed a clean slate when he'd agreed to come to Colorado. Whatever had happened to my brother, he'd already wanted to leave his old life behind.

Aiden had offered to give up a life he'd been happy with.

A life he'd worked for years to build. For *me*. But his happiness was just as important as mine.

"I told you," he said, "I don't get attached to things easily. Guess I'm an asshole like that. My friends and family can survive without me, and I'll be okay seeing them less often." He kissed my hand again, then held it against his heart. "But I am attached to you, Jessi Novo. I am so damn attached to you."

And I *melted*. Swooned. Seriously, my stomach dipped like I was in mid-air.

I had fallen so far for Aiden Shelborne, and there would be no way back up. But I didn't care. I wanted to go wherever this would lead.

———

I rested my head against his arm as we drove. No police cars followed us. The road was clear, with the last storm's snow piled up against the edges of the barriers. The sky brightened more with each minute that passed. We were both quiet, tension ebbing away as we left Hartley behind.

After half an hour of driving east, my phone pinged with a message from Scarlett. We'd climbed out of the canyon. "Scarlett says she and Trace are at her house," I reported, scrolling through my texts. "They've spoken to Owen. The fire in the building next to the diner is out. The police also found Chester in your jail cell, so they know you're gone."

"Is there going to be a BOLO for us? Colorado Highway Patrol chasing us down?"

"No. Owen is pissed off about everything at the moment, but he's a lot angrier at the Rigsbys. He's putting Chester under arrest, as well as one of the county correctional officers. But Owen decided that the paperwork for *your* arrest is strangely incomplete, and in light of new evidence, you're just being considered a witness." I looked over at him and smiled. "I'm sure you'll have to make a statement."

"I can do it when we get back to Hartley."

Smiling wider, I kept texting with Scarlett. It sounded like things were a mess in Hartley right now, between the fire and the events at the jail and the state authorities' imminent arrival. But the investigation was now focused entirely on the Rigsbys. Meanwhile, Scarlett was in the process of telling everybody in town that Chester and Jeremy Rigsby had planted Mitch's body at the diner to frame Aiden, and that they'd tried to kill him. Scarlett was hailing Trace as a hero for rescuing Aiden from the plot. Poor Owen. He had a lot of legal stuff to clean up, I had no doubt.

But in the war for public opinion, the scales were tipping.

"What about Jeremy?" Aiden asked. "What's he up to?"

I continued texting with Scarlett and grumbled as I read her message. "No sign of him. He, Spencer and Dale have gone quiet." I looked over at Aiden. "But several trucks were seen leaving the Hart-Made warehouse during the night. They're probably moving out whatever illegal stuff they delivered. Maybe they're pulling everything off Refuge Mountain, too. Without enough evidence for a search warrant, nobody can stop them."

"If they're running scared, that's a good thing. Means they won't be *your* problem. Or Owen's." Aiden squeezed the steering wheel. "I didn't tell you about the offer Sawyer Rigsby made me. He came to see me in jail."

"When?"

"A few hours before Chester showed. Sawyer offered to get me out of jail if I would leave Hartley and never come back. I told him no."

"But you didn't decide you wanted to stay until after that."

He shrugged. "Deep down, I already knew. Just took my conscious mind a little longer to catch up." Aiden reached for my hand again. "I think when we hiked up Refuge Mountain and you told me its story, told me your dreams for that place, I knew."

"But that day, you said you weren't the kind of man who could stay for me," I reminded him. "What changed?" I still didn't fully understand it.

"I did," he said softly. "I can't let you go, so I'll have to be the kind of man who deserves you."

"I never asked you to change for me. I wouldn't want that. This is a big decision. Maybe we should try dating long distance for a while, and then—"

"Stop trying to undermine my grand romantic gesture." He smirked at me. "I'm doing this because *I* want to. That much about me hasn't changed. I'm still pig-headed and not always nice. I'll probably do something that infuriates you any minute now."

"Good. I kinda like when you're pig-headed. But I also think you're nicer than you claim."

"Maybe. For you."

I leaned in for a quick kiss. I was bursting with happiness and possibility. *This is happening*, I told myself. *It's really happening*.

"If Sawyer is smart, he'll cut his losses and get his operation out of Hartley," Aiden said a few minutes later. "If not, we can deal with him when we're back. You and me. And Trace and Scarlett, too. We make a decent team. I don't know what me staying in Hartley will look like, or even what you'll want. But we'll figure it out. If you'll have me."

"I can't imagine anything better."

He was going to try to make this work. When Aiden said something, he meant it. And I wanted the same. A chance to make this dream into something real for the *both* of us. It wasn't a guarantee, because that wasn't realistic. But it was enough for now.

We needed food and gas, so we pulled off in another tiny town. Aiden went to a drive-through to get us some breakfast, and then we parked the truck on a deserted scenic overlook. We ate egg-and-bacon sandwiches, which Aiden complained about because they really were terrible, and then we popped breath mints and bundled up in his backseat.

Aiden grabbed his puffer coat from his duffel. He wrapped it around the both of us, and I sat in his lap and we kissed. A lot. Kissed each other's mouths and necks and hands and wrists. Any bare skin we could reach. My cold hands ventured beneath Aiden's shirt, getting warm against his firm stomach and chest.

With the way our plans had gone sideways, Aiden was on the road far earlier than he'd scheduled. We would travel east another hour or so before heading north. We had plenty of time before he was expected, so we could relax a little. We both needed this. A chance to be close and stare at one another and just be happy. To push away the rest of the world and be *us*.

Today was supposed to be the end. But this was our beginning.

"When we get to Steamboat," I said, "can I help you in the kitchen?"

His eyes turned smoldering, as if I'd made a far more scandalous proposal. "I'm the boss in the kitchen when I'm working. Can you handle that?"

"I like when you're the boss, if it's the right moment. I think you know that already." My tongue flicked out to lick his lower lip. Aiden growled.

"Then I insist on you helping me."

We kissed for a while longer. The windows of Aiden's

truck had long since fogged up. I moved to sit in between his thighs, my back to his chest. Aiden's arms were wrapped snuggly around me.

"Will you be my date for the wedding reception?" he asked. "I wasn't planning to make an appearance, but I'd like to dance with you."

"I would love to dance with you. But I can't go to a wedding. I have nothing to wear except what I have on right now." And that was just jeans, a sweatshirt, and mud-speckled boots.

"I bet one of my sisters will pack an extra dress. But if they don't, who cares? You look beautiful as you are. Or naked."

I gave him a sardonic glare over my shoulder. "It's a good thing they relegate you to the kitchen for this wedding-planning stuff. You'd probably throw carnations into buckets for the centerpieces and call it a day."

He cocked an eyebrow. "Sounds cost efficient. Then they could spend more on the food."

I laughed and shook my head. After that, it was more kissing and murmuring sweet things until we had to get back on the road. He also switched out his jail-issued shirt and shoes for comfier ones of his own.

Aiden swung by a gas station to fill up the tank. It was a huge travel stop, serving regular vehicles and semis. The shop sold all kinds of adorable Colorado themed souvenirs. I went in to use the restroom. When I got back to the truck, I relaxed in my seat, feeling unbelievably content as Aiden pumped the gas.

Then a familiar logo caught my eye. It was on the side of a box truck parked across the lot.

Hart-Made Candy Co.

I remembered what Scarlett had texted. She'd said the

Rigsbys had moved delivery trucks out of their warehouse during the night, spiriting away whatever secret contraband they'd brought down from Refuge Mountain.

And here was one of their trucks. Just sitting and waiting. Right in front of us.

CHAPTER TWENTY-EIGHT
Jessi

I GOT out of the pickup and circled around to where Aiden was pumping the gas. He'd just finished up and was putting the cap on the tank. "Look over there," I said, pointing at the red Hart-Made logo. "It's got to be one of the trucks that left Hartley overnight."

Aiden looked. We kept ourselves behind his quad cab, using it to provide cover. The Hart-Made truck had a shredded rear tire, and two men were arguing over it. I assumed those were the truck's drivers. Whatever problem they were having, it was more than a simple flat, and it had caused a delay. Maybe they were waiting for someone to bring them a part so they could make repairs.

Aiden put a hand on the small of my back. "Both of those guys are armed. They're wearing gun holsters."

"How can you tell?" I hadn't seen any sign of a weapon.

"The way they're standing. And the way their jackets fall."

"If they only have candy in that truck, then why would they need guns?"

"Good question."

"I want to know what they've got in there," I said.

Aiden rubbed his forehead. "I knew you were going to say that."

We got in Aiden's pickup, and he parked it in one of the spaces in front of the travel shop. But we continued to watch.

"We still have a lot of time before you have to be in Steamboat," I reasoned. "If they've got something illegal, we can call Owen. Or even Jake. I'm sure the federal government would want to know about verifiable evidence that the Rigsbys are transporting illegal drugs. Owen and Jake said they needed more proof, and this is our chance."

Aiden turned to me and rested his hand over mine. "I know this is important to you. The Rigsbys deserve whatever is coming to them. Eventually, they'll mess up and the law will catch up to them. But you don't have to be the one on a crusade. That's not your responsibility."

I thought about what my brother had asked me last night. How much I was willing to risk for Aiden. I'd told Trace that I would risk everything. I didn't have a single regret about that. But I was willing to risk a lot for Hartley, too. That town was my home, and I intended to fight for it. This wasn't just my personal vendetta against the Rigsbys. It was about what was *right*.

Aiden seemed to think Sawyer was just going to leave Hartley. But why would he, when he owned so much of the town? He owned my diner. He had the loyalty of the mayor and plenty of other people, too. If anything, Sawyer and the rest of his family would dig in and redouble their efforts to exploit the people of Hartley. Could I stand by and let that happen?

If that box truck hadn't blown a tire, then it would've been long gone by now. And if I hadn't come with Aiden, he might not have stopped here and we never would've seen it. But we *were* here. Maybe it had all lined up for a reason, and maybe it was pure luck. But either way, we couldn't ignore it.

"This could be the only shot we get to stop what the Rigsbys are doing," I said. "I'm going to try. Because if I don't, who will?"

Aiden studied me. His gaze had gone soft, and he brushed a few strands of hair away from my cheek. "Then I'll go with you. Since that first night at the diner, I've stood with you. But there are two of them with weapons against the two of us with none. Unless you count my chef's knives, and knives are no good in a gun fight."

One of the men wore glasses, and he was now smoking a cigarette. The other had on a blue Yankees cap, and he was speaking angrily into his phone. "We need to separate them," I said. "Or wait for them to split up on their own. We get the keys to the cargo area of their truck, and we get inside. See what they're transporting."

Aiden didn't say anything. His jaw was hard as we continued to watch the two men.

Then the guy in the blue cap jammed his phone in his pocket and walked toward the travel store.

I reached for the handle to the passenger door. "This is it. You follow that guy into the shop. I'll go over to the other one. I'll sweet-talk him."

Aiden's eyebrow arched so hard it almost reach his hairline. "Sweet-talk him *how*?"

"Don't worry about it. I've never seen the guy before, so he doesn't know me. He's not from Hartley. I'll get him to trust me and figure out some way to grab the keys."

"Absolutely not. No freaking way." Aiden stopped me before I could get out of the truck. "We're sticking together, or we're not doing this at all."

"Fine. Then how is this supposed to work?"

"Two on one. We both take the guy who's in the shop. Then we handle the other."

That sounded a lot less efficient. But I could tell Aiden

wasn't going to compromise. Perhaps this was one of those moments when I was being a little too impulsive.

Slow down. Be careful.

"Fine, we'll do it your way. But we'd better get moving. The guy's already inside."

We both got out of the truck and headed into the shop. Aiden leaned toward me and whispered, "He's going to the bathroom."

We followed him to the back, where the restrooms were located. But there were people streaming in and out of both the men's and ladies'. There was no way we could subdue the guy with a crowd watching.

This wasn't going to work.

Being careful was all well and good. But sometimes, you just had to jump.

Before the guy in the Yankees cap could enter the men's room, I dashed forward and grabbed his wrist. "Sir? There's something I need to show you. It's right over here."

I pushed him toward a closet. The door was barely ajar, and I could tell nobody else was inside. It was full of cleaning supplies for the bathrooms. The guy started to protest, but we had surprise on our side. And though Aiden was probably furious at me, he didn't waste a moment. He rushed in front of me, forcing the guy in the Yankees cap against the back wall of the closet.

He kicked the door shut. There was a muffled crash.

"Is everything okay in there?" a random woman asked on her way to the bathroom.

I spun around. "This place has a rat problem," I stage-whispered. "You wouldn't believe how big they are." Behind me, another thump came from the closet. "See? *Huge.*"

A look of pure horror contorted the woman's face. She turned around and went back toward the exit like she couldn't escape fast enough. It didn't seem like anyone else had heard the noise in the closet.

And a couple of seconds later, Aiden emerged, flexing his hand like it was sore. He was carrying a *Caution - Wet Floor* sign, and he set it up in front of the closet door after he closed it. "Yankees cap will be out of our hair for a little while. I got his gun and his phone. Plus a nice tactical knife, which is more my style." He pulled a knife in a leather sheath partway from his pocket, then tucked it away again.

"Keys?" I asked.

"No. The other one must have them."

That was too bad. I bit the inside of my lip. "But at least it's the two of us against one now. We can take him."

Aiden tilted his head fondly. "The Rigsbys had no idea what a mistake they were making when they got you on their bad side."

"But you and I are even better as a team. We can credit Chester and his brothers for helping us get together. We should send a thank-you card to them when they're in prison." I turned toward the front of the store.

Aiden's arm wrapped around my stomach and he pulled me back against him. "I hate it when you're anywhere near danger. But you have no idea how much it turns me on when your vicious side comes out."

I grinned at him over my shoulder. "I'll keep that in mind."

"For now, you've done enough," Aiden said. "I'll handle the guy outside."

But as we stepped into the main part of the store, there he was—the other driver of the Hart-Made delivery truck. The one in the glasses. He went straight for the snack and drink options.

Now what? I thought. I doubted our closet trick would work a second time.

"You're plotting something," Aiden murmured to me.

"Remember how you said the Rigsbys underestimated me?" He hadn't used those exact words, but that had been the gist. "Just watch."

I walked toward the man. His head was down as he chose between two different kinds of bottled tea. Just as I got close, I veered straight into him. We collided, and my fingers dipped into his coat pocket as I grabbed his shoulder with my other hand.

"Oh my gosh, I'm so sorry. My fault completely." I gave him a sweet smile. He frowned and shook me off. I kept apologizing, and the guy backed away. From the next aisle, Aiden shook his head at me, his mouth in a deep frown. I shrugged and tucked my new key ring safely in my jeans pocket.

Aiden quickly walked over to me. "Give me the keys. I'll check the cargo area of the Hart-Made truck."

"I'm coming too."

"No, you're staying in the store and keeping watch. If the guy in the glasses tries to leave, do some of that sweet-talking to distract him. But stay *here*, in public, where there are other people. No unnecessary risks. I'll be back in five minutes."

"But—"

He plucked the keys from my pocket. "Stay here," he barked. Then Aiden rushed out the door before I could do a thing to stop him.

I huffed in exasperation. Aiden had said he didn't like taking orders, but he had no problem issuing them.

I glanced around, trying to spot the guy in the glasses. If it was my job to watch him, then I had better do it. I pretended to examine a display of postcards, while the man in glasses went to the register to buy some chips and a pack of cigarettes.

I felt the presence behind me a split second before something hard pressed into my lower back. Hard and circular.

The barrel of a gun.

"Hey there, Jessi. It wasn't very smart of your boyfriend to leave you all alone."

It was Jeremy Rigsby.

Icy terror froze my limbs. But that brief surge of fear was quickly replaced by white-hot fury.

The gun barrel dug in even harder. "Don't even think about it," Jeremy said. "If you ever want to see Aiden alive again, you'd better keep your mouth shut."

CHAPTER TWENTY-NINE
Jessi

JEREMY MARCHED me into the parking lot, holding the gun against my side. "Uncle Dale told me to come help the idiots who'd screwed up their axle. Then imagine my surprise when I saw you and your asshole boyfriend here."

"That's because we know all about the illegal stuff you and your family are up to."

"Really? Then why aren't the cops after us?" He was keeping the weapon hidden inside the pocket of his jacket, but I could feel the muzzle and its implicit threat. I knew Jeremy was reckless enough to use it, despite all the witnesses. The risk of getting caught hadn't stopped him from hurting me before.

Where was Aiden?

"The cops *will* be after you," I said. "Any minute."

"I don't think so. I think you and Aiden are all on your own. You clearly broke him out of jail somehow, but you should've kept on running when you had the chance. You just can't resist trying to screw things up for me, can you?"

The guy in the glasses rushed out of the convenience shop, catching up to us. "I can't find Luther. Or my damned keys!"

"That's because Jessi and her boyfriend decided to cause trouble. It's going to be the last thing they ever do. Please tell me you still have your gun?"

The guy in glasses nodded. He eyed me. "*You.* You took my keys, you little bitch." He edged closer to me. I was trapped between the two men. I was determined to stay brave, but my confidence started to waver under this newcomer's hateful gaze.

Just who were the men the Rigsbys had recruited into their operation? They were armed. Probably ruthless.

"Her boyfriend's poking around the truck," Jeremy said, "but we have Jessi to play our bargaining chip. But there are people around. We need to keep this quiet." He jabbed me again with his gun muzzle. "If you try to warn him, you'll be very sorry."

What do I do? I asked myself. I was racking my brain, but no solution came. Maybe I should warn Aiden anyway. If I screamed, he might be able to get away. Get help.

I sucked in a breath, and Jeremy's free hand clamped over my mouth. And suddenly the other guy grabbed my throat so tightly I couldn't breathe.

"Easy, Walls," Jeremy said, until the other guy released his grip. "Take care of the boyfriend first. Then we can teach Jessi the lesson she has coming."

Aiden, I thought. *Please, please hurry.*

Jeremy shoved me around the side of the Hart-Made truck, where we were out of sight from the rest of the parking area. We were at the far edge of the lot, nearly to the woods that grew along a slope leading uphill. A huge bank of snow had been piled up here by a snowplow.

"Hand over your phone. I don't want you getting any creative ideas."

I got my phone from my back pocket and handed it to Jeremy. He threw it on the asphalt and stomped on it. The plastic shattered into ever-smaller pieces as he ground it with his heel. *Ugh*. That was painful to watch.

Jeremy nodded his head at Walls, who proceeded around the back of the box truck, his gun drawn. "The cargo door's open. But nobody's in there."

"Are you sure?" Jeremy pulled me along with him, getting closer to the rear of the truck. "Get in and check."

Walls climbed up into the cargo area. I held my breath, hoping that Aiden would burst out of a hiding place and take the guy out. But then Walls jumped back down. "Nobody's fucking *in* there. Like I said."

"Then find him!"

"I don't even know what the dude looks like. I'll take Jessi. *You* find him."

I trembled. I'd never thought I would prefer my ex to someone, but this Walls guy was very bad news.

Jeremy scowled and cursed under his breath. "He's a huge asshole with a beard. How hard can it be? He'll be the one gunning for us, so *hurry the hell up*."

Scowling, Walls stormed off. Jeremy pointed his gun at me as he glanced around anxiously. But I exhaled, regaining a small amount of confidence now that I had just one threat to deal with. Jeremy didn't intend to let me walk away from here alive. So I had to keep him busy for as long as possible. Buy time for Aiden to get to me.

Because he *would*. I knew he would.

That Walls guy couldn't get the jump on Aiden. *Right?*

"What are you transporting in the truck?" I asked.

"None of your fucking business." Jeremy fixed his scowl on me again. "All you had to do was go away. Why can't you understand that you're not wanted? Aiden was going to get sick of you anyway. You realize that, don't you? Maybe it's already happened. He probably left you here because you're not worth the trouble. Walls will come back, and we'll get to have all kinds of fun with you."

I swallowed my fear. "Hartley is my home. That's what I told Chester when he tried to intimidate me. And I have more of a right to be there than you do."

"How the hell do you figure that?"

"Because I care about that town. I care about the people who live there. Unlike you and your family. All you care about is what you can get for yourselves. Do you think your father would be proud of you for that? Proud of the way you've treated me?"

He shoved me against the side of the truck. "Shut your mouth. You don't know anything about my father."

Aiden, get here, I thought. I was playing a dangerous game with Jeremy. Provoking him to keep him distracted. But I couldn't push him too far, either.

"I know your dad was a war hero," I said. "And I'm sure he'd be ashamed of what Sawyer and Dale have been doing. Processing some kind of drugs on Refuge Mountain? We know all about it. Owen's been watching you. Aiden and I have been helping him."

Panic lanced through Jeremy's expression. Then it returned to smugness. "That was you outside the warehouse the other night, wasn't it? But you haven't got anything on us. All you've done is cause a few headaches. Like that bullshit with Mitch. You've won a few victories. But we always manage to turn it around on you. Dropping Mitch's body in your dumpster was the cover we needed to move our delivery trucks."

"Sure, getting Aiden thrown in jail worked so well for you. Where is Chester right now? You'd better hope he's not ratting out your entire operation to Owen and the DEA."

Now, Jeremy smiled. "Oh, don't worry. Owen and his

deputies will get a nice, loud surprise when he pokes around in the wrong place. We've already seen to that. If the DEA gets caught up in it too, that's even better." He leaned in and whispered, "*Boom*."

"Are you talking about a *bomb*?"

"Chester's going to keep his mouth shut, and Owen will get his surprise. And now that we've moved our product out of Hartley, nobody will have a shred of evidence against us. Our plan is buttoned up nice and tight. The only part I couldn't figure out was how to get to you. I figured I would have to wait. But here you are. I'll get to repay all the pain and humiliation you've caused me."

I had never hated anyone so much as I despised Jeremy Rigsby.

Jeremy pulled me along with him so he could peek out from behind the truck at the rest of the parking lot. He took a couple of steps away from me, still aiming his gun as he checked his phone. He pressed a button and a number dialed. There was no answer.

"You can't find Walls, right?" Elation filled me. "He's not answering. Why do you think that is?"

He kept punching at the phone.

"You saw what Aiden did to Chester and Mitch. One of them is dead, and the other's sitting in jail with a concussion. What do you think he'll do to you?"

The vein on Jeremy's forehead was pulsing. "Shut up," he said through gritted teeth. He pulled back his free hand in a fist, but it had the opposite effect than he intended. Any last shred of fear fled from my mind. Fury took its place. He thought *I* had caused *him* pain? I wanted him to suffer in every way possible. He would *never* silence me.

"Which one of your uncles is really in charge?" I asked. "It's obviously not you. Everything you touch turns to a disaster. Like when you hit *me*. But I hurt you back. Do you remember? I see the scar on your chin from those stitches you needed."

"Quit running your mouth, Jessi. I'm warning you."

"You've always liked to make yourself feel big, but you're small, Jeremy. You think beating me up and pretending to be a drug kingpin makes you important. But you're sad and pathetic and *small*."

"That's *it*." Jeremy grabbed me. The gun dug into my back. His other hand tightened at my throat. He pushed me forward around the edge of the huge snowbank and into the woods. Our boots sank into the slush. "You think I'm pathetic? You're less than nothing. I knew it from the moment I met you. You had your stupid little dreams, and I took pity on you. Brought you to Hartley because nobody else wanted you. You couldn't even be grateful. All you were was an easy lay, which is clearly all Aiden sees in you. It's all you're good for."

I stumbled and caught myself against a tree trunk. "Nothing you say can hurt me," I said defiantly. "You're weak and sad."

"No? I've got plenty of other ways to hurt you." Jeremy spun me around and pushed my back against the tree. Grabbed me again by the throat. "I've imagined this moment so many times over the last two years." His grip tightened. I couldn't breathe. The gun dug into my stomach. Then he let go of my throat only to drag his hand down between my legs. He tugged at the button of my jeans.

"Make a sound, and I'll kill you," he said.

I was about to fight back any way I could. But my eyes went wide as a huge, looming shadow stepped in behind Jeremy. "Get your fucking hands off her," Aiden said, so low I felt the vibration in my own chest.

A knife blade pressed against Jeremy's windpipe, and he tried to raise the gun, but it was wrenched out of his fingers. Aiden yanked him backward and shoved him onto his knees in the snow. The tip of the knife dug in below Jeremy's chin. Drops of blood welled from the cut.

Aiden's expression was hard. Fire raged in his eyes. "I'll give him exactly what he deserves. Say the word, Jessi. I'll do it."

"You can't. You're not going to kill me!" Jeremy's head lifted as he tried to escape the knife, but Aiden dug it in even further.

"Oh, I will," he said darkly. "If she wants me to."

Aiden's eyes didn't move from Jeremy. He waited. And I believed him. I could see it radiating from him, *feel* it. If I gave the okay, I had no doubt that Aiden would gut him right here. Damn the consequences.

I almost said yes. But Jeremy Rigsby wasn't worth that.

I gave Aiden the slightest head shake. The fire dulled to embers in Aiden's eyes.

"He said there's a bomb somewhere in Hartley. It's supposed to blow up Owen and any other law enforcement that goes near. We have to stop it."

Jeremy's terrified gaze shifted from Aiden to me. "It's true. Let me go, and I'll tell you where it is. I'll do whatever you want!"

"We don't need you for any of that." Aiden leaned in. The tip of the knife bit even deeper, and Jeremy whimpered. "It's either on Refuge Mountain or Sawyer's shipping warehouse. And I doubt Sawyer would want to damage a perfectly good building. I'm not going to kill you, but I've got plenty of other ways to hurt you."

Then Aiden's mouth spread in his most vicious, sharklike smile.

With a violent movement, Aiden lifted the knife and stabbed it deep into Jeremy's thigh. He brought his hand over Jeremy's mouth to muffle the man's screams. My ex writhed and bucked like an eel out of water.

"Looks painful," I said. "I'd keep pressure on that wound if I were you."

"We'd better wrap this up." Aiden had three handguns, one taken from each of the men he'd subdued, and he chucked two of them out into the woods. He gave the last to me. "I'm keeping the knife," he added. "This thing is handy."

Next, Aiden had me walk ahead to make sure no bystanders were watching. Then he dragged Jeremy out of the woods and hefted the bleeding, crying man into the cargo hold of the Hart-Made truck. We'd yanked off Jeremy's gloves and shoved them into his mouth to act as a gag. He was doing his best to keep pressure on his thigh, which had to be excruciating. He'd left a trail of blood in the dirty snow. Aiden kicked away the red as best he could, churning up the snow to hide the evidence.

Meanwhile, I took Aiden's phone and tried to call Owen. No answer. I left a harried voicemail, telling him there was probably a bomb on Refuge Mountain. "We have to get back to Hartley," I said. "If Owen or anybody else goes on the mountain before we can warn them, they'll be killed."

We were an hour away. Jeremy had destroyed my phone, and half the time, Aiden's phone didn't get reception at all in the mountains. What if the Rigsbys had figured out some way to lure Owen to Refuge Mountain? What if he was already there? Jeremy had sounded so sure of his plan.

What if we were already too late?

"We have to go," I said.

"Just a minute." Aiden stuck Jeremy behind a pallet of Hart-Made Candy Co. boxes. Aiden took off Jeremy's coat and then his belt to secure his hands. Then Aiden used Jeremy's jacket to tie up his injured leg. "Had to make sure he'd stay put."

"What about the other guy?" I asked. "Walls?"

"He's in a dumpster behind the convenience store. Not dead, just knocked out. So we'd better get out of here before he or the one we left inside can wake up. Though I doubt they'll be eager to call the police, since they've got contraband on this truck somewhere."

I didn't like the idea of leaving Jeremy and the truck here, since they could find a way to escape, but we didn't have much choice. And I *still* hadn't figured out what these boxes were really carrying. The cargo area had an odd smell, but I couldn't put my finger on it.

"Did you get a chance to find out what they're transporting?" I asked quickly.

"No. Right after I unlocked the cargo door, I changed my mind and decided to go back for you. That's when I saw Jeremy bring you outside. I hid." Aiden strode over to me and pulled me in close, tucking my head against his chest for a quick but thorough hug. "I'm so sorry, Jessi. I had to wait for the right moment. It makes me sick that he was hurting you. If you'd given me the go ahead…"

"I know. But you're worth a thousand of him. His blood doesn't belong on your hands." I basked for one more second in Aiden's warm, comforting embrace. Then I stepped back. "We have to hurry."

Aiden used the tactical knife to slice away the plastic from the pallet of cardboard boxes. It looked like each large box could fit a couple dozen decorative candy boxes within. "We'll take one of these bulk boxes with us," he said. "Maybe it'll have the evidence we need to uncover the Rigsbys' drug operation."

We jumped out of the delivery truck. Aiden replaced the

padlock on the cargo door, locking Jeremy inside, and pocketed the truck keys. Even if Walls and his partner Luther woke up, they couldn't drive it away.

Then Aiden tucked the cardboard box under his arm, and we both ran for his pickup.

CHAPTER THIRTY
Aiden

I GUNNED the engine as we hurried back toward Hartley. My knuckles were pale as I squeezed the steering wheel. But I pretended it was Jeremy Rigsby's neck.

I couldn't stop thinking about how he'd put his hands on Jessi.

Truly, I had been one flick of my wrist away from ending that guy, despite Jessi's decision to give him mercy. But letting him live had been the right call. Hiding the dead body would've been annoying, and I might've had a bunch of police nonsense to deal with... Too much effort.

He wasn't going to bleed to death. I'd avoided any vital arteries when I'd stabbed his thigh. But at least I had the satisfaction of knowing he was in a world of hurt at the moment. The man deserved so much worse.

"Have you tried Owen's number again?" I asked. "Or the main Hartley police lines?"

"Your phone still has no service. It hasn't had a single bar since the travel stop." She threw up her hands in frustration. *"What the heck is wrong with this thing?"*

"My phone sucks. I'm sorry. I'll switch carriers when I make the move to Hartley official."

"You'd better," she grumbled. But it seemed like the mention of my staying in Hartley had soothed Jessi's anxiety, just a little.

"What about Jeremy's phone?" I asked. "Or the others?" I'd taken the phones off the two clowns who'd been working for Jeremy, in addition to their guns.

"Good idea. The screens are probably locked, but maybe I can make an emergency call."

I couldn't believe what a mess this day had turned into. I'd escaped from jail this morning, narrowly rescued Jessi from Jeremy Rigsby, and now we were trying to save Owen and maybe a lot more people before a bomb blew up Refuge Mountain. Meanwhile, I was supposed to be on my way to Steamboat Springs for that catering gig. I'd have to sort that out later.

Hartley, Colorado was like quicksand. Ever since I'd driven inside its borders, I hadn't been able to escape. Not really. But the truth was, I didn't want to. So long as Jessi Novo called Hartley home, then I would give in to the pull.

We would save Hartley. Together. No way in hell would I let Jessi down.

After a few minutes of fiddling with the phones, Jessi shook her head. "Nothing's going through, but I'll keep trying. We're in the canyon now. Even my phone, if Jeremy hadn't stomped on it, wouldn't have service here."

I was pushing the engine as fast as I could go without risking an accident, but it still felt like we were crawling.

Jessi kept trying. Finally, when we were nearing Hartley, she cried, "It's working!" She had it on speaker, so I heard it ringing.

A voice answered, "Hartley Sheriff's Department."

"Scarlett?" Jessi asked.

"Jessi? Is that you?"

"Why are you answering the sheriff's department line?

Never mind." Jessi shook her head. "Explain that later. Scar, we ran into Jeremy Rigsby. Long story, but he admitted there's a bomb hidden somewhere in Hartley. Probably Refuge Mountain."

"*What?*" Scarlett screeched. "But—Chester said he wanted to cooperate in exchange for immunity. He said there's evidence on Refuge Mountain, and that's where Owen is going right now, along with his deputies and the state investigators who just arrived. They left fifteen, maybe twenty minutes ago."

"Chester set a trap." I pressed the gas hard, and my truck lurched forward even faster. "This was their contingency plan." And with Chester in jail after trying to kill me, it was all the more believable that he'd offer up info in exchange for a deal.

"Oh no, Jessi, Trace is with them, too! Owen deputized him. That's why I'm here at the station working the phones. Everything's a mess around here, and—"

"*Listen*," Jessi said. "You have to get Owen on the radio. Warn him."

"Okay. I'm working on it." There was a pause, followed by murmurs as Scarlett spoke, trying to get Owen to come in. We heard her gasp. "The radio's not connecting. But it should be. It's like it's broken."

"*Shit*," I muttered. "Scarlett, get out of there."

There was rustling. Other voices. The sound of Scarlett's heavy breathing.

Jessi glanced over at me, fear making her eyes shine. "Scar?" she asked quietly into the phone. "What's happening?"

In the windows, the canyon walls flew past. Another mile closer to Hartley.

"I just saw Dale Rigsby," Scarlett whispered. "He's here at the sheriff's department. I'm hiding in Owen's office. Dale must have gotten help from one of Owen's officers. They're looking around. I think they're looking for *me*."

So Sheriff Douglas had more traitors in his department than he'd even realized.

"They might be taking over the sheriff's office," I said. "Getting Chester out of jail and who knows what else. Get out of there, Scarlett."

"Okay. I—I can climb out of Owen's window."

Jessi sat forward, cradling the phone close to her mouth. "You have to take your Jeep to Refuge Mountain. You hear me? You have to catch up to Owen."

Scarlett was breathing heavily. "I'll do it. I promise."

"If you beat us there," Jessi added, "just go after Owen. Warn him and the others." Her voice wavered, and I knew she was thinking of her brother. "But Aiden and I aren't far. We'll try to meet you there."

"All right. I've gotta go now."

"Be safe, Scar." Jessi ended the call. "Please hurry, Aiden."

"I'll get there as fast as I can."

But we both knew it might be too late.

"This exit." Jessi pointed. "It'll get us to the national forest roads faster." She chewed her lip as we took the curves a bit too fast. I wanted to reach for her hand, but I needed both of mine on the wheel. At least the roads were completely dry and clear of snow.

Finally, we pulled up to the turnoff leading onto the unpaved forest access roads. And Scarlett's Jeep sped toward us from the other direction, her dark-red hair blowing wildly in the open windows.

Jessi was out first. I followed her quickly. Scarlett braked to a stop for us to get into the Jeep. Then she raced onto the turnoff and took the unpaved access road toward Refuge Mountain.

With a vehicle like this, I had to assume that Scarlett was

the outdoorsy type. "Do you have binoculars?" I asked from the backseat. Jessi was in the front, riding shotgun.

"Glove box."

Jessi got the binoculars out and handed them to me. I couldn't see anything yet. We were still hemmed in by trees. The Jeep bumped along the unpaved path. But much of the snow had now melted, leaving two wide tracks for Scarlett's wheels to follow.

"What about flares?" I said.

"I've got an emergency kit on the floor back there." Scarlett jabbed a thumb in my direction.

I felt around and located the box.

Mitch's rifle was also tucked partway below the seat. Earlier, Scarlett had been carrying it after she and Jessi had created their diversion and Trace had broken me out of jail.

I got the flares out of the kit, then made sure the rifle was loaded. The Jeep continued to bounce along the road.

We came to the padlocked gate that Owen and I had seen a few days ago. It was wide open, which made sense, since law enforcement was heading up the mountain.

"*Hurry*," Jessi said. "Please."

We followed a curve in the road, and the trees opened up, along with a panorama of Refuge Mountain. The road narrowed up ahead into a smaller trail that snaked back and forth along the side of the mountain.

About halfway up, colorful shapes moved. Owen and his group. They were on ATVs.

"That's them!" Scarlett shouted. "Oh sweet Lord, there's no way we'll catch up before they reach the top."

Jessi put a hand on her friend's shoulder. "Then stop the Jeep. Quick. Before we lose our line of sight." Jessi turned back and looked at me. It was like our brains had melded. I knew exactly what she was thinking, and it was the same idea that had occurred to me.

I handed Jessi the emergency flares. "Scarlett, once we stop, watch Owen's party with the binoculars," I said. "Let us know if we get their attention."

"Got it."

The moment Scarlett stopped the Jeep, Jessi and I leaped out. Jessi aimed the first flare into the sky. Fired. It made an arc of smoke high in the air. But I couldn't tell if Owen's group had spotted it.

"They're still moving," Scarlett shouted from the driver's seat, binos up to her face.

That bomb could be anywhere on the mountain. We had to make them stop in their tracks.

With the rifle slung across my body, I clamored up onto the hood of the Jeep to gain elevation. I hadn't shot a gun like this in years. It wasn't my thing. Give me a sharp knife any day. But I didn't have to hit some impossible target. For this, a simple pull of the trigger was all I needed.

I lifted the rifle and flicked off the safety. Braced it. Fired. The crack echoed against the mountainside, the sound traveling for miles.

Scarlett waved a hand through her open window. "They stopped! They're scrambling around like they're freaking out, but they stopped."

"Jessi, another flare."

She fired off her second, and that time, Owen's group definitely saw it. And they saw *us*. Scarlett got out, and she and Jessi both jumped up and down. A few minutes later, an ATV made its way down to us. Trace was riding it, with Deputy Marsh behind him on the seat.

Jessi ran toward her brother. Hugged him and told the deputy in rapid-fire sentences about the Rigsbys' trap. Marsh radioed to Owen. While their connection to the station had been cut off, their short-range comms were intact.

Then Jessi raised her head, looking around until her eyes

locked on mine. I went over to her as I opened my arms. Jessi sank into my embrace, and I held her tight against me. I felt her heart racing.

"Thank you," she murmured. "I'm so thankful you were there. For *everything*. Aiden, I...I'm so thankful for you."

"Me too, baby," I said against her hair. "But we did it together. You and me."

She lifted her gaze and nodded. I knew we were thinking the same thing.

You and me.

It was the two of us now. Fused by fire into a single unit. We were never letting each other go.

I had to call my family and the wedding planner in Steamboat Springs with the unfortunate news: I would be late. I wasn't even sure I'd make it. And I felt like shit about it. Missing an important work gig was a jackass move, and while I had my moments, that wasn't the kind of guy I liked to be. My sous chef and our assistants would be scrambling as they tried to make up for my absence. But it couldn't be helped.

For the moment, Jessi and I both had some witness stuff to deal with. But even if I could've found a way to sort out the paperwork stuff on the road, I knew that Jessi wasn't ready to leave Trace and her friends just yet. And if Jessi was sticking around in Hartley, that meant *I* was staying.

Nonnegotiable.

After we told Owen that Dale Rigsby was trying to take over the sheriff's station, he and the state police rolled in heavy. But Dale, Chester, and the remaining officer who'd helped them had already disappeared. Owen issued a warrant for their arrest, and hopefully highway patrol would pick them up soon. Meanwhile, a bomb-defusing team would arrive in Hartley any minute to handle the explosives on Refuge Mountain. State forensics teams would examine everything left behind and piece it together.

Highway patrol had also been called to arrest Jeremy Rigsby for his assault on Jessi. The other two guys I'd left unconscious might've proved a slight headache for me. But I wasn't worried. It was self defense. Or at least, close enough.

We still didn't know exactly what those Hart-Made trucks were carrying, or even how far they'd gotten across state lines. We would have to wait until the state police searched the truck where Jeremy was currently tied up and awaiting rescue. And if that search didn't prove enlightening, the state investigators would find evidence on Refuge Mountain to prove what the Rigsbys had been making.

Answers hadn't arrived yet. But we'd get them soon. That was guaranteed.

One of the biggest remaining mysteries was Sawyer Rigsby himself. I'd expected him to run with the rest of his family. But instead, he'd called for a town hall meeting.

And that was where I headed now.

What explanation could Sawyer possibly have after everything that had happened? Better yet—how did he intend to weasel his way out of responsibility?

Owen and I pulled up in front of the Hartley High gymnasium, where the meeting was being held. Jessi was already inside with Scarlett and Trace. I didn't like separating from her even for a few minutes, but Trace was watching over her. And Owen and I had an important task to manage.

We were in Owen's official sheriff's department truck. The sun shone brightly from a clear blue sky. Dirty snow was still piled up here and there on the street, but the sidewalks were dry. I had my windows open, and we could hear voices booming from the gym.

Owen radioed the police cruiser that had just pulled up behind us. "Deputy Marsh, are you ready?"

"All set, sir."

"Stand by for my signal." Owen lowered the radio and heaved a sigh. "This has been a real shit show. I'll be cleaning up this mess for a long time to come. I don't even know half the things you and Jessi and her brother really did, and I don't want to."

I chuckled quietly. "I'm more than happy to keep those details to myself unless absolutely necessary. We should head inside before the show is over."

"Hold on." Owen bumped my shoulder with the back of his hand. "Thank you, Aiden. You and Jessi saved my life and that of a lot of other people. I know I was skeptical of you at first—"

I snorted.

"*But* I was wrong. You're a good man. And from what I've seen so far, you're good for Jessi. I'll be sorry to see you leave Hartley."

"Oh, did nobody tell you?" Actually, it wasn't surprising given the madness of the last half day. "I've decided to stick around Hartley. You'll be seeing plenty of me."

His eyes bugged. "*What?* But your job and your life are back in California, aren't they? What will you do here?"

Aside from spending every minute I can with Jessi? "I haven't figured that out yet. Get on your nerves, I'm sure."

"Could you not? I need some new deputies. You know more than the average person already about law enforcement. You've proven you can stay cool under pressure. I'd much rather have you working for me than being a thorn in my side."

"No way. I'm no cop. That's a job I *definitely* don't want."

His expression turned cautious. "Please tell me you'll stay out of trouble from now on. You and Jessi both."

"You know I can't speak for her. Jessi finds trouble even more often than I do." And when she did, I would stand by her.

Owen groaned. "I guess that's heartburn for another day. Let's get this done."

On our way, I grabbed the cardboard box from the truck's cargo. Then we strode into the gym. Sawyer Rigsby was holding court, the mayor standing timidly by his side. Hartley residents filled the bleachers. I spotted Jessi and her brother up front. She winked at me. I lifted my chin in acknowledgement. Pride filled me at the knowledge that she was mine. Hopefully, mine for a very long time.

"I know you all have questions," Sawyer was saying, "and I will answer every one to the best of my ability. But I assure you that I had *no knowledge* of anything that my brother Dale or his sons were doing. I'm as innocent in all this as you are, and I'm horrified that my family could've done the things the police are saying. *If* they're true."

Fifty different people spoke at once. Then Jessi jumped up to standing and shouted over the hum of voices. "Mr. Rigsby, what about all the Hart-Made Candy delivery trucks that left your warehouse overnight? What were they carrying?"

Sawyer blinked and recovered quickly. "Those were our regular product shipments."

I stepped forward, carrying the cardboard box, while Owen hung back near the gym doors. My shoes squeaked on the wood. "Like this?" I asked. I set the box on the floor in front of Sawyer, within view of everyone there. The box was stamped with the Hart-Made Candy Co. logo on the side. "If it's all so innocent, then go ahead. Show us what's inside."

Everyone in the gym had gone quiet. Watching and waiting.

Sawyer's eyes widened. "How do I know you haven't tampered with this?"

"Isn't that your factory seal?" I pointed at the logo-printed tape. I hadn't opened this box, and neither had Owen. But I was virtually certain now what was inside. "This came directly from one of your delivery trucks just this morning."

A muscle in Sawyer's jaw pulsed. "Fine. I don't see the point of this display, but if this is what it takes to clear my name." Pressing his lips together in defiance, Sawyer bent forward. He pulled his keys from his pocket and used one to cut a jagged line in the tape. He pulled apart the cardboard flaps, revealing a neat layer of red-and-white rectangles. Hart-Made's brown sugar brittle, their signature product.

"See?" Sawyer asked, flourishing his hand.

"Open one."

He took out one shallow box and lifted the lid. The inner tray was wrapped in plastic, but Sawyer sliced the protective cover and selected a piece of golden-brown candy, popping it into his mouth. "Delicious. Are you satisfied?"

Everyone else in the gym watched us. There were a few whispers. Owen stepped forward, frowning uncertainly.

I dug deeper into the stack of candy boxes, pulling out one from the middle. I handed it to Sawyer. Immediately, the odd smell we had noticed in the Hart-Made truck this morning was more pronounced.

And now that I'd realized what it was, I couldn't believe I hadn't placed it before.

"Try a piece of this one," I said.

Sawyer's face was turning all sorts of colors. "What is the point of this?"

"That's a good question," someone else from the crowd called out.

Jessi turned around to face her fellow Hartley residents. "If you're hiding contraband, it makes sense to put it underneath your legitimate products." She faced Sawyer again, crossing her arms. "If you have nothing to hide, then prove it. Try this candy, too."

Sawyer made no move to open the new box of candy. So I took it from his hands and did it for him, breaking the plastic seal. Now the smell was even stronger. I held out the tray to him. It was full of golden-brown shards, similar to the brown sugar brittle. But a slightly different color.

And that smell was *definitely* not sweet.

Sawyer stared. His lips trembled.

"It's called shatter," I announced to the people gathered in the gym.

I'd figured it out a couple of hours ago. Yesterday, when we had been on the phone with my brother Jake, he had explained the different kinds of marijuana concentrates that were easiest to transport. Shatter was formed in thin sheets and was a golden-brown color. I couldn't believe I hadn't made the connection before. *That* had been the smell in the truck. It had been faint because the illicit packages were wrapped in plastic and surrounded with actual candy, which helped to obscure the scent.

"It's a highly concentrated form of cannabis," I went on. "It's produced using flammable solvents, and manufacturers employ liquid nitrogen to keep the volatile mixtures under control. But those methods aren't foolproof, as Dale and his crew found out on Refuge Mountain. That's where they've been cooking up this stuff underground in the caves. Jessi and I felt an explosion there a few days ago from a cave-in, probably after some of those solvents ignited. You grew the marijuana plants on the national forest land over the summer, right? Relying on the fact that it was rarely patrolled. All of which makes this one hundred percent illegal, especially if you're shipping out of state. Which I'm sure you are."

The murmurs in the room increased. Shocked glances and angry faces.

For a long moment, Sawyer just stared at the golden-brown shards. Then he pushed the candy box away. "I'm as shocked as you are. I had nothing to do with any of this. Even if there happened to be illegal substances on my delivery trucks, you have no evidence that I was involved with it."

Now, Owen came forward. "Actually, we do, Uncle Sawyer." He nodded, and Deputy Marsh entered the room, along with Theo Rigsby. Dale's youngest son. Chester and Mitch's younger brother. He had helped them harass Jessi, but it had turned out he was the weak link in their operation. He hadn't known about his family's plan to blow up Refuge Mountain, and for him, that had been a step too far. He'd agreed to confess everything he knew. Including his uncle Sawyer's involvement in every aspect of the scheme.

"Theo is going to testify that you were in charge of the whole thing," Owen said.

Sawyer scoffed. "That's ridiculous."

Then he suddenly broke for the exit.

I grabbed hold of his coat, while three state police officers descended on him. They wrenched his hands behind his back and slapped cuffs on his wrists.

"You're under arrest, Sawyer," Owen said. "For conspiracy. Distribution of illegal substances. Attempted murder for the plot to blow up a bomb on federal land. And who knows what else. I'm going to let the state and federal prosecutors figure that part out."

The state police led Sawyer away, reading him his rights.

Owen went forward, holding out his hands to calm the crowd, while the mayor stood sheepishly by his side. While Owen and the mayor answered questions and tried to calm everyone down, Jessi rushed over to me.

"Hey, sweetness," I said.

I hugged her, spinning her around before we made our way outside. At the curb, Sawyer was trying to argue with the police officers, who were pushing him into a cruiser. But we turned our backs on him. He had received enough of our attention.

Jessi put her hands on my face and pulled me down to kiss her. "What do you say? Should we try to make it to Steamboat and get things back on track for the wedding tomorrow?"

"You want to?" I asked.

I was sure the whole investigation and prosecution of Sawyer and the other Rigsbys would take a while. They had a ton of evidence to gather and witnesses to interview. I was going to do my best to stay out of it as much as possible. Well, except for Jeremy. I couldn't wait to testify against his ass. He would be heading back to prison, hopefully for much longer than two years.

The stab wound to his thigh? Once again, self defense on my part. *Clearly*. Jessi would back me up on that.

It was still possible to make it to Steamboat before the wedding. But Jessi had been through a lot today. If she didn't feel up to travel, I would understand.

She frowned at me disapprovingly. "We can't disappoint the bride and groom."

Scarlett and Trace had just stepped through the gym doors onto the sidewalk, and they'd overheard. "You should go," Scarlett said. "Don't let the Rigsbys screw up your plans. We can help Owen with everything here. Not that he needs us, considering that Hartley is swarming with state police. And probably the DEA will show up soon enough, from the sound of things."

I nodded at Trace. "Are you going to dive back into the fray? Owen deputized you. He's hiring more permanently, too. You've got an inside track."

"Hell, no. I'm done playing deputy. I don't have a clue what I'm doing with my life, currently. But joining Owen's department isn't going to be it."

"Then that makes two of us." I turned to Jessi. The stunningly brave woman that I got to call mine. "I'm up for getting on the road again. If you're with me. I'm not going anywhere without you."

She laced our fingers together and gazed up at me. "Then we'd better go. I don't know about you, but I have a lot of cooking to do when I get there. I hear the head chef for the wedding didn't even show up, and that's just not right."

"You're going to swoop in as their hero, huh?" I asked.

"It's the kind of thing I do."

My face hurt from how much I was smiling at her.

CHAPTER THIRTY-ONE
Aiden

WE WERE LATE. *Really* late.

By the time we reached the resort in Steamboat, it was almost midnight.

We went straight to the resort's ballroom kitchen, which was closed by then. But I found the notes my sous chef had made, along with the trays of prep work and the ingredients that still needed to be dealt with. I examined it all with a critical eye. My people had done a decent job following the instructions that I'd given them. But they were behind, and I was more of a stickler about certain things than my sous chef.

"What do you think?" Jessi asked.

I set down my knife roll on a prep table. I'd gotten it from my duffel on our way in. "The prep isn't where I wanted it to be tonight. But with you helping me, we can get there."

She smiled, her cheeks turning pink like I had just said something mushy and romantic. She kissed me.

And we got to work.

Jessi crashed in my hotel room with me. There was no hanky-panky, just a few hours of sleep, which was nowhere near enough even added to the nap we had taken at the sheriff's station in between interviews.

In the morning, we were back in the kitchen. I introduced Jessi to my team. "Meet my girlfriend, Jessi Novo," I said, to shocked silence. Dropped jaws. "I've had girlfriends before. It's not *that* interesting." But I'd never brought one into my kitchen.

Finally I glared, and everyone returned to their prep. Jessi smirked, covering a laugh, but her eyes twinkled with pleasure. I hadn't exactly cleared the girlfriend designation with her beforehand. But I'd wanted to claim her. And she seemed okay with it. After that, I was surprised how little awkwardness there was between Jessi and the rest of my team. She folded into the line like she'd been there for ages.

We were actually going to get this done.

Around lunch, we took a break. And that was when my brother Jake strolled in with my sister Madison trailing him. "Well, well," Jake said, pulling Jessi into a hug. "The rumors are true. Aiden brought his new girlfriend with him. I figured that had to be you. It's great to meet you in person."

"Wait," Jessi said, "Aiden, you didn't tell your family I was coming?"

"There was a lot going on yesterday," I protested. "Jake knows that already. He talked to Owen about the DEA sending agents to Hartley."

Madison tilted her head sardonically at me, folding her arms. "Could you introduce us properly? Also, we need photos to mark this occasion."

"What occasion?" Jessi asked.

"Aiden has *never*, not *once*, brought a woman to meet us before."

"I'm the first?" Jessi smiled at me.

"Probably the last, too," I whispered. Of course, my sister heard. Madison gasped.

"You two are *cute*." My sister opened her arms. "Jake got a hug, so that means I need one. And I want to hear every detail about Hartley and the whole conspiracy you guys uncovered. And I have to know everything sweet and romantic that Aiden has done, so I can make fun of him for pretending to be such a hardass all these years."

Here we go, I thought.

I really hoped Jessi could handle my family, because they could get animated. I didn't want to scare her off already.

"He's a hardass all right," Jessi said with a smirk. "But I wouldn't change a thing."

Okay, she can handle it.

Within a few minutes, Madison whisked Jessi away to try on dresses with our younger sister Regan. "Oh yeah, I'm going to take Jessi to meet Mom and Dad and everyone else too," Madison said over her shoulder. "Bye!"

I groaned.

"You're surprised by any of this?" Jake asked.

I was still on break, and we were hanging out in a quiet hallway outside the kitchen. I rested my weight against a table. "Not in the least. This is why I haven't brought anyone to meet you idiots before." Mom and Dad would have endless prying questions. Regan and Beau, my twin younger siblings, would cause drama. Madison would probably get Jessi out of there quick enough, but knowing her, she'd have my girl drunk and doing something crazy in the hotel bar within an hour. At least Madison's husband Nash and Jake's wife Harper were sensible. And all the kids, my nieces and nephew, were back in West Oaks, staying with other family.

But Harper had a wild side like Madison. With Jessi in the mix, there was no telling what those three women would get up to once they'd joined forces.

"Then Jessi must really be special," Jake said.

"She's...everything."

Jake's eyebrows lifted. He and I didn't look much alike, especially given that smile Jake usually wore, but otherwise our facial expressions were spot on.

"I tried to drive away from her, and I couldn't. I've rarely needed anyone but myself in my life—"

"No kidding," Jake interrupted.

"But I need her. I'm falling for her. I'm going to try to make this work. " I crossed my arms. "Lay it on me. Tell me I'm stupid, falling for a woman I've known less than a week."

Jake stuck his hands in his pockets and leaned against the wall next to me. "I can't do that. I fell for Harper just as quickly when we met in high school. Took us a very long time to figure things out. But when you've found your perfect match, your heart has a way of telling you. And you'd be a fool to let that go."

"Thanks." My older brother and I had never been very close, but I had the feeling that was changing. I was glad for his approval. And his advice, even if I'd never welcomed it before.

"When are you bringing her back to West Oaks?" Jake asked. "If you need help getting her settled, you know we'll all be there for you."

"Uh, no. I'm moving back to Hartley with Jessi. Permanently." The idea was still solidifying in my head, but I had no doubts that I wanted this. I'd have to get my stuff moved out of the house I shared with my roommates. Pack up thirty years' worth of life in California. It was worth it, but it was still going to be a headache. Hopefully Jessi would come with me. I wanted to show her around West Oaks. Romance her on the beach.

Jake's expression froze. He blinked at me. "Mom is going to flip out."

I pressed my hands to my eyes. "I know. I can start putting out feelers about an executive chef to replace me. I'll run the interviews over Zoom if I have to. I won't leave Mom in the lurch."

Jake grabbed my shoulder. "Are you kidding? I'm not talking about the company. Mom is going to demand *details*. Like Jessi's life story and proposed wedding dates for the two of you."

Oh, jeez. He was right. "Jessi needs to take things slow on that front."

"News flash, but moving to another state to be with her? Introducing her to this circus? Not moving all that slow." Jake laughed at my expression. "I'm happy for you, man. Amazed that you found a woman who could stand you, but really, really happy."

"Yeah. Me too." I chuckled. "On both counts."

―――――

I had to head back to the kitchen. The wedding dinner was in just a few hours. And now that we were all caught up and running like the well-oiled machine that I usually expected in my kitchen, I didn't need Jessi as an extra set of hands.

I hoped she was enjoying herself and that my family was taking it easy on her.

As soon as the last entrée was out of the kitchen, I wrapped things up with my team. The servers still had to do cake, coffee, and dessert, but that wasn't my domain. I was off the clock. I hurried to take a shower and change my clothes.

The moment I stepped into the ballroom where they were holding the reception, I saw my beautiful girl. Her dark hair fell around her shoulders, and her eyes were accentuated with liner. She was wearing a long, shimmery black dress that hugged her curves. She looked absolutely incredible. I was stunned all over again.

Jessi's eyes landed on me, and she looked even more gorgeous as she smiled.

But before I could reach her, my parents accosted me. I gave them each a hug, and my mom scrutinized me like she always did. Her gray-blond hair was styled up in a twist, and her dress blinded me with glittery sequins. "Aiden. We need to talk."

"Yes, Mom. We will. I have a lot to share." I'd already planned to spend all day tomorrow with my family. I would break the news about my move to Colorado. Jessi could either join me or hide in the hotel room. I preferred the first, but I was fine with either. "Sorry I was late," I added. But my mother's frown told me I wasn't forgiven for that yet. I probably owed her a few more details. Maybe omitting the fact that I'd gotten arrested.

"Jessi's lovely," my dad said. He was the peacemaker of the family.

"I know."

Mom sighed. "That's all you're going to say? Impossible as ever, aren't you?"

Dad leaned into her and said, "We should let him off the hook. Just for tonight."

"I guess I can be merciful. We'll talk, second son of mine. *Tomorrow*."

"Yes, boss," I said.

She swatted my arm. "Such a little shit."

"Guilty as charged," I said, hiding a smile. Just like she was. Then I relented, swooping in to kiss my mom on the cheek. "You look very pretty tonight, by the way."

"Shush." She shook her head at me. "Go on, then."

I dodged more family members and acquaintances on my way across the room. My sisters and Harper were smirking at me, probably about to launch into something sarcastic, so I grabbed Jessi's hand and steered her straight onto the dancefloor.

I pulled her against me. *Finally.* "I missed having my arms around you."

Jessi beamed at me. "I've been having a *great* time."

I grumbled. "What did they say about me?"

She rested her head on my shoulder, laughing softly. She didn't answer my question. "They're all so Californian. Blond and tan. Like they're from a magazine. You're the only one who looks like your dad."

I turned, and every other Shelborne had their eyes on us. "I hear that a lot."

"The wedding was gorgeous, and dinner was amazing," Jessi gushed. "Somebody canceled at the last minute, so there was a spot for me. It's been kinda magical, actually. Right now most of all."

I shrugged. "Of course dinner was amazing."

She snorted. "Out of all I just said, that's what you're focused on? Your food?"

"What else do you expect?"

"I did have some thoughts on your béchamel, though."

My brow wrinkled. "That sauce was on point."

"Yes, but it could've been better."

"Oh *really*." I tugged her closer, glowering.

"If you're trying to distract me by being ruggedly sexy, it's working."

I bent down to kiss her neck. "Actually, I'm the one who's been distracted. I was worried my family would make you have second thoughts about me."

"Not at all. They've been wonderful."

"So they didn't tell a million stories about me as a kid?"

"Oh, they did. Jake and Madison had the most. You sounded pretty awful."

I narrowed my eyes. "Good thing I'm moving to Colorado. I'm going to disown all of them."

Jessi laughed, snuggling into me. "They love you, Aiden. It's obvious. I don't want to take you away from them."

"But I want to go. I told Jake how I feel about you, and he gets it. The rest of them will too."

I would be starting over. So much was uncertain right now. But somehow, I was sure about what Jessi and I could have together. If we worked for it. Now that I'd had a glimpse, I wanted that future with every fiber of my being. I was going to take hold of the possibilities we were building in both my hands, and I was going to hold on tight.

Her eyes flicked up to mine, and they reflected the fairy lights that the wedding planner had strung all over the venue. Shining like stars. "I can't believe this is my life," she whispered. "Things like this aren't supposed to happen to girls like me."

"Things like what?"

"The perfect man showing up in town and sweeping me off my feet."

"I'm hardly perfect."

"Perfect for me."

I kissed her nose. "Then that's what I'll aim to be."

CHAPTER THIRTY-TWO
Jessi

OVER THE NEXT weeks and months, I often felt like I was swept up in a whirlwind romance. Something worthy of poems and heartfelt country songs. But other times, my story with Aiden felt like the slowest of slow-burns.

I loved every minute of it.

What I *didn't* love was the everyday logistical stuff that followed in the aftermath of Sawyer and Dale Rigsby's downfall. All the legal and administrative mess. Mostly, that wasn't my problem. It was Owen's. And the teams of state police and federal agents who occupied Hartley for a while. But they brought business to the diner and to Scarlett's sweet shop, so that was a benefit.

As soon as Aiden and I got back from Steamboat Springs, we reopened the diner and got back to it. We worked together on planning menus. We fell into a natural division of labor. He handled the cooking, while I worked the front of the house and made all the desserts, which quickly grew a reputation. And as the media attention caused by the scandal brought in more tourism, online reviewers raved about my tarts and Aiden's upscale diner cuisine.

To fund their legal defense, Sawyer and Dale sold nearly

all of their holdings in the county at bargain prices, including the building that housed my diner. Somehow, I scraped together the funds for a down-payment, with some help from my Hartley friends. It was the same with the sweet shop, which Scarlett bought with some local business partners, including Marco. She got rid of the Hart-Made branding, and she stopped making brown sugar brittle. But aside from those changes, the sweet shop was just as charming as ever. She sold some of my tarts, and I had a display of her signature sweets on my counter at the diner.

Eventually, the investigators wrapped up their work, and the government finished its cleanup efforts on the national forest side of Refuge Mountain. The Rigsbys faced multiple state and federal charges, and were awaiting trial in a federal detention center without bond.

Hartley settled into a more normal pace.

We were still rebuilding after everything that had happened, but the increase in tourism was making a difference. There was a fresh sense of optimism around town as well. New businesses opening up. Transplants moving to town after seeing the scenic photos of our little corner of Colorado online.

Every day with Aiden was new to me, too. An adventure.

But I couldn't help it. My dreams grew bigger. Even bigger than myself. I wanted to give back somehow, to share my happiness and newfound prosperity with others who needed help.

I just didn't know yet how to make that happen.

Aiden took me to California for a long weekend. It was my first time out of state. The first time I'd ever seen the ocean and felt the surf lapping at my bare feet on the shore. It was incredible, but it also solidified my conviction that I was a mountain girl. I visited with Aiden's family, met Aiden's friends, and helped him pack up his things to ship to

Colorado. I loved getting to see those parts of his life. Finding out more about this man I'd fallen for so quickly, yet was still discovering.

Though we'd spent nearly every single day together since we'd first met, we chose to live separately. Aiden rented a room above the saloon, while my brother slept on the floor in my studio.

And every Sunday night, we closed the diner, and Aiden took me out on a date.

Now that Aiden and I were really trying to make this work, I was all the more determined to take things slow. Aiden seemed to feel the exact same way. He took me out to restaurants in nearby towns. Took me dancing. He invited me over to his place and made me dinner, kissing me breathless over dessert. But I always left to go back to my own apartment, never spending the night.

After months of dating and little more than sultry goodnight kisses, I started to get impatient. By then, it was Aiden who was adamant about taking our time. As if he wanted to prove how committed he was to his life in Hartley, his life with *me*, before we took that next step. So that when we got intimate again, we would both be absolutely sure.

It took a full three months after we'd come back to Hartley after the Steamboat Springs wedding. And I was *dying*.

That Sunday night, Aiden made French food for dinner. Beef bourguignon, potatoes roasted in duck fat, jewel-toned Burgundy wine. He kept our fingers entwined during dinner, his eyes burning into me, and my heart was going so crazy that I could barely manage to eat even though it was all delicious.

And finally, he kissed my knuckles in that way that made all my nerve endings go haywire. "I love you, Jessi. I am very much in love with you."

It was the first time he'd said it. Everything inside me was spinning around in ecstatic, dizzying circles. It was all the emotions and all the words I'd been holding in, because I had known that I loved him for a while now.

"I love you, too. With my whole heart."

He pressed a kiss to the inside of my wrist. "Can I make love to you?"

I launched myself at him, jumping into his lap right there at the table.

Our kiss didn't break as he carried me into his bedroom. A few seams got ripped and buttons popped as we tore at each other's clothes. That first time after our long hiatus was a little desperate. Tongues battling and hands groping, trying to get our bodies as close as possible. We were finally naked together again after so much waiting, skin to hot skin. His erection nudged insistently against my stomach as we made out, and his thumbs caressed the curves of my breasts before his hand dipped between my legs. His fingers circled my core, finding the wetness there that was just for him.

"No condom," I managed to say. "I don't need it."

His eyes flashed, and a growl rumbled out of his chest.

I dug my fingers into his hair as his bare cock pushed inside of me. My legs wrapped around him. Aiden made love to me with all the passion we'd been keeping in reserve. Wild, vigorous strokes. Nothing held back. He pressed my hands over my head against the mattress and stared down at me with intense, fiery need, just the way I liked. I was pinned in place, delirious. Completely at his mercy.

Aiden's fingers sought out my clit and massaged it right above where we were joined. But it was the look of ecstasy on his masculine face and the tight clench of his muscles, the knowledge that my body was giving him that much pleasure, that sent me right over the edge. We came at the same moment. Together. Sharing kisses and gasping each other's breath.

Then Aiden settled on top of me, warm and solid. My shield against anything that might hurt me. I had never felt so satisfied or safe. Our need for each other was sated, at least for the moment, and we cuddled and talked about what would happen next.

And I still had those dreams swirling around in my head. *Should I tell him?* I wondered. *No. Not yet.*

"Do you want to move in with me here?" he asked, twirling a lock of my hair around his finger.

I smoothed my hand over the dark hair on his chest. "What if we do some renovations on the apartment over the diner?" That wasn't my big dream, but I had been thinking of it a lot. Planning out where some new walls could go. A small kitchenette. The apartment was a studio, but it had enough space to be more, if we planned it right. Sawyer Rigsby hadn't bothered to invest in fixing it up. But now, the building was mine. I wanted to make it into a home for us.

He smiled softly. My heart still skipped whenever he did that. Aiden's smiles were rare, but so expressive. "I like that idea. But what about your brother?"

"I don't know what to do about Trace. I think he's ready to move out, though." Trace was still technically living with me, though he often disappeared. Now that it was summer, he'd been camping in the woods off and on, sometimes for days at a time. He wanted space of his own, and he also wanted freedom. What my brother *needed*, I had no clue. "I've tried talking to him, but you know how he is. He still won't tell me what happened to him before he abandoned his old life and came to Hartley."

"I doubt he ever will."

I huffed, not liking that answer.

"Trace will figure it out," Aiden said. "If he wants to take over this apartment for a while, he can. I can keep covering the lease."

"I'll talk to him." I inched up higher to kiss Aiden on the lips. "You're very sweet."

"That's not true. I'm far more salty than sweet."

I laughed and shook my head. "Trust me, I know desserts. And you're my favorite one."

"You're my favorite everything." He rolled us both over, kissing me in earnest.

We spent the rest of that night making love, drawing out each moment like we could create our own world, just us, and make it last forever. It was the best dream I'd ever had, and even when dawn light turned Aiden's bedroom hazy at the edges, I was still wide awake.

―――

In June, just over five months after we'd first met, we set out on a hike to Refuge Mountain.

It was sunny, with a morning chill in the air. It wouldn't get above sixty-five degrees today, which I considered perfect. By the time we hiked up to the old ruined cabin, I'd stripped off my top layer and tied it around my waist. Aiden looked ridiculously sexy in hiking shorts and a skintight T-shirt, all his muscles on display. He had an Anaheim Angels baseball cap that he liked to wear, which was the only signal to most people that he was from Southern California. Except the ocean tattoo. That tended to be a giveaway.

We stopped at the cabin to take a water break. A panoramic view of the valley lay before us. Green trees and red canyon walls. Distant purple mountains like something out of a painting. Wildflowers grew in abundance all around the clearing that surrounded the cabin.

Aiden picked a columbine and tucked it behind my ear. "I have a surprise," he said.

"Is that why you were so determined to go on a hike today?" Not like I'd been hard to convince, given the ideal weather.

"Yep, I've got an ulterior motive. I want to ask you a question."

My breath caught. The last couple months of living together and renovating the studio had been everything I could've wanted. I was so in love that it shocked me sometimes. But if he was going to ask a certain big question, I didn't think I was ready.

One of his thick eyebrows lifted slightly. "Don't worry. It's not that. I wanted to ask if you still think about building a business here on Refuge Mountain. Like you told me about before."

"*Oh*." I hadn't mentioned that idea in months. We'd had enough to deal with. Not just helping Hartley recover from the Rigsbys' schemes, but starting our life together. Getting Aiden settled. Plus dealing with my brother, who continued to be an enigma to me. I was so happy that it seemed greedy to want even more.

But I did want it. "I still think about it. Yeah." A restaurant, a cozy hotel. Not as fancy as a resort, but special… And over the months, that dream had morphed and grown into something even more far-fetched, and I hadn't shared that with a single soul. Not even Aiden.

It was my big dream. My *big idea*.

Maybe this was the moment to finally share it.

Aiden glanced around the clearing full of wildflowers and then at the valley lying below. "I've been thinking about it too. A lot. What would you say to going into business with me? I put out some feelers about buying the land. A friend of mine in California who's a lawyer put me in touch with a real estate guy. It turns out, the owner of this side of the mountain is willing to sell. They're asking a fair price."

I was beyond shocked. I didn't know what to say. "Are you kidding?" I pushed my hair off my forehead. "I would want that. Absolutely. But I don't have any money." Especially after buying the diner and taking out loans to make it happen. And the amount of land we were talking about, even at a fair price, would cost a *lot* of money. More than I might ever see in my lifetime.

A mischievous smirk curved Aiden's lips. "I do. I had a stake in my family's catering company, and they agreed to buy me out. But they also want to invest. I told them about your ideas for this place, and they love it. They want in on the ground floor. But keep in mind, that's also the downside to this proposal. The whole Shelborne clan would have a stake in whatever we build here. Trust me, my mom drives a hard bargain. So does Madison. She's a hostage negotiator, remember? She can be brutal."

"But," I sputtered. I was still trying to get my head around all of this. "You're saying we would have enough? Your family… They actually want to invest in building a hotel and a restaurant? At the site of the ranch here on Refuge Mountain?"

"If you're the one running it with me. Then yeah."

I gawked at him. How was this even real?

"I told them that your vision had to trump everything else," Aiden said, "and they agreed to be passive investors. I'm sure they'll still find ways to be annoying. But they believe in you."

"*Why?*"

"Because I do."

I hugged him. I was shaking and overwhelmed. I wanted this so badly. I'd figured I would need investors to ever have the possibility of making this dream happen, but I hadn't known where I would find them. "You're sure? They really want to do this?"

"I wouldn't have brought it to you otherwise. You'll need to hire your own lawyer to look over the contracts. It's that kind of thing." He rolled his eyes. "But once we get that part done, they're ready to do it. We'll need to get banks involved too, for financing and all of that. But we'll make it happen. If you want to do this with me."

I looked into the dark brown eyes of my personal hero. My very own cowboy-prince. The man who'd swept me so thoroughly off my feet that I still hadn't touched the ground.

"This is my dream," I said. Part of it, at least. "But what about *you*? You've given up so much for me. Remade your entire life."

His thumb moved along my cheekbone. Followed the curve of my lower lip. "Before, I never had big dreams like yours. Not until I met you. Baby, *you* are my dream, and I've got everything I could ever want right here."

Aiden dipped his head for a soft, slow kiss. I tried to memorize this moment. The smell of the wildflowers and the gentle movement of the breeze across my skin. And my Aiden, making every other sensation fade to the background. His warm, comforting presence. My rock. Who knew he could spin such pretty words, too?

"I didn't know you were such a romantic," I murmured against his lips.

"I know. I can barely stand myself. I'm so fucking sweet." He said this like a lament, and I burst out in giggles.

"I love you. I love you so much."

Aiden picked me up and spun me around, both of us laughing. We sat on a rock and started brainstorming ideas. Logistics. Possible designs and concepts.

But then I had to stop him. This was it. I couldn't keep it in anymore.

"There's something else I need to say. A requirement, actually. If we're really going to do this."

"Tell me."

I took in our surroundings again, thinking of all the times I'd come to Refuge Mountain when I needed peace. The stories people told about this place. The idea of a *refuge*, and the inherent promise of that word.

"I want to set aside space here for people who have nowhere else to go. Some rooms that we reserve for people who've been abused, especially women, who need to get back on their feet. Like I did after Jeremy hurt me."

"A shelter?"

"Yes, like a shelter. But bigger than that, even. A place that feels safe and beautiful. Healing and liberating." I gestured at the view around us. The gentle rush of the nearby creek and waterfall. The birds singing, aspen leaves rustling in the wind.

Aiden nodded encouragingly.

"And we could offer them jobs," I said in a rush. "Find them other opportunities in Hartley and nearby towns. A new beginning. I think we could run the business and give back, too. But for me, creating a safe space for people who need it would be the real purpose."

"You've really considered this."

"I have. It means a lot to me." I reached for his hand. "What do you think?"

"I'm on board. A hundred percent. My family will be, too. They'll love it." Aiden kissed my forehead, wrapping me up in his arms. "You are absolutely amazing, you know that? If I was the type to settle down, I'd be thinking seriously about asking you to marry me."

"But you're not the marrying kind, huh?"

"Sometimes I surprise even myself. Guess we'll just have to wait and see." His expression was placid, but his eyes shone down on me, so full of love and fondness and more things than I had words for. "Do you have a name for this wonderful place you're envisioning?" he asked, our hands linked together.

"I do. I want to name it Last Refuge. So that anyone who feels they have nowhere else to turn will know. They can come here."

CHAPTER THIRTY-THREE
Aiden

I LIFTED THE SLEDGEHAMMER. "Do you want to do the honors, Jessi?"

She grinned and took the sledge in both hands. Our audience of friends and supporters cheered.

We were back on Refuge Mountain. And today was the day. We were breaking ground—and some walls—on the Last Refuge Inn & Tavern. Jessi's idea was going to become a reality. On the surface, a new gathering place for the people of Hartley. We certainly needed it with the way the population had been growing.

But underneath, Last Refuge would be a beacon for people who needed help. We were going to keep it quiet. Let word of mouth slowly spread. There were some rules to follow for running a shelter, and we'd do what was necessary to keep it aboveboard, as least as far as the state was concerned. But for those who truly needed it, we would make sure they were provided for. Regardless of anyone's rules.

Jessi was the heart and soul of this entire enterprise. I was just the muscle when the occasion called for it, and more often the cook. Because everybody would have to eat.

Our friends counted down while Jessi took practice

swings. *"Three. Two."* When they reached zero, the sledgehammer crashed into one of the walls we were breaking down inside the old ranch. There was clapping, more cheers. And I took the sledgehammer from Jessi's hands, giving her a kiss as I did.

"Your turn," she said.

I swung, taking out a larger chunk of the wall, and Jessi whooped. I hooked her waist with my free hand, tugging her close. Jessi had been floating on air for days, looking forward to this. She'd really shown her appreciation to me last night, and of course, I'd returned the favor. Such a hardship. It was a tough life I led.

"Okay, that's enough," I said. "Better let the pros take over from here."

She pouted. "It's so cathartic, though."

"I'll have to find you something else to smash. But not this. We have big plans for this place."

She grinned. "We do indeed."

We had spent all summer finalizing the land purchase, working with architects, and getting our contractor in place. The fact that we were starting so soon was a minor miracle in itself. But it helped that this county had virtually no regulations, and the financing had come through in a snap, thanks to an additional silent benefactor that Trace had connected us with. As with everything concerning Trace, it had been mysterious. Some ex-Army friend of his who wanted to remain nameless. But I didn't care. The money came with no strings except that we establish Last Refuge according to Jessi's proposal. And that was all I wanted.

We'd purchased the old ranch, as well as much of the surrounding mountainside, including the old cabin that the legends spoke about. The main building of the ranch would become our restaurant, and a row of existing cabins would be converted into guest cottages. Eventually, we would repurpose and expand the barn into an event venue, and a new building would house the hotel. It was a major undertaking. But we hoped the construction on the restaurant itself might be finished this fall, if everything went perfectly.

But Jessi had been working her butt off on this project along with me, and when she put her mind to something, I was amazed what she could do. We already had a party in the works for the restaurant's grand opening, date to be determined, and my family all planned to visit Hartley to attend.

For today, we had champagne waiting back at the diner, as well as some appetizers and desserts that Jessi and I had whipped up. As soon as everyone had finished here, we would head down to Main Street.

While Jessi and Scarlett bent their heads together to chat, I stepped outside and walked over to the barn, where Trace had retreated. He made me look social by comparison.

"How're you doing?" I asked.

"Fine." His voice was gruff. And it was a non-answer, as always. I got it. I did. But I knew how much Trace's reticence was getting to Jessi.

For the last few weeks, he had been living in one of the cabins up here. Trace had volunteered to be security for the work site during off hours, as if that was necessary in Hartley. But if more people got ideas like the Rigsbys, then maybe it was. We wanted Refuge Mountain to be a safe place.

That had been on my mind a lot too, actually.

Trace cleared his throat. "It's commendable, what you and your family have done for Jessi."

"Your benefactor friend helped. Whoever he is. But Jessi's doing a lot of it herself. She's the heart of Last Refuge."

He nodded. "She is. It's a good name. A good idea, too. A place for people with nowhere else to turn."

"Jessi said you volunteered to help out around here?"

Trace chewed his lip and glanced at the barn. His hair was

still long enough to cover half his face, and the sun had added bleached highlights from all the time he'd been spending outdoors. "As much as I can. I'm no construction expert. But I'd like to be a part of this. I could tend bar and wait tables when the place opens, too. Whatever you guys need."

He'd been doing odd jobs like that for months. I ran my palm over my beard. "Maybe there's another role you could take on once it's built. Something that would play to your skills."

"And what skills would those be?"

"Whatever skills you honed while you were overseas doing 'aid work'." I added air quotes with my fingers. He didn't take the bait, and he likely never would. I had no doubt his stories were all classified.

"What role are you suggesting for me, exactly?"

Over by the main ranch house, Jessi and Scarlett had emerged, joining the rest of their friends. There was conversation and smiles, the same thing that always followed when Jessi was around. But when Last Refuge opened, we would be welcoming people who needed help. Who might even need justice.

They would be escaping *from* something. What if that something followed?

"Jessi wants to provide a safe space for women who've been abused. And for other people who have nowhere else to turn. Once those people start arriving at Last Refuge, they'll need protection if the things they're running from come looking. You can't have a true refuge without someone to defend it."

"Like you protected Jessi before I got here?"

"More or less. And you know what they say. Best defense is a good offense."

I was still using vague terms, but I was sure Trace understood what I meant. He was quiet as he considered this. "What about the police? Sheriff Douglas?"

"You know that official avenues aren't always the best option. We might have to use...other methods. Things that Sheriff Douglas wouldn't want to know about."

His eyes turned hard. Shrewd. "You're talking about becoming vigilantes." Trace seemed more amused than shocked. As I'd expected, because he had no problems breaking rules.

"If that's what it takes. If they fight dirty, so will we. But I'd rather call us Protectors."

"Us?"

I nodded. "You, me. Other guys with the right kind of training who want to take this on. I'm going to call some of my Army brothers. See if they're interested."

"They still talk to you?"

"Ha. You're funny, Novo." I flipped him off.

He shrugged. "I might know some guys too. If *they'll* talk to *me*."

"We need people we can trust. We'll have to be careful, and I don't want to jeopardize anything else we're building here. But I've spoken to Jessi about it, and she agrees."

Trace and I both watched as Jessi and Scarlett hugged.

"I'd like to have something worth defending," Trace said quietly.

"So you're in?" I held out my hand. We shook.

Eventually, I would want Trace to lead the Protectors. He'd be a far better point person than me, given his training and experience. But I wasn't sure he was in the right headspace to take that on. Not yet.

Trace wandered over to Jessi. They spoke briefly. Then she came over to me. "We're supposed to meet everyone down at the diner," she said.

"We can head there soon. I need a minute with my girl." I

wrapped my arms around her, and she rested her head on my shoulder.

"You asked Trace about the Protectors?" she said.

"Did he mention it just now when he spoke to you?"

"Yes. He wanted to make sure I was on board. I'm glad he's going to help. We'll need him."

"I agree." But I suspected Trace would need this, too. I liked that he was still looking out for his sister, checking in with her. But I thought of what Trace had said to me. *I'd like to have something worth defending.* He wasn't talking about Jessi. Defending his sister was a given. Trace was hoping to find more. Answers, maybe. A purpose. Whatever had happened to him before, it had shaken his confidence to the core. I guessed the injuries to his psyche were much worse than the one to his knee that had left him limping. The Protectors could give him that.

I already had a lot worth defending. And if left to my own devices, I might've been satisfied with a simple life with the woman I loved by my side. But she was better than me. She wanted to do more for others. So I would do absolutely everything in my power to make it a reality for her.

People in desperate need of a hero were going to come to Last Refuge. I would step up and provide one, along with Trace and whoever else we could recruit. Perhaps Owen would join in too, as long as we weren't breaking too many rules for his sensibilities as sheriff. Besides, I did get satisfaction from righting wrongs when they were in front of me. I was a loner, but I valued having people I cared about around me. It had been too long since I'd spent quality time with my Army buddies.

Hell, this might even be fun.

But the truth was, there was only one woman I *wanted* to play hero for.

"What were you and Scarlett talking about?" I asked. "Did

you ask if she's interested in running the diner after the new restaurant opens?"

Jessi had been toying with that idea. But she shook her head. "Not yet. Scarlett had something else on her mind. She asked how soon we can start accepting people for Last Refuge. For our *real* purpose, I mean."

"It'll be a while. These cabins are in bad shape." Trace was okay staying in one, but he could rough it more than any soldier or operator I'd ever seen. If not for his sister, I suspected he might've disappeared into the mountains by now without looking back. "Trace and I have barely gotten started on the Protectors. We'll need more people, procedures, gear. Weapons. All we've had is one handshake."

"I know, but Scarlett has someone who needs help *now*. A girl from the town where Scarlett grew up. It's even more remote than Hartley. And..." Jessi frowned. "It sounds complicated."

Of course. "Is this girl in danger?"

Jessi's dark blue eyes lifted. She nodded. "Scarlett said her friend needs to escape from a bad situation. You know how Scarlett is. She played it off like the whole thing will probably turn out okay, no big deal, but I can tell she's scared."

"Then we'll figure something out. Give me the details, anything and everything that Scarlett knows. I'll talk to Trace and see what we can do. Sounds like the Protectors have their first assignment." Whether we were ready for it or not.

"Thank you." Jessi was looking at me like I'd hung the sun and stars and planets in the sky. If she had asked me to, I would've done my best to make it happen.

"If this girl needs a hero, she'll find one in Hartley," I said. "I've certainly found mine."

The End.

Author's Note

While I've spent much of my life in Southern California, Colorado has been home for about fifteen years now. The mountains speak to my soul, much as they do to Jessi. I'm a mountain girl through-and-through.

If you know Colorado geography, you might have noticed that Hartley doesn't correspond to any exact place. It's roughly situated in the southwestern part of the state, but I take a lot of liberty with the landscape, placement of highways, and mountain ranges. It's a mash-up of many beautiful Colorado towns. So please take those aspects of Hartley with a literary grain of salt.

Thank you so much to my writing group, my advance reviewers, and the fans who've joined me on this journey. It feels so good to finally bring my characters to Colorado! I can't wait to find out what's in store as the Last Refuge Protectors turn Hartley into a safe place for those who need it...and a very unsafe place for the bad guys.

Until next time, when it's Trace and Scarlett's turn in BENT WINGED ANGEL!

-Hannah

Also by Hannah Shield

LAST REFUGE PROTECTORS

HARD KNOCK HERO (Aiden & Jessi)

BENT WINGED ANGEL (Trace & Scarlett) - Coming soon

WEST OAKS HEROES

THE SIX NIGHT TRUCE (Janie & Sean)

THE FIVE MINUTE MISTAKE (Madison & Nash)

THE FOUR DAY FAKEOUT (Jake & Harper)

THE THREE WEEK DEAL (Matteo & Angela)

THE TWO LAST MOMENTS (Danny & Lark)

THE ONE FOR FOREVER (Rex & Quinn) - Coming soon

BENNETT SECURITY

HANDS OFF (Aurora & Devon)

HEAD FIRST (Lana & Max)

HARD WIRED (Sylvie & Dominic)

HOLD TIGHT (Faith & Tanner)

HUNG UP (Danica & Noah)

HAVE MERCY (Ruby & Chase)

About the Author

Hannah Shield once worked as an attorney. Now, she loves thrilling readers on the page—in every possible way.

She writes steamy, suspenseful romance with feisty heroines, brooding heroes, and heart-pounding action. Visit her website at www.hannahshield.com.

Made in United States
Orlando, FL
06 February 2025